Violet's Bold Mission

Violet's Bold Mission

BOOK FOUR
of the
A Life of Faith:
Violet Travilla
Series

Based on the characters by
Martha Finley

MCP
Mission City Press

Franklin, Tennessee

Book Four of the *A Life of Faith: Violet Travilla* Series

Violet's Bold Mission
Copyright © 2004, Mission City Press, Inc. All Rights Reserved.

Published by Mission City Press, Inc.

This book is based on the characters in the *Elsie Dinsmore* series written by Martha Finley and first published in 1868 by Dodd, Mead & Company.

Cover & Interior Design:	Richmond & Williams
Cover Photography:	Michelle Grisco Photography
Typesetting:	BookSetters

Unless otherwise indicated, all Scripture references are from the Holy Bible, New International Version (NIV). Copyright © 1973, 1978, 1984 by International Bible Society. Used by permission of Zondervan Publishing House, Grand Rapids, MI. All rights reserved.

Violet Travilla and *A Life of Faith* are trademarks of Mission City Press, Inc.

For more information, write to Mission City Press at P.O. Box 681913, Franklin, Tennessee 37068-1913, or visit our Web Site at:

www.alifeoffaith.com

Library of Congress Catalog Card Number: 2004106056
Finley, Martha
    Violet's Bold Mission
    Book Four of the *A Life of Faith: Violet Travilla* Series
    ISBN: 1-928749-20-8

Printed in the United States of America
1 2 3 4 5 6 7 8 — 08 07 06 05 04

— FOREWORD —

*V*iolet Travilla's recent adventures have taken her to exciting places — Rome and New York City — and shown her what life is like beyond her beloved Ion. Now, Vi is back home in the South. In the coastal city not far from the Travilla estate, she will bring what she has learned from others to the fulfillment of her own commitment to service. But achieving her goal won't be easy. There are many people who will not trust her motives, and some will go to dangerous lengths to stop her progress.

This book is the fourth in the *A Life of Faith: Violet Travilla* series. It is based on the characters created by Miss Martha Finley in her best-selling nineteenth century novels about Vi's mother, Elsie Dinsmore, and her family. Miss Finley was dedicated to providing young people of her time with models of Christian faith and living. In the late 1800s and early 1900s, her stories about the Dinsmore and Travilla families both entertained and inspired millions of young readers and their parents throughout the United States and around the world.

In order to bring Miss Finley's timeless message of faith, hope, and love to modern readers, Mission City Press has drawn on her characters and their fictional lives to create stories about the nineteenth century that have special relevance to challenges and opportunities facing young Christians today. We are pleased to carry forward Miss Finley's mission of service with the latest *A Life of Faith* novel, *Violet's Bold Mission*.

∞ WOMEN MAKING CHANGES ∞

Vi's commitment to serving the poor was unusual for a young woman of her time and social position. In the 1880s, girls from wealthy and well-to-do families were expected, by many people, to only concentrate on the ladylike arts of needle-work, drawing, and music. In some quarters, the idea of a young lady receiving a good education or seeking work outside the secure world of home and family was unimaginable. Women were regarded as weak and passive creatures, fit *only* to be wives and mothers. They were not supposed to take interest in politics or the important events of the day, which were the business of men.

By the 1880s, however, things were changing. In an 1887 article in *Godey's Lady's Book*—the most popular American women's magazine of the Victorian period—an author wrote: "The woman of today is the miracle of today, she is a wonder even to herself. She had been told through so many generations that she could not do this and could not do that, could not do or be anything in fact but what man proposed, that she believed it, and even asserted it of herself. . . ."

The author went on to say that something new was happening in the 1880s—"a great change, a great awakening"—and women were discovering their own voices and coming together to improve life for themselves and other women: "...already we have women in the majority as teachers, women who have won fame as preachers, lawyers, doctors, and artists, women in plenty, who hold their own and support themselves and others in every evocation [sic] of life."

In many ways, women were the greatest untapped natural resource America had. Young women like Vi Travilla were applying their talents and their energies to wider interests than simply finding husbands. Many parents, like Elsie Travilla, were beginning to encourage their daughters' ambitions and hopes to use all of the gifts God had given them.

Of course, women had always worked. The contribution of women to the settling of the nation was every bit as important as that of men. Poor women, widows, and unmarried women were often the sole support for their families. Factories and shops depended on the labor of women, though female workers were rarely paid wages equal to those of men, even when their jobs were the same or harder. In the South, after the Civil War, many women (like Vi's Aunt Louise Conley) had lost their old fortunes and had to find ways to earn a living for themselves and their children. Former slaves had the added burden of trying to pull together families that had been separated by slavery. From the loftiest mansion to the lowliest cottage and tenement house, women were seeking to gain better treatment for themselves and other women. Whatever their situation, however, the law and social custom made the struggle very difficult.

∞ THE STRUGGLE FOR WOMEN'S RIGHTS ∞

Today, it's hard to imagine a time when the majority of American citizens were not allowed to vote, but that was just the case during the country's first 130 years.

In a representative democracy like the United States, "suffrage" means the right to vote for elected officials—from the local mayor and school board to the President. "Universal suffrage" means that every citizen can vote. (Another word for the right to vote is "franchise.")

There are always some limits on voting, such as the age at which a person is considered an adult and may vote. When the U.S. Constitution was ratified by the states in 1787, only men who owned property (and therefore paid taxes) were allowed to vote. The property requirement was eventually removed by the states, and in 1870, the right to vote was extended to African-American men by the Fifteenth Amendment to the Constitution. But women, regardless of their race, were excluded.

Many women accepted this state of affairs, but as early as the 1830s and 1840s, women like Lucretia Mott and Elizabeth Cady Stanton were beginning to call for women's suffrage. Many of the campaigners for women's right to vote were activists in the cause of abolition (the end of slavery). They believed that all citizens—regardless of race or gender—should have equal rights. In July 1848, the first convention to discuss women's rights was held in Seneca Falls, New York. This convention issued a declaration calling for female suffrage, as well as equal rights in education and employment. The women who gathered at Seneca Falls cited the words of the Declaration of Independence and the even more precise language of John Adams (the country's second President) in the Massachusetts Constitution: "All people are born free and equal and have certain natural, essential and unalienable rights; among which may be reckoned the right of enjoying and defending their lives and liberties."

The movement for suffrage gathered more followers, men as well as women. The leaders and organizers were in the main women of faith, supporters of abolition, and believers in education, social justice, and the betterment of living and working conditions for the poor. Changing the voting laws was a difficult process, requiring tireless efforts. The women who joined the movement were often subjected to ridicule, threats, and sometimes physical violence. A number were arrested and jailed for their protests.

The first victories came at the grassroots level as a few cities and municipal governments granted voting rights to *all* citizens in local elections. In 1869, the Territory of Wyoming gave women the right to vote in all elections. When Wyoming became a state in 1890, it was the first to include the right of women to vote in its constitution; three years later, Wyoming adopted the state motto "Equal Rights." But it would be another thirty years before all American women would be guaranteed suffrage.

Other countries moved much earlier to grant universal suffrage. The first modern democracy to give women the right to vote in national elections was tiny New Zealand when it became a nation in 1893. During the next decade, Australia,

Finland, and Norway followed New Zealand's lead. Women's suffrage was granted in Canada in 1919. At last, in 1920, the passage of the Nineteenth Amendment to the U.S. Constitution guaranteed American women the right to cast their ballots in national elections. In England, where the battle for suffrage had lasted longer and been even more difficult than in the U.S., the full rights of universal suffrage weren't extended to women until 1928.

Travilla/Dinsmore Family Tree

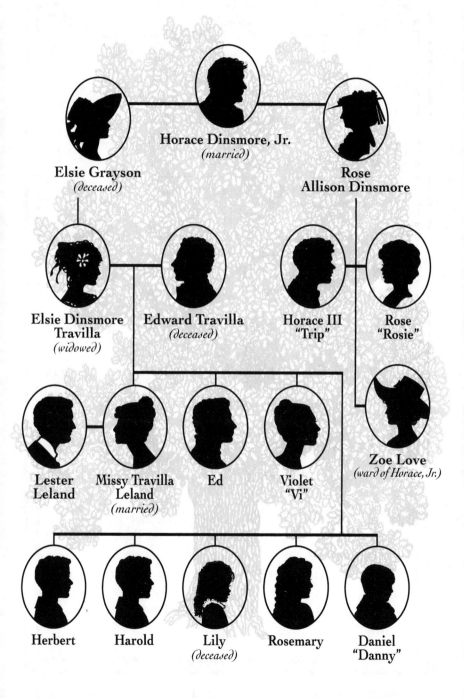

Horace Dinsmore, Jr.
(married)

Elsie Grayson
(deceased)

Rose
Allison Dinsmore

Elsie Dinsmore
Travilla
(widowed)

Edward Travilla
(deceased)

Horace III
"Trip"

Rose
"Rosie"

Lester
Leland

Missy Travilla
Leland
(married)

Ed

Violet
"Vi"

Zoe Love
(ward of Horace, Jr.)

Herbert

Harold

Lily
(deceased)

Rosemary

Daniel
"Danny"

SETTING

$\mathcal{T}$he story begins in India Bay, the seaport city near the Travilla family's large country estate, Ion. It is late summer, 1883.

CHARACTERS

∞ ION ∞

Violet Travilla (Vi) — age 20, the third child of Elsie and the late Edward Travilla.

Elsie Dinsmore Travilla — Vi's mother; a wealthy widow and the owner of Ion and other properties in the South.

Missy Travilla Leland — Vi's elder sister, married to **Lester Leland**. They live in Rome, Italy.

Edward Travilla, Jr. (Ed) — age 24, Vi's elder brother, a university graduate.

Herbert and Harold Travilla — age 17, Vi's twin brothers.

Rosemary Travilla — age 13, Vi's younger sister.

Danny Travilla — age 9, Vi's youngest brother.

Mrs. Maurene O'Flaherty — widow of a now famous composer and Vi's companion and friend.

Aunt Chloe — Elsie Dinsmore's childhood nursemaid and lifelong companion; a former slave now in her eighties.

Ben and Christine — longtime household servants at Ion.

Enoch and Christine Reeve — valued employees at Ion.

∞ THE OAKS ∞

Horace Dinsmore, Jr. and his wife, **Rose** — Vi's grandparents and owners of The Oaks estate.

Zoe Love — age 18, the daughter of a deceased American diplomat and now the ward of Horace Dinsmore, Jr.

∞ INDIA BAY ∞

Dr. Silas Lansing — an eminent surgeon, and his wife, **Naomi**, prominent citizens of India Bay and old friends of the Travilla family.

Miss Emily Clayton — a professional nurse.

Dr. Bowman — a young physician.

Mr. Archibald — a master carpenter.

Mr. and Mrs. Marvin Nelson, Miss Crane, Mrs. Denton, Mrs. Mary Appleton and her daughter, **Polly** — residents of Wildwood, a district in India Bay.

Tobias Clinch — owner of the Wildwood Hotel.

Jess Jenkins — an employee of Mr. Clinch.

Sergeant Peevy — a policeman.

∞ THE OTHERS ∞

Tansy Evans — age 11, and her sister, **Marigold**, age 6.

Dr. Marcus Darius Raymond — a university professor and friend of Ed Travilla.

Ebenezer Greer — a landowner from South Carolina.

Mr. Bartleby — a lawyer in South Carolina.

A House in Need

For every house is built by someone, but God is the builder of everything.

A House in Need

*I*t was a bright Monday morning in early September—still like mid-summer in the South. The sounds of hammering and men's voices drifted up the stairs to the third floor where two young women—wearing cotton aprons over their everyday dresses and colorful scarves covering their hair—were working.

"Where is my washing cloth?" Rosemary Travilla demanded with impatience. She stood up, gazed around the half-furnished bedroom, and frowned.

"Where did you have it last?" Zoe Love asked.

"In my hand!" Rosemary exclaimed with a stamp of her foot.

Zoe smothered a laugh and said, "It's here somewhere, but there are plenty of rags in that basket on the bed. Just get another one."

Rosemary sulked, but she took a fresh rag and dipped it into a bucket of soapy water. Then she returned to her task, washing an old but sturdy spindle-legged table. Rosemary, who was thirteen years old, had been very pleased when Violet, her older sister, requested that she help with the cleaning. But Rosemary had always been given to complaining.

After a few minutes of hard scrubbing, she said, "I don't know how things can get this filthy."

"No one has lived in this house for years," Zoe replied. "It's not like Ion where people clean and dust every day. We're cleaning away years of neglect. But it must have been a beautiful house when people were here. And it will be a clean house when all the work is done."

"It won't be beautiful, though," Rosemary said.

"That isn't what Vi intends," Zoe said. "This house is going to be a mission, and Vi wants it to be clean and comfortable for the people who come here — not a showplace. It's going to be a place where everyone is welcome and people work together to serve others."

"Well, I don't see why she couldn't have chosen a new house for her mission," Rosemary said in a whining tone.

The house was indeed to be a place of service — the fulfillment of Violet Travilla's years of dreaming and planning. It was an old house, built in the 1820s in what was then the main residential section of the seaport city of India Bay. The place had been enlarged over the years, until the grounds occupied almost an entire city block. But the wealthy owners had been bankrupted in the Civil War, and parts of the land were sold off to pay taxes. No matter their financial hardships, however, the owners would never agree to sell the house, the stable and carriage house, and the greatly reduced patch of ground on which they stood.

A brother and sister — all that were left of the original family — inherited the house a few years after the War, and they had lived there alone, rarely seeing anyone other than a grocer who brought food and took away an occasional letter to be mailed. About five years earlier, the two reclusive siblings had died during an epidemic of cholera. The house had gone to some distant relatives, and they had been trying to sell it ever since. But no one wanted a ramshackle house in a down-and-out neighborhood.

During Reconstruction, the city's well-to-do residents had moved in another direction — away from the port and the railroad tracks and toward the rolling green hills to the west. The old neighborhood became increasingly poor and disreputable, and the house, like those around it, fell into disrepair. Many of the old homes in the area were divided into boarding houses and apartments for the poor and unemployed. Others had been torn down or destroyed by fire.

Somehow, this house survived. Over the years, its once beautiful gardens became thick with weeds and tangles of woody vines. Without pruning, the shade trees grew twisted and shaggy, and the neat evergreen hedges along the boundary lines spread upward and outward, forming an impenetrable wall. The effect was to hide the house from view. Dark and overgrown, it became the subject of gossip and rumor. Some called it a "ghost house," and after the brother and sister died, people began telling stories of strange noises and lights coming from inside the house on moonless nights. Each year, the tales became scarier, so that not even the most adventurous boys and men would dare approach the tall wrought-iron gates at the entryways to the property.

Then Vi Travilla discovered it. For several months, she'd been searching the city for a suitable building for the mission. She had seen a few places that might work, but she was never really satisfied with the sites shown to her by the land agents. Then one of the agents had said casually, "Well, there's always the 'ghost house' on Wildwood Street. It's been on the market since the last of the old owners died five years ago."

Though the agent was merely jesting, Vi had been intrigued. Hearing about the dilapidated house and its spooky reputation roused Vi's curiosity, and she determined to see it. Against the agent's better judgment, Vi prevailed.

The first time she walked through the dark and dirty rooms, littered with abandoned furniture, she knew that she had found her mission.

The very next day, she'd returned there with her mother and Ed, her elder brother. Ed had been more than doubtful; he thought that renovating the old house was highly impractical. But Elsie Travilla looked at it through her daughter's eyes and saw what Vi saw—a commodious house that could be rescued and transformed.

A good deal of family discussion followed. Ed raised his objections, and Vi took them into account. Compromises were made, and at last they all agreed. Elsie would purchase the property, and when Vi, who had just turned twenty, came of age in another year, she would receive the deed in her own name. At Ed's insistence, no work on the house could begin until it had been inspected by a professional architect, and a reputable building contractor was hired.

"I don't want you falling through those old floors, little sister," he'd said, only half-jokingly. "Really, Vi, the house hasn't been updated since before the War. It needs plumbing and heating and lights. The roof is in bad shape, and the old cookhouse is falling down. There's an enormous amount of work that must be done before you can begin to think about opening it to anyone. It's going to take a lot of money."

"Money spent in the Lord's service," Elsie reminded him. "Don't worry. I will supervise the spending, and you and Vi will supervise the work. I expect you to account to me for your expenditures and keep me informed of your progress, just as I would in any business. But otherwise, I leave the decisions to you both."

Ed's demands were soon met. The house was pronounced sound in structure, and a contractor was engaged. The architect worked closely with Vi to plan the house's interior. Rooms that had once been filled with family and servants and important guests—it was said that General Robert E. Lee had been a frequent visitor—were assigned new purposes. The old double parlor would become a meeting and dining room. The old dining room would be transformed into a modern kitchen. The old library and a sitting room would be converted to an office and storage for supplies. The second floor would be devoted to schoolrooms, a playroom, and a medical clinic. And so on up to the attic.

Workmen plied their trades throughout the spring and summer, and by the first day of September, the house had a new roof, running water and bathrooms on every floor, gas lighting, and a huge coal-fired furnace. The old chimneys were cleaned, and the house's many fireplaces made ready for winter fires. Now, the work of renovating the interior was well underway. Old walls were being removed and new ones built. Old doors were rehung, and windows that had not been opened for decades were repaired.

The people in the neighborhood watched the workmen coming and going, and stories quickly spread about what was being done with the old place. A hotel? Another boarding house? As the work progressed, people realized that someone was spending a great deal on the old house, and a rumor spread that rich folks were moving back in and intending to drive the poor out of the area. That caused a brief flurry of fear and anger, until a local man finally asked Mr. Archibald, the head carpenter, what was going on. The curious man was informed that a Christian lady was making the house into a mission and a school. Most of the older residents of the area welcomed this news. But many others remained suspicious, and some were quietly hostile — for reasons that Vi would not learn about for some time.

Zoe and Rosemary were still cleaning in the third-floor bedroom when Mrs. O'Flaherty came in.

Rosemary started to complain again, but Mrs. O'Flaherty said, "Hush, girl, and take a look around at what you've accomplished this morning. That old table looked like a piece of junk, and now you have washed it and polished it and made it handsome again. Look at the woodwork you've cleaned and the floor we've scrubbed. They shine like new."

Rosemary did consider the room. "It does look better," she admitted at last.

"What about the old wallpaper?" Zoe asked. "It's faded, but now that it's been washed, I think it's lovely. It must have been bright when it was first put up, but I really like the way it has become so soft looking. It's like a garden on a misty morning."

"I believe that Vi agrees with you," Mrs. O'Flaherty said. "The rest of the house is undergoing such changes that she wants to preserve as much of its history as possible on this floor. And speaking of the house's history, we have another task this afternoon."

"Please, not more washing," Rosemary groaned.

"No, we are going to hunt for treasure," Mrs. O'Flaherty replied. "Vi wants to explore the attic for useful items. It's filled almost to the rafters with old furniture and boxes and stacks of paintings. Rosemary, there are trunks that haven't been opened in thirty years. Who knows what we may find in them?"

The idea of opening old trunks intrigued Rosemary, and she declared herself ready to proceed to the attic.

"Not quite yet," Mrs. O'Flaherty said. "You and I are going to wash these windows first, while Zoe cleans the mantel over the fireplace. When we finish, we'll have lunch. Vi should be back by then, and we can all inspect the attic together."

Rosemary was not thrilled about more washing, but the prospect of lunch cheered her.

Mrs. O'Flaherty brought in a bucket of water, which emitted the tart odor of vinegar, and a small bundle of newspapers. She had Rosemary tear the papers into large pieces.

"Why don't we just use rags?" Rosemary asked as she tore. "The papers make my hands black with ink."

"We'll wash the windows first with the rags and vinegar water. Then we'll polish the glass with the papers. That way, there will be no lint left behind, and these old windows will sparkle," Mrs. O'Flaherty explained.

"What about the outsides?" Rosemary wondered. "The glass is dirtier outside than inside."

"That's a job for men on ladders," Mrs. O'Flaherty said.

Rosemary was soon washing away, and as she got each pane of glass clean, Mrs. O'Flaherty polished it, her paper making little squeaking noises that brought Rosemary to giggles.

"It sounds like mice singing," the girl laughed. "What songs would a mouse sing, do you think?"

" 'Three Blind Mice'?" Zoe suggested.

"Of course!" Rosemary exclaimed. And she began to sing the old nursery song in her musical soprano voice. When she finished, Mrs. O'Flaherty started another song, and soon they were all singing merrily as they washed and polished.

When Vi entered the room some time later, she was laughing. "I wondered who was brightening our mission with song," she said. She looked around the room. "If singing brings results like this, sing on. This room looks wonderful! I can really see how beautiful this house must have been. Why, I could move into this room today."

Rosemary seemed startled. "But you're not moving, are you?" she asked with obvious concern. "You're not going to leave Ion?"

"I just meant that anyone could live in this room now," Vi soothed.

"Not until we find a mattress for the bed," Zoe said. "That's really the only thing lacking, but it's indispensable if anyone plans to sleep here."

Then Mrs. O'Flaherty asked, "Now tell us, Vi. What was the result of your visit to the oculist?"

Vi's smile instantly turned to a frown. She took the little purse that hung over her arm and opened it. Reaching inside, she drew forth a small item and held it out.

"These," she said in consternation.

"Spectacles!" Zoe exclaimed.

"Put them on!" Rosemary joined in. "I want to see you in spectacles."

Reluctantly and with her head lowered, Vi raised the glasses to her face and hooked the handles over her ears. She fiddled with the frames and then slowly raised her head.

"You look like a schoolteacher!" Rosemary burst out in a giggling laugh.

"Thank you very much," Vi replied with a heavy dose of sarcasm.

"I just meant that you look older," Rosemary said apologetically. "More—more mature."

"I think you look splendid," Zoe said. "The spectacles suit you. They don't hide your eyes at all. And can you really see better?"

"Well, it's easier to read," Vi replied. "The letters on the page aren't fuzzy, and the eye doctor said my eyes won't get tired now and I won't get those little headaches. He says that I'll get used to them, but I don't think so. They feel so odd and uncomfortable, like I have something pasted to my head."

"You will get used to them," Zoe said. "My Papa had spectacles for reading, and he never went anyplace without them. But they weren't pretty like yours."

Mrs. O'Flaherty cocked her head to one side, studying Vi. "You don't look older, Vi girl, but Rosemary was right when she said 'more mature.' Very intellectual, I'd say. A very pretty young woman with brains."

"If that's the effect," Zoe said, pulling off her kerchief and shaking her blond curls, "then I want spectacles for myself. I have the hardest time making people understand that I have brains and not goose feathers in my head."

That remark made Vi laugh again. She took the little glasses off and laid them on the table. "Well, I'm not reading, so I don't have to wear them now," she said firmly. "Are you hungry? The basket that Crystal packed for us is waiting in the kitchen."

Rosemary was out the door before another word could be said.

"If that girl is ever lost, I know how to find her," Mrs. O'Flaherty chuckled. "All we need to do is shout 'Food!' and she'll come running."

A House in Need

Sitting in the partly finished kitchen, they ate the delicious lunch prepared by Ion's head housekeeper. After Rosemary finally announced that she was full, they washed their dishes and then climbed the narrow, creaking back stairway that led to the third floor. The attic was reached through a doorway off the third-floor hallway.

The attic was indeed filled almost to the rafters. Mrs. O'Flaherty and Vi managed to open one of the louvered windows that served as vents, so that the fresh air could make its way inside. But the room was still almost dark, so they lit several oil lamps.

"Ugh! I've never seen so many cobwebs," Rosemary said as the light came up. "Shouldn't we dust or something before we start looking at this stuff?"

"It's better not to raise the dust too much, or we won't be able to breathe," Mrs. O'Flaherty said. "We can go through everything and see what is useable. Cleaning can wait for another time."

They began to explore, and it was not long before they found treasures. Under a ragged and torn mattress, Vi and Zoe discovered a handsome sofa of carved maple. Behind some stacks of boxes, Vi saw what seemed to be a child's bed set up in a far corner. Peeking beneath a blanket, Mrs. O'Flaherty found a rolltop desk, and Rosemary located a swivel chair that must have gone with the desk.

"These will be perfect for the office," Mrs. O'Flaherty said. "The desk is large with deep drawers and good storage. I can almost see you, Vi, working here at your record keeping."

"Don't remind me," Vi answered. "Keeping books and records? I know I must, but I don't look forward to it."

"Maybe you could hire a secretary," Rosemary said as she carefully raised the lid of a battered trunk.

"After we hire a cook and a nurse and someone to manage the grounds and stoke the furnace, and after we buy desks and books for the schoolroom and Bibles and hymnals for the meeting room and..."

"I understand," Rosemary cut in. "I wasn't thinking about all those really important things. But look what I've found! I think it's curtains and bedspreads, and they're very pretty."

Mrs. O'Flaherty examined the contents of the trunk and said, "Most of these are in good condition. If they can't be used as they are, they can be cut and sewn for other purposes. An excellent discovery," she added, patting Rosemary's shoulder.

Once they'd made a survey of the attic, they decided to take some things down to the third floor. They wanted to clear space in the attic so that the carpenters could more easily move the heavy pieces of furniture. Working almost like a factory line, they carried out boxes filled with fabrics and bed linens, clothes, china and drinking glasses, books, and quaint old toys. Very carefully, they took away the several dozen framed paintings and etchings that had been stacked in the attic. Everything was stored in a bedroom that had not yet been cleaned.

They sorted through the items, deciding how and where each might be used. Zoe's attention had been caught by a painting in a square frame. It was a portrait of a young boy and girl whose faces were so alike they had to be brother and sister. The little girl sat stiffly in a chair and held a doll on her lap. The boy stood beside her, and a small dog played at his feet.

"Their clothes are so odd," Rosemary said.

"Not odd," Zoe replied. "Just of another time. I wonder who they were. I wonder if they lived in this house when it was new and beautiful."

"Maybe they're the brother and sister who owned the house and died here," Rosemary said.

Vi had come to look at the painting. "If they are," she said softly, "I hope they're happy with what we are doing to their home."

"I'm going to clean that frame tomorrow," Zoe said in an excited way. "And then I will put the portrait over the mantel in the bedroom we finished today. That way, the brother and sister can see what is happening to their house."

"You mean like ghosts watching us?" Rosemary asked.

"Of course not, silly," Zoe laughed. "You know there's no such thing as ghosts."

"I know," Rosemary said, "but people call this a 'ghost house,' so I can't help but imagine."

"Well, put your imagination away, young lady," Mrs. O'Flaherty said in a tone that sounded like scolding but was full of amusement, "and open your ears. What do you hear?"

Rosemary lifted her head and listened. After several moments she said, "Nothing. Oh, I hear some birds chirping, and some noises from the street. But no hammering or sawing or banging. The workmen must have finished for the day."

As if in answer, a man's voice called to them. "We're going home now, Miss Travilla!"

Vi hurried into the hallway and leaned over the banister. "Thank you, Mr. Archibald," she said. "We will see you tomorrow."

"Yes, ma'am," the voice replied, and a few moments later, Vi heard the front door close.

Vi was looking at her little watch as she returned to the others. "It's a quarter past four. Ben is to arrive at four-thirty with the carriage, and you know he's never late. Since we have the carriage today, I'd like to take some of these old books with us. "

She sent Rosemary downstairs to keep a watch for Ben, and she, Zoe, and Mrs. O'Flaherty spent a few more minutes clearing away the debris from the day's work. They brought the oil lamps down from the attic, making sure that the wicks were completely out. Then they packed two small boxes with books, collected their purses and jackets, and went down to the first floor. The carriage from Ion was waiting at the entrance, and Ben was helping Rosemary put their luncheon basket inside.

Vi retrieved a ring of keys from the kitchen, and she and Mrs. O'Flaherty made a quick tour of the first floor—checking that all the doors and windows were locked tight. They were about to close the front door when they heard steps running quickly and lightly above them.

"One of the ghosts?" Mrs. O'Flaherty smiled.

Vi looked outside and saw Rosemary sitting in the carriage. "It's Zoe," she declared. "She must have left something behind."

A few seconds passed, and they heard the same light footsteps descending the stairways. Zoe came into view, holding her skirts high and hurrying down the steps.

"What did you forget?" Vi asked as Zoe reached the ground floor.

"I didn't forget anything," Zoe replied with an expression of mock sternness, "but *you* did, Miss Violet Travilla."

Zoe held out the wire-framed spectacles.

"We shall have to watch our friend very carefully," Zoe said to Mrs. O'Flaherty. "She seems to be growing absent-minded in her old age."

Sheepishly, Vi took the glasses and put them into her little purse.

They stepped out into a beautifully clear afternoon and breathed in the fresh air. Vi turned back to lock and check the front door. In another hour, they would be home again, at Ion.

CHAPTER

Back at Ion

They broke bread in their homes and ate together with glad and sincere hearts.

ACTS 2:46

Back at Ion

hen the carriage arrived at Ion, Rosemary hopped out before Ben could alight from his seat to help the ladies down. On the long ride from the city, she had declared her intention to have a long bath, and now she ran inside in search of her goal.

"You'd think my little sister had been laboring in a coal mine," Vi said with a laugh.

"The wonder is that she has been laboring at all," Mrs. O'Flaherty replied. "But she worked hard today, and she worked well. She has earned her tub of soap and water."

"Rosemary's a funny girl," Zoe said as they mounted the steps to the front door. "She moans and groans, but she never shirks her duties as far as I can see. And she does make me laugh. All her questions and comments are phrased in such a comical way. Will she come with us tomorrow?"

Vi replied that Rosemary would not accompany them, for she had lessons to do with their mother. Vi was glad to hear that her sister was helpful; she hoped that all her family would be able to participate in the mission.

Inside the familiar entrance hall of her home, Vi sighed happily as she removed her bonnet. "We accomplished a good deal," she said with satisfaction.

"I'm glad to hear that," said a lovely voice, and Vi turned to see her mother coming out of the library.

Elsie Travilla joined them and gave her daughter and Zoe hugs. "So you are making progress," she said.

"We are, Mamma," Vi replied. "The work has reached the point where we can really see what the mission will look like. Mrs. O and Zoe and Rosemary finished cleaning one of the upstairs bedrooms today, and we made a very good start on the attic."

Violet's Bold Mission

"It is full of useful things, Cousin Elsie," Zoe added with excitement. "And I found an old portrait that we think might be the brother and sister who lived in the house."

"I can see that you worked by the dirt streaks on your faces," Elsie said with a warm smile. "Rosemary ran in like a whirlwind and claimed the downstairs bath, but you two can use mine if you like. There's plenty of time for you to bathe and dress before supper. Then you might visit with Aunt Chloe for a bit. She enjoys hearing about your progress."

Eager to clean away the day's dust and grime, the two young women hurried up the stairs.

Elsie turned to Mrs. O'Flaherty and said, "Tell me, Maurene, do you have any regrets about volunteering for Vi's project? You've been back with us for a month now, and your stay has not been a holiday. I don't think you've missed a day of work with Vi at the mission."

Mrs. O'Flaherty smiled her widest grin, displaying her gold tooth, and said, "I haven't a single regret, nor even a second thought. I enjoyed my brush with celebrity in New York. It was thrilling to be there, helping to bring my husband's music to life. But as soon as I was certain that his work would be recognized as it deserved, I began to wonder what to do with myself. Despite my privileged upbringing, I fear I was not meant to be a lady of leisure. I can't see myself living out my life as just the widow of the acclaimed composer. This would sound strange to most people, but I don't think I'd be comfortable just being comfortable. I need to be part of something bigger than myself, and Vi's request for my assistance with the mission was exactly the opportunity I was hoping for. Besides, I've watched your daughter's commitment to service grow and ripen over the years of her girlhood. How could I miss this chance to be at hand when her dream is about to become real?"

"Somehow I knew you would say that," Elsie responded. "But I had to ask. I'm not as young as I used to be," she went

18

on with a soft chuckle, "and at times those girls are too energetic for me. I wanted to be sure that you were not being run
ragged."

Mrs. O'Flaherty took Elsie's hand and said, "I never was a
mother, so I'm truly grateful that you have shared your family
with me. Your children are like a fountain of youth. Every day,
they remind me that God is always opening doors to us—giving
us opportunities to please Him by doing what is good and right,
whatever our stage of life. I have a world of experience to draw
on, and that's how I can be of help to Vi. In turn, I get to share
in her ideals and energy. I think that's a fair trade."

"More than fair," Elsie said, slipping her hand through
Mrs. O'Flaherty's arm. "Would you like tea? There's a fresh
pot in the library."

"I'd like that very much," Mrs. O'Flaherty said. "But first,
I must wash my hands. Rosemary and I cleaned windows
today, and I can still smell the vinegar."

"Rosemary cleaned windows?" Elsie said in surprise.
"Well, come to the library as soon as you've freshened up. We
can enjoy our tea, and I can hear more about Rosemary's first
day of work."

Mrs. O'Flaherty was not the only one who had come
back to Ion. Ed Travilla had made his return some nine
months earlier—after graduating from the University and
taking a six-month tour of Europe. He'd been surprised at
the many offers of employment he'd received when he had
earned his degree. Had he chosen, he could have made a
career in business in New York or Philadelphia. Several of
his professors had urged him to stay at the University and
teach. There had also been serious suggestions that he might
enter the ministry.

But for Ed, there was never any question of what he would do. Ion was where his heart lay, and he never doubted his commitment to carry on for his late father. His days now were devoted to learning how to manage such a large farming operation as Ion, plus his mother's Louisiana properties and many investments. He was a conscientious student—working with Elsie and his grandfather, Horace Dinsmore, Jr., to master all the tasks of running a large and complicated business. Some nights, his head would throb with the information he was absorbing.

But his "education" was not limited to books of figures and lessons in accounting and economics. Like his father before him, Ed believed that work was done with the hands as well as the head. He made the effort to labor alongside Ion's employees as often as possible so that he might learn from them. He enjoyed physical labor, and after a day like this one—spent cutting hay in the fields—he felt tired but also exhilarated. Walking up the hill from the stables, he found himself smiling at the prospect of sharing supper with his family, hearing about the day's work at the mission, and then reading his new book on modern agricultural science. He thought to himself, *Two years ago, I read myself to sleep with the works of the Greek philosophers. Now I read of plows and thrashers and the market values of corn and wheat. And there is pleasure in both.*

The family was gathering in the dining room and taking their places at the table. As Vi surveyed them, it struck her once again how many changes had taken place in the past few years.

Ed now occupied the seat at the end of the table that had been their father's. She marveled at how much Ed had grown like their Papa. It was a resemblance that went well beyond Ed's tall, dark good looks. After a day in the fields, Ed seemed to shine with good cheer. *Look at how he jokes with Danny, so like the way Papa used to make me laugh*, she thought with a smile.

There was Zoe in the place once reserved for their dear cousin Molly, who now lived in Louisiana with her husband and children. And Mrs. O'Flaherty, sitting where Molly's mother once had. *Friends depart*, Vi said to herself, *and more friends come in their place. It is like a circle that is never broken.*

Vi thought about her elder sister, Missy, who had not dined with the family for almost four years, since her last visit after her marriage to Lester Leland in Rome. Missy was a mother now, and there was some talk that the Lelands might return to the United States in another year. Vi hoped it would come to pass, for she missed her big sister and her brother-in-law terribly and couldn't wait to see her new nephew.

It made Vi feel warm inside to look around the large table and see so many loved ones. Her twin brothers, Herbert and Harold, were as tall as Ed but more fair in coloring, like their mother. At seventeen, they attended the Boys' Academy in the city, and in another year, they would both leave for college. Vi realized how she would miss their easy jesting and the funny way they had of speaking as if their thoughts came from the same mind.

And Rosemary and Danny and Mamma… Her thoughts were interrupted by a gentle poke from Ed.

"You're daydreaming, Vi," her brother said. "I can tell by your expression. You were smiling that secret smile that brings out your dimple."

"She ain't daydreaming," said Danny, who sat next to Vi. "It's getting dark outside, so she must be night dreaming."

From across the table, Rosemary frowned and said, "Don't say 'ain't.' Vi *isn't* daydreaming. Except that she *was* daydreaming. I could see that. What were you thinking about, Vi?"

"Oh, nothing really," Vi replied with a trace of embarrassment. "I was just thinking about family and friends."

Violet's Bold Mission

"You're never short of those at Ion," Ed remarked. Then seeing that Crystal and a maid had entered, carrying trays of food, he said to everyone, "Let's bow heads now and thank our gracious Father in Heaven for all His many gifts to us."

All heads were lowered and hands were clasped as he prayed, "Dear Lord, we ask Your blessing on the food we are about to receive and on those who have prepared it for us. Tonight, we thank You especially for the presence of our loved ones at this table. And we ask for Your blessing on those who cannot be here with us. Although distant, they are always in our hearts, and we pray that You will watch over them and keep them safe. Thank You, Lord, for the gift of family and friends, and for Your Love that knows no bounds. Amen."

The others echoed his "Amen."

Then Crystal and the young maid began passing platters and dishes. Plates were filled, and the meal commenced.

"Slow down, Rosemary," Harold said to his little sister. "You're eating as if you haven't seen food in a week."

Rosemary tried to reply, but her mouth was so full that she could only glare at her brother.

"You'll blow up like a balloon," Herbert joked. "Only you'll be too full of roast beef and gravy to float away."

"Stop teasing, boys," Elsie said a little sternly. "Rosemary worked very hard at the mission today. It's no surprise that she's hungry."

Rosemary, who had been chewing furiously, swallowed hard. Able to speak at last, she said, "Thank you, Mamma." And she shot a grimacing look at the twins.

Elsie saw the look and said to Rosemary, "Still, my dear, you must eat at a reasonable pace. Eating too quickly will upset your stomach."

"I'll try, Mamma," Rosemary said, going back to her supper.

It was, as always, a delicious meal, and for a time everyone concentrated on eating. Then the conversation picked up.

Leaning toward Vi, Ed asked, "What were you thinking earlier, about family and friends?"

Laying her fork on her plate, Vi said, "I was thinking how fortunate I am. Ever since I was a little girl, I've always looked forward to mealtime, but not just because of the food. I love coming together like this and talking and laughing and—well—just being together. I used to think that every family in the world was doing the same thing, all eating their meals together at the same time as us."

"Millions of families do, though not at the same time," Ed said. "But now you know that others do not. Many don't have good food and safe shelter, and loving families and friends to share with."

"I want the mission to offer the kind of fellowship that we've always had," Vi replied, her eyes bright with anticipation. Then her eyelids dropped, her long black lashes brushing her cheek. "I sometimes wonder if it will ever really happen. We have a building, but will we ever have the hearts of the people we want to serve?"

"Don't lose faith now, Vi," Ed said. "Trust God and trust yourself. It won't be long before you can open the mission doors. I'm not sure that people will come in easily at first, but have faith. They will come. Remember Dr. Frazier. She told you how hard it was to start her practice and earn the trust of the people she serves."

"Every time she writes to me, she reminds me that I must be realistic," Vi responded, looking into her brother's face. Then she said, in a business-like tone, "I need to talk to you and Mamma about something important. Would you have time after supper?"

"I'm always at your service," Ed smiled. "But dessert first. I passed the kitchen when I came in, and I smelled apple pie. Crystal has promised me a nice wedge of cheddar cheese to go with it."

"Did you say apple pie?" Rosemary asked eagerly.

"I told you," Mrs. O'Flaherty laughed merrily as she nodded at Zoe. "Just mention food, and our young window-cleaner will come running!"

The family retired to the sitting room after their meal. The adults had their coffee, and the twins, Rosemary, and Danny worked for a while on a difficult jigsaw puzzle they had recently received from Missy and Lester. Then Elsie announced that it was time to go to their bedrooms, for everyone had lessons to prepare.

Zoe had some reading to do. At the end of the week, she would be returning to The Oaks and her studies with Horace Dinsmore, her guardian since her father's death. Unknown to anyone except Mr. Dinsmore, Zoe had formed a plan to attend college. They were working very hard to prepare Zoe for the scholastic rigors of college, and after taking several weeks off to help Vi, Zoe was anxious to get back to her books.

As for Mrs. O'Flaherty, she excused herself when she finished her coffee. She had several important letters to write to her friends in New York. Then she had promised to help Rosemary with her French lesson.

So Vi had Ed and their mother to herself.

"Now, little sister," Ed began, "what is this important matter you need to discuss?"

"You might have guessed that it's about the mission," Vi said. "I talked with Mr. Archibald this morning, and he said that most of the work on the house will be finished in another few weeks. There's still some painting, but the kitchen is the only big job left. Then Mr. Archibald and his men will begin the renovation of the carriage house. The stable is in full working order and the area behind it has been cleared to make a small pasture. All the repairs to the outside of the house are done, and the painters come next week."

"So you are on schedule?" Elsie asked.

"Yes, Mamma," Vi smiled. "I'm very confident we can be open by December."

"But you still have employees to hire," Ed noted.

"I've been working on that," Vi said. "As you know, Dr. and Mrs. Lansing are helping us find a nurse for the clinic. I don't think it will be too difficult to find a cook, and the headmaster at the Boys' Academy has agreed to help me with the search for a teacher."

Vi took several sheets of paper from her pocket, and then slowly she removed her new spectacles from the same pocket. Without raising her face to her mother and brother, she quickly hooked the glasses over her ears and began to scan the papers.

Amused looks passed between Ed and Elsie.

"Will you bite my head off if I say something nice about your new spectacles?" Ed asked his sister.

Vi looked up, and there was just a hint of defiance in her expression.

"Well?" she asked.

"Well, that's it. Your spectacles look very nice," Ed replied. "They don't hide your face in the least."

"They really are quite attractive, dear," Elsie added. "I was afraid they might obscure your beautiful eyes, but they do nothing of the sort."

"They feel very strange," Vi replied, pushing at the piece that bridged her nose. "Luckily I only need them when I read."

She handed the sheets of paper to her brother. "These are bills. I've gone over them all, and as far as I can tell, all the charges are accurate."

"There will be plenty more of these coming in as the work is completed," Ed said.

Violet's Bold Mission

"Which raises one of the issues I wanted to discuss," Vi responded. "We've always known that we would need to raise money to run the mission. I have little idea how to solicit contributions, but I know it is time to learn."

Her remarks set off a lengthy conversation about the how's and when's of seeking funds to support the project. Elsie had long experience of working with charitable organizations, and her daughter and son listened with rapt attention to her every word. They talked on for nearly an hour, making some decisions and setting tasks for themselves.

At last, Elsie asked, "Is there anything else we need to address tonight?"

"Just one, Mamma," Vi replied a little hesitantly. She sat up straighter and cleared her throat. Then she said in a rush, "I want to move into the mission as soon as possible. Mrs. O'Flaherty wants the same. We can achieve so much more if we're there all the time—not driving back and forth every day. We have to get to know the neighborhood better. Right now, we're a curiosity to most of the people. All they see is ladies coming and going in a buggy every day. Word about the mission has gotten around, but we're strangers, and there's no reason for the people to trust us or our motives. We can't help anyone until we know what they really need. And we can't know what's needed until we know the people of Wildwood and live with them."

She stopped suddenly. She had planned out what she would say, but now that it was spoken aloud, her words didn't seem nearly so convincing as they had in her head. Vi was certain that both her mother and Ed would object.

Ed did so instantly. "Two single women alone in that unfinished house—in that neighborhood?" he exclaimed. "You're not being reasonable, Vi. Surely you must know how dangerous that area is, especially at night."

He stood up and began to pace. "I understand your motives," he went on, "but you're rushing things. It was all agreed. You could stay there after all the work on the mission was done and all the employees were hired—including at least one man to guard your safety. But you and Mrs. O by yourselves? It's too big a risk!"

Vi just listened. She knew that Ed's concerns were valid. The mission's neighborhood was not just poor. It included some of the most disreputable hotels and saloons in the city—places were gambling and drinking led almost daily to violence and lawlessness. Even the police avoided the area as much as they could, so that the good people in the neighborhood were plagued with crime. But she also thought about Dr. Amelia Frazier's clinic in New York City, located in the heart of an area that was much more dangerous, and Dr. Frazier wasn't afraid to live with the people she served.

Ed finally appealed to their mother for support.

Elsie responded slowly. "Yes, I agree that it isn't safe for Vi to move to the mission now," she said.

Vi opened her mouth to speak, but Elsie held up her hand. "I also agree that it is not practical for Vi and Mrs. O to be traveling back and forth to the city every day, now that the opening of the mission is so near," she said. "My dears, I want us to find a compromise."

Ed stopped his pacing and said, "That would be fine, Mamma, so long as we don't compromise Vi's safety."

"Do you have an idea, Mamma?" Vi asked hopefully.

"I may," Elsie said. "I understand your eagerness, Vi. To go among the people, that is the model of our Lord. But you must use your head as well as your heart. We are now in early September. It will be another month at least until the house is really finished and you have employed your workers. It is likely to take a month more to complete the conversion of the carriage house to comfortable living quarters for your employees."

Two more months to wait, Vi thought dejectedly.

"But you report that the work on the first two floors of the house is almost done, excepting the kitchen," Elsie went on.

"Yes, ma'am," Vi said.

"And that includes a rather large room and a small sitting room off the kitchen, as I recall from the plans," Elsie said.

"It does," Ed confirmed. "Those rooms will be for the cook."

"But they might have another purpose," Elsie said with a smile, "until the living quarters in the carriage house are complete."

"They could," Vi said, beginning to get the drift of her mother's thinking. "They could be sleeping quarters for anyone."

"So if we can find the right man to guard the house," Elsie said, turning at Ed, "it would seem possible for Vi and Maurene to occupy the mission."

"If we can find the *right* man," Ed repeated firmly.

"Then we may have a solution," Elsie said. She turned to Vi and asked, "Would you agree to let Ed conduct the search for your household guard?"

"Oh, yes, Mamma," Vi said with a happy grin. "As long as my brother agrees not to prolong his search."

Ed came to her side and put his hand on her shoulder. "If you can compromise, so can I, little sister," he said.

"I have another idea, but I don't want to speak of it yet," Elsie said. "Will you allow me a few more days, my dear, to explore some possibilities I have in mind?"

"Of course, Mamma," Vi said, adding, "but not too many days, I hope. You've made me very curious."

Elsie put her arm around her daughter's shoulders and said, "You know the dangers of too much curiosity, Vi. I will not keep you in the dark for long, but you have important work to do in the meantime. Don't let yourself become distracted. The Lord has work for you, and now is not the time for detours, no matter how curious you are."

CHAPTER

3

A New Name

*Your beginnings will seem
humble, so prosperous
will your future be.*

JOB 8:7

A New Name

Vi, Zoe, and Mrs. O made the drive into the city and continued their work on the mission every day for the rest of the week. Herbert and Harold pitched in, too, coming to the house each afternoon after school and then riding home with the ladies. With the twins' strong backs at their service, the attic was soon cleared of its useful items, and the third-floor bedrooms were furnished with beds and dressers. Ed took a half-day to come to the city, inspect the work on the old carriage house, and confer with Mr. Archibald. Before Ed could take his leave, Zoe drafted him into the task of hanging all the pictures she'd found in the attic.

The cleaning proceeded at a furious pace, and by the following Saturday, four bedrooms on the third floor were missing only the new mattresses that Vi had ordered, and just one bedroom remained to be cleaned. Surveying the results of their hard work, the ladies agreed that their Sunday should indeed be a day of rest. They would attend church and enjoy the company of the family at Ion.

Vi hadn't forgotten her conversation with her mother and Ed, and she was churning with curiosity. What was her mother's idea? Had Ed done anything about finding a man to live at the house? It had been almost a week since their talk, and neither had said anything to her. Again and again, she reminded herself to be patient. Whatever her mother and brother were doing, it was for the benefit of the mission.

Following services at their country church, the family were all at the dining table, enjoying their Sunday lunch at Ion, when Danny asked, "What you gonna call the mission, Vi?"

"I'm not sure," she answered. "I could use some ideas."

"I've got an idea," Danny said with uncharacteristic shyness. "I don't think you should call it a mission."

"But why not?" Rosemary asked. "That's what it will be."

"Well, it's gonna be a school," Danny said. "And there's gonna be a nurse to help sick people. If I were a kid who lived there, I might be afraid to go to school or see a nurse at a *mission*. It sounds too grown-up or something."

"Danny has an interesting point," his mother said.

Encouraged by this comment, Danny went on, "I've been thinking that it's a house, like our house. And people feel good when they go to somebody's house."

"It could be Wildwood House," Rosemary said. "That's the name of the street."

"Or perhaps Bell House," Harold suggested. "Bell is the name of the family who owned it for so long."

"That name has a certain *ring* to it," Herbert joked, poking his twin, as everyone groaned at his pun.

"I like those ideas," Vi said. "But what were you thinking, Danny? Have you got an idea?"

"I've been reading my favorite Bible story," he said. "Remember the Good Samaritan—how he helped someone else without thinking of himself? That's what the mission's gonna do, isn't it?"

"The Good Samaritan," Vi mused thoughtfully.

Mrs. O'Flaherty was instantly taken by Danny's idea. "Samaritan House," she said. "Now that does have a nice ring."

They all began talking, and there was general agreement that Samaritan House was a very good name.

"But the choice is up to Vi," Elsie reminded them. And everyone turned to look at Vi. Her face was serious as she contemplated. For some moments, no one made a sound. Forks were held in midair, and even Rosemary stopped eating as the family awaited her response.

Then it came — the dimpled smile.

"I think it's perfect!" Vi declared. "After Jesus told the story of the Good Samaritan, He said, 'Go and do likewise.' That's what the mission will be about — following our Lord's command to love our neighbors as ourselves. It will be a house of love and hope and help. So yes, it should be Samaritan House!"

Danny couldn't help grinning. He'd been feeling somewhat left out of the planning for the mission. He'd listened to all the talk for so many months, and he wanted very much to be a part of it. But what could a nine-year-old contribute to such a grown-up project? He'd thought about it more than anyone realized, and one day it occurred to him that the mission didn't have a name. Everyone said "the mission," but that wouldn't do for Danny. It was like a person, he decided, and a person had to have a name. He thought about it more and tried out many ideas in his head. Then today, his thoughts had just popped out. Nobody made fun of him; they liked his ideas. What boy wouldn't grin with pride when he found a way to help?

"Three cheers for Danny!" Harold declared, and everyone joined in a happy round of hurrahs.

"Thank you, Danny," Vi said. "Our mission has a name now. Every time I say Samaritan House, the name will remind me what the real purpose is. It feels right, doesn't it? Just saying it feels right."

"It feels right to me," Danny replied. And though it hardly seemed possible, his grin grew even wider.

That afternoon, Ed found Vi and Mrs. O'Flaherty taking a stroll in the garden, and he asked them to go to the library with him. Vi wondered what he wanted, but Ed said she'd just have to be patient. Elsie was already in the library when Vi and Mrs. O'Flaherty arrived, but even she had no knowledge of Ed's purpose. The three ladies had some minutes to indulge in speculation before Ed joined them.

"I have a proposal," he said, "but only you can make the decision. I promised to conduct a search for the man to guard the mission. I considered a number of possibilities. I even contemplated hiring someone with training in the police or perhaps the military. Then a couple of days ago, I was working in the fields again, and the right man walked up to me and said 'hello.' "

He paused, having a little fun at drawing out the suspense.

"Who was it?" Vi finally demanded.

Smiling, Ed said, "Someone whom I trust completely. The strongest man in our employ and one of the smartest."

Vi knew immediately. She cried out, "Enoch! It has to be Enoch Reeve!"

"You got it on the first guess, little sister," Ed smiled. "Who would be better? We've talked about a guard, but what you really need is a first-rate caretaker."

"But what of Enoch's wife and baby?" Elsie asked anxiously. "He would not be separated from Christine and little Jacob."

"No, Mamma, it is we who must be separated from Christine and the baby," Ed replied. "My proposal is that the Reeves move to the mission—to Samaritan House. They would become caretaker and housekeeper. We know how capable Christine is. She was such a wonderful nursemaid to Danny, and with her experience she'd be a superb assistant with small children. I know how valuable she is here, and we would miss her and Enoch. But think what an opportunity this would be for them. Higher pay, of course. And when the renovation of the carriage house is completed, they'd have their own home—larger than their place in the servants' quarter now."

"But have you discussed this with Enoch?" Elsie asked.

"Yesterday," Ed said. "I made it clear that it was only a possibility, but he was very interested. I learned some things I never knew before. It turns out that he was raised in India Bay. He left in 1862 when he was sixteen. He made his way north and joined the Union Army. He was in one of the all-Negro regiments—brave men who never got the recognition they deserved. During Reconstruction, Enoch came back to the city, but all his family were either dead or gone. He considered moving west, but he said that he wanted to plant himself here, where his roots are. Then he heard about Papa, and he sought work at Ion."

"I remember when he first came to us," Elsie said with a wistful smile. "From the start, Edward trusted Enoch implicitly. Your Papa was so pleased when Enoch began to court Christine. And we all know how happy Enoch and Christine are, especially now they have baby Jacob. You're right that I shall miss them very much, but if they would agree—what do you say, Vi?"

"I say that Ed is almost as clever as Danny," Vi teased. "If the Reeves want to be part of the mission, it would be wonderful. When can you talk to them, Ed?"

"First thing tomorrow."

In her excitement, Vi had almost forgotten her own goal to move to the house as soon as possible. But it came back, and her face fell.

"This means we can't live at the mission until the carriage house is done and Enoch and Christine can move in," she said.

Elsie patted Vi's hand and said, "Surely that is a small sacrifice compared to having the Reeves at Samaritan House."

"And Mr. Archibald has promised to hurry the work on the carriage house," Ed added. "So maybe it won't be too long a wait."

Vi nodded, though she couldn't completely dispel her disappointment. Still, there was no question about her decision. If they agreed, Enoch and Christine Reeve and their son would join her project soon enough.

Violet's Bold Mission

Vi's expression changed to a lovely smile. "Clearly God is reminding me that patience has its rewards," she said brightly. "What are two more months of bumpy rides compared to having the Reeves join our Samaritan House family?"

<hr />

The new week dawned bright and early the next morning. Zoe came to Vi's bedroom almost as soon as it was light. She was going to The Oaks that morning and wanted to say good-bye.

"I'm torn between helping you and getting back to my lessons," Zoe said. "But Uncle Horace says that if I study very hard for the next two weeks, then he will allow me another week to stay here and go to the mission."

"That will be splendid," Vi said with a happy smile. "I know Grandpapa and Grandmamma have missed your presence at The Oaks. I can give you up for two weeks, if I must. It's a good compromise, isn't it? I've been learning a great deal about compromise lately."

"So long as you don't compromise your principles, that's a good thing," Zoe replied. "I came in so early because I was hoping we might share our devotion this morning. I was thinking about John 15, when Jesus talks to the disciples and tells them that He calls them friends and commands them to love each other, as He loves them."

Vi picked up her Bible and turned quickly to the passage. She read it aloud. Then the two girls discussed its meaning for them.

"It is an awesome promise," Zoe said gravely. She quoted, " 'Remain in me, and I will remain in you. No branch can bear fruit by itself; it must remain in the vine. Neither can you bear fruit unless you remain in me.' "

"Jesus was preparing His disciples for His death," Vi said. "He was strengthening them for what was to come. He was telling us of His eternal love for all who love Him. I'm glad you chose that passage, Zoe. It seems sad, on the surface, but what a great depth of hope and love it offers us."

"That's my feeling too," Zoe said. She put her hand over Vi's and continued, "You're taking on such a challenge, but our Heavenly Friend will be with you no matter what. I wanted you to know that I will as well. I will always be your friend, and you can count on me."

Vi saw tears glistening in Zoe's eyes. But Zoe quickly blinked them away and smiled. "Oh, don't mind me. I'm just being sentimental. Whoever would have thought that I could enjoy scrubbing and sweeping so much? After my days at Samaritan House, I fear I may have difficulty settling back into my bookish ways."

"In two weeks, I'll have to retrain you for housekeeping," Vi laughed warmly.

At that moment, there was a knock at Vi's door, and Elsie came in. "I guessed you were here, Zoe, when I found your room empty," she said. "I received a note from Papa last night. He's sending a carriage from The Oaks to get you this morning. He told me to warn you that he plans an American history lesson today and to mention Marbury versus Madison. Do you take his meaning?"

At that, Zoe jumped up from her seat and exclaimed, "Chief Justice Marshall and the Supreme Court! Oh, it is a most important topic in American history! Did you know what a good teacher your father is, Cousin Elsie?"

Elsie smiled and said, "He was my teacher, too, but I'm afraid that history was not my best subject. You girls finish dressing and come downstairs. Don't dawdle now. Breakfast is waiting."

Violet's Bold Mission

It was not quite nine o'clock when the Dinsmore carriage arrived for Zoe. Then Vi and Mrs. O'Flaherty took the buggy for their trip into the city. Despite the bumps in the old country road, Vi always enjoyed driving the buggy herself. She already missed Zoe, but being at the reins raised her spirits and renewed her energy.

An hour later, they reached the city, and Vi steered toward Main Street and their now daily route to the Wildwood district. They passed through the business center with its many shops and office buildings—the hub of India Bay's commercial interests. The carriage then rolled southward by the railway station and along streets that ran parallel to the railroad tracks. Within a single block, the new commercial buildings (most of them built since the Civil War) gave way to shabbiness and decay. It always jarred Vi to see the sudden change from prosperity to poverty. *How does this happen?* she asked herself, and as usual, she could find no logical answer for the literal divide—almost like an invisible wall—that existed between the people of India Bay.

As they approached the house on Wildwood, there were a number of people out on the street, but as usual, most paid no attention to the passing buggy, and some turned their backs in a deliberate way. The few who looked did so with hard, suspicious stares. Vi had come to dread this final part of the drive—with their feeling battered by those hard, mistrusting eyes.

Just before they reached the gates to the house, Vi reined the horse from a trot to a walk. Out of the corner of her eye, she glanced toward the broken sidewalk and saw a young mother holding a little girl by the hand. The child, who was no older than five or six, looked at the buggy and began to wave. The mother, who might have been expected to hurry her child away, paused. Then she smiled—a lovely, kind smile that drew an immediate and equally warm smile from Vi. Mrs.

A New Name

O'Flaherty had also noticed the little family, and she waved gaily to the little girl.

Vi guided the horse and buggy through the gates of Samaritan House, and the moment was over. But Vi would always remember it: the bright smiles, the child's waves—their first genuine greeting from the world of Wildwood Street.

One of Mr. Archibald's workers came forward to take the buggy to the back of the house and unhitch the horse.

As she and Mrs. O'Flaherty entered the house, Vi's heart was pounding a little. She took a deep breath.

"At least two people seemed glad to see us, Mrs. O," she said to her companion. "It's a beginning."

"Our first neighbors," Mrs. O'Flaherty replied. "It's indeed a beginning, Vi girl."

When Vi and Mrs. O'Flaherty returned to Ion that afternoon, they were surprised to see an elegant brougham standing in the driveway. A driver in full livery stood beside the handsome carriage, talking to a young stableman. The stableman took the buggy from Vi, and the liveried driver bowed politely to the ladies as they walked up the steps.

An elderly women was sitting in a chair in the hallway. Vi rushed to hug her old nursemaid and friend, who responded with a chipper smile. "How are you today, Aunt Chloe?" Vi asked.

It wasn't a casual question. Chloe, who had been with the family since before Elsie Dinsmore was born, was in her eighties. The year before, she had lost her husband, Joe, and his death had weakened her. Not in mind or spirit. And never in her faith. But her body—always so strong—had grown thin and fragile. Chloe was still a revered presence in the household, but her activities had been greatly curtailed, and it was impossible not to worry about her health.

Violet's Bold Mission

"I'm doin' good," Chloe told Vi. "I like to sit in this chair and feel the sun on my face. Remember how Joe used to sit here in the afternoons, keepin' a lookout for Mr. Ed comin' home from school and Missy from her errands in the city? Well, your Mamma asked if I'd mind watchin' out for you and Mrs. O'Flaherty today. There's an important visitor in the parlor, and I think you might hear some news. Elsie says don't worry 'bout washin' up."

"What news?" Vi asked as she untied her bonnet.

"That's not for me to say," Chloe chuckled. "But nothin' bad, for sure. Fluff up your hair a bit and go on in."

Vi did as she was told and gave her hair a quick toss. Then she and Mrs. O'Flaherty entered the parlor.

Elsie was sitting on the couch with an older woman whom Vi instantly recognized. It was Mrs. Silas Lansing, the wife of India Bay's most respected surgeon and a dear friend of all the Travillas.

"Here they are," said Mrs. Lansing cheerfully. "Vi, Mrs. O'Flaherty, I have come to see you. Your mother has kept me delightfully entertained, but you two are the objects of my visit."

Elsie was smiling at her friend with great affection. "Naomi has brought an invitation," Elsie said. "Take your seats and let me serve you tea while she tells you what is on her mind."

Vi and Mrs. O'Flaherty sat down in chairs across from the couch.

"I wish we could chat, but I must return home very shortly," Mrs. Lansing said. "First, I have business to take care of. I have found three well-qualified candidates for the nursing position at the mission. You can interview them this week if you will be in town."

"We go to the house every day now," Vi replied. "As long as they can meet during the day, then any time will be fine."

"Excellent," Mrs. Lansing said. "If it's all right with you, I'll go ahead and make the appointments. I will send you a note tomorrow regarding the days and times. I think they should come to the mission to meet with you. All three women are experienced nurses, and nothing shocks them. But they need to see the area and the house. Whoever you choose should know just what she is in for. Is that agreeable?"

"Yes, ma'am," Vi said quickly. She adored Mrs. Lansing's brisk manner, though she had to be quick to keep up with the pace.

Mrs. Lansing smiled. "Very good," she said. "With the Lord's help, you should have a nurse by the end of the week. Now as to my invitation. Your mother wrote to me about your desire to move into the mission. It makes perfect sense to me that you should not have to make that long drive to and from the city every day. But it is not sensible that you two should stay there alone. I discussed it with Dr. Lansing, and he agreed totally. You want to get to know the people in the area, which is admirable. But until they get to know you and your purpose, it is not safe. I understand that a couple will be moving to the mission, but not for at least a month."

Vi's eyes flew wide open, and she looked at her mother.

"It's true," Elsie said. "Enoch and Christine have agreed to take the positions."

Vi started to express her delight, but Mrs. Lansing spoke first.

"Until the couple can move in," she said, "I want you and Mrs. O'Flaherty to stay with Dr. Lansing and me. You can work from dawn to dusk if you like, then come to our home and eat and sleep. We have no intention of monitoring your movements. I just want our home to be your safe harbor until the mission is ready. What do you say?"

Vi was almost dumbfounded. So this was her mother's idea!

Vi looked questioningly at Elsie.

"It seems a perfect alternative to me," Elsie said. "All I ask is that you come home on Sundays."

Vi turned to Mrs. O'Flaherty who said, "It is a grand invitation, girl. And I would be happy to accept."

Vi looked back to Mrs. Lansing and exclaimed, "Oh, yes! We accept! You and Dr. Lansing are so kind to invite us. I prayed that I might find a way."

"Well, our Good Lord must have whispered your prayer in my ear," Mrs. Lansing replied. "Your mother wrote to ask if I knew of a private home that might take temporary boarders. I read her words and thought, 'Of course, I do. Our home!' Dr. Lansing thinks it's a brilliant idea, but then he is always so surprised by female common sense that he thinks it is brilliant. He's very interested in your project, you know. You'll need to pack, of course. Will Thursday be too soon to join us?"

"Thursday would be fine," Vi said.

"Then plan to come around eleven," Mrs. Lansing said. "You can unpack and have lunch with Dr. Lansing and me and still have a full afternoon at the mission."

Mrs. Lansing stood. "I'm really quite excited about this," she said, cocking her head slightly to the side and seeming to study both Vi and Mrs. O'Flaherty. "Our houseguests are usually other surgeons and medical professors — all geniuses in their fields, I suppose. But it is very difficult entertaining guests whose only interests are innards and germs. You two are doing me a favor. I shall enjoy the company of charming, intelligent ladies for a change."

Vi laughed and gave Mrs. Lansing a hug. Mrs. O'Flaherty thanked the lady graciously and shook her hand. Then Mrs. Lansing retrieved her purse and gloves and strode across the room — with Elsie just behind her.

"Remember," Mrs. Lansing said. "Look for my note about the nurses tomorrow. I shall expect you both on Thursday.

Oh, yes, tell that young brother of yours that he's a very bright lad. Samaritan House—it's perfect."

Vi could not find words to express her delight. Her eyes still round as saucers, she looked at Mrs. O'Flaherty.

"The Lord has surely provided for us," Mrs. O'Flaherty said. "When we saw that young mother and her child today and they reached out to us with their smiles and waves, I had the feeling that a good wind was blowing our way. And now we have Mrs. Lansing's invitation. I do like that good lady very much. For all the Lansings' wealth and social position, she is as down-to-earth as can be."

Elsie had just returned to the parlor. "The Lansings weren't always wealthy," she said. "They married when he was still in medical college, and she has told me that their early years together were a struggle. One of the reasons she gives so much of herself to causes for the poor is that she never forgets what it feels like."

Elsie sat down again and refilled their cups. "We'll have some packing to do, but first, enjoy your tea and tell me about your day at Samaritan House."

Vi and Mrs. O'Flaherty resumed their seats, and Vi described the ride into India Bay and the mother and child they'd seen on the street.

"It is a beginning," Elsie said when Vi finished. " 'The kingdom of heaven is like a mustard seed,' " she quoted from the Book of Matthew, " 'which a man took and planted in his field. Though it is the smallest of all your seeds, yet when it grows, it is the largest of garden plants and becomes a tree, so that the birds of the air come and perch in its branches.' "

Elsie took a sip of her tea and then continued, "I have always loved that parable. Jesus tells us again and again to

43

have faith—that faith as small as a mustard seed can move mountains. You must hold that knowledge in your heart, Vi dear. Your real work has not yet begun. Restoring the house and transforming it into a suitable home for the mission will be as nothing compared to the tasks ahead. The people you hope to help will not all welcome your efforts. They have probably seen other people, including many well-intentioned Christians, come and go. Sadly, they have too often been disappointed by offers of aid that failed to materialize. Some will never trust you and the mission, no matter what you do. You must be prepared for that."

Vi's expression had turned serious as her mother spoke. "I think of that a lot, Mamma," she said. "I know I have to be realistic in my expectations. Reverend Carpenter told me so. Dr. Frazier is even more adamant. One time when I was at her clinic, a woman brought her father in. He looked very old to me, but Dr. Frazier told me he was not yet fifty. He had a cancer, and there was nothing that could be done to save him. I could see how much his case saddened Dr. Frazier. All she could provide was medication that would dull his terrible pain. I asked her how she kept up her spirits, and she said, 'By trusting God.' She told me that when she truly accepted Jesus as her model for life, she was able to see that it was not up to her to decide what was a failure and what was a success. Her duty was to use the gifts God had given her to the best of her abilities and trust the outcome to Him."

"I hope to meet Dr. Frazier sometime," Elsie said. "From everything you tell me of her, she is clearly a woman with wisdom beyond her years."

"Yes, wisdom and experience. I learned so much from her. She told me that people who help the poor need to remember that although their situation in life might be better than those they help, they *themselves* are not better," Vi said with passion. "I hope the people of Wildwood will know that I truly believe *all* people are of equal worth before God."

A New Name

"We will pray that they do, Vi," Elsie replied. A moment passed between the women, then Elsie said thoughtfully, "Dr. Frazier, Dinah and Reverend Carpenter, Mrs. O'Flaherty— you have many good teachers. The Lord always guides us to people who can help us as we plant the tiny mustard seed and nurture it into a tall tree."

Looking down at the watch pinned to her blouse, Elsie then said, "My timepiece is telling me that it is late, and you two have had no chance even to wash the dust from your faces."

Elsie and Mrs. O'Flaherty both stood, but Vi didn't stir.

"Is there something else, Vi dear?" Elsie asked.

Vi looked up. There was a strange, intense expression on her face.

"Something just dawned on me," she said. "The woman and her child today—it was *they* who planted the mustard seed. It was *their* faith that enabled them to greet us as no one else on Wildwood Street has before. Our mission really did begin today—because of *them*. I've been thinking in terms of helping others. But I was the one who needed help. The mission really isn't just a place, is it? The mission has been growing there all along in the hearts of a mother and her child, and who knows how many others."

Her face brightened with a smile as she added, "I don't know their names, but I must add them to my list of teachers. I have so very much to learn."

CHAPTER

4

Just the Right Person?

Find rest, O my soul, in God alone; my hope comes from him.

PSALM 62:5

Just the Right Person?

$\mathcal{T}$he preparations for the move to the Lansings' were accomplished on time, thanks in the main to Elsie and Mrs. O'Flaherty. Vi's days were taken up with interviewing and choosing a nurse for the clinic. Mrs. Lansing set three interviews, as she promised; then at the last minute, she added a fourth name to the list of candidates.

Vi met with two women on Wednesday and one on Thursday morning. They were all as well qualified as Mrs. Lansing had said. Each had many years' experience, plus sterling letters of recommendation from their former employers. One had nursed soldiers during the War, another had spent several years as a missionary nurse in Asia, and the third had only recently retired as the matron at a large hospital in a neighboring state.

Vi spent several hours with each of these candidates. She explained the goals of the mission and solicited the women's thinking. She showed them about the house and grounds, and they discussed what the work at Samaritan House would entail. But after each meeting, Vi found herself with doubts. With only one more candidate to see, she worried that she might have to begin the search over again.

By the time she arrived at the Lansings' at a few minutes after eleven o'clock on Thursday morning, Vi was well aware that she needed advice. She was very glad to see the large carriage from Ion parked beneath the Lansings' portico when she pulled her little buggy up to the house.

Rosemary ran out to meet her. "Mamma let me come with her today," Rosemary bubbled. "We're going to visit with Mrs. Lansing until we can get the twins at school. Ben took all your bags inside, and Mrs. O'Flaherty has unpacked for you, and you have such a beautiful room. We'll have lunch when Dr. Lansing comes and—"

Vi held her hand up and said laughingly, "Let me put my feet on the ground, sister. You're talking like a runaway train."

"Sorry, but I have important things to tell you," Rosemary replied with a little huff. "Mrs. Lansing said to tie the horse to that metal thing over there." She pointed to a wrought iron railing. "Someone's coming to take care of him."

"I'll tie the *reins* to the hitching post," Vi said. "I don't think I am strong enough to tie up a horse by myself."

"I'm to show you to the parlor," Rosemary went on, not noticing that she had been corrected.

Everyone was waiting when Vi and Rosemary entered. Vi greeted her mother and Mrs. O'Flaherty and Mrs. Lansing. Then getting straight to business, Mrs. Lansing asked Vi how the interviews had gone.

Frowning slightly, Vi said, "I'm not sure I know," she said. "All the women are very nice and more than qualified. But..." She hesitated, uncertain what to say next.

"But you have not met just the right person," Mrs. Lansing said with an understanding smile. "I think that Mrs. Black may have seemed a bit too stiff, and Miss Vine a little too anxious to please. Perhaps Matron Jones appeared somewhat too determined to do things her way."

Vi looked at Mrs. Lansing with wonderment. "Then I'm not imagining possible difficulties?" she asked.

"No, my dear," Mrs. Lansing replied. "You are simply encountering the problems that every employer must deal with. The ladies you've met are all superior nurses and very fine people. That doesn't mean that they are the right choice for the mission. Any can do the work you need, but whether they are temperamentally suited for your project is another issue entirely. I guess, however, that your interviews have given you a better idea of what you *do* want in the person you hire."

Vi nodded in agreement. "That's true," she said.

"Well, you still have one candidate to see tomorrow," Mrs. Lansing said. "And if she is not what you seek, then we'll arrange more interviews. I have a long list of names, and I'm sure your nurse is among them. Don't worry. You must trust your instincts, Vi, and the Lord will provide."

"I trust Him completely, but I'm not so sure of my instincts," Vi said with a little laugh.

"Well, let us turn to other matters now," Mrs. Lansing replied. "Your mother and Mrs. O'Flaherty and I have been discussing the issue of finances for Samaritan House, and we have some ideas that are, I think, quite interesting."

As they waited for Dr. Lansing to arrive—the ladies talked about ways to raise money and build community support for the mission. Indeed, the ideas were interesting, and Vi tried to pay close attention. But despite Mrs. Lansing's admonition that she not worry, Vi couldn't put the problem of finding a nurse from her mind. *What is it that I'm really looking for?* Vi asked herself. *And do I have the wisdom to recognize it when it comes along?*

Vi and Mrs. O'Flaherty immediately settled into their temporary home with the Lansings. The eminent surgeon and his briskly capable wife were surprisingly easygoing hosts—not at all formal as one might expect two of the leading citizens of India Bay to be. Their whole household seemed to take its lead from the couple, and by the end of the first day, Vi felt almost as comfortable as if she were at home at Ion.

She awoke feeling strangely excited after her first night in the Lansings' spacious guest bedroom. It was going to be a busy day at Samaritan House. The architect was coming to check the progress of the construction. The painters would be there, raising their ladders and beginning the work of painting

the outside of the house. Vi and Mrs. O'Flaherty planned to finish their cleaning of the third floor, where only one room was left to do. And in the afternoon, Vi would conduct her interview with the fourth of Mrs. Lansing's candidates for nurse.

Vi's mind was humming as she dressed in a simple calico frock, suitable for the day's labor. She considered taking a change of clothes so that she might look more impressive for her afternoon interview. But, no, she decided. It would be best for Miss Clayton—that was the nurse's name—to see the real life of the mission.

Vi and Mrs. O'Flaherty breakfasted with the Lansings, who were early risers, and joined in their morning devotion. The little buggy was waiting at the door for them, and they made the drive to the mission in good time, arriving not long after Mr. Archibald and his crew.

They chatted with the head carpenter about the day's plans, and then Mr. Archibald told them something that might have been disturbing, if Vi hadn't been in such good spirits.

"I don't want to worry you," Mr. Archibald began, "but I think there's been someone in the house. In the kitchen. When I came in this morning, there were some things out of place. There's an old tin plate on the table with some crusts of bread in it. And it looks like somebody lit a fire in the fireplace. I found some half-burned twigs and bits of charred paper. I thought maybe one of the men might have left things there yesterday. But they all say they didn't. They say the kitchen was cleared up when they finished work and nobody burned so much as a match—not with all the sawdust around."

"Is anything missing?" Mrs. O'Flaherty asked.

"Not that I can see," replied Mr. Archibald. "I looked all around the downstairs and the second floor, and I didn't see anything gone."

"How would someone get in?" Mrs. O'Flaherty pressed.

"I closed up good when we left yesterday," Mr. Archibald said, shaking his head in a gesture of frustration. "But one of the windows in the kitchen wasn't locked. The window that we put the new panes in. I guess I missed it when I was checking. I'm mighty sorry about that."

Vi concentrated for several moments. Then she said, "If nothing was taken, perhaps someone was just seeking shelter. It was cool last night, I noticed. Maybe someone only wanted to stay inside. I'm not worried, Mr. Archibald. After all, the purpose of this house is to serve those in need."

"It likely wasn't a thief," Mr. Archibald responded. "But it's dangerous all the same. That fire bothers me. An old house like this is — well, I don't want all the work we're doing to go up in flames. I'd like to put in new locks, Miss Travilla. Doors and windows. I'd feel better getting good, strong locks on everything."

Vi gave her approval, and Mr. Archibald vowed to complete the installation that very day.

When Mr. Archibald had excused himself, Mrs. O'Flaherty headed straight for the stairway. She wanted to look around the upper floors, just in case there was any sign of disturbance.

"You're not really concerned, are you?" Vi asked.

"It can't hurt to check," Mrs. O'Flaherty said. "Better safe than sorry, Vi girl. That's always a good motto."

The older woman mounted the steps, but Vi went to the kitchen. There were several men working there, and they greeted her. But all signs of a "visitor" had been cleared away. The fireplace had been swept and the old kitchen table was now piled with the carpenters' tools and materials.

Vi thought little more about it as she went to join Mrs. O'Flaherty.

Violet's Bold Mission

In anticipation of the interview, Vi finally laid aside her rags and broom at a little before three. She washed her face and hands, brushed her hair, put on a clean apron, and went to await Miss Clayton.

At three on the dot, there was a knock at the door. Vi opened it to find a young woman in a trim, dark blue suit and a pert little straw hat.

"Miss Travilla?" the young woman asked.

"I am," Vi responded. "And you must be Miss Clayton. Please come in. As you see, we are still under construction. But welcome to Samaritan House."

Miss Clayton entered, looking this way and that at the house. Vi tried to read her expression, but the young woman's rather plain and decidedly pale face revealed nothing as her eyes scanned the entry hall and the rooms beyond. She followed Vi into the old parlor, where a couple of chairs and a small table had been placed near the front window.

"This will be the meeting and dining room," Vi explained.

A loud round of pounding suddenly came from the rear of the house.

"The carpenters are working on the new kitchen," Vi said, "so we may be interrupted off and on by the hammering. I hope it isn't too disconcerting."

"Not at all," Miss Clayton said pleasantly.

Vi gestured to the chairs, and they sat down. Miss Clayton reached into her rather large purse and withdrew an envelope, presenting it to Vi.

"My credentials," she said, "such as they are."

Vi took a sheet from the envelope and began to read. She didn't notice Miss Clayton's quick eyes moving about the large room, taking in every detail.

Miss Clayton's credentials were hardly as extensive as the three earlier candidates', but Vi immediately noticed a name.

"You trained at the Homeopathic Hospital in Pittsburgh," she said.

"I did, and I could not have asked for better. But I'm surprised you've heard of it."

"I have cousins who did their medical studies in Philadelphia," Vi said. "They've spoken of the Homeopathic as one of the leading hospitals in Pennsylvania. I believe it serves many of the poor there."

"It does," Miss Clayton confirmed, her expression brightening just a bit. "Both the poor and the laboring classes. It is a place where factory injuries often outnumber illnesses."

"Did that bother you?" Vi asked bluntly.

Miss Clayton's eyes widened for a split second. "Bother?" she repeated. "It bothers me that hardworking men, women, and children were so often maimed as the result of injuries that could easily have been prevented. But if you are asking whether I was bothered by working in a city hospital that treats the poor and working people, then my answer is no. It often exhausted me, and it could be discouraging. But it was both humbling and inspiring to help people who faced misfortune with more fortitude than I ever thought possible."

"Why did you leave, then?"

"My own health," Miss Clayton said, lowering her head slightly. "As you see there, I stayed at the hospital for two years after I finished my training. I was very interested in public health, and I had ambitions to join the public health service. But the atmosphere of the city finally made me ill. The city's air is so thick with the black soot of the giant blast furnaces that it became agony for me to breathe, and I was advised to move away before my health was broken beyond repair. I have an aunt who lives here in India Bay, and she asked me to come live with her. I've been here for several months—recuperating as my doctors in Pittsburgh ordered. Now I'm restored and very anxious to return to nursing. I've had several offers of private positions, but when Mrs. Lansing told me of your mission and your need for a nurse, I knew that I had to apply. I'm younger and probably far less experienced than your other applicants, but this is the kind of work I want to do, Miss Travilla. The wealthy can always find good care when they are ill, but the wealthy won't come here, will they? The people who will come here deserve care every bit as much as those who purchase it."

Miss Clayton spoke these words in an even tone, but Vi heard passion beneath her steadiness.

"Private nursing would be easier, I assume," Vi said.

"It can be," Miss Clayton agreed, "but what I have done of it is not satisfying for me."

Then for the first time, she smiled. "I'm selfish, Miss Travilla," she said. "I want to feel happy, and I'm happiest with hard work. I need to believe that I'm part of a larger purpose — serving a cause that is bigger than myself. Are you familiar with the Book of Ecclesiastes?"

Vi nodded.

"Then you'll know these words: 'Whatever your hand finds to do, do it with all your might.' My hands are good at nursing. I need to put them to work. I can see what you're doing here, and for the first time since I left Pittsburgh, I feel that I'm in a place where I can work with all my might."

"It will often involve long hours," Vi said. "Your health?"

"I'm recovered," Miss Clayton said, "but I understand your concern. Please, talk to Dr. Lansing. He and Mrs. Lansing are friends of my aunt, and he has been my physician since I arrived. He has my permission to speak frankly to you."

"I think I know what he will tell me, but I'm obliged to inquire," Vi said. Folding the sheet of paper and putting it in her pocket, she asked, "Do you have time for a tour of the house? I can tell you our plans, and there's someone I'd like you to meet."

Miss Clayton stood instantly. "I'd like that very much," she said. Then her sharp eyes surveyed the old parlor once again. "It must have been a beautiful house in its youth," she said in a soft tone. "Do you know its history?"

Just the Right Person?

Vi couldn't have been more pleased by that question. None of the other candidates had exhibited any interest in the house, and Vi now realized that omission had disappointed her. Over the months of renovation, she had come to think of the house as a symbol of her goal—a thing of beauty that had been ignored and left to crumble, yet was now being saved and given a new purpose. Miss Clayton's simple interest revealed that she, too, had a sense of place. It was the beginning of a bond.

This tour lasted longer than any of the previous ones, for Miss Clayton had many questions—all of which, it seemed to Vi, were highly intelligent. They walked about the garden, and Vi showed her guest the carriage house. Returning to the house, Vi explained the uses to which each of the rooms would be put. They spent a good deal of time in the second-floor room that would be the clinic. Miss Clayton made several excellent suggestions, and then asked a question that no one had raised before.

"What will you do about people who cannot walk up the stairs?" she asked. "I believe that this part of the city includes many elderly and infirm people, including veterans of the War. It is never easy for them to get around."

Vi's hand flew to her mouth. "Oh! I haven't thought of that! You are so right, Miss Clayton. I cannot imagine how we were so thoughtless."

"It's not beyond cure, Miss Travilla," Miss Clayton said in her even way. "I can give you some ideas—arrangements that have been made for hospitals and convalescent homes. It's not necessary to change your plans. There are ways to make your clinic open to all."

"Miss Clayton, I can obviously use your help," Vi replied with a smile. "I want to talk about this further. But first, it's time for you to meet Mrs. O'Flaherty."

Violet's Bold Mission

Without more explanation, Vi led the young woman from the clinic area and up the stairway to the third floor. Mrs. O'Flaherty was in the hallway. She stood on a small stepladder and was polishing the glass chimneys of the new gaslights. She turned when she heard the young ladies approaching and carefully backed down the ladder—revealing the heavy boots and bright stockings she always wore when she worked.

"I'd like to present Miss Clayton," Vi said. "She has applied for the nurse's position."

Miss Clayton put out her hand, and Mrs. O'Flaherty took it in a firm grasp.

Vi then said, "Miss Clayton is already helping us. She has a concern about the clinic, and I want her to explain it to you. If you have the time, Miss Clayton, would you mind telling Mrs. O'Flaherty the ideas you shared with me? We can go back to the clinic room, so you can point out things as we talk."

In truth, Miss Clayton was a little bewildered, for she had no idea who this Mrs. O'Flaherty—dressed like a housemaid and wearing bright green hose!—was. But the young nurse was more than happy to discuss the clinic, and not only because she had applied to work there. In her tour of the house and grounds, Miss Clayton had almost forgotten her own objective as she was caught up in Vi's vision of the mission and her dedication to serving the poor. It was clear that Vi was doing what Miss Clayton herself strove to do: acting on her Christian faith and living her life as Jesus had commanded. Without hesitation, she agreed to stay and talk about the clinic.

Following Vi and Mrs. O'Flaherty back down to the empty white room that would soon be opened to people in need, Miss Clayton had another idea. Whether or not she was employed here, she wanted to be part of this mission.

Unknown to her, Vi was having similar thoughts.

"I'm sorry we're late," Vi said as she and Mrs. O'Flaherty entered the parlor where Dr. and Mrs. Lansing were sitting. "We took Miss Clayton to her aunt's house, for it was growing dark when we ended our interview."

"Supper isn't for another hour. Besides, I told you that we don't expect you to follow our schedule," Mrs. Lansing replied. "But was Miss Clayton late? I thought the interview was at three o'clock. That was almost four hours ago."

"She arrived exactly on time," Vi said. "It was we who kept her so late."

Dr. Lansing smiled and said, "Can I assume that she impressed you?"

"I believe that Vi has found our nurse," Mrs. O'Flaherty replied.

"She told you of her health problem?" the doctor said inquiringly.

"She said I should ask you about her condition," Vi said.

The doctor laid aside the newspaper he'd been reading. "She has no condition now, aside from good health. The air of Pittsburgh caused her problem, but in her months here she has completely recovered. She is a strong young woman and very hopeful of returning to her profession."

"Good," Vi said with a happy sigh. "You said the Lord would provide, Mrs. Lansing, and He has. I will write Miss Clayton tonight and offer the position. But I've been wondering about something. Was there a reason that you arranged for me to see her after the other ladies?"

Mrs. Lansing smiled slyly. "I thought merely that you would benefit from comparing all the options. Miss Clayton is not a showy young person and on first meeting she may seem a bit plain, both in appearance and in speaking. If you'd met her before the others, you might have been inclined to think her experience lacking. I simply thought it more fair to you and Miss Clayton if you talked with the older ladies first. That way you could have a better sense of what you want in a nurse for the mission. If you'd selected one of the other ladies, I still had some ideas for Miss Clayton."

Dr. Lansing laughed out loud and said, "My clever wife always has her reasons, and I've learned never to question them."

"Well, you were right, Mrs. Lansing," Vi said. "I'm not experienced at hiring anyone, and I might not have spent so much time with Miss Clayton had I seen her first. I admit she is not what I had in mind when I pictured a nurse for the mission. But she is exactly what we need. What she lacks in experience she more than makes up for in good sense and determination. Now that I've met her, I can't imagine anyone else at Samaritan House. Oh, you do think she'll accept, don't you?"

"I feel sure that by this time tomorrow evening, Samaritan House will have its nurse," Mrs. Lansing said.

"And that is a prediction which, as my business friends say, you can take to the bank!" Dr. Lansing declared with another jovial laugh.

5

Moving Days

*My people will live in peaceful
dwelling places, in secure
homes, in undisturbed
places of rest.*

ISAIAH 32:18

*T*ime seemed to fly by. The work on the house was completed, and the transformation of the carriage house proceeded ahead of schedule—thanks to a streak of clear weather that allowed Mr. Archibald's crew to work without interruption. Vi and Mrs. O'Flaherty—with help from Zoe during her week of respite from her studies and also from the twins, who came every day after school—completed the cleaning of the house. Carpets were laid, draperies were hung, and the new furnishings began to be delivered. Ed, who visited the mission several times each week now, was often closeted in the office with Vi, ordering supplies and setting up the mission's record-keeping system. Rosemary also came a number of times, working energetically and amusing everyone with her comments.

"Why don't you just hire somebody to do all this?" she asked one day as she was rubbing the new desks in the schoolroom with wax.

"Because we have you, my girl," Mrs. O'Flaherty said.

Rosemary pouted, "That's not funny, Mrs. O."

"I meant it as a compliment," Mrs. O'Flaherty replied. "You are a good worker, and when everything is done, you'll have the satisfaction of knowing that you've contributed to the preparation of the mission. You can take pride in that."

"But pride is sinful, isn't it?" Rosemary asked.

"False and arrogant pride is," Mrs. O'Flaherty said. "But remember what the apostle Paul wrote to the Galatians: 'Each one should test his own actions. Then he can take pride in himself, without comparing himself to someone else, for each one should carry his own load.' The Lord doesn't deny us the feeling of pride, when it's deserved."

"Well, I'll be satisfied when these desks are done," Rosemary said, rubbing harder than ever. "When I was little, Papa used to tease about sending me to the shop for some 'elbow grease' when I complained about picking up my toys or making my bed. I believed there really was a shop where you could buy elbow grease. If there were, I would buy some now."

"You have that pot of bee's wax instead," said Mrs. O'Flaherty with a grin. "And your youthful energy. There's no need to waste money on elbow grease for you."

Miss Clayton—Emily—had accepted Vi's offer as speedily as Mrs. Lansing predicted, and she became a daily presence at the house. But after a week, Vi noticed a change in her new colleague. At first Vi worried that Emily might be ill or overworked. The young woman's face lost its pallor, and her cheeks were flushed with pink. Her eyes, which were a clear gray-blue, seemed almost to glow. The young nurse looked like someone with a fever.

Privately, Vi expressed her concern to Mrs. O'Flaherty.

"She's not ill," Mrs. O assured. "She is happy. She is working again, and the flush in her cheeks and shine in her eyes come from the happiness she feels inside. I went to the clinic yesterday to leave a box of linens. Emily was there, washing out the large medicine cabinet. And do you know what she was also doing? Whistling. I don't believe she was conscious of it. It was soft, but I recognized the tune. People don't whistle when they're ill, Vi girl. That young lady is happy to be here, and there's no doubt about it."

At last, the day came when Mr. Archibald announced that the carriage house was ready for its new occupants. He was beaming when he entered the office, where Ed and Vi were bent over a stack of bills.

"It's done," he said. "That old carriage house is going to be a mighty nice dwelling for somebody. We have a few more days of finishing work on the new storage shed, and then we'll be packing up. I've got to say, I'm going to miss coming here. It's not often I get to be part of saving one of these fine, old places — and for such a good reason."

"It's work you can be proud of," Ed said. He rose from his chair and went to shake Mr. Archibald's hand.

"I can't believe that we have reached this day," Vi said. "It would not have happened without you, Mr. Archibald. I thought we would not be able to move in until November, yet you have completed the work a month ahead of schedule."

The man blushed with pleasure. "We knew how anxious you were to get in, and my men didn't mind pushing themselves for you. I have to tell you that I wasn't too happy about working in this neighborhood at first. And some of my men were a little spooked by the stories about this being a 'ghost house.' Usually we're working on new offices and putting up those big houses folks are building out in the western district. But this job — well, it's been something special. All the men are saying how good it feels being part of it."

"I'd like a look at the carriage house," Ed said. "Do you have time for a quick inspection, Mr. Archibald?"

"I do, sir, I do," the head carpenter replied with enthusiasm. "I want to show you how we did the ceilings so the old oak beams show."

"Coming, Vi?" Ed asked.

Vi shook her head. "I'll join you in a few minutes," she said.

So the men left, talking about beams and trusses and such.

Vi sat in her chair and slowly became aware of how quiet it was. She had grown so used to the sounds of construction that the absence of hammering and sawing seemed strange, almost eerie.

"The house is done," she said aloud, "and now the real work begins."

Violet's Bold Mission

A tingling sensation filled her. Her hands had grown cold and began to tremble. Though she was sitting, her legs felt weak. She almost gasped. What was she feeling? Excitement, joy, and — fearfulness. *The real work*, she thought to herself.

She yanked off her spectacles and shut her eyes tightly. Then she prayed aloud from the depth of her heart: "Dear Father in Heaven, thank You for bringing us to this day. Thank You for guiding Mr. Archibald and his men and all the people who have built this house to Your service. But, Father, we need You more than ever. The house is finished, and now we must fill it with love and hope and help. We have trust to earn from the people of Wildwood, and I know the time ahead won't be easy. Strengthen me, Lord, so that I won't be fearful to venture forward on Your path. Make me strong and help me know what is right. Please grant me a humble heart and an open mind. Please lift me when I stumble and enlighten me when I make mistakes, as I know that I shall. And if it is Your will, help us make Samaritan House a home for all, where there are no walls between rich and poor, young and old, sick and healthy — just people helping each other and sharing all the blessings You bestow on us. Bless this house, Lord, with Your love and under-standing. And guide our steps as we follow Your path."

Vi sat very still, her eyes still closed. She felt the tingling disappear — replaced by another sensation. Her muscles relaxed. Her breathing was steady. Her strength returned; she felt warm again, and at peace.

She stood and walked to the open window. The trees were in the full glory of their first fall color — luminous in the afternoon sun. Vi looked out and realized with astonishment that she had been so absorbed in the work on the house that she'd barely noticed the change of season. Yet all around her, God had been working His miracles. Summer had ended; autumn had begun. One led to the other as it always had, just as the first step in the building of Samaritan House would lead naturally to the next.

A soft breeze touched her face. As she gazed at the garden, the little breeze caught the gold and green leaves of the trees, causing them to rustle and move in a festive dance. Unaware that she was smiling, Vi watched the leaves shimmering and twisting and dancing in the shifting light. It was as if the busy leaves were reminding her to celebrate what had been accomplished even as she looked forward to what was to come.

Thank You, Lord, she thought, *for reminding me that there is a time for everything and for helping me put my fear away. It's time for me to rejoice and praise Your name.*

A few days after the builders departed, Enoch, Christine, and their son were moved to the city and into their new home. The very next day, Vi and Mrs. O'Flaherty said good-bye to the Lansings and moved to the house. Both Elsie and Ed came to help and make sure they had everything they might need. Elsie brought a huge basket of food, prepared by Chloe and Crystal.

"Is that for our lunch?" Vi laughed as Ed hoisted the heavy basket onto the table in the kitchen.

"I think they made enough for a month of lunches," Ed replied.

"Aunt Chloe was very concerned when she heard about your new oven," Elsie explained. "She cannot imagine how it will work, so she wanted you to have plenty of food in case you couldn't cook for yourselves. I think I will ask her to accompany me the next time I come here. She can see the house and be assured that you are safe and comfortable."

"That will be wonderful, Mamma!" Vi exclaimed.

"You can issue the invitation personally when you come home on Sunday," Elsie said. "It will be all the more meaningful to Aunt Chloe, coming from you."

"Do you realize that I now have *two* homes?" Vi said. "Ion and Samaritan House."

"When you're at Ion this weekend, you'll get a treat," Ed said. "There will be someone new for you to meet. I have a guest coming, and he'll be staying with us for several weeks."

Vi had taken a bag of apples from the basket and was dividing them between two bowls.

"A guest," she said absentmindedly. "Who?"

"One of my professors at the University," Ed replied. "Dr. Raymond. He's an archeologist. I think you'll find him fascinating."

In her mind, Vi pictured a dusty old man teaching a dusty old subject. She was glad that her brother would have company, but her thoughts were too firmly focused on the future to allow much interest in Ed's visitor.

"I look forward to meeting him," she said. She picked up two fruit pies from the table and stacked them on top of one of the bowls of apples. Then she handed the stack to her brother.

"Will you take these to Christine?" she said. "Aunt Chloe and Crystal have baked enough for a small army."

Ed took the bowl and pies and went outside. He was a little disappointed by his sister's lack of interest in his news. Still, he was smiling to himself as he walked to the carriage house.

Vi and Elsie had almost finished putting all the food in the pantry when Mrs. O'Flaherty came into the kitchen.

"Well, Enoch has his first task as caretaker," she said. "The window near the coal chute in the basement is broken out. I found it when I was walking in the garden. Enoch propped a board over it, to keep any curious little creatures out. He'll replace the glass tomorrow."

"I wonder how it was broken," Elsie said, a trace of concern in her voice.

"Doubtless during the work," Mrs. O'Flaherty replied. "Or perhaps when the coal was delivered. I'm sure the men simply forgot to repair it."

"Still," Elsie said, "I think it might be wise to have iron bars installed, perhaps on all the basement and first-floor windows. This place may be a tempting target for thieves."

"Oh, Mamma, you worry too much," Vi said, putting her arm around Elsie's waist. "No thieves would dare enter once they see Enoch. Only a fool would take on a man of his size and strength. Besides, this house must be open in appearance if people are to feel comfortable coming in."

Elsie smiled at her daughter and said, "You're right. I'm just being an overly cautious mother. No bars on Samaritan House. Let everyone feel free to 'enter his gates with thanksgiving,' " she added, quoting from Psalm 100.

Elsie and Ed left after lunch, and Vi and Mrs. O'Flaherty set about unpacking their clothes and settling in for their first night as residents of Samaritan House. At Christine's insistence, they ate supper with the Reeves in the carriage house, enjoying an excellent meal and equally fine company. Christine had volunteered to prepare meals until a cook was hired and the mission began providing food for all who needed to eat.

Vi was surprised at how tired she was when she and Mrs. O'Flaherty returned to the house around eight o'clock. She simply couldn't stifle her yawns.

"It's the good kind of fatigue," Mrs. O'Flaherty said. "It comes when one hard task has been completed well and another is about to begin. I feel it too. An early night will do us both good."

So together, they went through the house, checking that all the doors and windows were securely locked and turning off the gaslights that gave the house a warm, golden glow.

Bidding each other good night, Mrs. O'Flaherty retired to her room on the third floor and Vi to the room across the hall—the one with the portrait of the young boy and girl hanging above the fireplace. Vi was tempted to skip her devotion, but her heart was too full of joy. She read her Bible for a while, and then said her prayers. On this night, she felt no doubts about what lay ahead, and her prayer was one of gratitude and praise for her Heavenly Father.

As she was turning out her light, a bit of verse from Psalm 84 came to her: "I would rather be a doorkeeper in the house of my God than dwell in the tents of the wicked." In the dark, she smiled to herself. *That's what I am*, she thought just before she fell asleep, *a doorkeeper in the house of my God. Tomorrow, we will open the door and begin to invite those in need to come in.*

Vi awoke with a start. It was dark, and she had no idea what time it was. Groggy with sleep, she wondered what had wakened her. *Just the creaking of the house,* she thought as she settled back onto her pillow. *Or the wind.*

But she'd no sooner closed her eyes than a thumping sound brought her fully awake. She sat up and listened.

There! It sounded again. A thump or bump that seemed to come from over her head. Could one of Mrs. O's "curious creatures" have gotten into the attic? A raccoon or a possum? The thump came once more, and this time it was accompanied by a low cry that might be an animal but sounded almost like a human voice.

Vi was out of bed in an instant and fumbling for matches to light her lamp. She heard another, different noise, and she jumped in fear when her own door opened.

"Did you hear something?" Mrs. O'Flaherty asked in a whisper as she entered.

Vi didn't have a chance to answer. The low crying came again—definitely from the attic.

"I suppose it's an animal," Mrs. O'Flaherty said softly. "Something that climbed up that old oak tree and over the roof and got in through the vent."

Her hands quaking, Vi finally managed to light the wick of her oil lamp. "Should we get Enoch?" she asked, trying to keep her voice steady. She was remembering what her mother had said about thieves. She recalled Mr. Archibald's evidence that someone had been in the house. And she thought about the stories of strange noises coming from the house at night — the "ghost house" stories that had kept people away for so many years. A shiver ran through her even as she told herself not to be such a silly goose.

"I'm sure it's just an animal," Mrs. O'Flaherty replied, as the cry came again. "A cat maybe. It could be injured. We should probably see if we can find it. Here, Vi, take my hand."

Vi handed the lamp to Mrs. O'Flaherty, clasped her hand, and followed her down the hallway toward the closed attic door. Mrs. O'Flaherty reached for the handle and turned it. The door opened noiselessly.

They had left a gaslight burning low in the hall, but the narrow attic stairway was completely dark and the light of Vi's lamp barely penetrated the blackness. On tiptoe, the two women mounted the steep steps — Mrs. O'Flaherty in the lead.

The attic had been cleaned and cleared of many objects. Instead of the jam-packed room that Vi and the others had encountered weeks earlier, it now seemed like a cavern in the faint light of the little lamp. The furniture and chests that remained had been stacked around the walls and covered with dust sheets. Now they seemed to Vi like ominous, shadowy heaps rather than the chairs and boxes she knew they really were. Slowly, Mrs. O'Flaherty moved the lamp in a half circle, casting its glow from one side of the room to the other. But they saw nothing.

71

Vi realized that she was trembling, but whether from the night chill or fear, she couldn't guess. She clung to Mrs. O'Flaherty's hand as they moved forward cautiously. Mrs. O'Flaherty continued to move the lamp in a slow arc from side to side, looking for any sign of movement.

Then they both stopped in their tracks. A voice spoke from the far end of the long room — a high, small voice that seemed to say, "Help."

It was followed immediately by a pitiful, moaning sound.

Vi all but froze on the spot, but Mrs. O'Flaherty pulled her forward. The light caught a pair of dark eyes, and as they neared, a small face was revealed. A young girl's face. She was sitting on the old child's bed that had been pushed against the far wall. On the bed was a lumpy jumble of bedding and blankets.

Hardly aware that she was speaking, Vi asked, "Who?"

"Please help," the girl said. "Marigold's awfully sick."

Just then the jumble on the bed moved and moaned. Mrs. O'Flaherty dropped Vi's hand, and both rushed to the bed.

Vi fell to her knees before the child and asked, "Who are you?"

"Tansy," the child said flatly. "My sister's really sick. I'm scared she's going to die." At that, tears flowed from her wide eyes, caught like dewdrops in the lamplight. But her voice remained soft and flat. "You can take me to jail if you'll just help Marigold. I don't know what to do."

Vi reached out and took Tansy's hand. It seemed to weigh no more than a dry autumn leaf.

Mrs. O'Flaherty had pulled a stool near the bed and set the lamp on it. She was tending to the bundle on the bed.

"This child is burning with fever," she said. "We must get her downstairs and send for a doctor."

She lifted the bundle and commanded, "Vi, bring the light and the other child."

Without loosening her hold on the girl's hand, Vi stood and took up the lamp. When Tansy seemed to pull back, Vi said in a soothing tone, "We're going to help your sister, I promise. But we need for you to tell us what has happened. Come with us and we'll get help for her. Take hold of my nightgown and don't let go."

The girl nodded and stood up. She grabbed Vi's gown but said nothing.

Vi lighted the way for Mrs. O'Flaherty and within a minute they had all descended the stairs. "My bed," Vi said. And Mrs. O'Flaherty carried the sick child into Vi's room and placed her in the bed. Ever so gently, she removed the dusty blankets from the girl, tossing them on the floor. Vi hurried to light the room—the older girl still hanging on to her nightgown and following her every step. Mrs. O'Flaherty had poured water from Vi's jug into a basin, which she placed on the bedside table. She wet a towel and began gently bathing the sick child's face and neck.

"Vi girl, you'll have to wake Enoch and send him for Doctor Lansing."

Vi got her robe, which lay on the end of the bed, and began to put it on. But still the older child held tightly to her gown. Vi took her little hand again and said, "I have to go get help now. You stay here with your sister and Mrs. O'Flaherty."

The girl looked up at Vi and asked in her soft, flat voice, "Then you'll take me to jail?"

Vi instantly embraced the girl's shoulders. "Oh, no, darling! You'll stay here with us and help us make your sister well. You stay right here with Mrs. O, and I'll be back very soon."

Vi let go of the girl and got the chair from her dressing table. She placed it near the bed and then set the girl on it. "Stay here where you can see your sister and talk with Mrs. O."

The girl sat, turning her bright eyes to the little figure who lay under the covers, and said nothing else.

Vi put on her slippers, grabbed up the lamp once again, and hurried out. She ran down the two flights of stairs and through the dark house to the kitchen. She fumbled in a drawer, found her keys, and unlocked the back door. Dashing across the driveway, she was soon banging on the carriage house door.

It was opened, and Vi saw Enoch, dressed and obviously wide awake.

"You're up," she said with surprise.

"Yes, ma'am," he replied in his deep, rich voice. "I'm always up by four o'clock."

As quickly as she could, Vi explained what she needed. Enoch got his jacket and said, "I'll take the buggy so I can bring the doctor back with me. You want Christine to go to the house?"

"Not right now, but we can use her help getting breakfast. I don't know when those poor children last ate."

Enoch disappeared into the house again, and Vi could hear him speaking to his wife. Then he reappeared, saying, "You go to the house now, Miss Travilla. I'll have the doctor back here real soon."

He set off to the stable, and Vi returned to the house. In the kitchen, she lit a fire in the stove, filled a kettle, and put it on to heat. She prepared a tray of food from Chloe's basket—some cold cornbread and fruit preserves and three slices of pie. Then she made tea in a large pot and filled a small jug with milk. She carried the tray upstairs.

I didn't expect this, Lord, she thought as she ascended the steps. *I didn't expect our first new friends to be two lost lambs.*

CHAPTER

6

A Strange Story

He gathers the lambs in his arms and carries them close to his heart.

ISAIAH 40:11

*W*hen the doctor arrived, it was not Dr. Lansing, whom Vi expected, but a physician she had met several times during her stay at the Lansings' home. Dr. Bowman was Dr. Lansing's assistant and "protégé," as the older surgeon liked to say. He was an attractive young man with a bright sense of humor that sometimes masked his profound commitment to his profession.

He examined the child thoroughly and made his diagnosis. "She's very weak, but I think the worst of the fever has passed," he told Vi and Mrs. O'Flaherty. "The problem is an ear infection, but it seems to be healing itself. Her fever should be normal in a day, maybe two. I want to keep checking her until I'm sure it's past. Otherwise, she and her older sister are badly undernourished. Good food and rest will take care of that. They may not be able to eat much at first, so feed them when they're hungry and they'll be back to regular meals soon enough. They're lucky children to have found your attic. I don't think that the streets are their real home. Do you know where they came from?"

"No," Vi said, "we didn't want to question Tansy while she was so worried about her sister. Tansy wouldn't stir from Marigold's bedside until you came. Mrs. O'Flaherty is cleaning her up a bit now. Would you assure her that her sister will get well?"

"Of course," Dr. Bowman smiled. "I'm quite good with children, if I say so myself."

"That's because you like them," Vi said. Then she added, "I'm sorry we had to rouse you so early."

"No problem at all. I was up working on some research for a paper that Dr. Lansing is preparing for the medical journal. That's why I was at his house. We worked late last night, and I stayed over. Frankly, I was glad for the call," he replied. "By the way, I understand you've hired a nurse. I'd like to meet her and give her some instructions for our young Marigold."

Vi looked at her watch. "Miss Clayton should be here in another hour or so. She'll be glad to have her first patient."

Dr. Bowman withdrew a card from his pocket and handed it to Vi. "My time is not entirely my own, Miss Travilla, but I would like to lend you a hand whenever I can. Maybe we could arrange a half-day when I could work here—strictly volunteer, of course. I'm very impressed by what you're doing. I took a quick look at the clinic, and it is extremely well set up."

Vi smiled and said, "That is Miss Clayton's doing entirely."

"Well, well," the doctor said, rocking back on his heels. "This nurse of yours clearly knows her business."

"She will be glad to hear that you said so, Dr. Bowman," Vi replied.

Just then, Mrs. O'Flaherty returned with Tansy. The doctor smiled at the girl, and she smiled back—the first smile that Vi and Mrs. O'Flaherty had seen. He spoke with her in a kind and gentle fashion. Dr. Bowman explained what was wrong with Marigold, and the young girl clearly accepted his words. She asked some questions, which pleased the doctor.

"See how your little sister has fallen asleep," he said, leading Tansy to the bed where her sister lay curled up peacefully under the covers. "Now you must do the same. You needn't worry about Marigold. Miss Travilla and Mrs. O'Flaherty will watch her carefully. And in just a few minutes, a very clever nurse will be here. She knows just what to do to make little girls get well."

"Can I sleep here, on the floor beside my sister?" Tansy asked.

"You could," the doctor replied, "but I think you might prefer a nice bed with a soft pillow."

"You can sleep in the next room," Vi said. "It's very comfortable, and you'll only be a few steps away from Marigold. Would you like that?"

The girl nodded and smiled again. "Yes, ma'am, that would be nice."

Perhaps it was just the mention of sleep, or perhaps it was the sense of security that she felt from all three of the adults in the room, but something made Tansy yawn widely at that moment. Her hand flew to her mouth, and she said, "Excuse me! That was rude."

"Not rude at all, Miss Tansy," the doctor said. "That is your body's way of telling you that it wants to be off to that comfortable bed."

Mrs. O'Flaherty came to the girl and put an arm around her thin shoulders. "I believe that I can find a nightgown that will just fit you," she said as she took Tansy's hand and led her from the room.

"That's curious," the doctor commented almost to himself.

"What is?" Vi asked.

"That child is very well-mannered," Dr. Bowman answered. "Her sister's clothing is filthy and torn, but finely made. They're not street children, for certain. I wonder where they came from. I wonder if there are parents somewhere."

That thought had not occurred to Vi in her anxiety about the two little girls.

"Oh, dear," she said. "If there are parents, they must be terrified. We shall have to talk with Tansy and find out where her home is."

"Yes, but let her sleep first," Dr. Bowman cautioned. "Whatever her story, she needs rest before she tells it."

Tansy slept until the late afternoon. Vi, Mrs. O'Flaherty, and Emily Clayton took turns watching both children. Little Marigold woke first, very surprised to find herself in a big bed in a pretty room. Emily was with her and gently explained what had happened and that her sister was sleeping in the room next door. Marigold took the news serenely. She told Emily that she knew they would be all right.

"Sissy was scared, but I knew Jesus was watching over us," the little girl declared with perfect calm. "He always watches over us. Even when my ear hurt so bad, I knew He'd help us."

"He brought you here, little one, where you'd be safe and sound," Emily replied, her heart opening to the girl. "He loves you always."

"I know," Marigold said. "And I love Him."

By the time Tansy awoke, Marigold had eaten a bowl of Christine's chicken soup and a slice of bread and butter, and drunk a small cup of warm, sweet tea. Emily had bathed her and put her in a clean gown, and remade the bed with fresh sheets. Marigold was sitting halfway up in bed, listening to a story Emily was reading, when Tansy came in—Vi right behind her.

Tansy ran to the bed and hugged her sister. "You're all right," she said. "A nice doctor was here, and he said you'd be all right."

"Jesus took care of me," Marigold said.

Emily, ever the watchful nurse, said to Tansy, "Your sister has had a good meal. I'm sure you must be hungry. I'll go to the kitchen and bring you a tray of food, if you like."

"Yes, ma'am," Tansy replied politely, "that would be very nice."

When Emily had left, Tansy whispered to Marigold, "Who's that lady?"

"She's a nurse," Marigold said, her eyes widening. "A *real* nurse who knows how to make people not feel sick. I like her."

"Then I like her too," Tansy said.

She sat down on the bed, pulling her feet under her, and Vi took the chair next to the bed.

"I know that you are Marigold and you are Tansy," she said. "My name is Violet Travilla and your nurse's name is

Emily Clayton. My other friend's name is Mrs. O'Flaherty, but she'd like it if you call her Mrs. O, as I do. We're all very glad to have you here with us. But tell me, do you have a last name?"

"Evans," Marigold said.

"I like that name," Vi smiled. "Now, how did you get here? It must be an interesting story."

Tansy cast a glance at her sister, and Marigold said, "You tell her, Sissy. I'm too tired."

So Tansy began the story, and it was far more interesting than Vi could have imagined.

The two little girls had come to India Bay from a place in South Carolina, hundreds of miles to the South.

"Our Granny was a slave," Tansy explained. "And our Mommy, too, when she was a little girl. They lived on a big plantation that was owned by a nice lady named Mrs. Greer. After 'mancipation, Granny and Mommy stayed with Mrs. Greer, and Mommy married our daddy, Mr. Evans. But Granny and Daddy died of a fever just before Marigold was born. We grew up on the plantation, though it wasn't nice at all after Mrs. Greer died last year. Her son took over, and he's a hard, mean man. Mommy said that he didn't seem to know that there were no slaves anymore because he treated all the workers like he owned them. Mommy wanted to take us away, but she didn't have enough money. Then she got sick, and she wrote to our daddy's family and asked if we could come live with them. They said yes and sent some money, and Mommy had a little money too. She paid a man she knew to take Marigold and me north in his carriage. Mommy was going to follow us as soon as she got better."

"Do you know where your father's family lives?" Vi asked.

"In the North, but I'm not sure where," Tansy said. "I had a letter with their address, but somebody stole my bag when we got here. I know the letter was from Pennsylvania. That's where our daddy grew up. But I can't remember the place."

"That's all right," Vi said.

"Tell her how we got here, Sissy," Marigold piped up. She was clearly enjoying the story of her own adventures.

"Well, the man who was taking us just left us in a town we'd never heard of," Tansy said. "We didn't know what to do, but I remembered Granny telling me about the Underground Railway and how the slaves traveled it to the North and freedom. So we found the railroad station and somebody told us which train was going north. We couldn't buy tickets because the man took our money. But we got on the train, and nobody seemed to notice us. We hid away in a little closet, but a man in a uniform found us. He said he was a porter. He was mad at first, but when I told him what had happened, he was kind. He let us stay on the train till it got here. Then he gave us some money and a letter to the minister at a church. He told us where the church was, but we got lost. We just walked around for a couple of days. Then we found this house. People were here during the day, but it was empty at night and we could get in through a window. We'd sleep here and leave before anyone came in the morning. We didn't know it was your house, Miss Violet. Honest we didn't," she said, her voice rising with anxiety.

"I'm glad you came," Vi said laying her hand lightly over Tansy's. "This isn't just my house. It's a place for people who need help. We call it Samaritan House."

"Like the Good Samaritan?" Marigold asked.

"Exactly," Vi said with a wide smile. "People here want to be like the Good Samaritan and help others."

"But we shouldn't have come in without asking," Tansy said. "And we shouldn't have broken that window in the basement after the other one was locked up. That was wrong, and I thought we'd be punished, like going to jail."

"Well, put that thought from your mind," Vi responded firmly. "No one will be punished here. You're our guests now, and I hope we can all be friends."

"I'd like that," Marigold said instantly.

"Me too," Tansy agreed, though her voice was shy.

Emily returned with Tansy's tray—and a glass of apple cider for Marigold—and Vi told her some of the girls' story while Tansy ate.

"But there's still something very important that we don't know," Emily said with feigned seriousness.

"Important?" Marigold asked curiously.

"Your birthdays! We must know your birthdays and how old you are," Emily replied in a tone more merry than Vi had heard before. "Good friends always know that."

Marigold clapped her hands and exclaimed, "My birthday's in January, and I'll be six years old!"

Tansy laid down her spoon and said in a ladylike manner, "My birthday is June nineteenth, and I'm eleven years and four months old."

Vi laughed and said, "My birthday's in June too, and very nearly the same day as yours. And two of my brothers were born in February, which is almost the same as Marigold. They're twins, and they're seventeen years old."

"How old are you, Miss Violet?" Marigold asked.

Tansy frowned and said, "That's a rude question, Marigold."

"Not so rude among friends. I'm twenty years and four months," Vi replied.

Marigold's eyes grew wide again, and she said, "Ooooh...that's pretty old, isn't it?"

"I'm even older," Emily said gaily. "Twenty-four. That's very, *very* old."

Marigold was already giggling, and now they all laughed together. It was not that the joke was so very funny. But clearly it had been a long time since the two Evans girls had felt free to laugh as happy children do. Safe and secure now in Samaritan House, their happiness bubbled up and burst into joyful sound.

Violet's Bold Mission

In spite of what she now knew about the girls' misfortune, Vi began to feel hopeful for them. She was certain she could find their mother and their Pennsylvania family and restore the girls to those who loved them. She imagined the mother's fears, and determined to start the search the next morning. Surely it would not take too long to reunite the family. Surely not.

Under Dr. Bowman's care and the attention of the ladies of Samaritan House, Marigold quickly recovered. Both girls were soon eating better and looking much healthier. It turned out that they had been on the streets for about three weeks and had lived on food given to them by several shopkeepers and (much to Vi's surprise) a saloon cook.

"I thought the good weather was God's gift to Samaritan House," Vi said to Dr. Bowman on the day he pronounced Marigold ready to leave her bed. "But perhaps our Heavenly Father had two little lost lambs in mind when He blessed us with so many clear, sunny days. I can't imagine how they would have managed if it had been wet and stormy."

"Indeed," mused Dr. Bowman. "He kept his eye on those two young sparrows. Despite not eating properly, they're both in very good condition. Tansy is perhaps more underfed than her sister. I suspect that she sacrificed her food, what they had of it, for Marigold. By the way, Miss Travilla, have you learned anything about their mother?"

"Not yet," Vi replied. "Given what the girls told us about Mr. Greer, I didn't want to contact him, but Mrs. Lansing has written to a friend in Columbia, which isn't too far from the Greer plantation. He's a lawyer, and Mrs. Lansing asked him to investigate discreetly. Hopefully he will help us get in touch with the girls' mother. I also wrote an aunt of mine in

84

Philadelphia asking her how we might go about locating the family in Pennsylvania. I'm afraid it will be a difficult task, but my Aunt Adelaide and her husband have excellent connections. Of course, the girls will stay here until their mother and family are found. Mr. and Mrs. Reeve, our caretaker and housekeeper, have practically adopted them already, as has Miss Clayton."

The doctor gave a little cough and seemed almost to blush. Then he said, "Miss Clayton is an excellent nurse. Really excellent. She and I have arranged for me to come every Friday morning from now on, if that suits you."

"Of course it suits me," Vi declared happily. "It is very generous of you, but as yet we have no patients for you to attend."

"Oh, that makes no difference," the young doctor replied, making that little coughing sound again and dropping his head a bit so that a lock of hair fell forward over his brow. "Miss Clayton and I have some matters of procedure to work out — organizing things, you know. So I'll have plenty to do in anticipation of patients."

Vi thanked him again for his kindness, but she said nothing about a tiny little question that had formed in her mind.

Ed's Visitor

*Welcome him in the LORD
with great joy.*

PHILIPPIANS 2:29

Ed's Visitor

When Sunday came, Vi was up early and ready for her drive to the country church near Ion. She would join her family for the service, spend the day with them at home, and return to the city the following morning. Mrs. O'Flaherty had decided to stay at Samaritan House to keep watch over the little girls and to be available should any of the mission's new neighbors come by.

It was a warm, late October morning. The bright blue sky was cloudless, and Vi looked forward to the drive. With herself the only one in the small buggy, she gave the horse its head once she reached open road, and he trotted like a racer. Away from the sights and smells of the city, Vi took deep breaths of the tangy autumn air and drank in the country landscape, where nature seemed to have attired the trees in the brightest shades of the season. Her cheeks were flushed pink, and her eyes were sparkling by the time she reached the church.

She saw the Travillas' carriage arriving as she was hitching her buggy. Everyone was there except Ed, and Vi questioned her mother about his absence as they entered the church. Elsie quickly explained that Ed had gone into India Bay to meet his guest, the professor, at the train station. Vi had forgotten all about Ed's visitor, and a thought flashed through her mind: *I hope this professor is not too stuffy and dull.* Immediately she rebuked herself for her unkindness, asked forgiveness, and settled into the family's pew—determined to devote her full attention to the morning's lesson.

When the family returned to Ion, Ed had still not arrived, but Elsie decided not to inconvenience the servants by delaying the family's luncheon. They had just concluded the meal when Ed and his friend finally appeared.

"The train was an hour late," Ed explained as he entered the dining room, followed by a man who was not in the least what Vi expected.

89

Violet's Bold Mission

He was tall, several inches above Ed's six feet, and much younger than most university professors—about thirty, Vi guessed. Below a crop of thick sandy-brown hair, his lean face was deeply tanned, making his blue eyes almost seem to glow. There were lines radiating from the corners of his eyes, the kind that come from spending a great deal of time in the sun. His jaw was square, and he wore a heavy mustache, which didn't quite hide his slightly lopsided smile. Vi thought him interesting-looking, though hardly handsome, and not like any of the professors she'd met during her visits to Ed's university.

Ed began the introductions with a cheerful, "Travilla family, I'd like to present my friend, Professor Marcus Darius Raymond."

The man nodded and smiled as he was then introduced to each member of the family.

When Ed reached Danny, the boy said, "How do you do, Professor Raymond? Are you the man who studies old bones?"

"Not exactly," the professor replied. "My subject is ancient civilizations, and I try to learn how people lived hundreds and thousands of years ago. You might say I study the bones of times long past—but not the kind of bones you mean."

"Oh," said Danny with a hint of disappointment, for he had lately become very interested in the new science of dinosaur study.

Elsie rang a little bell, and a maid appeared. Elsie requested that food be brought for the men, and then she suggested that the family adjourn to the parlor while Ed and the professor had their lunch.

Instead of waiting for her brother, Vi asked her mother if she might take a walk down to the lake. "It's such a glorious day," Vi said, "and I haven't visited my favorite spot for many weeks."

"Can I go with you, Vi?" Rosemary asked.

"You may both go," Elsie said. "But don't stay too long. We have a guest, and it would be discourteous not to keep him entertained."

Vi promised that they would be back in an hour, and she and Rosemary hurried to get their jackets.

The lake, which their father had constructed just after the Civil War, lay in a small depression not too far from the house. It was fed by cold springs deep in the ground, so even in times of drought, it was never dry. Over the years, the saplings that Edward Travilla had planted around its shore had grown tall and lush. On the far side of the lake was a boathouse, where several rowboats and a canoe were kept, and a pebbly beach, from which Edward Travilla had taught all his children to swim.

On the near side of the lake, a wooden dock extended into the water, and this was where Vi was headed.

"Ouch!" Rosemary cried out as they tramped through the overgrown field that sloped down to the lake. "Oh, I hate these thistles! They scratch my arms and catch at my clothes."

"Well, walk around them," Vi laughed. She looked up and saw the water through a break in the trees at the edge of the field. A little thrill of pleasure ran up her arms and shoulders. "Oh, I always forget how beautiful the lake is in the autumn," she said softly.

"What?" Rosemary asked.

"Look at how beautiful it is," Vi said. "The water is like a silver-blue mirror. See how it reflects the trees — golden trees in a silver mirror. I forget from year to year how incredibly beautiful it is, and each time I see it again, it is new to me — a gift from our Heavenly Father."

"You've always come here more than anyone else," Rosemary said. "Why?"

Vi didn't reply at first. They'd reached the break in the stand of trees. Just beyond, there was a stretch of green grass that went to the water's edge. The dock extended from the grassy shore for about twenty-five feet into the water. Weathered gray, the dock looked like a narrow roadway floating on the gently rippling water.

"It's so peaceful," Vi said at last. "I come here to be alone and to sketch and to think. And because it reminds me of Papa. When I was little and the dock was new, he'd bring me here, and we'd sit on the dock and fish. I had a little fishing pole he made for me. The first time I caught a fish, Papa had it cooked for our supper, though it barely amounted to a mouthful. Usually I didn't catch anything, but that didn't matter because I was with Papa. He'd tell me stories about growing up at Ion and about his mother and our own Mamma when she was a girl. I wish we had known our grandmother Travilla, for she must have been an amazing woman. She ran Ion all by herself after her husband died, and she raised Papa on her own."

"I wish we still had Papa," Rosemary said softly. They had walked to the far end of the dock, and now they sat down on the planked surface, warmed by the sun.

"We do in a way," Vi said. "We have such good memories of him."

"But I don't have as many memories as you," Rosemary replied. "And Danny hardly remembers him at all. Sometimes, I feel as if I was cheated—that Papa died before I could really know him."

"I understand that," Vi said gently. "We all miss him so much. But look around. This place was something he made for us. And Ion is so full of him. For me, Ion will always be a source of strength, for there's not a corner or cabinet that doesn't remind me of Papa. You may not have so many memories, but don't you cherish them and learn from them?"

"I guess so," Rosemary said slowly. "Whenever I go riding, I think about Papa putting me up on my first pony and walking me around the paddock and telling me not to be afraid. I remember him reading to me at bedtime and helping me to learn the words. I remember how funny he was and how he could make me laugh no matter how mad I was."

"Memories are another of God's gifts to us," Vi said. "We have them whenever we need them to remind us of how much Papa loved us."

"And how much we loved him," Rosemary added in a brighter tone. "I guess that's what matters—that we all love each other, and that God loves us."

Vi reached over and began carefully removing some brambles that had tangled in Rosemary's stockings. "I always feel so close to God when I come here," she said. "It's like a church to me—the lake, the trees, and the sky overhead. It's a sanctuary for me."

"I like it, too," Rosemary said, looking around. "Maybe I should come here more often."

Then Rosemary asked Vi about Samaritan House, and Vi began telling her about Tansy and Marigold. But their conversation was interrupted by a manly voice shouting their names. It was Ed, and the girls saw him approaching, with Professor Raymond at his side.

Vi waved, and she and Rosemary got to their feet. As the men came near, Rosemary whispered quickly, "The professor reminds me of a giraffe."

Vi shushed her sister, but she couldn't help smiling. He did look a bit like a giraffe—tall, thin, with the straight posture and long stride of the stately animals she had seen in the zoo in New York.

"Mamma sent us to escort you back," Ed said, "and I thought Mark might enjoy seeing the lake."

"It's quite charming," the professor said, scanning the area quickly. "A pretty place for water sports."

Charming? Pretty? Vi felt an odd surge of irritation to hear her special place—her sanctuary—described as if it were a lady's bonnet.

Violet's Bold Mission

Ed was telling his friend how his father had built the lake so the young Travillas would have a place to swim and boat and fish.

"All of you?" the professor asked in a surprised tone. "Girls as well as boys?"

"Of course," Ed said. "It was especially important to him that we all be strong swimmers. My older sister once rescued someone from drowning in this lake."

"It's not very deep, I think," the professor said dismissively.

"Deep enough to drown in," Vi said sharply. "And very cold. Too cold for most people."

"Yes, I see," the professor said, as if he were acknowledging the remark of a not-very-bright pupil.

Vi felt the heat of anger in her face. She grabbed Rosemary's hand and said, "We should be getting back—now!"

Ed seemed not to hear the sharpness in her voice, but Rosemary did. She wondered whatever had caused this sudden change in Vi's mood. Rosemary knew that her sister could get angry, but not often and always for a very good reason. She was so startled that she allowed herself to be pulled away.

"Wait for us," Ed called at his sisters, who were almost running back to the shore.

Vi stopped at the end of the dock, but she kept hold of Rosemary's hand—unconsciously squeezing it until Rosemary yipped, "Oww!" and Vi let go.

Hearing Ed's and the professor's footsteps behind them, Vi began walking away from the lake, her pace more measured. Rosemary dropped back a bit and started chatting with Ed and the guest. But Vi made a point of walking ahead of them and saying nothing.

"Ed said your name is Darius. Is that for the King of Persia?" Rosemary was asking.

"There were actually three kings of Persia named Darius," the professor replied. "I claim to be named for the first, who was both a great conqueror and a great lawgiver. My father was a student of ancient history, and my names were his choice."

"Then is Marcus for Mark Antony?" Rosemary questioned.

"No one so ancient," the professor said. "My first name honors an American physician and missionary. His name was Marcus Whitman. He traveled west in the 1830s and served the Indians of the Pacific Northwest. He was a pioneer rather than a conqueror. My father met him several times, and named me to honor his work."

The professor's remarks raised Vi's curiosity, and she slowed her steps, falling back and joining her companions.

"Speaking of names," Professor Raymond was saying, "the choice of Ion for your home is quite interesting. Do you know its origin, Ed?"

"It was named by my grandfather Travilla, who died long before I was born," Ed answered in a tone that sounded, to Vi's ears, more like a student's than that of a grown man who would someday own the estate.

"I assume it is from the ancient Greek region of Ionia," Ed continued. "The columns of the portico are certainly Ionic in style."

Vi could not stop herself from speaking up. "Ion was supposed to have been an early king of Athens," she said pertly. "In mythology, he was the grandson of Hellen, the ancestor of the ancient Greeks and Hellenic culture."

"Someone has taught you well, Miss Travilla," the professor said with a low chuckle. "That is indeed one of the ancient myths about Ion. Do you know how your own name is associated with Ion?"

Vi looked at him quizzically.

The professor stopped walking and seemed to stare off at the house, which had come into full view at the top of the rise. The others stopped too, and stood silently — waiting for whatever he had to say.

Still gazing into the distance, Professor Raymond quoted something in Greek.

Vi recognized the language but not the meaning.

"Do you remember that one, Ed?" the professor asked.

Ed hesitated, then said, "Not really. Should I know it?"

"Perhaps not," the professor replied in a tone Vi thought was distinctly condescending. "It is from the great playwright Aristophanes. It is a phrase he used to describe noble Athens — 'city of the violet crown.' "

He turned to Vi. "Ion means 'violet' in ancient Greek," he said with a smile. "The legendary Ion was crowned the king of Athens, hence his city was *violet*-crowned. Do you not think that an interesting connection, Miss Travilla?"

It was interesting, Vi thought. But before she could speak, Rosemary sang out, "It's *fascinating*! Really, Professor, just fascinating! I wonder if Papa knew that story. Maybe that's why you were named Violet, Vi."

"Did your father read Greek?" the professor asked.

"He did," Ed answered. "I must show you the library. Papa had a very good collection of Greek and Latin texts."

The others resumed their walk toward the house, but Vi didn't move for some moments. She was thinking, and whatever was on her mind caused the shadow of a frown to settle on her face.

"Come on, Vi!" Rosemary called out.

Vi looked up, and her frown faded as she headed up the rise.

Reaching the house, Ed and the professor went directly to the library. Vi and Rosemary sought out their mother, who was in the sitting room with Aunt Chloe.

Rosemary excitedly told them about the information that the professor had imparted, and Elsie also found it most intriguing.

"That professor's a right smart man, is he?" said Aunt Chloe.

"Oh, very smart," Rosemary replied in a serious way. "He studies ancient civilizations, Aunt Chloe, to find out how people lived back then."

"I learn about that by studying the Bible," Chloe said with a smile. "It goes back to the very beginning."

"From what Ed tells me, Professor Raymond's first interest was the classic writings of the Greeks and Romans," Elsie said. "He has traveled to Greece and Egypt and throughout the Holy Land. It was during his travels that he changed his field of study to ancient cultures."

"The Holy Land!" Chloe exclaimed. "You saying that he has walked the same ground where our Lord and Savior walked?"

"Indeed," Elsie replied. "He has visited Jerusalem itself."

"My, my," Chloe said in amazement.

"I wonder if he saw the pyramids in Egypt," Rosemary said.

"I would imagine that he did," Elsie replied, "but you should ask him, dear."

Vi sat quietly during this discussion. She was thinking that the professor was probably a very interesting person. But there was something about him…

Elsie interrupted Vi's thoughts with a question. "I understand that Mrs. Lansing has plans for an event in support of Samaritan House. Has she discussed her idea with you?"

Vi immediately forgot about the professor. She responded, "Mrs. Lansing wants to have a party for Samaritan House. She says it would be a good way to introduce the political and business leaders of India Bay to the work we're doing. I guess it's a good idea, but she wants me to make a speech."

"You can do that, Vi," Rosemary said with enthusiasm. "Nobody would be better to tell people about Samaritan House."

"I can talk people's ears off about Samaritan House," Vi laughed. "But that's not the same as making a speech. Just thinking about it makes my knees weak."

Violet's Bold Mission

"Well, dear," Elsie said, "we will all help you. Naomi wrote me that she is thinking of a small ball at her home. No more than a hundred guests for dancing and supper. She'd like it to be early in December. That should be plenty of time for you to prepare for your speech."

Vi had no chance to reply, for Rosemary had jumped up from her seat. "A ball!" she exclaimed. "Oh, Mamma, will I be able to go? I've never been to a ball, and I know it will be just beautiful if Mrs. Lansing is planning it."

"I think you should go," Elsie said with a smile. "After all, you washed windows and scrubbed floors at Samaritan House. You deserve to go to the ball."

"Would it be all right with you, Vi?" Rosemary asked.

"Of course," Vi smiled. "You must be there."

Rosemary clapped her hands and began to waltz around the room. Caught up in the prospect of her first "grown-up" party, she didn't hear Vi say, "Maybe you should make the speech, little sister. I wish I could share your excitement."

But Elsie heard the remark. She leaned over to Vi and said, "Do not be troubled, dearest. Just keep the objective in mind—Samaritan House. Your speech will serve Samaritan House and the purposes of our Lord."

"I know, Mamma," Vi smiled back. "Now, let's forget speeches. I want to tell you all about our two new residents."

Supper was very pleasant that evening, and Professor Raymond kept everyone spellbound with his stories of visiting the excavation site of ancient Troy near the coast of Turkey. Rosemary was delighted to learn that he had, indeed, seen the pyramids in Egypt and had traveled on the Nile River. He told them as well of his journeys in the Holy Land and painted a vivid word picture of the arid beauty of the landscape of the region.

Ed's Visitor

Listening to him, Vi understood why he had been one of Ed's favorite teachers. As he spoke, she could almost see the dusty roads and villages of the ancient land of the Bible.

The others had many questions for their guest, but when dessert arrived, Professor Raymond said, "Forgive me. I have held forth for almost this entire meal. As much as I enjoy talking, I learn from listening. Tell me, Miss Violet, about this project of yours—the mission that your brother has mentioned."

His question surprised Vi, and she could hardly imagine why he cared. But she replied politely, describing Samaritan House and its purpose.

"So you are something of an explorer yourself," the professor commented when she had finished.

"How do you mean?" she asked.

"You are exploring ways of life and people that are new to you," he said. "You are using your resources to unearth treasures where most people see only poverty and desolation."

"That is a romantic way to put it," Vi rejoined, uncertain whether his remarks were meant as a compliment or not.

"You must see Samaritan House while you are here," Elsie said.

"I would like that, Mrs. Travilla, if it's not an inconvenience for Miss Violet," Professor Raymond said.

"Our doors are always open," Vi said.

As if on cue, the door of the dining room opened at just that moment, and Horace Dinsmore entered, with his wife, Rose, and Zoe.

They were warmly greeted by the family, and soon everyone was gathered in the parlor. The conversation was certainly lively that evening. Horace thoroughly enjoyed himself as he talked with the young professor about his travels and his work. A dedicated historian himself, Horace was particularly interested in the work at Troy, which had only recently passed from the realm of myth into historical reality as the result of excavations by the German-born businessman Heinrich Schliemann.

Zoe surprised even the professor by revealing that she had once met Herr Schliemann, when he had visited the American Embassy in Paris. It had been a meeting that her father had always enjoyed recalling. Professor Raymond questioned her closely about her recollections of the famous man. And Zoe did her best to remember details, though she'd been only eleven at the time, and Herr Schliemann was not yet a world-famous explorer.

Eventually Elsie had to remind her younger children and the twins of their approaching bedtimes and rather firmly insisted that they say good night. Noticing the lateness of the hour, Horace, Rose, and Zoe also bade their farewells, but not until Horace had gained the promise of his daughter, grandson, and the professor that they would dine at Roselands the following evening.

Violet then excused herself, having remembered that she was to invite Chloe to visit Samaritan House and might not see her elderly friend before her early departure for the city in the morning. After receiving Chloe's grateful acceptance, Vi kissed her old nursemaid and went to tell her mother good night. She then retired to her own room. She was a little surprised at how tired she felt, for it had been a leisurely day. *Perhaps it is just the bracing autumn air that encourages me to sleep,* she thought as she took her Bible from the night table and considered several short chapters she might read. She was settling comfortably against her pillows when there was a light tapping at her door and Rosemary peeked in.

"Aren't you supposed to be tucked in bed?" Vi asked playfully.

Approaching her sister's bed, Rosemary said in a near-whisper, "I had to ask you something, Vi, in private."

Vi sat up and said, "What is it? Do you need my help with anything?"

Rosemary dipped her pretty head sideways and replied, "I just wanted to know what you were angry about today. At the lake. Was it something about the professor?"

Vi pinched her brows together in a mock frown and said, "Oh, you are a noticing girl, Rosemary. And a very curious one."

"Well, you were mad. You dragged me away and nearly squeezed my hand blue. I couldn't help noticing something," Rosemary said with a pout. She put both hands on her hips—a habit she had when she was most determined to get her way—and continued, "*I* didn't do anything, and *Ed* didn't do anything. So I guess it had to be the professor. Don't you like him, Vi? Don't you think he's just the most fascinating person?"

Vi sighed and then smiled. "I think he is very interesting," she said.

"Then why run away?" Rosemary asked, sitting down on the bed.

This was not a conversation Vi wished to have, so she said, "I wasn't running away. I promised Mamma that we'd be back in an hour, and it was time to go."

"But you don't like the professor, do you?" Rosemary queried with the doggedness of a puppy tugging at its leash.

"I hardly know the professor!" Vi exclaimed. "I think he is interesting. I just don't think he should speak to us as if we were his pupils. It's an arrogance of manner that irritates me. That's all, Rosemary. I don't like being lectured, but because he's a professor and used to lecturing, he probably can't help it. Anyway, he's Ed's friend, and that's all that should matter to me."

Rosemary tilted her head again, staring at her sister. After several long moments, she said, "That's all that matters to *me*. That and the fact that Professor Raymond seems quite friendly and so fascinating."

"So you've already said," Vi replied in a flat tone. She took up her Bible again and added, "I really need to do my reading and get to sleep. I leave very early tomorrow, you know."

Rosemary jumped off the bed and ambled to the door.

"What's your text, big sister?" she asked in a saucy way.

"I'm still deciding," Vi said.

Rosemary approached the door but turned back. "You might try John 7:24," she said, adding, "You know it, don't you?" as she disappeared from Vi's sight, and the door shut behind her.

"I do know it," Vi said to her now empty room. Then she quoted: "'Stop judging by mere appearances, and make a right judgment.'"

She started to laugh at Rosemary's little jest. But instantly her expression turned sober. *Perhaps you are wiser than you realize, dear sister*, she thought. *Hasty conclusions have always been a fault of mine. I must try to know the professor better if I am to make a right judgment. I must try to like him, for Ed's sake at least.*

With that in mind, she turned to John 7, and as she read the chapter, she carefully considered its meaning for her.

CHAPTER

8

Introductions

*I will get up now and go about
the city, through its streets
and squares. . . .*

SONG OF SOLOMON 3:2

Introductions

*B*y the time Vi reached Samaritan House the next morning, she had resolutely put all thoughts of the professor and his manners away. Her mind was focused on the mission and what she now regarded as the next phase of its work.

"How do we encourage people to come here?" she asked Mrs. O'Flaherty and Emily as they sat in the mission office.

Mrs. O'Flaherty had made coffee, and the aroma filled the room. Outside, Christine was teaching Tansy and Marigold a skipping game, and the girls' happy laughter drifted through the open window. In the company of her friends, Vi was thinking how much she wanted to share this feeling of companionship with others.

"That," said Mrs. O'Flaherty, "is the most important question we have to answer. This is not like opening a dress shop on Main Street. We cannot put our pretty wares in a window nor place enticing advertisements in the newspapers. We know that there are people who will benefit from our services, but we do not know the people of Wildwood. They have seen us, but as yet they have shown little interest in what we do."

"Then we must introduce ourselves," Vi said.

"I have been thinking about that," Emily said, "and I've also discussed it with my aunt. She has lived in India Bay all her life, and she's told me a great deal about the city's history. She says that there are leaders in every community, and that we must make allies of the leaders of Wildwood."

"What does she mean by 'leaders'?" Vi asked.

"My sense is that the leaders in Wildwood are not people who would wish to help us," Mrs. O'Flaherty said. "From what we have been told, control of this area seems to be in the hands of the saloon and gambling house owners—men who will surely

105

resent our presence. They will assume, quite correctly, that our work may take customers away from their bars and gaming tables. Such men will doubtless regard us as a threat to the profits they earn from their misguided customers."

"That's true," Emily replied. "But my aunt says that there is another side to the community. Aunt Erica suggests that the churches are where we should start, for their support is crucial. She told me about several previous efforts to establish missions in Wildwood. She says those efforts failed in large measure because the people who came to serve didn't befriend the local congregations. There were conflicts between established congregations and the newcomers. For instance, she remembers that one of the ministers who came here decided to hold meetings on Sunday mornings, and attendance at the local churches dropped—until he left Wildwood for some reason. Aunt Erica says that if we are to succeed, we must bear in mind that we are outsiders and tread lightly lest we offend those whose support we need."

"Your Aunt Erica sounds like a woman of uncommon good sense," Mrs. O'Flaherty said.

"She is," Emily agreed. "Her family—my mother's family—was among the original settlers of the city. Aunt Erica's late husband was a city councilman for years, and she has a real understanding of city politics."

Vi sighed heavily. "Politics," she said in a disheartened tone. "If the politicians were doing their job, there would be no places like Wildwood."

"Not all politicians are concened about the poor," Mrs. O'Flaherty said. "But the idea of going to the churches is a very good one. We could call on the pastors and ministers who serve this area."

"And their wives," Emily added. "Aunt Erica says that the wives of ministers often know more about the people than anyone."

"Then we shall make calls," Vi said, her voice conveying renewed energy. "I'm sure that Mrs. Lansing can provide us the names of the religious leaders whom we ought to see. What else can we do to introduce ourselves?"

"Christine and Enoch have already started," Mrs. O'Flaherty said with a smile.

Vi turned questioning eyes on her friend, and Mrs. O'Flaherty explained: "Christine goes into the streets every day to shop. She has found local suppliers for our milk and eggs. She has also met a woman who does laundry and another who bakes bread. Enoch has set up an account for the mission at the feed and grain store. We have been in residence here for but a week, and they have already met more people and learned more about the workings of Wildwood than I could have learned in a month."

"They should be meeting with us right now," Vi stated.

"I asked them, but Enoch had an errand to run and Christine had already promised to play with Tansy and Marigold this morning."

"Oh, I nearly forgot!" Vi exclaimed at the mention of the little girls. "Mamma sent presents for Tansy and Marigold. I left the box in the kitchen when I arrived. But when the girls came down to breakfast, I was so happy to see them that I forgot all about the box."

"What did Elsie send?" Mrs. O'Flaherty asked.

"Clothing," Vi smiled. "Mostly items that Rosemary and I outgrew. But they're all in excellent condition. And Mamma and Aunt Chloe are already at work sewing some new things."

"The girls will be pleased," Mrs. O'Flaherty said. "We have purchased the basics for them, but if they are to be here for some time, they need a more extensive wardrobe. Have you heard anything about their family, Vi?"

Vi replied that she had not, but that she hoped Mrs. Lansing might receive news from South Carolina soon.

The women continued to discuss various mission business for a while, until sounds coming from the kitchen ended their meeting. Christine was starting to make lunch while Tansy and Marigold played with little Jacob.

When Vi, Emily, and Mrs. O'Flaherty entered, the girls began to tell them all about the new games they'd learned. Then Vi told them about the box she had brought from Ion, and the girls were immensely curious about what it might contain.

"Why don't you open it now?" Vi said, pointing to the corner where the plain box sat unnoticed.

"Oh, may we?" Tansy asked.

"Certainly," Vi said gaily. "It is from my Mamma, and she wanted me to tell you that she looks forward to meeting you both very soon."

The girls went to the box, and Tansy untied the string that held it closed. Carefully, she raised the lid and removed the layer of paper that covered the contents. She lifted out the first item — a pink muslin dress with an apple green sash.

"Ooooh," Marigold breathed in awe. "It's so pretty."

"Is it yours, Miss Violet?" Tansy asked, holding the dress high above the floor.

"No, dear, it's yours," Vi laughed. "Everything in that box is now yours and Marigold's."

"Hold it to your shoulders, Tansy," Christine said. "Yep, it looks like it'll be a perfect fit."

Mrs. O'Flaherty had taken another dress from the box. It was similar to the first, but yellow with a white sash.

"This seems to be in Marigold's size," Mrs. O'Flaherty said.

The little girl cried out with joy, "It is my size! Just my size, Mrs. O!"

"Then it must be yours," Mrs. O'Flaherty said.

Soon they were taking more clothes from the large box, each item earning a round of ooh's and ah's and giggles from the girls. There were several dresses of muslin and light wool, jackets, pinafores, undergarments of the softest white cotton, stockings, nightgowns and a robe for each girl, and a bundle of colorful sashes and hair ribbons.

"I think we have time before lunch to take these things to your rooms," Emily said. She gathered most of the clothing into her arms, and the girls divided the rest between them.

"Your Mamma must be a very kind lady," Tansy said to Vi. "We want to thank her. Do you think we could write her a letter, Miss Violet?"

"That's a wonderful idea," Vi replied. "I know Mamma would be so pleased to receive a letter from you. Why don't you and Marigold think about what you'd like to say. Then we can write your letter tonight, after supper, and we'll post it first thing tomorrow morning. Now, take your things upstairs, and Miss Emily will help you put them away."

"We will, Miss Violet," Tansy said.

"Thank you, Miss Violet," Marigold said.

They followed Emily out the door, Tansy walking with stately grace and Marigold hopping and skipping behind her.

That afternoon, having convinced the little girls to take naps, Vi and Mrs. O'Flaherty decided that they should take a walk about the neighborhood. They had ventured out before, but for the most part, their forays in Wildwood had been by buggy or carriage, not on foot.

They decided to head toward the main shopping area, which constituted a couple of blocks of stores, small shops, and hotels. It was a far cry from the business district in the center of the city. For the people of Wildwood, shopping was a matter of necessity, not fashion and entertainment. The streets were wide compared to those Vi had seen in the very poor areas of New York

City, but no better maintained. Wildwood Street was paved with brick — a reminder of its better days — but now most of the side streets that ran off the main road were no more than rutted dirt tracks that would turn to thick mud in rain. There were no sidewalks, though in some places wooden platforms had been erected to give pedestrians a place to walk.

The day was warm and breezy, but it gave little comfort. Because the fall had been so dry, dust seemed to cover everything, giving the buildings a dull, brown tone. The breeze blew the dust about and rustled the dead leaves and trash that had piled up in every nook and cranny.

The shopping area was full of people, though Vi soon realized that most of them were not shopping. Clusters of men of all ages stood outside the hotels and in the darkened alleyways between some of the older buildings. There was a listlessness about these men, almost as if they could not move at a normal pace. They did not even glance up when anyone tried to pass, so that people who had destinations were forced into the street to get by. Vi saw groups of women as well, outside the grocer and the butcher shop and gathered round the street sellers' carts. The women, often with children at their feet, were more animated, and occasional hoots of laughter rose from their midst.

The laughter of the women and the low drone of the men mixed with the other street noises — the shouts and cries of children, the barking and growling of dogs, the clopping of horses' hooves, the clatter of passing wagons, and the distant whistle and roar of trains leaving the city for the journey southward. Mingling with it all was the sound of music, the tinny, high-pitched playing of a piano coming from one of the hotels. Vi tried to make out the tune, but it was nothing she had ever heard before.

Vi and Mrs. O'Flaherty decided to go into the dry goods store, which stood opposite the most notorious hotel and saloon in the district. Mrs. O'Flaherty wished to purchase some needles and thread and a paper of pins for her sewing box. The store was fairly well stocked, and on seeing the women enter, a man came forward to offer his assistance. He was of middle age, stocky, with a round face and bright eyes.

"May I help you?" he asked pleasantly.

Mrs. O'Flaherty told him what she needed, and he quickly found the items and placed them on the counter.

"Are you ladies new to Wildwood?" he asked as he wrapped the sewing goods in brown paper and tied the little package with string.

"We've just moved into the old Bell house," Vi replied.

The man paused for the slightest moment. Then he said, "We heard that it was being made into some kind of a mission."

"That's right," Vi said. "It is called Samaritan House now, and we hope it will become a place of help and refuge for those in need."

Then she introduced herself and Mrs. O'Flaherty. The man's name was Mr. Nelson, and he was the owner of the store.

"If I might inquire, what is the nature of the services you offer?" he asked.

"We have a clinic with a full-time nurse and a doctor who comes once a week," Vi said. "And we plan to start a school for children. We want to help families, and anyone else really."

"A school?" Mr. Nelson said with interest. "There's a great need for that here. I don't have children myself, but I'm a great believer in education."

"So are we," Mrs. O'Flaherty said. "Perhaps some of your customers would be interested in our school. We'd like to have a full class by January."

"There's more than enough children in Wildwood, but I'm not sure how interested their parents will be," Mr. Nelson replied. Then he leaned forward a bit over the counter and lowered his voice. "People here tend to be suspicious of education. They tend to be suspicious of many things in Wildwood, especially outsiders."

"Well, we can understand that feeling, Mr. Nelson," Mrs. O'Flaherty said, lowering her voice in a way that matched his. "Everyone resents the kind of do-gooders who try to take over and tell others how to live. I can see that you have great knowledge of this area. Perhaps you might be willing to advise us on occasion."

Mr. Nelson stood straight and beamed happily. "I'd be most honored to offer advice," he said. "And my good wife as well. She's often here in the store, and we'd be delighted to assist you ladies in any way we can."

"Thank you so much, Mr. Nelson," Mrs. O'Flaherty said with her most gracious smile. "We shall look forward to meeting your wife. Oh, yes," she added as if it were an afterthought, "I noticed a nice piece of lace over there."

Gesturing to one of the far counters, she said, "I should like to buy that as well."

Mr. Nelson hurried to get the lace and wrap it for her. He totaled her purchases on a small pad. Mrs. O'Flaherty paid, and promising to return soon, she and Vi bade Mr. Nelson a pleasant farewell.

He escorted them to the door, making a slight bow as they exited. It was quite a nice sale, he thought, with the addition of the lace. And he told himself that he'd just made a very good connection. He could hardly wait to tell his wife of his new acquaintance with the ladies who had purchased the "ghost house."

Walking back toward Samaritan House, Vi asked her companion, "Did you really need that lace, Mrs. O?"

"Oh, yes. It's a nice piece and will make a pretty collar for one of the girl's dresses," Mrs. O'Flaherty responded. "But I admit that I also wanted to make a good impression on Mr. Nelson."

"Did you have a particular reason?" Vi wondered. "Do you think he's one of the leaders of Wildwood?"

"No, probably not a leader. But I wouldn't be surprised if he is a gossip, and I would like him to speak well of us to his customers. He seems like a nice man. Since Wildwood has no newspaper," continued Mrs. O'Flaherty, "we need friends like Mr. Nelson who know what is happening among our new neighbors. It's through connections like Mr. Nelson that we will learn about the day-to-day life in our community—the marriages, the new babies, the people in need and in sorrow. Yes," Mrs. O concluded thoughtfully, "Samaritan House will benefit from his knowledge and his advice, I think."

As they neared the mission, Vi asked, "Did you see how the people outside the stores stared at us?"

"We are new to them and natural objects of interest," said Mrs. O'Flaherty. "By now, most of the people of Wildwood have probably heard about 'the mission ladies.' But it seemed to me that the stares were not so hostile as ones we have encountered before. Perhaps we have become curiosities only, and that would be a step forward."

" I hope so," Vi said. "I hope we will be accepted here."

Vi and Mrs. O'Flaherty's first visit into the center of Wildwood had certainly been noticed by a great many people. Numerous simple meals that evening were enlivened by reports of the ladies who had walked to Mr. Nelson's store. Opinions were greatly divided. Some people were genuinely interested in what was happening at the old "ghost house" and welcomed the arrival of anyone who might bring help to their benighted neighborhood. But a good many others were doubtful that these ladies could accomplish anything where previous efforts had failed. There were cynics who laughed at the "Christian do-gooders" and their "highfalutin manners." And a few people still had fears that the restoration of the old Bell house might signal a return of the wealthy to the old neighborhood.

But in one quarter, the appearance of the ladies on the street that day roused only anger. In the back room of one of the hotel saloons, a few men were discussing the threat these "snooty society women" might pose. These men, who profited handsomely from the weaknesses of others, had carefully watched the developments of the summer and fall—the transformation of the old house and the recent arrival of the women and their servants. There was low talk about "taking measures" and "making things unpleasant" for the newcomers on Wildwood Street. Then one man said to his fellows, "We've done it before. We've driven the do-gooders back where they came from. I don't think that a bunch of women and one black man can stand up to us for long." With a malevolent laugh, he calmly reassured his associates, "Don't worry, boys. We'll soon have them running back to their fancy parlors and ballrooms."

9

Disturbing News

*The righteous care about justice
for the poor, but the wicked
have no such concern.*

PROVERBS 29:7

Disturbing News

The very next morning, Vi called on Mrs. Lansing. After some discussion of Mrs. Lansing's preparations for the ball, which was now set for the first Friday in December, Vi revealed her plan to meet the church leaders of Wildwood and asked Mrs. Lansing's help.

"I know several personally and can write notes of introduction for you," Mrs. Lansing said. "I will put together a list of the others, with their addresses. There are at least a half-dozen active congregations in Wildwood, and perhaps that many in Boxtown as well."

"Boxtown?" Vi questioned.

"Have you not heard of Boxtown yet?" Mrs. Lansing asked.

Vi indicated that the term was unknown to her, and Mrs. Lansing said, "That is probably because you have not hired servants locally. Boxtown is a section of the city on the east side of the railroad tracks. It is where most of the Negroes live. It is called Boxtown because after the War, many of the freed slaves moved there and built small shanty houses that looked like boxes. On the map, Boxtown seems to be a part of the Wildwood district, but it might as well be another country. Boxtown isn't an official name, but that is how it has been known for almost twenty years."

"Do you mean that no black people live in Wildwood?" Vi asked incredulously.

"They wouldn't want to, for very good reasons," Mrs. Lansing replied sadly. "You must understand, Vi, how deep the divide is between black and white. The War bred resentment, but Reconstruction has created a kind of hatred that smolders in the hearts of many white Southerners of every station. The Ku Klux Klan, which your late father fought so courageously, was one of the most vicious expressions of that feeling. But there are many more white people, inside and outside of the church, who harbor the most terrible prejudices. They have made scapegoats of our Negro brothers and sisters by blaming the victims of slavery for problems not of their making—the defeat of the South in the War and the depredations of Reconstruction that have followed. Scapegoating is an all-too-human sin, my dear. We try to blame others for our own failings and misfortunes. Here it has led to a separation of whites and blacks."

"But I see black people in Wildwood," Vi said.

"You see people who work there, usually in the lowest-paid jobs, but black and white do not live together or eat together or, perhaps saddest of all, worship together," Mrs. Lansing replied with a sad shake of her head.

"I know about the prejudices that were used to justify slavery," Vi said. "I'm not so naïve that I haven't seen the problems between black and white. But I had not realized the separation was so complete. That black and white people should live entirely apart from one another. That the churches should be so divided. It is a violation of everything our Lord and Savior taught us! How can this happen? We learn that all believers are one in heart and mind. The apostle Paul tells us, 'There is neither Jew nor Greek, slave nor free, male nor female, for you are all one in Christ Jesus.' The knowledge that such segregation is tolerated makes me ashamed." Tears welled in Vi's eyes, and her cheeks burned with indignation.

Mrs. Lansing laid her hand on Vi's arm and said, "I share your feeling, but shame and anger will accomplish little. There are people in Boxtown who need your help every bit as much as the residents of Wildwood. You must reach out to them, but do so in the understanding that you cannot fully know the nature of what they endure. The separation is not of their making, yet they deal with it bravely. You must approach the people of

Boxtown as a humble student approaches a great teacher. The truth is that you and I enjoy many privileges based solely on the color of our skin. We have much to learn from those who are denied those same privileges for no reason other than the color of their skin."

Vi and Mrs. Lansing continued this conversation for some time, and Vi realized how much she did have to learn — not only about Boxtown and the separation of the races in India Bay, but also about the people of Wildwood and their feelings and fears.

"I want to run a school for poor children," Vi said, "yet today, I am reminded of my own ignorance. Is it presumptuous to want to help others when I have so little comprehension of their lives?"

Mrs. Lansing thought for a moment before she said, "I think it would be presumptuous if you assumed that you have all the answers for everyone. There is only One who ever walked this earth who possessed that knowledge — Jesus. Your work will help lead people to Him. It is possible that the mission will become a place where people of all colors can gather in the Spirit of the Lord, but that has to be their choice, my dear, not yours."

Mrs. Lansing rose from her chair and went to her desk. She withdrew several sheets of paper and took up her pen. "Now, I shall write these notes of introduction," she said. As her pen began to scratch over the pages, she asked, "Have you decided what you will say to our guests at the ball?"

"Not yet," Vi confessed, "but I've been thinking about it a great deal. It is so hard to find the right words."

"So long as your words come from your heart, they will serve the purpose," Mrs. Lansing said. "Speak to others as you speak to me, and they will hear what is in your heart."

"That is perhaps easier to say than to do," Vi laughed.

Mrs. Lansing looked up from her writing. "If you need an example, look to the speech that President Lincoln gave at the dedication of the military cemetery at Gettysburg on that cold November day in 1863. He spoke for a mere two minutes. The speech includes but 266 words. Yet how the words of his Gettysburg Address still ring in the hearts of all Americans. Think of how beautifully and simply he expressed the longings of our divided country—'that this nation, under God, shall have a new birth of freedom. . . .'"

"I cannot hope to match Mr. Lincoln's eloquence," Vi said.

"If a speaker's goal is eloquence alone, then a speech may impress when it is uttered, but the words will soon be forgotten. I have sat through many an eloquent speech that was as light as a feather and swiftly blown from my mind," Mrs. Lansing said. "From the heart, Vi. That's the secret of all true eloquence. Speak straight from your heart."

When the notes were done, Mrs. Lansing informed Vi that she had received a letter from her lawyer friend, Mr. Bartleby, in South Carolina. No, there was no word about Tansy and Marigold's family. Mr. Bartleby had acknowledged Mrs. Lansing's request and promised to report to her as swiftly as possible. It might be a week or more, but he assured Mrs. Lansing that he would spare no effort.

"Like the farmer who sowed his seeds in our Lord's parable, we have tossed out an appeal for help," Mrs. Lansing said. "I trust that our request has fallen on good soil. We must have patience now, and I have every confidence that Mr. Bartleby will produce a crop."

"Remind me of that often," Vi said with a wry laugh. "Patience has always been a virtue that too easily slips from my grasp, and I worry about what is beyond my power to control."

"Well, concentrate on what you need to do now," Mrs. Lansing replied kindly, "and leave the rest to our Heavenly Father. When you feel anxious, remind yourself of the words of Psalm 55 and 'cast your cares on the LORD and he will sustain you . . .'"

Disturbing News

Vi left Mrs. Lansing a half hour later with three neatly addressed envelopes and a great deal to think about. The news about Boxtown had surprised and disturbed her. She wondered why she had not known about this literal divide between black and white. Had she simply closed her eyes to such an appalling situation? Well, her eyes were open now; she was determined to know more, and she wanted to talk with Christine and Enoch.

But that intention was swiftly driven from her thoughts when she pulled into the mission. The sight that greeted her sent a wave of fear through her. Under one of the maple trees at the edge of the driveway, Mrs. O'Flaherty and Enoch were bending over Emily, who was crouching close to the ground. Standing close to Mrs. O'Flaherty were Tansy and Marigold, and both girls were sobbing and clearly frightened.

Vi dropped the reins, jumped from the buggy, and ran to the little group.

"What has happened?" she asked.

"A cat has been hurt," Mrs. O'Flaherty said, and Vi heard a slight tremor in her friend's voice, "but I'm sure it will be all right."

Mrs. O'Flaherty put her arms around the shoulders of the girls and drew them close. "Miss Emily is an excellent nurse, and she knows how to help the poor creature," she said, more for the benefit of the children than of Vi.

Vi said, "How did this—" but her question was interrupted by a warning look from Mrs. O'Flaherty.

"An accident," Mrs. O'Flaherty said.

"It was up in the tree!" Marigold exclaimed in a fresh burst of tears.

"Oh, dear," Vi said. She looked at Emily and saw her hands gently stroking what appeared to be an orange ball of fur.

121

"I think we should take it inside," Emily said, looking up at Enoch. "Can you find something we might use as a bed?"

"I've got a sturdy wood box that'll do just right," Enoch replied, and he hurried away in the direction of the tool-shed.

Carefully, Emily gathered the animal in her arms, and Vi reached out to help her friend stand. The cat was small, Vi saw, and lay as limp as a rag doll. Emily was cradling one of its front legs in her hand and there were flecks of what appeared to be dried blood on its face and back.

"Is it dead?" Marigold shrieked in terror.

"Oh no," Emily said in a quietly reassuring tone. "It is unconscious, like being asleep. But it is alive."

Enoch reappeared, holding a square box that had once contained nails.

Mrs. O'Flaherty took the box and spoke softly to the girls. "We must make this into a bed. If you come with me, we can find a soft blanket and a pillow to make the little cat comfortable. Will you help me?"

"We want to help very much," Tansy said fervently.

"Very, *very* much," Marigold added through her tears.

Mrs. O'Flaherty used her handkerchief to wipe the small child's cheeks. Then she took the girls' hands and led them to the house—both girls glancing anxiously back over their shoulders until they entered the kitchen door.

Emily followed, walking slowly so as not to jostle the little animal in her arms.

When the children were beyond hearing, Vi turned to Enoch. "Did it fall from the tree? Who found the poor thing?"

"It wasn't a fall, Miss Violet," Enoch said, a dark frown coming to his face. "And it wasn't any accident. That animal was tied there in that branch"—he pointed to one of the lower limbs of the maple tree—"tied by its legs. The little girls found it first. They'd just finished lunch and come out here to play.

Disturbing News

I was in the shed, and I heard them screaming. It was an awful sight, ma'am, and I got the poor thing down as fast as I could. I thought it was dead, but I felt its breathin'. Miss Clayton was here by then, and she took over. I don't think it was in that tree for too long, but long enough to put up a struggle and break one of its legs and bang itself up pretty bad. It takes a mighty lot of evil in a person to do that to one of God's innocent creatures," he concluded with a sorrowful shake of his head.

"Are you sure it was deliberate?" Vi asked, for she could not conceive of anyone committing such cruelty against man or beast. "Might the cat have accidentally become entangled?"

"No, ma'am," Enoch said firmly. He picked up some rope that lay on the ground nearby. "See here," he said, showing the rope to Vi. "These knots were tied by human hands. And this rope is new, not a piece of string the cat mighta picked up in the street."

"Oh," Vi sighed softly, for she could think of nothing else to say. She just stood and stared at the rope in Enoch's hands. Finally she asked, "Who might have done such a thing?"

"It coulda been boys," Enoch said. "This is the kinda sport that boys with no brains sometimes get up to. But doin' it in broad daylight, when we'd be sure to find the poor cat right quick—that strikes me as too bold for cowardly boys. I've seen this kinda thing before, Miss Violet. Back in the days when the Ku Klux Klanners roamed these parts, they'd often harm the pets and hunting dogs that belonged to black folk. It was a first warning, meant to scare the folks into leaving."

"Do you think this is a warning to us?" Vi questioned.

"Could be," Enoch replied. "There's people in this area that don't want this mission to succeed. I've picked up some talk at the livery stable and the feed store. I've…"

A little voice cut off what he was about to say. Marigold's head poked out from the kitchen door, and she was calling to

Vi. "You must come, Miss Violet! The kitty's awake now! Please come see!"

Vi waved and called back, "I'll be right there, Marigold."

The little face popped back inside. Vi turned to Enoch and said, "I want to know more about what you've heard, and I have several other things I need to discuss with you and Christine. Do you think we might have some time after supper tonight?"

"Sure thing, Miss Violet," he agreed. "We'll come to the house so Jacob can have a play with the girls 'fore his bedtime."

In the kitchen, the little girls and Mrs. O'Flaherty were standing round the table watching Emily work. The old nail box, which had been converted to a comfortable bed with the addition of a small pillow covered by a piece of woolen blanket, sat on the table, and Emily was bent over it.

Vi walked in, and Marigold ran to her, saying, "It's awake, Miss Violet. Kitty's waked up."

"How is the poor thing?" Vi asked.

Emily straightened and smiled. "I've never had so small a patient before, but I think it has a chance now," she said. "I've set the leg and splinted it and cleaned the cuts. Luckily they were no more than scratches and should heal quickly. I can find no other injuries, but then I am not an animal doctor."

Vi observed the cat, which was no more than three or four months old, and then she carefully stroked its little head with a finger. The cat moved its head slightly, but made no sound.

"It's been thoroughly traumatized by the ordeal," Emily said, "but in a way, that is good, for it would be difficult to keep an older cat still. If that bone is to knit, we must keep it quiet for as long as possible. I'd like to move the kitten to the clinic so I can keep an eye on it."

"Of course," Vi said, still stroking the cat's soft head. "And it can come to my room at night."

"Do you think it's hungry, Miss Emily?" asked Tansy. "Would the kitty like some milk?"

Emily thought this an excellent idea. She got a tiny saucer and poured a few teaspoons of milk in it. She held it so the cat could lap without moving its body. It sniffed at the saucer, took a small taste with its quick pink tongue, and then began to lap greedily. When the milk was gone, Emily refilled the saucer, and the cat finished all but a few drops.

She said, "Hunger is a good sign, I think. It would be if it were a little boy with a broken leg."

"Then it'll get well?" asked Tansy, looking at the nurse with bright, worried eyes.

"I cannot promise that, but I am hopeful," Emily replied.

"You said like 'a little boy.' Is it a boy, Miss Emily?" Tansy questioned.

Smiling, Emily said, "Actually, I believe it's a girl."

"Can we pray for her?" Marigold wanted to know.

"We can and we will," said Vi. She sat down on a kitchen chair and lifted Marigold onto her lap. "God created all the living creatures on this earth, and He gave humans rule over all His creatures. Of course we must pray for any one of His creations that has been hurt."

Marigold clasped her hands together, shut her eyes tightly, and said, "Please God, help the kitty get well. She didn't do anything wrong to anybody. I just know she's a good cat, and we love her very much. Thank You, God. Amen."

Then Marigold looked into Vi's face and asked, "Do you think God heard me?"

Vi hugged her close and said, "God always hears you, darling. He listens to every prayer. And He will do what is right for the kitty."

Violet's Bold Mission

The cat had fallen asleep, and Emily lifted the box with great care. In a whisper, she said, "Come, girls. We'll take her up to the clinic, and you can keep watch over her."

Marigold hopped down from Vi's lap. Dashing around the table, she took her sister's hand, and they followed Emily.

Mrs. O'Flaherty was about to go as well, when Vi said, "Can you stay a few minutes, Mrs. O? There are some things I need to talk over with you."

"About the cat?" Mrs. O'Flaherty asked.

"That, yes," Vi sighed, "and about some disturbing information I got from Mrs. Lansing. Have you ever heard of Boxtown?"

Vi and Mrs. O'Flaherty talked for some time. And that evening, the discussion was continued with Enoch and Christine, who knew a great deal about Boxtown and the inviolate line of separation between the black and white residents of the city. Enoch told Vi all about the Boxtown community. He had lived there for a year when he returned to India Bay after the War, and he still had friends there, including the minister of the church that he and Christine planned to attend. He explained that Boxtown was in many ways like a small city unto itself — peopled by the poor and the well-to-do alike.

"After the War, black folks who left the plantations didn't own any land, and they couldn't buy property in white neighborhoods," he explained. "Boxtown back then wasn't any bigger than a block where a few free blacks had settled. It's not what you'd call good real estate, just a strip of land between the railroad tracks and those bogs that border on the seashore. No white folks would live there, so the land was cheap, and our people moved in. There's quite a few of those original shacks left, but the people have built real houses and shops and churches and made it a community. The people work all around the city, but when you go to a rich person's house and see their maids and butlers and the like, you can be sure those servants go back home to Boxtown. Same for the black men who work on the docks and in the mills. Cross those railroad tracks, Miss Violet, and you're in a different world."

"But would we be welcome there?" Vi asked.

"Not welcome or unwelcome, I expect," Enoch said. "People would be curious about why you were there, sure enough, but I don't think you'd find them unfriendly."

The conversation was an education for Vi. Enoch explained that the South was unlike the North in that relatively few foreign immigrants were coming south of the old Mason-Dixon line to settle. In her time in New York City, Vi had seen how the poorest of the new European immigrants tended to cluster together in neighborhoods with those of the same nationality and ethnicity—German with German, Irish with Irish, Italian with Italian, and so forth. She had also learned how these groups often clashed, acting out old national animosities and conflicts on new soil, and she'd heard about the gangs of young men who fought for supremacy and made some parts of New York City as dangerous as a battle-field.

"The big difference," Enoch said, "is that most of those immigrants you saw in New York can rise above their poverty if they got a mind to and melt into the American way 'cause they're white. Just think about your friends, Miss Violet. Unless they tell you, you probably got no idea where their grandparents and great-grandparents came from. Mighta been England or Scotland or France or anywhere, but to you they're just Americans. It's not the same for black folks 'cause all you gotta do is look at us, and you know we came from slaves brought here from Africa. I don't mean *you*, Miss

Violet, just in general. Point is, we don't look the same and 'cause of that, it's nigh on impossible for us to just melt in. Add in all the history of injustice, the prejudice, and the crazy superstitions, and you can see why the people of Boxtown keep to themselves."

Vi did see, and she knew in her heart that everything that Enoch told her was true.

"I ain't sayin' that the mission can't serve Boxtown, ma'am," Enoch went on. "Just that you gotta take a different kind of approach. I could introduce you to Reverend Williams if you like. That's my friend, and he can tell you a lot more than I can and maybe help you understand the ways of Boxtown."

Vi was very grateful for this offer. Then she asked Enoch and Christine about what they had heard in Wildwood. The gist of it was that the people were afraid to venture inside the mission grounds. The rumor was that somehow or another, the "mission ladies" would be leaving soon. This news left Vi more concerned that the incident of the cat might well have been an attempt to scare them into giving up the mission.

"Don't want to jump to conclusions though," Enoch said cautiously. "It's still most likely that it was a prank."

"Well, whoever did it, they have not succeeded in frightening us, whatever their motives," Mrs. O'Flaherty declared with determination.

"No, ma'am, they haven't," Christine agreed. "But that doesn't mean they won't try something else, another prank or something worse."

"We all gotta be extra watchful from now on," Enoch said gravely. "I know you want the mission to be open at all hours, Miss Violet, but for the time being, I'd like us to keep the gates locked up at night. And I'll be taking a few extra turns round the grounds after dark."

Vi thought for a minute. Then she said, "I also think we should be sure the children are never left outside on their own. I'd hate for them to see anything like that poor cat in the tree again. For the time being, we had better be safe than sorry."

Just before bed that night, Mrs. O'Flaherty came to Vi's room. "Do you plan to tell your mother and Ed of this incident?" she asked.

It was a question Vi had been pondering.

"I don't think it's necessary yet," Vi replied. "I believe we should take precautions. But I don't want to worry Mamma and Ed without good reason. There is every chance it was just a cruel joke and will not be repeated. Do you think I'm wrong?"

"No," Mrs. O'Flaherty said slowly. "I think we have done what needs to be done for the present. But should anything of this kind occur again, you must inform your family immediately."

"Oh, I agree with you, Mrs. O," Vi said firmly. "I agree absolutely."

At just the time the adults at Samaritan House were breaking up their meeting and setting out to secure the mission house and property against more unwanted intrusions, another meeting was taking place in the back room of Wildwood's most notorious hotel.

"We did it, Mr. Clinch," a small, wiry young man was saying. "I won't bother you with the details. I didn't hang around to see the fireworks, but I can assure you those mission ladies got themselves a fright this day."

"I said no one was to be hurt," a tall man replied with a meaningful look.

"We didn't hurt *no person*, and that's the truth," the wiry man said with a sneer.

Clinch opened a metal box on his desk and began counting out dollar bills. He pushed the stack forward and said, "Then here's your pay, Jess, and a little extra for following my special orders."

The wiry man greedily grabbed up the money. His instinct was to count it, but he knew better than to offend Mr. Tobias Clinch, the most powerful man in Wildwood.

"I have another job for you," Mr. Clinch was saying. "This one is for someone of my acquaintance, but you should regard me as your employer as usual. You must do the job to my satisfaction if you want to collect your fee."

"Yes, sir," the small, weasel-like man responded in an oily tone. "You got more scarin' for me to do?"

"Maybe later," Clinch said.

From the same metal box, he took a small, framed photograph and handed it to Jess.

"These two little Negro girls," he said, "they're missing, and my, er, my friend is looking for them. Their names are on a paper inside the frame. My friend has good reason to believe that they may be in India Bay, possibly here in Wildwood. I want you to look for them. Find them, and my friend will pay you a generous reward. But you are not to approach them or endanger them in any way. Do you understand?"

"Just find them and tell you where they are," Jess said.

The tall man sat down at his desk. He turned his swivel chair so that he no longer faced the little man and said curtly, "You can go now."

Jess was slipping the photograph into his jacket pocket as he backed toward the office door.

"We'll find 'em, Mr. Clinch, sir," he said. "My boys got eyes in every corner of Inja Bay. We'll spot 'em soon enough."

"See that you do," Clinch said without looking around. "And close the door on your way out."

Hearing the door click shut, Clinch swung his chair back, locked the box on his desk, returned it to a bottom drawer, and locked that as well.

Disturbing News

The sickly sweet smell of Jess's hair oil still hung in the room, and Clinch made a disgusted face. To deal with petty criminals like Jess Jenkins always made him uncomfortable. But for Clinch to maintain his tight grip over Wildwood, Jess and his gang of scoundrels were a necessary evil. Just as doing favors for good customers was necessary. This made him think again of Mr. Ebenezer Greer of South Carolina — an exceptionally good customer who regularly lost large sums of money at Clinch's gaming tables and always came back for another try. Briefly, Clinch wondered why such a man would be searching for two children. *But that's not my worry*, he thought, and put the whole matter out of his mind.

CHAPTER

10

More Developments

Nothing in all creation is hidden from God's sight.

HEBREWS 4:13

More Developments

The rest of the week proceeded without further incident—at least, nothing of a negative kind. It was with great joy that two days later, everyone at Samaritan House greeted a very special visitor. They were all gathered before the house when Ion's finest carriage slowly entered the gates and came to a halt at the front door. Ben climbed down from the driver's seat, and he and Enoch with the greatest of care assisted Chloe from the carriage and up the steps to the porch. Leaning on Ben's arm, Chloe was welcomed by Vi, Mrs. O'Flaherty, and Christine, who was holding baby Jacob in her arms, and then introduced to Miss Clayton and the two Evans girls.

Tears came to the old woman's eyes at the sight of the little girls, and she told them to call her "Aunt Chloe" just as all the children of Ion did.

Seeing the elderly nursemaid's tears, Marigold asked with concern, "Are you sad, Aunt Chloe?"

"Not a bit, child," Chloe smiled. "I got tears of gladness to see you and your sister and the baby. It makes me happy to know that you children are part of Vi's mission. Children are the hope of the world, and our Lord gives us no greater gift or higher responsibility in this earthly life than the raising of children to know His love."

Elsie, who had accompanied Chloe, then introduced herself to Tansy and Marigold, saying, "I am pleased to meet such brave girls. Vi has told me all about how you cared for one another, and how glad she is to have you here."

The two little girls curtseyed prettily, and they fairly glowed with delight at meeting Mrs. Travilla and Chloe, for Vi had already told them several stories about growing up at Ion in the care of these two loving, godly women.

Chloe was given a full tour of the lower floor of the house. She expressed approval of all the renovations, including the kitchen, which she inspected with great diligence. Christine's thorough explanation of how the new stove and ovens worked seemed to satisfy Chloe and banish her fears about its safety.

The tour was followed by tea in the parlor, and Chloe asked Marigold and Tansy to sit beside her as they enjoyed their tea and cakes. The visit was relatively brief, for Chloe tired easily, but it could not have been sweeter.

Mr. Archibald, the carpenter, also made another appearance at Samaritan House that week. Vi had asked him to come and discuss a new building project—an elevator to the second-floor clinic. After a lengthy meeting with Vi and Emily, Mr. Archibald agreed that an elevator could be installed, and he promised to return soon with building plans—after he had made a careful study of the engineering required.

Because there were no more frightening occurrences, the residents of the mission began to think that the hateful treatment of the cat had been a viscious prank after all. Under Emily's nursing and the constant attention of Tansy and Marigold, the animal was recovering. When Dr. Bowman visited on Friday, he was astonished to learn what had happened and truly amazed to see the little cat actually moving about on the floor of the clinic. Its movements were comically awkward—a combination of three-legged hops, scooting on its belly, and rolling from side to side.

"It's a resourceful little thing," the doctor said as he observed the cat. "I see it's a marmalade."

"*She* is," Marigold corrected him with a playful grin. "What's a mar-marmu—?"

"A reference to her coloring," Dr. Bowman replied. "She would have been born with dark fur, but it has changed to orange and acquired stripes of darker hue. She's a tabby—a striped cat—orange with orange stripes. And that, my girl, reminds some people of orange marmalade, which is a sweet jam made from the fruits of the orange tree. Have you ever eaten marmalade on your toast?"

"I don't think so," the little girl replied. "What does it taste like?"

"People without much imagination would tell you it tastes both sweet and tart, like oranges," Dr. Bowman said with a twinkle in his eye. "But I think it tastes like tropical islands, far away in the Mediterranean Sea, and of ocean breezes and blue skies and adventure."

"Oooh, that does sound good," Marigold said with a grin. She bent down to stroke the little cat's head and back, and the kitty curled against her hand and purred contentedly.

"You're a mar-made cat," Marigold said. "A pretty mar-made cat."

"*Marmalade*," Tansy said, correcting her sister.

Marigold tried again. "Mar-mu-made," she said. Then, "Ma-lu-raid."

With a frustrated shake of her head, she declared, "Oh, I can't say it right! I'll just call her Jam!"

"Jam the cat," Dr. Bowman said. "I like that very much, Marigold."

He too bent down and gave the cat a gentle rub under her chin. "Hello, Jam," he said. "You are a brave little creature. Sweet, too."

~~~

After examining both girls, Dr. Bowman reported to Vi and Mrs. O'Flaherty that they were in excellent shape. Marigold's ear infection had entirely disappeared and, he was pleased to say, her hearing was not damaged. Both children were gaining weight, and he had no reason to expect that their arduous few weeks on their own would have any lasting effect on their physical health. He also praised Emily's skill in caring for the cat, owning that he could not have done nearly so well.

Vi had her own news, and she invited the doctor and Mrs. O'Flaherty into her office. A letter lay open on her desk. It had been delivered by Mrs. Lansing's driver while the doctor was examining his young patients.

"She has heard from Mr. Bartleby, her lawyer friend in Columbia, and she enclosed his letter with her own," Vi said, taking the sheets of paper from her desk.

"Mr. Bartleby has learned a good deal about Mr. Greer. Indeed, he inherited a large plantation from his mother about a year ago. The plantation is located near a mill town about fifty miles north of South Carolina's capital city, and Mr. Bartleby says that it has been owned by the Greer family since before the Revolutionary War. From his contact in Bethel—the town near the Greer plantation—Mr. Bartleby learned that the plantation has been very poorly managed since the elderly lady's death and that Mr. Greer is seeking to sell it. There are also stories that he is an unpleasant man and treats his tenants and employees badly."

Putting on her spectacles, Vi read aloud a passage from Mr. Bartleby's letter. The lawyer had written:

I cannot confirm these reports by personal observation. At your request, Mrs. Lansing, I have not visited the town of Bethel nor made my inquiries public. But I telegraphed an old college friend of mine who is a judge there now, and he wrote back with a good deal of background. Mr. Ebenezer Greer had left his mother's home some fifteen years ago and paid her no visits until he returned for her funeral. My judge friend did not preside over the probating of the lady's will, for he did not live in Bethel at that time. But he says there is no question of the son's inheritance. Mr.

Greer has not gained much goodwill since his return to Bethel. He seems to be a greedy and uncivil person — unlike his mother, who was much loved in the community for her kindness and Christian generosity. There are stories that Mr. Greer rules his workers and tenants like a tyrant and pays them almost nothing. His tenant farmers are forced to give him the entirety of their crops each year in exchange for the rent of their dwellings, and he provides them with the barest of provisions to feed their families. He is also reputed to treat his house servants as if they were still slaves, demanding heavy labor and compensating his employees with little more than food and board.

Vi stopped reading and looked up.

"That substantiates what the girls have told us," Mrs. O'Flaherty said. "Tansy has confided that her mother worked such long hours that she barely had time to sleep. That surely contributed to the poor woman's illness."

"Does the letter contain any word of the girls' family?" Dr. Bowman asked, his face now darkly clouded with concern.

"There is just a bit," Vi said.

Then she read again from Mr. Bartleby's letter:

The judge has no personal knowledge of a family named Evans. However, his law clerk — a young man who grew up in Bethel — recalled a farmer named John Evans who worked a large place that was either part of the Greer plantation or adjacent to it. He remembers Mr. Evans as a Northerner, from Pennsylvania or perhaps New York — who came to the community as a free man and was initially rejected as a "carpetbagger" and an "uppity black Yankee." But by the time Mr. Evans died, he had earned a reputation as a fine, hardworking Christian man. Unfortunately, my friend's clerk, who was a boy at the time, knows nothing about Mr. Evans's family and cannot say whether Mr. Evans had a wife or children. He does recall hearing that Mr. Evans died in an epidemic that swept the community some five or six years ago.

Vi laid the letter aside. She told her friends that Mr. Bartleby had expressed his willingness to proceed with his investigation, should that be Mrs. Lansing's wish.

"There is more than enough in that letter to attest to the truth of everything the girls have told us," Mrs. O'Flaherty commented, adding, "not that I ever doubted them. But this certainly seems to explain their mother's desire to send her daughters away from the plantation and to make her own escape. How can a man like this Mr. Greer be allowed to treat people with such meanness and disregard?" she asked, anger flashing in her sapphire eyes.

"Because the law supports him," Dr. Bowman responded with indignation.

Vi removed her glasses and sighed heavily. "My Papa always said that for all the horrors of the Civil War, the peace that followed was even more difficult. Reconstruction promised justice and compensation for the victims of slavery, but it has not turned out that way."

"Be that as it may, we have two little girls to think of, Vi," Mrs. O'Flaherty said, her tone practical now. "What is our next move?"

"I think we should ask Mr. Bartleby to continue his investigation," Vi said. "I've already written a note to Mrs. Lansing requesting as much. We shall pay for his time, of course."

Dr. Bowman said that he was going to the Lansing home as soon as he left the mission, and he offered to take the note.

Then Vi said, "I'd planned to stay here this weekend and attend Sunday services at one of the churches on our list. I thought it a good way to meet the minister and present the letter of introduction from Mrs. Lansing. But now I think I should go to Ion. I want to present this new information to Mamma and Ed and get their counsel."

"I can take your place at church," Mrs. O'Flaherty said. "Enoch and Christine have already asked for the girls to join them for services at the church pastored by Enoch's friend in Boxtown."

With furrowed brow, Dr. Bowman said, "In light of the incident with the cat, I don't like the thought of leaving Samaritan House unattended even for a Sunday morning. Would you allow me to serve as guardian while you are all away? The only payment I request is to share luncheon with you, Mrs. O'Flaherty, when you return from church."

Mrs. O'Flaherty agreed with pleasure, and Vi expressed her thanks. She said that she would go to Ion the following day, Saturday, and return to Wildwood by lunchtime on Sunday. That way she could join them.

"Perhaps I will have more ideas from Mamma and Ed when I get back," she said. "At any rate, it will be a pleasure to dine with you on Sunday, Doctor…and productive perhaps to discuss our thinking after we all have some time to mull over this news from South Carolina."

Dr. Bowman's concern for the safety of the occupants of Samaritan House was not without reason. On arriving that morning, he had noticed a small man, wearing dark clothing and a bowl-shaped hat, who was lounging against a crumbling section of wall in an empty lot opposite the mission. On seeing the man, the word "snake" had popped into the doctor's mind. Dr. Bowman chided himself for so hateful a thought (though it had not been deliberate) and told himself to forget about the man.

Violet's Bold Mission

But as he was examining little Jam and congratulating Emily on her expert care for the injured animal, the image of the small man reappeared in his consciousness. Had he just been loitering on the street, Dr. Bowman wondered, or could he have been watching the mission? The doctor had paid a number of visits to Samaritan House in the past two weeks, and he was sure he'd never seen the man before.

Dr. Bowman said nothing to the ladies of the house, for he had no wish to worry them about something that was doubtless just a product of his active imagination. He left the mission soon after his meeting with Vi and Mrs. O'Flaherty was concluded. He'd taken a few extra minutes to say good-bye to Tansy, Marigold, and Emily, lingering a bit longer with the latter to discuss a few matters regarding supplies for the clinic.

At length, he drove his buggy through the mission gates and turned in the direction of the Lansings' home. He made a point of closely scanning the streets for the snakelike man. But he saw only a few women with shopping baskets, some small children trailing behind them, and a couple of young men stretched out on the grass of the empty lot, talking and smoking cigarettes. But no small man in a derby hat.

Dr. Bowman had to laugh at his own wild imaginings. Still, he did not waver in his decision to watch over Samaritan House in the absence of its residents. Then another thought came into his head without being invited. *At least Miss Clayton will be safe at home with her aunt on Sunday.* He wondered why that knowledge seemed so comforting.

CHAPTER

11

More Warnings?

The LORD is a refuge for the oppressed, a stronghold in times of trouble.

PSALM 9:9

he next afternoon, Vi arrived at Ion just after the family had finished their midday meal. Elsie, her father and mother, Ed, Zoe annd the professor were sitting in the parlor. Vi was so glad to see them all that she didn't notice Professor Raymond at first. She greeted him politely, and he returned her greeting. Then everyone asked for a recounting of the week's events at Samaritan House.

Soon they were all riveted by the news of what the South Carolina lawyer had learned about Mr. Greer.

"What a terrible man!" Zoe exclaimed. "How is such treatment of people possible after millions died or were wounded in the Civil War to end the evil of slavery? Why, his plantation sounds like something from the Middle Ages—cruel master and helpless serfs."

Everyone else agreed with Zoe's assessment, though their language was more tempered.

"It is just possible we do this Mr. Greer an injustice by rushing to make a judgment," Horace Dinsmore cautioned. "What the lawyer has reported consists mostly of rumor."

"That's true, Grandpa," Vi said, "and that is why I've asked Mrs. Lansing to have Mr. Bartleby continue his investigation. But still, I cannot rid myself of the feeling that Tansy and Marigold's mother may be in jeopardy. I feel an urgency that I cannot explain."

"Perhaps you should talk to the police in India Bay," Rose Dinsmore suggested. "They should be alerted in case anyone makes inquiries about the children. It is possible that their mother is searching for them even now."

Vi smiled gratefully at her grandmother. "Thank you, Grandmamma," she said. "I knew that I could count on my family for wise ideas."

"Should we send someone to South Carolina?" Ed asked.

"It might be necessary later," Elsie replied, "but it sounds to me as if this Mr. Bartleby is quite adequate for the task at hand. If you will have Mrs. Lansing send me his address, Vi, I shall communicate with him directly and have him bill me for all his expenses."

"Oh, that's so kind of you, Mamma," Vi said. She gave her mother a hug and kissed her cheek, and Elsie returned these gestures with equal affection.

Then Elsie said, "I must say that I was very impressed by your two young guests when Aunt Chloe and I visited the mission. Tansy and Marigold have excellent manners and qualities that make it clear they have been raised in a good Christian home. In fact, what I observed in them seems to belie the possibility that they have been treated as slaves, or serfs as Zoe says."

"Are they educated?" Zoe asked.

"Yes, quite well," Vi replied. "Marigold is not yet six years old, but she already reads and can write a bit. Tansy is an avid reader and knows history and arithmetic far beyond the level one would expect of the child of a poor tenant farmer. She has told me that the late Mrs. Greer taught her mother and then Tansy and Marigold. And the girls' mother continued their education after Mrs. Greer's death. Tansy said it was one of the reasons Mr. Greer was always angry with her mother, after he took over the plantation. According to Tansy, he said learning was wasted on the poor, and he didn't want his employees thinking they were better than their master."

"There is most definitely something strange about this situation," Elsie remarked almost to herself. "I think there is more to the story of our two little lambs than any of us can guess. Perhaps more than the girls know themselves."

"Is that your woman's intuition, Mamma?" Ed asked with a chuckle.

"Do you mock intuition, Ed?" Zoe said. Her tone was light, but Vi heard a slight edge of indignation in her friend's voice.

This led to a few minutes of banter. Ed refused to concede to Zoe's argument that intuition was a characteristic not limited to women.

"What do you say, Mark?" Ed finally appealed to his friend.

The professor had said nothing during the conversation. Now he smiled and replied, "I would be a foolish man to set myself between you, Ed, and the ladies. I will venture, however, that I am not as inclined to dismiss intuition as I once was."

"Surely you as a scholar would not trust entirely to feelings as a guide?" Ed asked incredulously.

"No, but I do not ignore feelings—intuition if you will—either. After all, God has gifted us with the ability to feel and the ability to reason. Might not intuition fall somewhere between the two? We often praise people for their skill at reading other people's characters—recognizing the scoundrel who hides behind a façade of seeming goodwill, for instance. I do not believe that intuition is necessarily reliable, but I think we would be close-minded to ignore it entirely."

"Thank you, Professor Raymond," Zoe said, struggling to keep the note of triumph out of her voice.

This led to a lively conversation about several philosophical points. As the talk progressed, Vi noticed how the professor spoke rather little, but always seemed to ask questions that enabled the others to focus their thoughts and argue their points without conflict. For the first time, she understood why Ed was so fond of his former teacher. She tried to imagine what it would be like to be a student in the professor's classroom, and suddenly it dawned on her. She had had such a teacher—her own father! Edward Travilla had often taught not by lecturing but by just such questioning. It was a method, her father said, that had come from the ancient Greeks. *So there is something to admire about Professor Raymond,* she thought. *Papa would have liked him, I'm sure. And for that reason alone, if no other, I should be more tolerant of his arrogant manners. Perhaps he hides other unexpected qualities behind that pompous façade. Perhaps I have jumped to hasty conclusions yet again,* she thought, recalling her summer in New York City when she had so nearly misjudged the actions of Zoe and their friend, the French Ambassador.

On her way to Ion that day, Vi had decided that she should share the story of the cat with her big brother. So after the pleasant evening with her family, Vi managed to get Ed to herself for a time, and she told him everything. She assured him that they were taking extra precautions at the mission, but since nothing else had occurred, they had reason to believe it had been a terrible joke by neighborhood boys. She did, however, confide Enoch's concern that it might be an attempt to scare the residents of the mission away.

Ed was, as she'd expected, furious at the idea that someone would attempt to frighten his sister and their friends, and in so terrible a manner.

Vi calmed him, and then she asked him not to repeat the story to their mother. "Since it was in all likelihood a prank, I do not want Mamma needlessly worried. I don't mean that it is a secret, Ed—just that I don't want to unsettle her unless there is reason."

Ed agreed to her wish, for he was just as mindful of their mother's well-being as Vi was.

"How is the cat?" he asked at last.

"Doing surprisingly well," Vi said with a grin. "Emily and the girls fret over the little thing as if she were the Queen of

England herself. Assuming that all continues to go well, I think Samaritan House has another permanent inhabitant."

Ed's face turned serious again and he said, "You have to promise me that you will be careful, Vi. All of you. The torture of the cat may have been just a nasty joke by mean-spirited boys. But you can't drop your guard. If there is another such incident, you must let me know immediately. Will you promise me that?"

"I will, big brother," Vi said.

They talked a while longer, and Vi learned that the professor would be returning to the East in another week.

"He misses his children," Ed remarked.

"Children!" Vi declared. "I didn't know he is a father."

"Yes, he has three little ones," Ed said. "The eldest is a boy about Danny's age, and there are two younger girls. Mark has endured great sadness in the past few years. His wife died suddenly when the youngest child was only two years old. Mark was so distraught that he sent the children to live with a relative in Boston. He threw himself into his work and travels, and I'm sure that is how he survived his tragedy. The children still live apart from him, but he sees them as often as he can."

"They live apart?" Vi questioned. "But surely he does not blame them in any way for the loss of his wife."

Vi was thinking of her own mother and grandfather. She had often heard the story of Horace Dinsmore's coldness to Elsie after the death of his first wife—Elsie's mother—and before Horace opened his heart to the healing grace of the Lord Jesus.

Ed said, "No, Mark does not blame the children at all. He loves them dearly. But I think he may blame himself, for he was away in Europe when his wife died and not there for his children when they needed him so. He must feel great guilt, and for that reason he doesn't think himself fit to be a good father to them."

"You've talked about this with him?" Vi questioned.

"Mark has told me about the children, but he does not speak of his wife's death. I have only picked up hints here and there," Ed replied. Then he smiled softly and added, "Zoe would say that I am using my intuition. Perhaps she is right that it is not a trait exclusive to the female mind."

"Shall I tell her you said that?" Vi asked in a teasing way.

"Don't you dare, little sister!" he commanded with a laugh. "Zoe would never let me forget it."

"Would that be such a bad thing?" Vi inquired.

"Yes — no — I don't really know," he replied in an odd tone, and Vi realized that he was blushing.

"I've never known quite what to make of our little friend," Ed was saying, trying to steady his voice. "Zoe is as impetuous as a child one minute, then almost as wise as Mamma the next. Oh, well, I should be grateful that Grandpapa is her guardian and not I."

"She is probably just as glad of that as you," Vi said in a playful way. *But perhaps not for the reasons you imagine*, she thought.

Vi went to bed that night thinking that her few hours at home had been surprisingly revealing. Professor Raymond and then Ed. She had seen sides of both that challenged her understanding. "Are all men so complicated?" she said out loud as she turned out her light and snuggled under the covers of the bed that had been hers for so many years. "I haven't the skills to figure them out. But dear Father in Heaven, please help me to be more understanding," she said as her words became a prayer. "Give me the strength to resist making snap judgments, because it is not my place to judge anyone but myself. As You know, I need lots of help in this area, for I am all too often tempted to draw conclusions without evidence. I also ask Your blessings on the professor and his motherless children. And on my big brother. And Zoe. And Tansy and Marigold. And everyone I love..."

Comforted as always by her conversation with her Heavenly Friend, Vi drifted off into a deep and peaceful sleep. When she awoke the next morning, she felt wonderfully refreshed and ready to return to the city. Whatever challenges awaited her at Samaritan House, she was ready to meet them with the confidence of one who knows that the Lord is always at her side.

Vi was looking forward to lunch with Mrs. O'Flaherty and Dr. Bowman. Vi's visit with her family had sparked new ideas that she wanted to discuss with her friends, and she was especially anxious to act on her Grandmamma Rose's suggestion that they speak with the police about the little girls. Vi had never visited a police station before, and she thought Dr. Bowman might be able to tell her how to proceed.

She hardly expected to see a policeman in uniform at the front door of Samaritan House as she guided the buggy into the drive at a little past noon. He was standing on the steps, talking with Mrs. O'Flaherty, and he seemed to be writing something in a notebook.

Vi quickly dismounted and tied the buggy reins to the post in front of the steps. Mrs. O'Flaherty and the policeman came to meet her. "We've had more trouble," Mrs. O'Flaherty said. "Sergeant Peevy will explain. But thanks be to God, no one has been hurt."

She introduced the policeman to Vi. "Sergeant Peevy, I would like you to meet Miss Travilla."

The officer tipped his hat and bowed slightly, but he didn't extend a hand.

"Pleased to meet you, Miz Travilla," he said. "I'm sorry to report that the new shed behind your house was set afire, and the circumstances appear suspicious."

"Someone set a fire?" Vi asked in disbelief.

"That appears to be the case," Sergeant Peevy said. "Mrs. O'Flaherty here tells me that the shed was clean and that all the building materials were taken away after the work on this place was done. But we found wood shavings outside, and it's not likely they got there by accident."

Vi could hardly take this all in as the policeman continued, "It's a good thing the young doctor was here when the fire started. It could've spread real fast to the stable and the carriage house."

"Dr. Bowman?" Vi asked.

"Yes, Vi girl," Mrs. O'Flaherty replied with evident pride. "Dr. Bowman arrived before we all left for church this morning. He was patrolling the house when he looked out a window and saw the smoke. He ran out and turned himself into a one-man bucket brigade. Then a stranger on the street saw what was happening and he came to help. Between them, they extinguished the fire before it did too much damage. But someone reported it to a policeman, and Sergeant Peevy was here when I returned from church."

"The girls? And the Reeves?" Vi asked anxiously.

"They aren't back yet," Mrs. O'Flaherty replied. "Christine said that they might dine with their friend Reverend Williams after services."

"Mrs. O'Flaherty told me about the cat in the tree," the sergeant said, looking at his notepad. "That was last Monday. I don't want to alarm you ladies, but there appears to be a pattern here. Have you had any trouble with people in the neighborhood?"

"No, sir," Vi said. "We are aware that people are curious about us, and some seem openly suspicious. But no indeed, there has been nothing to explain these incidents. You believe the fire was deliberate?"

"I couldn't testify to it in court," the sergeant replied with a frown. "But if I were you, I would be on the alert. People like you have come to Wildwood before, and they've all left. We never had proof that they were driven out, but there are people here who do not want a Christian mission in their midst."

"Do the churches have such problems?" Mrs. O'Flaherty asked.

"No, ma'am, they don't," the officer said, "because they keep their heads down, as we used to say in the War, and tend to their own flocks. But a mission's different. Mission people like yourselves reach out to everyone. You must know what goes on in Wildwood," he added, lowering his tone. "There's bad folks making money off the misery of poor people, and a mission is going to affect their business."

"Just who are these bad people?" Vi asked.

"It wouldn't be proper for me to be naming names without evidence," the sergeant said officially. Then he lowered his voice again and said, "But take a look at who owns those hotels and saloons farther down the street. They're rough men, Miz Travilla, rough and cunning. And they're the head of the snake in Wildwood. That's who you've got to look out for."

"But can't you do something?" Vi demanded.

"We do what we can, miss," the policeman replied defensively. "But we can't do anything until there's been a crime, and few people in Wildwood are brave enough to report to us. We wouldn't have heard about your fire 'cept for that young woman who ran into the station this morning."

Vi looked inquiringly at Mrs. O'Flaherty.

"No one seems to know who the woman is, and she didn't give her name," the older woman said. Then she addressed the policeman. "Is there any more information we can provide for you, Sergeant Peevy?"

The sergeant said that he had all he needed for the time being and thanked the ladies for their help. Then he indicated that he would try to get an extra patrol or two for the mission.

"Do you lock those gates at night?" he asked.

Violet's Bold Mission

"We don't want to, but yes," Vi said. "After what happened to the cat, our caretaker, Mr. Reeve, insisted that the gates be locked at sundown, and he inspects the grounds at night."

"He's right, ma'am," said Sergeant Peevy.

The policeman then bade the ladies good-bye. He walked around the side of the house to where his horse was hitched, and the women did not move until the sound of clopping hooves disappeared.

"Where's Dr. Bowman, Mrs. O?" Vi asked. "And the stranger who helped him?"

"The stranger has gone," replied Mrs. O'Flaherty gravely. "Like the young woman who went to the police, he wouldn't tell us his name, though I made every effort to learn it. But he did let me pack a basket of food, and he accepted it for his family. I asked him to stay until you arrived, but he'd have none of that. I thought at first he was embarrassed by our gratitude, but I saw soon enough that he was afraid."

"Afraid of us?"

"Not really. It was more that he was afraid of being here — of being seen at the mission."

Mrs. O'Flaherty's expression then brightened, and she said, "As for Dr. Bowman, he is inside cleaning up. I returned just as the fire was put out, and I hardly recognized our hero. He was covered in smoke and ash and water."

"I hope you can recognize me now," came a cheerful voice as the doctor emerged onto the porch. "I have washed my face and hair and cleaned my hands, but I'm afraid I can do little about my suit."

"You look grand to me, young man," Mrs. O'Flaherty said with a wide smile that revealed her gold tooth. "Come in, now, both of you, and let's eat. You have more than earned your meal today, Doctor Bowman."

Vi excused herself to take her horse and buggy to the stable. She put the horse in its stall, noting that Dr. Bowman's mare was in a second stall, and she poured out some grain for both horses. Then she went to examine the damage to the shed. It wasn't too bad, she realized. The fire had been lit on the side of the shed — out of direct view from the street. The outside wall was darkly scorched, and the new paint was blistered and peeling. She thought that several boards needed replacing, but luckily the blaze had not reached the shed roof. If it had, the fire would have jumped quickly to the stable. Looking at the ground, now muddy from the buckets of water tossed on the fire, she saw the wood shavings that Sergeant Peevy spoke of, as well as some bits of greasy rag and torn newspaper that had not been burnt. She disposed of the suspicious scraps.

Heading to the house, she raised a quick, silent prayer: *Thank You, dear Lord, for Dr. Bowman's presence of mind and quick action. And thank You for the strangers who risked themselves to help. Please bless them all with Your abundant love and protection, and give us Your strength as we face whatever trials lie ahead.*

Then she thought of a verse from Job 12: "He reveals the deep things of darkness and brings deep shadows into the light."

Help us, Lord, by revealing the truth about those who want to harm Samaritan House, she prayed. *Please lift this shadow so we may go forward with Your good work.*

Naturally the fire was the main topic of conversation over lunch. Dr. Bowman told them everything that had occurred. He had not seen anyone near the shed before the fire, but like Sergeant Peevy, he was convinced that the blaze was deliberately set. They all agreed to tell Enoch and Christine exactly what they knew, although it was quickly decided to tell the little girls only that the fire was an accident. They didn't want the girls to be afraid.

Dr. Bowman, who should have been exhausted after his efforts, was in fact full of energy. He refused to leave

Samaritan House until the Reeves had returned. The meal being finished, he helped Vi and Mrs. O'Flaherty clear the table and sat with them in the kitchen while they washed the dishes.

Vi mentioned her intention to tell the police about the girls. "I could have spoken of it to Sergeant Peevy," she said, "but it flew from my mind as soon as I heard about the fire."

Dr. Bowman asked permission to return to Samaritan House the next afternoon and escort Vi to the police station, and his offer was gratefully accepted.

"Soon you will be moving in with us, Doctor," Mrs. O'Flaherty joked. "The cook's rooms are still empty."

"I'm afraid my landlady would not allow that," the doctor replied. "She is a dear woman but given to a great variety of aches and pains. It gives her great pleasure to have a doctor in the house, and she treats me attentively in exchange for my professional advice."

He tugged at the sleeve of his dress shirt, now grayed with smoke and dirt. "I have every confidence that this shirt will be as white as snow and starched and ironed to perfection tomorrow," he said. "To return the favor, I shall spend a great deal of time discussing the shooting pains in her shoulder, the weakness of her knees, and the bunions on her feet."

"Is she really ill?" Vi asked.

"Healthy as a horse," the doctor replied with a chuckle. "But I do not begrudge the time we spend chatting, for she is a kind and generous woman in all respects. She lost her husband in the War and her only child, a son, in an accident some years ago. In a small way, I believe she has adopted me to help fill the void in her life that their deaths created."

It was not long before the Reeves returned with Tansy and Marigold. Vi quickly explained about the "accidental" fire. Mrs. O'Flaherty took the girls and Jacob outside to see the shed, and Dr. Bowman then acquainted Enoch and Christine with the full story, including the evidence that the fire was deliberate. Vi added Sergeant Peevy's remarks about the hotel owners and their possible interest in seeing that the mission failed. It was now clear to them all that someone was attempting to frighten the residents of Samaritan House and drive them out of Wildwood.

"Well, they won't succeed," Vi declared indignantly. "I am my father's daughter, and I will be guided by his example. He did not cower from the Ku Klux Klan. I shall certainly not bend to the will of a few saloon keepers! Whatever these men may have in mind to do, we must all remember the words of King David: 'It is God who arms me with strength and makes my way perfect.'"

She pounded her fist upon the table so hard that some bowls rattled and a large spoon fell to the floor. It might have been a funny scene, but Vi's determination was so real and so true that no one doubted her seriousness. To Enoch and Christine, it was as if Edward Travilla himself had been speaking. They heard the father in his daughter's voice and saw him in the set of her jaw and the flash in her eyes. She was prepared to do battle for the mission, and so were they.

A little later, as Dr. Bowman was getting his horse, he had an opportunity to speak to Enoch alone and confided his suspicion about the small man he'd seen in the lot opposite the house on the previous Friday.

"I'm probably being fanciful," the doctor said as he cinched his horse's saddle, "but I can't shake the feeling that he was watching this house."

Enoch thought for several moments. Then he said, "Somebody was watching close enough to know that we were all away this morning."

"But I was here," the doctor objected.

"You came in the back way, and you didn't drive your buggy today," Enoch said. "If they're watching the front, they'd have missed seeing you. I drove the carriage to the front door to get Mrs. O'Flaherty and the girls. Then I took Mrs. O'Flaherty to the church, and we went on to Boxtown. Anybody across the street woulda seen us leave. And if somebody's been watching closely, they'd know that Miss Violet goes outta the city on Sundays. I'm thinking they didn't see you come in from the back gate, and that's what made them bold enough to set that fire in the daytime. It woulda been quite a trick, sir, having the shed and maybe the stable burned to the ground when we all got back from church."

"Well, let's keep a sharp eye out," Dr. Bowman said in a solemn tone. "I haven't mentioned the man to anyone else, for I see no need to worry the ladies about what is just a vague feeling on my part."

"No need, sir," Enoch agreed. "At least, not yet."

The next few days were unmarred by any more incidents. Vi and Dr. Bowman paid their planned visit to the local police station and made the report about the two girls. No one had contacted the police about two missing children, but the captain with whom Vi and the doctor spoke promised to alert the mission if he or any of his officers had news.

Keeping her promise to Ed, Vi wrote to him about the fire and left it to his good judgment whether to tell their mother. Vi didn't want to keep secrets from her Mamma, but neither did she want to cause Elsie needless anxiety.

A day later, Harold and Herbert came to the mission after their school let out.

"Ed got your later before breakfast, and he asked us to stop by to see how you are," Harold explained. "He told us about the fire."

More Warnings?

"Ed couldn't come because he and the professor are doing something this week—visiting some people at India Bay University, I think," Herbert added. "It's been jolly fun having Professor Raymond stay with us. At first, I thought him a bit stuck-up. But he's really a fine fellow, and his stories about all the places he's been are just ripping good."

"Did he tell you he's going to Mexico on an expedition next summer?" Harold asked his sister.

When Vi said that she hadn't heard this news, Harold and Herbert eagerly filled her in on the details. The professor, they said, would be working with an archeologist who was searching for the remains of an ancient North American culture.

"But is that dangerous work?" Vi asked.

"It could be," Herbert said with an edge of excitement. "They're going deep into the jungle, I think. But what an adventure!"

"He's leaving us on Friday, you know," Harold said. "He's going to Boston to see his children. I wonder why his children don't live with him?"

"Probably because he travels so much. I just know that it's going to be too quiet at Ion without him around," Herbert added with a little sigh of disappointment.

Then they talked of other things before the twins took their leave. Vi told her brothers about her plans to visit with the ministers of the local churches and seek their support. She also went over the details of the fire and showed them the shed, which Enoch had already repaired and repainted. As she waved good-bye to the twins, Vi hoped with all her heart that their report to Ed would be reassuring.

She also found herself thinking about the professor and his impending departure. She wouldn't see him again, she supposed, but she raised a prayer for God to watch over him on his journey home and for his safe return from all his future journeys, wherever they took him.

159

CHAPTER

12

A Test
of Courage

*But the LORD is faithful, and he
will strengthen and protect
you from the evil one.*

2 THESSALONIANS 3:3

A Test of Courage

he rest of the week passed quietly. Vi and Mrs. O'Flaherty paid a call on the minister of the church Mrs. O had attended the previous Sunday, and they were most encouraged by his reaction to the goals of Samaritan House. The minister said that he would inform his congregation about the clinic. And his wife was very pleased to hear about Vi's plans to start school classes in the winter and even volunteered to assist when help was needed.

In her letter to Ed, Vi had told him that she wouldn't be coming to Ion the next weekend, for she and Mrs. O'Flaherty would be attending Sunday services at another of the churches on Mrs. Lansing's list. Vi prayed that her reception there would be in the same spirit as at the first church.

Two callers came to the mission that week — Mrs. Nelson, the wife of the dry goods dealer, and her sister, Miss Crane. They were quite jolly ladies, though both shared Mr. Nelson's penchant for gossip. From them, Vi, Mrs. O'Flaherty, and Emily learned a good deal more about the community of Wildwood. Both Mrs. Nelson and Miss Crane exhibited a healthy distaste for the hotel owners and their saloons and other businesses.

"Be especially careful of that Mr. Clinch," Mrs. Nelson confided. "He owns the Wildwood Hotel, and he's the real power in Wildwood. A few years ago, Marvin — that's Mr. Nelson — tried to start a store owners association. A group, you know, to try to clean up Wildwood Street and improve the neighborhood. Well, Mr. Clinch put a stop to Marvin's idea quick enough."

"How did he do that?" Emily asked.

"Oh, nothing out in the open," Mrs. Nelson replied. She drew herself up in a posture of indignation and said, "Mr.

Clinch never said a word to my husband, like an honest man would have. But his henchman—a dreadful little person named Jess Jenkins who always wears a derby hat—he paid visits to the other shopkeepers. Nobody would tell us what he said, but all of a sudden, nobody wanted any part of an association. Well, Marvin—Mr. Nelson—knew better than to cross Mr. Clinch, so he dropped his idea like a hot coal."

"Mr. Clinch has driven people like you out of Wildwood before," Miss Crane said in an excited little voice. "He's as bad as they come, Miss Travilla, and he wants Wildwood to stay just as it is. You should be careful to stay out of his way. *Very* careful, I can tell you," she added with a knowing nod.

Mrs. Nelson and her sister took their leave soon after imparting this information, leaving the ladies of Samaritan House to speculate.

"Do you think this Mr. Clinch could be behind our troubles?" Vi asked.

"It's possible, though we shouldn't be too quick to judge," Mrs. O'Flaherty said. "I'd hate to condemn anyone based on local gossip."

"But what Mrs. Nelson said about the little man in the derby hat…" Emily began. Then she paused. Her forehead wrinkled with thought for several moments.

"What?" Vi asked.

"I think I've seen him," Emily said slowly. "I've seen a person who matches that description in the lot across the street. I have a good view of the lot from the front window of the clinic, and I sometimes gaze out upon it. I can't help thinking what a good children's play yard it would make. It's terribly overgrown and full of rubbish, but—"

"But the man!" Vi burst out in a tone that was half impatient and half amused. "The man in the derby hat? You've seen him?"

"A number of times," Emily replied. "I've seen him there with two or three young men. He doesn't stay long, though

the other men do. They lounge and smoke cigarettes, sometimes all day. I just thought they were jobless and had nothing
to do—like other men I see so often on the streets. But now
that I think of it, the man in the derby almost seems to bring
them to the lot."

"I wonder if anyone is there now," Mrs. O'Flaherty said.

The three women quickly made their way up to the clinic
and gathered at the front window. Indeed it offered a clear
view of the empty lot, but instead of several men, they saw
only one. He was sitting on a broken bit of wall, and he
appeared only to be watching passers-by. He was small, wiry,
and dressed in dark clothing. In one hand, he held a black hat
that was shaped like a bowl, and he was casually polishing the
hat on the coat sleeve of his other arm.

Whispering as if she feared the man might hear her, Vi said,
"We have to tell Enoch about this. Oh dear, I hope I'm over-
reacting, but we have to tell Enoch now."

The little man did not reappear in the lot the next morning,
and there were no other men there either. Emily made a point of
checking frequently from the clinic view, and Enoch kept his
eye on the lot all day, but nothing suspicious was seen.

"It's probably just a gathering place for the poor and unemployed," Mrs. O'Flaherty said hopefully as she and Vi prepared lunch. "I think we may get some rain today, for the sky
is gray with clouds. The young men Emily has seen have
probably gathered inside today."

Vi expressed her agreement, though she could not rid herself of the vague feeling that Samaritan House was being
watched. She'd felt it ever since seeing the man with the derby
hat. The fact that he hadn't returned did little to settle her
unease.

Violet's Bold Mission

Trying to take her mind off her troublesome thoughts, she asked, "Are you and the girls going for a walk after lunch?"

"If it doesn't rain, I thought we might walk to the greengrocer's shop," Mrs. O said. "I'd like to see if he has any winter squash or pumpkin for sale today. Yet I would welcome rain if it comes. Everything has been so dry this autumn. Have you noticed how quickly the leaves turn brown and how bare so many trees are? I hope this doesn't foretell a bad winter."

"A cold winter is especially hard on the poor," Vi noted.

"Well, this year they will have the sheltering warmth of Samaritan House to turn to," Mrs. O'Flaherty said.

"If people will only trust us," Vi replied. "I cannot bear to think that anyone might suffer because they do not feel safe coming to our door."

"It will happen, Vi girl, but we have to be patient," Mrs. O'Flaherty said. Then she quoted Galatians 6:9: " 'Let us not become weary in doing good, for at the proper time we will reap a harvest if we do not give up.' We cannot force the people of Wildwood to seek us out, my girl," she continued. "We just have to keep moving forward with what we know we're called to do here at the mission. Mrs. Nelson and her sister came to see us yesterday. That's a good start. Each time we walk in the area, each visit we pay to a local store, each time we smile and greet a neighbor we pass on the street — even the ones who don't smile back — we are building trust. It's a slow process, but you understood that when you undertook this mission."

Vi sighed and said, "I did, Mrs. O, but still I feel like a child waiting for her birthday party to begin. I want the door to open and everyone to come inside."

"Our Friend in Heaven understands human impatience," Mrs. O'Flaherty said with a smile. "He knows how hard it is for us to wait. The harvest will come, Vi girl. Just wait, and you'll see."

At that moment, Tansy and Marigold burst into the kitchen, followed by Emily.

"We've been dressing paper dolls," Marigold proclaimed, holding up two cardboard figures draped in colorful pieces of fabric and ribbon. "Aren't they pretty?"

While the girls were showing their creations to Mrs. O'Flaherty, Vi whispered to Emily, "Did you see anything?"

"Nothing but an empty lot. Hardly anyone is on the street today," Emily replied in an equally soft tone. "Perhaps we allowed Mrs. Nelson to frighten us without reason."

"Yes, perhaps we did," Vi agreed. But her sense of disquiet would simply not go away. She had to force herself to smile as she turned to the little girls and said, "I hope you like Irish stew. Mrs. O'Flaherty has taught me how to make it."

"We'll like it 'cause you made it, Miss Vi," Marigold replied with a grin so bright it could light the gloomiest day.

The sky had darkened even more after lunch, but Mrs. O'Flaherty thought the rain would hold off long enough to allow her walk with the girls. So after lunch, she sent them to their bedroom for their warm jackets and caps, and she went to the front porch to await them. She scanned the lot opposite the house. She couldn't see it entirely, for the hedge blocked part of the view. But the place near the old wall, where Emily had said that the men usually loitered, was deserted. No young men and no man in a derby hat. Not far from the front of the house, Mrs. O'Flaherty saw Enoch; he was pruning some of the fall-flowering bushes, which had lost their blooms, and—Mrs. O knew—keeping his lookout for intruders.

The little girls came out to meet her, and she took their hands. They walked down the porch steps and were only a few yards from the open front gate when Mrs. O'Flaherty suddenly realized that she'd forgotten her large umbrella.

"Wait right here, girls, and I'll be back in a jiffy," she said. "My umbrella is just inside the door."

Checking that Enoch was still in the yard, she hurried to the house and found Vi in the entry hall.

"Forgot my umbrella," Mrs. O laughed. "It's sure to rain on us if I don't have it."

"It's right there in the stand," Vi said. "I hope the rain holds off for you and the girls. They enjoy your walks so," she added as she began to climb the stairs.

Vi hadn't gone two steps before she heard a piercing scream followed by wild shrieking. It was the children, and Vi made out Tansy's voice crying, "Help! Don't! Don't!"

Vi flew down the steps and out the front door. Mrs. O was right behind her.

At the end of the drive, they saw a horrible scene. Two strange men were fighting with Enoch. A third man held the struggling children by their arms. Enoch struck one of the men with his fist, and the man seemed to fly into the air, landing hard on the gravel of the driveway. Then Enoch whirled around and grabbed for the girls. He loosened Tansy from the third man's grasp and pushed her aside to safety. Then he reached for Marigold. But the other man, the one who hadn't been hit, rushed up behind Enoch and raised something in his hands.

It was Enoch's hedge cutters! The blades were closed, so the implement was like a bludgeon, and the man brought it down on Enoch's head and shoulders. Vi screamed a warning to Enoch, but it was as if her words merely hung in the air as the blow was struck.

Enoch stood up straight for an instant and seemed to look toward the sky. Then he crumpled to the ground.

Vi was running at the men. Mrs. O'Flaherty, just behind her, was calling to Tansy, "Get away!" and Tansy, her eyes dazed with fright, moved toward Mrs. O's voice.

"He's got Marigold!" Mrs. O shouted to Vi.

"I'll get her!" Vi yelled back. "Take care of Enoch!"

By now, Emily had emerged from the house, and she was running to Enoch, who lay motionless in the drive.

Vi saw nothing except the third man, who had scooped up Marigold, thrown the screaming child over his shoulder like a sack of grain, and was running into the street. Vi's thoughts were incoherent, but she ran as fast as she ever had. Several times she came near tripping over her long skirts, but she pulled them up to her knees and ran faster.

The man was quick and agile, and he might easily have outdistanced Vi. But little Marigold was kicking with all her might and pulling at the man's black hair and pounding his back with her fists—all the time screaming at the top of her small lungs. Her hitting and kicking slowed the man, but he was still faster than Vi, and she couldn't catch up to him.

She didn't realize that she was also screaming. Over and over she yelled, "Kidnapper! Kidnapper!"

Curious faces appeared at the windows in the shabby houses along Wildwood Street. People started to go outside—perhaps even to help—but when they saw who the running man was, they melted away into the shadows of fear. Even without his derby hat, Jess Jenkins was known to everyone.

Vi saw none of this. She was in pursuit, running down the center of Wildwood Street—one block, two blocks, three blocks. Toward the shopping area. Suddenly a wagon turned into the street from a side lane. Vi almost crashed into the old horse pulling the wagon, but she veered sideways, avoiding the animal. She stumbled over some rocks and fell hard on her knees and hands. The pain was sharp and strong, but she scrambled up and ran on.

Where was the man? She dashed into the business section but couldn't see him anywhere.

A prayer battered her confused mind. *Oh, Lord, don't let me fail Marigold! Where is she? Which way should I go? Help me, Lord! Please, please show me the way!*

She looked around. There was Mr. Nelson's store, and across the street, the Wildwood Hotel.

Vi ran toward the hotel, and then she heard something. She stopped dead still and listened.

It was Marigold! The child's voice rang out through the open hotel door: "Let me go! Let me go, you bad man! Let me go now!"

Vi tore up the hotel steps and through the door. She expected to see Marigold and the man, but the lobby was empty except for a hotel clerk behind the desk.

She shouted at him, "Where's the child?" but the clerk only shrugged his shoulders and tried to look blank.

"Let me go!"

The yelling came from a side room—a kind of parlor with a glass door.

Vi threw the door open and came face-to-face with a man who was struggling with Marigold and attempting to stifle her screams by holding his hand over her face.

"Don't touch her!" Vi commanded. The man was so startled he dropped his hold on Marigold, and the little girl slipped away. She ran to Vi, huddling against her legs.

With the child at her side, Vi took a look at the man. It was not the one who had kidnapped Marigold, not the small, quick man whom Vi had chased for five blocks. This man was taller, heavier, older, and dressed like a gentleman. And he was taking Vi's measure just as closely as she observed him.

Mopping his brow with a handkerchief, he said in a harsh tone, "You have no business here, madam. This child is none of your concern."

"She is entirely my concern," Vi retorted. "And who are you to steal a child from her protectors?"

The man ignored her question, but Marigold tugged at her skirt and said hoarsely, "It's Mr. Greer. Bad old Mr. Greer."

"That's right," the man sneered. "I am Ebenezer Greer of Bethel, South Carolina. And I am legal guardian of this child and her sister."

"I do not believe you," Vi said. She was breathing heavily from her run and from anger. Quickly counting to ten, she lowered her voice and said, "Marigold's mother is her guardian, and we have been searching for her."

Mr. Greer's face grew red with anger as he blurted, "The child's mother is—is—"

He stopped himself suddenly and wiped his brow again. "The child's mother is ill, and she has given me legal guardianship of her two daughters until she is well again."

Marigold looked up at Vi with a puzzled expression. Vi squeezed the girl's shoulder gently and addressed Mr. Greer. "If what you say is true, why steal the children away? Have you proof of your claim?" she asked in a tone as hard as granite.

"I have," he replied with confidence. "The document is in my case, in my room."

"Then you have no claim until you produce proof," came a man's voice from behind Vi.

Vi turned her head and saw the last person she would ever have expected—Professor Mark Raymond.

"You must prove who you are and what you say. I doubt a piece of paper from South Carolina will be sufficient for the police here, in light of your attempt to kidnap this child. If you have a document, it will be necessary to verify its truth before anyone would put this child in your care."

"The p—police?" Mr. Greer sputtered. "Who are you to question my honesty, sir?"

"I am a friend of Miss Travilla and her family," the professor said with a calmness that was steely. "I am here to escort

her and this child to their home. If you have a claim, I advise you to take it to the police. And hire yourself a good lawyer, sir, for the stealing of this little girl and the assault upon Miss Travilla's servant are grave criminal offenses. I am sure the legal authorities will want to speak to you very soon."

Mr. Greer's face fairly glowed with his rage. He took a menacing step toward Vi and Marigold, but instantly the professor moved between them. He towered over the other man, and Mr. Greer stepped backward, bumping into a small plant stand and sending a potted fern crashing to the floor.

Vi couldn't see the professor's face, but she was certain he was smiling when he said to Mr. Greer, "What a shame. I know the proprietor of this hotel will want to add that bit of breakage to your bill, sir."

Professor Raymond turned his back on the man and quickly guided Vi and Marigold out of the room, through the lobby, and into the street. A saddled horse that Vi instantly recognized as her own favorite mare from Ion stood waiting.

A chill wind had blown up, and Vi shivered. Without saying a word, the professor took off his jacket and laid it around Vi's shoulders. Then he lifted her into the saddle and handed Marigold up to her. The little girl nestled comfortably against Vi and closed her eyes.

"Are you both all right?" he asked softly.

"Yes, I believe so," Vi responded. Everything had happened so quickly that she'd forgotten her bloodied hands and knees.

The professor took the reins and began walking the horse in the direction of Samaritan House.

On the way he explained his extraordinary appearance in the hotel parlor.

"My train leaves the city tonight. I came here early at Ed's request, to deliver your horse and a few things from your mother. I arrived at the mission just minutes after you left. I was delayed a bit, trying to understand what had happened. By the way, Enoch is recovering. He was knocked out, but your nurse doesn't think he is too badly hurt. She has sent for a doctor. Your maid…"

"Housekeeper," Vi interrupted. "Her name is Christine, and she is Enoch's wife."

"Ah," the professor sighed. "That explains her tears. At any rate, she and the nurse are caring for him. And your companion is comforting the older girl."

"Who did they send to get Dr. Bowman?" Vi asked.

"Your companion…"

"Mrs. O'Flaherty—"

"Yes, Mrs. O'Flaherty. She had grabbed a boy off the street and given him a dollar to go to the police and then find the doctor. She has great presence of mind, for she also gave the boy money for cab fare and promised him five dollars more when he returned with the doctor. That's a small fortune for a poor boy and a guarantee that he will carry out his task in the shortest possible time."

Marigold, who had been listening to all this, opened her eyes and asked, "How is Sissy?"

The professor looked back over his shoulder and smiled so lovingly at the little girl that Vi's heart nearly melted with gratitude.

"Your sister is absolutely fine," the professor said. "But she will be very glad to see you. I have two little girls of my own, and I know how much they worry about each other."

"Thank you," Marigold said, settling more closely against Vi.

"Yes," Vi said, "thank you so very much, Professor Raymond. I'm not sure I could have gotten us out of that hotel without you. How did you know where to look for us?"

"That was also the doing of your Mrs. O'Flaherty. In spite of everything, she was clear-minded. Somehow, she guessed that the man who took the child would go to the Wildwood Hotel, and she directed me. But the man I encountered was not whom she described as the one who took the little girl. Mrs. O'Flaherty said the kidnapper was small, lean, and young."

"I must assume the kidnapper was working in Mr. Greer's service," Vi said. Her voice sounded thin and soft, for suddenly she felt very tired.

"Well, we'll unravel this mystery later," the professor said, "after you have all had some rest."

They walked on in silence until they reached the gates of Samaritan House. Mrs. O'Flaherty and Tansy were there on the porch, waiting. The professor carried Marigold, and Mrs. O'Flaherty gave her strong arm to Vi.

The rain they had expected all day began to fall as they entered the house. It started with large drops that tapped at the windows like fingers. But soon it became a strong, steady stream that promised to wash away the dust and dirt of Wildwood.

In spite of the heavy rain that should have kept people in their houses, word about the young lady from the mission—chasing Jess Jenkins down Wildwood Street and rescuing a little Negro child—spread immediately to every corner of Wildwood.

Since no one had seen what actually happened in the hotel, it was at first supposed that the young woman had confronted Jenkins himself or maybe even Mr. Clinch. A tall man had taken her and the child away, but a good deal of time had elapsed between the lady's arrival at the hotel and the gentleman's. Somehow, it was assumed, the "mission lady" had stood up to Jenkins—the meanest, lowest man in Wildwood—and walked out in one piece.

A Test of Courage

The hotel clerk was soon giving his eye-witness account to anyone who would listen. He explained about the man from South Carolina—that he had paid Jenkins to nab the child and that this stranger had argued with the young lady. But the people of Wildwood seemed to prefer the original version—that a woman, a young woman in a passion to recover a child, had entered the hotel as surely as Daniel was thrown into the lions' den, and that she had overcome Jess Jenkins.

Vi and the others at Samaritan House knew nothing of what was being said, but that afternoon and evening, as the story was passed from one person to the next, the "mission lady" became something of a legend in the Wildwood district. A few people disbelieved the whole story. A few others decided that the young woman had to be crazy and ought to be avoided. But in most minds, she was pictured as a heroine—brave and bold and on the side of right. People who had lived in Wildwood for many years heard the gossip and smiled to themselves. A woman—a girl, really—had the courage to do what no one had done before. Maybe, they thought, her new mission was worth taking notice of. Maybe, they hoped, it would succeed where others had not.

Quite another kind of conversation was taking place in the office behind the bar room in the Wildwood Hotel. Mr. Clinch sat at his desk. Jess Jenkins lurked in a dark corner of the room. And Ebenezer Greer rapidly paced the carpet in front of Clinch's desk.

"Your man is an idiot!" Greer was yelling at Mr. Clinch. "He told me he could get the girls without being seen. 'Clean as a whistle,' he said. That's just what he said. Then he comes tearing in here with just one child and that wild woman right behind him!"

In a low tone, Mr. Clinch replied, "It was *you* who gave Jess his orders. I had no part in your harebrained scheme, Greer."

"He told me to grab the kids when I had the chance," came a voice from the corner, "and that's what me and the boys did. We

175

wuz hidin' behind the bushes at the front of the house, just watchin'. Then the old lady came out with the girls, and she left 'em standing there alone, so we grabbed 'em. Just like he said to."

"I didn't say to do it in broad daylight!" Greer raged.

"Regardless of what you intended," Mr. Clinch said to Greer, "Jess and his men did what you ordered, and you must pay them . . . and me."

"I won't!" Greer exploded. "Not a penny!"

Mr. Clinch rose slowly from his desk. His expression was dark, but his voice was quiet—almost a whisper. "You will pay, and pay now," he said. "Or you will not leave this hotel."

"You're threatening me with harm?" Greer responded incredulously.

"Not at all," Clinch said. "But as a good citizen of India Bay, it would be my duty to retain you here and summon the police. I could not in good conscience allow a kidnapper to escape, now could I?"

"But you arranged it all!" Greer screamed in his rage. "I'd tell them—"

"Tell them what?" Clinch interrupted, a sardonic smile playing on his lips. "That you were a guest at my humble establishment? That you hired some of the local boys to work for you? And how was I, a law-abiding business owner, to know your criminal plans? What reason had I to suspect you, a gentleman farmer from South Carolina, of such criminal intentions? Where is your proof, Mr. Greer? You have not even a scrap of paper with my name on it."

This questioning had completely deflated Mr. Greer. His anger had turned to a quaking fear, for he knew that Clinch was right. With quivering hands, he reached into his coat pocket and withdrew a roll of bills. He peeled off a large number and threw them onto Clinch's desk.

Nothing was said while Clinch carefully counted the money. Then he looked at Greer coldly and said, "I advise you to leave India Bay immediately. One of my employees will accompany you to the next station down the line from the city. He's waiting for you in the livery stable, and if you value your freedom, you will pay him generously for his service. It would not be wise for you to take a train from here, for I am certain the police have your description by now and may already be searching for you. I expect they will be coming here quite soon, and as a good citizen, I would be obligated to inform them if you are still in this hotel."

This last statement caused Mr. Greer to turn pale. Without another word, he turned and rushed away, slamming the door on his way out.

Mr. Clinch was still holding the money, and he separated some of the bills. "Take your payment," he said, holding out the money but not looking at Jess Jenkins, "and get out of town. The cops will be after you faster than Mr. Greer, so I advise you to put some distance between yourself and India Bay immediately. This might blow over in a few weeks, but you'd be smart never to return. I hear there are excellent opportunities in the West for a man of your peculiar skills."

The little man grasped the bills, saying, "Thanks, boss," in his oily way. "I 'magine it'll be safe enough for me to come back in a month or two."

Mr. Clinch turned on him, his face expressionless but his eyes glowing like fire in the light of the gas lamps.

"You misunderstand me, Jess," Clinch hissed in a low, icy tone. "You *are* an idiot, just as Mr. Greer said. When you first located those children, I told you not to let yourself be seen. I told you no one was to be harmed. That young woman who chased you today is a member of one of the wealthiest and most respected families in this state. You attacked her household today, and I haven't enough money to bribe the law to ignore your stupidity. I don't care a whit about Greer. You failed *me*, Jess. I wanted those mission people out of Wildwood, and now you've made them heroes. If you are foolish enough to return, don't let me ever catch sight of you in Wildwood. I do not like violence, Jess, but I can be more severe than the police when I have to be. You have your money. Now get out."

Jess wanted to say something in his own defense, but the cold fire in Clinch's eyes was enough to still his tongue. He had made a dangerous enemy, and he knew it.

When Jess was gone, Mr. Clinch sat down at his desk again. He thought about what he'd seen that day, for he had observed the whole scene in the parlor from a hidden vantage point known only to him.

That Travilla girl is tough and brave, he thought to himself. *She won't be frightened away by crude scare tactics. She won't give up her mission without a fight. And she's got friends who will fight for her. Important friends. I wonder who the tall man is. He looked like he would have fought for her and that child without a second thought for his own safety. These people aren't like the sniveling do-gooders who came before.*

Then he realized that he still held the remainder of Mr. Greer's money in his hand. He opened his bottom drawer and took out his tin box.

As he put the money inside, another thought struck him. *It's time for a change of strategy.* He had no doubt that he could deal with this bold young woman and her little band of Christian soldiers, but he'd have to think of a new approach. Yes, he'd have to consider all the possibilities very carefully. He needed to know a good deal more about Miss Violet Travilla and her friends before he made another move. Whatever he decided to do, he understood now that he had to be extremely careful.

A smile came to his lips—not the sneer most people were used to, but a genuine smile. He sat back in his chair and said aloud to himself, "You've got to admire a young woman with that much spunk. Even without the tall man's help, I don't believe anything would have made her give up that child. You're a worthy foe, Miss Travilla, a very worthy foe."

CHAPTER

13

Some New Questions

He rescues and he saves.

DANIEL 6:27

Some New Questions

When Vi and the professor returned to the mission with Marigold, Dr. Bowman had already arrived, and he was tending Enoch in the carriage house. So Emily examined Marigold and pronounced her physically unharmed, save for a few bruises from pounding her kidnapper with her fists. Vi, on the other hand, needed attention to her hands and knees, so Emily took her to the clinic, and Vi told her what had occurred while the nurse gently cleaned and bandaged her cuts and scrapes.

Downstairs, Professor Raymond was telling what he knew—between excited interruptions by Marigold—to Mrs. O'Flaherty and Tansy.

"It was that mean old Mr. Greer!" Marigold declared to her sister. "He said Mommy's sick, and she made him our guard!"

"Guardian," the professor kindly explained. "But he had no proof, and like Miss Travilla, I don't believe he was telling the truth."

"What happened to the men who grabbed us?" Tansy asked fearfully. "Will they come back?"

"Oh, no, dear," Mrs. O'Flaherty said, hugging the girl. "Because they are cowards, they are much more afraid of us than we are of them. We have the shield of our faith to protect us. The Lord is watching over us. He gave Miss Vi and the professor the strength to save Marigold. He gives us all the strength we need, and He makes us strong. Those awful men cannot stand up to Him, can they?"

"But I was so very afraid," Tansy said.

"Me too," Marigold said nodding her head rapidly. "I was so afraid the whole time. Till I saw Miss Vi. She was just like a 'venger angel. I saw her and knew that God sent her to save me."

Violet's Bold Mission

"An avenging angel," the professor said with a light laugh. "I'm sure Miss Violet doesn't think of herself in that way. And you needn't worry about Mr. Greer or the other men. Mrs. O'Flaherty is right that they are cowards. I am sure that they are running away from India Bay as fast as they can. Right at this minute, they're probably running like frightened bunny rabbits and hoping they never come face-to-face with Miss Violet ever again."

This image of the bad men as scared bunnies made the girls giggle.

"But how can we ever thank you for helping us?" Mrs. O'Flaherty said to the professor, and sudden tears filled her blue eyes.

"I did very little," the professor averred.

"Oh, but you did very much," said Vi as she and Emily entered the meeting room where everyone was gathered. "You got us away from Mr. Greer and out of the hotel. If you hadn't been there to bring us home…"

Professor Raymond cut her off by saying, "Then you and your little friend would have marched out on your own and walked proudly back here. And no one would have dared try to stop you. Of that I am absolutely certain."

"Can I be your friend, mister?" Marigold asked. She walked over to the professor and gently patted his hand.

"I'd like to be your friend very much," the professor replied gently. "Yours and your sister's, for you are very brave girls."

"What's your name?" Marigold asked.

"Professor Raymond. But my students all call me Professor.'"

Marigold carefully pronounced the word a couple of times. "I can say it," she proclaimed proudly. "I can say 'Professor' even if I can't say *mar-mu-rade*."

Everyone laughed at that, even the professor, who had no idea why it was a joke. It felt good to laugh after such a harrowing day.

Some New Questions

Dr. Bowman came in a few minutes later and added to their joy with his news that Enoch would be just fine. "He has quite a bump on his head, but he's awake and alert. We'll watch him for signs of concussion, but he should be able to get back to work in a few days. I cannot say the same of the man in the shed."

"What man?" Vi asked with concern.

"Gracious me, I forgot about him! It's the man Enoch knocked out," Mrs. O'Flaherty replied. "I tied him up when he was still unconscious, and after we got Enoch to the carriage house, Emily and I dragged the kidnapper to the shed and locked the door. The police can take him away when they come."

"But is he hurt?" Vi asked Dr. Bowman.

"He has a very sore jaw and two missing teeth," the doctor said, "but his only serious injury is his fear of the police and a jail sentence. He's young, no older than seventeen, and I don't think he had any intention of doing harm. What little he told me made me think he was just following along with the two men who got away. With some persuasion, I feel sure he will tell the police who his accomplices are."

Vi wanted to bring the young man inside, for the shed was sure to be damp, but Sergeant Peevy and two other policemen arrived a few minutes later, and they quickly took possession of the prisoner. Sergeant Peevy got the information he required to make the arrest, and he promised to return the following day for another interview with Vi.

"You need your rest now," the sergeant said. "We'll take charge of that young scoundrel so he won't cause you any more trouble. Don't you worry about him. We'll lock him up good and tight."

183

Violet's Bold Mission

With the police gone, Mrs. O'Flaherty said, "I think Marigold needs a good wash before supper. Will you come too, Tansy, and help your sister choose a clean dress?"

When they had gone upstairs, the professor said, "Young Marigold seems to have weathered her experience with remarkable good spirit."

"Those two little girls have weathered a great deal besides," Vi replied with a sweet smile. "Separated from their mother, abandoned by a trusted friend, wandering alone in this city for weeks…yet the Lord has watched over their every step and given them the courage to survive. They amaze me, for I cannot imagine myself bearing such hardships with their grace."

"I would like to know more of their situation, if that is possible," the professor said thoughtfully. "I have heard some things from your conversations at Ion, but there must be more to the story. Oh, but you are surely exhausted, Miss Travilla. Please excuse me for asking. I don't want to presume on your time."

Vi had felt very tired when they returned to Samaritan House, but in the company of her friends (and her rescuer), her energy was revived. The professor had risked his own safety to help her and Marigold, and she felt obliged to tell him all that she knew. Besides, she thought they might benefit from his fresh perspective. So she, Emily, and Dr. Bowman gladly informed him of the girls' story.

The professor asked a number of pointed questions, but when they had finished telling him everything, he responded with silence. Vi could see from his expression that he was concentrating on something.

After several minutes, the professor finally spoke. "Have you considered that the cat, the fire, and the kidnapping of the girls may be linked together?" he asked. "We have a set of facts — events that you know happened. And then we have circumstances. The facts may seem unrelated, but when you combine them with the circumstances, a wider picture seems to become clear. Everything that has happened appears to come together in one place—the Wildwood Hotel—and one man. Though none of you have encountered him directly, this Mr. Clinch seems to be the center of everything."

"From the gossip we heard from Mrs. Nelson and Miss Crane, I had begun to suspect him of being behind the efforts to frighten us. They told us that Jess Jenkins was Mr. Clinch's henchman," Vi said. "But what connection would Mr. Clinch have to the girls?"

"I don't know," the professor admitted, "but I think it odd that Mr. Greer would choose to stay at the Wildwood Hotel. He is obviously a man of means, and it is strange that he would stay in a seedy and disreputable hotel rather than one suitable for gentlemen. And how did those men come to be in Greer's employ? For that matter, how did Greer know where to find the girls? Could Greer and this Clinch person be acquainted in some way?"

"I see where you're going," Dr. Bowman said. "We know that miserable little Jess Jenkins and his cohorts have been watching Samaritan House for some days now. It seems likely they were responsible for the torment of poor Jam and the attempt to burn the shed. And we know that they grabbed Marigold and Tansy for that odious Mr. Greer. Jenkins is the link between Greer and Clinch."

"There is also the evidence of Mrs. O'Flaherty's instinct," Emily added. "Or you might call it intuition. Somehow she put the pieces together. She told you to look for Vi and Marigold at the Wildwood Hotel, Professor Raymond. I never thought of that."

"Nor did I," said Doctor Bowman.

"As I told Miss Travilla once," the professor said, "I do not dismiss the value of intuitions, though I do not necessarily trust them either. But it is interesting that in a moment when you must all have been feeling panic and fear, Mrs. O'Flaherty somehow put two and two together and came up with four. I should be very interested to know more about this Mr. Clinch and his connection to Mr. Greer."

"Perhaps I can learn more from Sergeant Peevy when he visits us tomorrow," Vi said.

The four adults continued their conversation until Mrs. O'Flaherty came in with the girls. Mrs. O promptly asked the professor and the doctor to stay for supper. "It will be simple fare," she laughed, "but well prepared. I was thinking of a dish I learned to cook when I lived in Italy."

Both men accepted her invitation eagerly, and Professor Raymond commented on his special fondness for Italian cooking.

"What time does your train depart?" Vi asked the professor.

"Oh, I've decided to leave tomorrow," he replied offhandedly. "I'll stay at a hotel tonight and get a morning train. My bags have already been delivered to the station."

"But you can stay with me," the doctor said. "I have an extra bedroom, and my apartment is quite comfortable. My landlady will be thrilled to have another gentleman for breakfast."

"That would be splendid," the professor said with a smile. "I am most grateful to you, Doctor Bowman."

Mrs. O'Flaherty excused herself and went to the kitchen to begin the evening meal. Emily followed, saying she would return shortly with tea and sandwiches for everyone. Tansy and Marigold intended to go with her, but the professor invited them to stay and talk.

He was seated on a sofa, and Marigold went to sit beside him, for she had taken an immediate liking to the tall man with the thick mustache. Vi meanwhile motioned to Tansy to come and sit on her lap.

Some New Questions

The professor asked the children a question about their home in South Carolina, and soon the girls were chatting happily about their late father's farm — how big it was and what their father had grown there and what their house had looked like. Under the professor's gentle questioning, they also spoke about Mrs. Greer. Marigold's memories were of a grandmotherly lady who was always very kind. But Tansy remembered Mrs. Greer well. Mrs. Greer, she said, had taught her to read, and they had lessons together every day.

Vi was amazed at the conversation. The professor carefully steered clear of any topic that might be painful for the girls. Yet Vi quickly realized that his questions elicited a good deal of new information. The girl's father, Mr. Evans, had not been a tenant farmer, as Vi supposed, but he was purchasing the land from Mrs. Greer. After their father and grandmother died, the girls' mother had worked for Mrs. Greer as head housekeeper, and Mrs. Greer had treated Tansy and Marigold almost as if they were her own.

Vi listened very closely to what the girls were saying, yet she could not figure out why Mr. Greer wanted to lay claim to the children. Mr. Greer clearly had none of the attributes of his loving Christian mother. That he had no concern for the girls' welfare had been made clear enough by his actions. So what did he want with two young children? And where was their mother? Vi's heart ached for the mother who had tried so desperately to get her children away from Mr. Greer. What terrible fear had driven her to entrust her two young girls to anyone else? Mr. Greer had said that Mrs. Evans was sick. But where was she?

Vi hugged Tansy close to her as she prayed silently: *Dear Father in Heaven, You are the Shepherd, and we are Your flock. Now one of us is lost, not to You but to us. Please help us find the girls' mother — please lead us to the answers and enable us to reunite this family. Bless us with the fortitude of these children, who have endured*

such hardship, and keep us straight on the path that will take them back to their mother's arms. For we are helpless without You to protect and guide us.

"Miss Travilla?" someone was saying.

Vi looked around and realized that the professor was addressing her.

"I'm sorry," she said. "What did you say?"

"Nothing of importance," he replied. "Just a question that interests me. But it can wait."

She heard in his tone a hint of the arrogance that had irritated her so when she first met him. He sounded as if he had caught a student napping in one of his classes. But this time, it didn't bother her. It didn't annoy her in the least. She looked at him closely, and she had to admit that Rosemary was right. He was a fascinating man, and attractive too—in a way.

Opening the Mission Doors

Jesus said, "Feed my lambs."

JOHN 21:15

The next day, Vi wrote to her mother and Ed about all that had happened, and her letter reached Ion with the Monday morning mail. Ed immediately set out for the city, and he was knocking at the mission door just as the residents of Samaritan House were finishing their breakfast.

Vi had an idea who might be banging so noisily, so she hurried to the door. She was ready to remind her brother to use the bell, but the look on Ed's face stopped any attempt at teasing. His expression betrayed his feelings — a mingling of worry and anger that clouded his handsome features. So before he could say a word, Vi assured him that she and the others were well, that the police were fully informed, and that everyone—from the captain of the police to Professor Raymond—agreed that there was no danger now.

She led him to the kitchen and persuaded him to sit at the table. Then she went through all the details once again — adding the news that Sergeant Peevy had come by before breakfast and informed her that the police were sure Mr. Greer and Jess Jenkins had fled the city.

Ed took quite a lot of convincing, but finally he calmed down and allowed himself a wary smile. Mrs. O'Flaherty fed him a generous breakfast, for he had left Ion in too great a hurry to eat anything, and the food seemed to lift his spirits considerably. Then Emily, arriving shortly after Ed, reported to him on everyone's medical condition in clinical detail: Enoch had a slight concussion and required only a few days' rest, though he could not do heavy work for another week; Vi's cuts were superficial and healing nicely; and little Marigold's bruises were already disappearing. Dr. Bowman, she said, would come every day until he was assured of Enoch's full recovery.

"Is that necessary?" Ed asked.

"Perhaps not," Vi said with a sly smile, "but he enjoys coming here, for a number of reasons."

Catching an odd look from Emily, Vi quickly said, "Oh, yes, Professor Raymond left in good order. He telegraphed me from India Bay station just before his train departed."

"Telegraphed you?" Ed quizzed.

"For some reason, he wanted the name of Mrs. Lansing's lawyer friend in South Carolina. The professor included an address in Boston, where his children live, and I've already posted my reply. It gave me another opportunity to express my gratitude."

Ed took a sip of the coffee Mrs. O'Flaherty had just poured for him and said, "Mark's an odd duck sometimes. I wonder what he wants with the lawyer's address?"

"Well, brother dear, are you satisfied now that we are not in danger here?" Vi wanted to know.

"Almost entirely," he answered with a little wink at her. "Mamma wanted me to come here as soon as she read your letter, but she also said she was certain you had everything under control. Now that I think of it, she seemed more worried about my anxiety than your safety. She trusts you completely, Vi. She really does. Most mothers would have fainted or had hysterics if they received such a letter from their daughter. But I remember Mamma saying—after Aunt Louise told her all you had done for Cousin Virginia in New York—that you had inherited Papa's courage and his reasoning in good measure."

Vi smiled, showing her dimple, and said, "She wouldn't have thought that if she'd seen me running down Wildwood Street in pursuit of Marigold and that awful little man. I must have looked like a mad person—hardly anyone's idea of reasonable." Vi continued, "I can't stop thinking about Tansy and Marigold's mother. I believe that she may have put herself in grave danger by sending her children away. Who knows how Mr. Greer may have threatened her to get the information that led him to look for the girls in India Bay."

Ed looked into his sister's face and said, "We'll find her, Vi. In the meantime, I shall be glad to report to Mamma that her faith in you is entirely justified."

The rain that had fallen on the afternoon of Vi's encounter with Mr. Greer was a harbinger of change. Breaking the drought of the summer and fall, November was a wet month. The temperature dropped, and Enoch lit the new coal furnace for the first time. Ed had several cartloads of cut wood delivered from Ion for the mission's many fireplaces, and that gave Mrs. O'Flaherty an idea.

She and Vi continued their calls on the local ministers, and with the coming of chill, damp weather, several of these men and their wives mentioned their concerns about the poorer members of their congregations who would face the difficulty of heating their homes.

"Do you think we might provide a cart of wood to each church?" Mrs. O asked Vi after one of their visits with a local minister's family. "I'm sure your mother and brother would donate, as would your relatives at The Oaks and Roselands."

"That's a wonderful idea," Vi agreed with enthusiasm. "The ministers will know who is in need, and they can distribute the wood. If everyone agrees, we could supply every church with at least two cartloads, and then replenish the supply as needed."

"But we must consult with the pastors first," Mrs. O'Flaherty said. "I believe that they will welcome such a gift, but we can't proceed on an assumption."

"No, we can't," Vi said thoughtfully. "Nor must we take credit. It has to be a gift freely given, without expectation of any reward."

Violet's Bold Mission

They needn't have worried. The local churches were most grateful for the offer. Elsie and Ed organized the deliveries from Ion and the other farms, and soon each church in Wildwood was furnished with wood enough to keep fires burning in many homes until the new year arrived.

Though scheduled to open formally in early December—just after Mrs. Lansing's ball—Samaritan House began to attract visitors as soon as word of Vi's confrontation with Jess Jenkins spread through Wildwood. Mrs. Nelson and Miss Crane brought several other women by, and each contributed an item for the mission's pantry—jars of homemade pickles and jams—in exchange for an account of Vi's adventure. Vi was happy to oblige, and she was privately amused by the ladies' undisguised curiosity.

Once they had heard her story and asked their questions, one of the women mentioned the mission school. Vi explained that she was still seeking a qualified teacher but hoped to open the school in January, if there were enough children to make a class. The woman, who was the wife of the greengrocer, shyly asked if her children—a girl of nine and a boy of seven—might be eligible.

"They're bright, my young 'uns. They can read and write a bit, and my husband's taught 'em to do their sums. But Mr. Denton and me spend so much time in the store, I ain't got the time to educate 'em like they oughta be. We want the children to have better lives than we do, Miss Travilla, and that takes gettin' educated. They're good children and won't be no trouble to you."

Vi was deeply touched by Mrs. Denton's hope for her youngsters. She said that the young Dentons should be the first names on the list of Samaritan House pupils. She thanked Mrs. Denton very graciously. Then she suggested a tour of the schoolroom, which delighted all the women.

After they left, Vi hurried to find Mrs. O'Flaherty to tell her that the school had its first two students.

"Then you've got two new reasons to get on with finding a teacher," Mrs. O'Flaherty said in her practical way. "And a cook, while you're at it, my girl," she added. "Those cooks' rooms have been empty for too long."

More people came by each day, most of them curious for a look at the mission and the brave young lady who stood up to Jess Jenkins. But there were several visitors who had heard about the clinic, and Emily acquired her first patients. She treated coughs, bandaged cuts, and provided soothing ointments for rheumatic joints. The problems were minor, for her patients were not yet so trusting as to confide their more serious needs. But they went away impressed by the young nurse and her kind and efficient manner. They were doubly impressed when they learned that a doctor would be available every Friday; few of the citizens of Wildwood could afford medical care, and many had never seen a doctor in their lives.

After several weeks, the flow of people to Samaritan House had increased from a trickle to as many as two dozen in a day. Though curiosity remained the principal motive for most of the callers, Vi was beginning to sense how busy the mission might be when more people began to come out of need—as they surely would. The visits to the clinic were increasing, and there were now ten names on her list of pupils for the school. But what began to worry her most was the people who needed food. When she went into the streets, as she did whenever the weather was not forbidding, she saw too often the hollow faces and dark eyes of malnourishment.

One afternoon, Vi finished some paperwork in her office and went to the kitchen to make herself a cup of tea. Emily was there, packing a small basket with tins of beef, a jar of pickles, some butter, and a loaf of bread.

"I'm robbing the pantry," Emily said. "It's for an elderly couple. They came to the clinic because the wife burned her hand while frying bread in bacon grease. She was more upset about burning the bread than her own hand. She told me it was all they had to eat. I've dressed her hand, and her husband will bring her back tomorrow so I can change the bandage. But I cannot send them away without food."

Vi went to the icebox and took out a bottle of milk. "Include this as well," she said softly. "And ask them to come back at noon tomorrow, for we would like them to share our lunch."

"I will," Emily said warmly. "I'm seeing more of this every day, Vi. People come in for a pill or a dose of tonic, but what really ails them is hunger. It's going to be worse as winter comes."

"I know," was all that Vi could reply.

From the day they moved to Samaritan House, Christine and Mrs. O'Flaherty had cooked for its residents. But for all their housekeeping skills, neither had experience preparing food for large numbers of people. Vi had thought it would be easy to hire a cook, that the friends of her family would know of a qualified person. But no one had been able to help. Mrs. Lansing had told her that a good cook was "worth more than gold" to the well-to-do matrons of India Bay, and she was correct. The friends of the Travillas and the Lansings were loathe to part with the cooks in their own households. And the few cooks Vi spoke with told her that no one would trade a secure position with a wealthy family or an elite hotel or restaurant for the arduous labor of running a mission kitchen.

So Vi had put the problem to the back of her mind, hoping that it would solve itself. But now the thin faces and bodies she saw in the streets, like the old couple who lived on stale bread and bacon grease, haunted her, and Vi determined to have the mission kitchen operating as soon as possible.

I need Your help again, Dear Lord, she prayed. *The people here are hungry in body, and I need someone to feed them, as You fed the five thousand. You did not send the people away when they were hungry. To*

follow Your example, we must find a cook, yet I don't know where to look. What I thought would be an easy quest has been hard, and I admit that I have made missteps. When the problem became difficult, I put it aside and delayed. I'm sure there are many roads left to search, but I don't see them. Help me, Lord, to clear my thinking. I know I should have come to You sooner, Lord, for no problem is beyond Your care. Please forgive my procrastination and guide me to search carefully and find the solution.

Vi knew that the Lord answers every prayer, but not always in expected ways. She had no revelation, but she did find herself considering her problem in new ways. She consulted Mrs. O'Flaherty and Emily, and they offered some novel ideas. Instead of talking to family and restaurant cooks, Mrs. O suggested, they should think of places where large numbers of people were fed. Schools and hospitals, perhaps. Emily mentioned India Bay University. Vi had a few thoughts of her own, and Emily also promised to speak to her aunt, who seemed to know more about India Bay than anyone.

The very next morning, Vi was busily writing notes to the heads of several city schools and hospitals, stating her requirements for a cook and requesting recommendations. She was at her desk in the little office off the kitchen, and it was very quiet. Mrs. O'Flaherty was upstairs with the girls, and Emily was in the clinic. The only sound in the office was the purring of Jam the cat, who was napping on the window ledge. Vi welcomed the silence, for it allowed her to concentrate on her letters. At first, she didn't hear the soft rapping at the kitchen door. But whoever it was persisted, and after a few moments, Vi raised her head to listen. Then she laid her pen aside and went to see who was there.

A young woman and a child stood on the steps. They were dressed in worn but clean clothing and shawls to protect them against the cold. Vi had a feeling that somehow she knew them. She asked them inside, and a little hesitantly, they entered.

"I don't want to impose on you, miss," the woman said. "I just come to ask about the school. I heard you're starting a school. My little girl here is six, and I was wondering if she might be old enough to attend. I haven't got any money to pay, but I could do work for you if you'd let my Polly learn in your school. I don't want any charity, you understand."

"Of course I understand," Vi said. "But our school is free, and Polly is just the right age. Please, sit down, and I can tell you about the school. I was about to make myself a cup of tea. Would you join me? Perhaps Polly would like a glass of milk."

The little girl nodded. She had a lovely face and bright, hazel-green eyes, but she was very pale—the paleness of a child who is not often out of doors.

Vi put the kettle on the burner and then poured a glass of milk. On the counter were two sweet buns left from breakfast, and Vi put one on a plate.

The mother and child were sitting at the kitchen table, and Vi placed the milk and bun in front of the child.

"I always think milk tastes so good with something sweet," she said to Polly.

The little girl smiled up at her, and Vi instantly recognized her. Polly was the little girl who had waved at her that day so many weeks before! Polly and her mother were the first two people who had welcomed Vi and Mrs. O'Flaherty to Wildwood.

Vi was nearly stunned to see them here now, sitting in her kitchen, but she quickly recovered her composure.

"My name is Miss Violet Travilla," she said to the mother.

"I'm Mrs. Mary Appleton," the young woman replied. "It's nice to meet you, Miss Travilla. We've seen you before."

"I know," Vi replied. "One day when the work on this house was still underway, you smiled at us, and Polly waved.

I hoped we would meet someday. I have never forgotten your kindness."

Mrs. Appleton blushed and smiled. "We just thought you looked like nice people," she said shyly.

"And we thought the same of you," Vi replied. "I am truly glad you came today. It will be so nice to have Polly as one of our pupils."

"Will you be teacher, miss?" Polly asked.

"No, but I will help the teacher," Vi said. "And if I have enough time, I hope to teach a class in art." Turning to Mrs. Appleton, Vi explained, "We haven't hired a teacher yet, but we will have someone before the class begins in January. Lessons will be three hours a day, from nine o'clock until noon. Then we'll serve lunch for all the children. Will that suit your schedule, Mrs. Appleton?"

"Yes, miss, it does," the young mother said. "It's very generous of you."

Mrs. Appleton lowered her head and said, "Maybe I could help with the lunches, Miss Travilla. I'm a good cook, and that would be a way of helping pay for Polly's classes."

"You're a cook?" Vi exclaimed in amazement.

"Yes, miss. Least I was till this week," Mrs. Appleton said, raising her head and looking into Vi's eyes. "I used to cook at the Wildwood Hotel. I know it's not a nice place, but the pay was fair and I never had to be around the customers. I stayed in the kitchen, and Mr. Clinch, he didn't mind if Polly stayed with me so long as the customers didn't see her. Then he let me go this week. But it wasn't 'cause of my work, miss. I'm a hard worker and a good cook. I learned from my mother. 'Good home cooking,' she called it. I have four sisters and five brothers, so Mama was always cooking, it seemed. Being the oldest girl, I naturally helped her. But you're not interested in that," she concluded, dropping her head again.

"Oh, but I am," Vi said. "I have an idea."

Violet's Bold Mission

She turned to the child, who was just finishing her milk, and said, "Polly, there are two girls living here now. Their names are Tansy and Marigold, and Marigold is your age. They're upstairs playing, and I know they'd like to meet you. Would you like to play with them?"

Polly nodded and then looked at her mother.

"That would be nice," Mrs. Appleton said, "if it's not putting you out, miss."

"Not at all," Vi said. "I'd like to talk with you more, and Polly can enjoy herself while we're chatting."

Vi went to a cabinet and took down the tea caddy, teapot, and two cups. "If you'll make tea for us, Mrs. Appleton, I'll take Polly upstairs and introduce her to the girls and Mrs. O'Flaherty."

"Who's that?" Polly asked.

Vi took the child's hand and led her to the door, saying, "Do you remember the lady who was with me on the day you waved at us? Well, that was Mrs. O'Flaherty, and she's one of the nicest and most interesting people you'll ever meet."

When the door closed, Mrs. Appleton sat staring at it for a few seconds. She asked herself what this young lady wanted to talk about, but she couldn't think of an answer. She'd find out soon enough, she decided. Because she was, as she'd said, a good worker, Mary Appleton rose from her chair, laid her old shawl over its back, and set about making tea.

Two hours later, Mrs. Appleton and her daughter left Samaritan House. They had been invited for lunch, but Mrs. Appleton had some things to do.

As soon as Vi had showed them out the front door, she ran up the stairs, calling for Mrs. O'Flaherty and Emily. Emily hurried out of the clinic and met Vi on the second-floor landing. "What has happened?" she asked anxiously, for she assumed there was an emergency of some sort.

Mrs. O'Flaherty's head appeared above, looking over the banister, and she voiced the same question.

"It's the answer to our prayers!" Vi exclaimed excitedly. "We have a cook!"

"Polly's mother?" Mrs. O'Flaherty inquired as she descended the stairs, with Tansy and Marigold trailing behind her.

"Yes! Polly's mother!" Vi replied, and she danced a few happy steps around the landing. "Her name is Mary Appleton, and she's perfect. She has experience, and she needs the work. And she brews absolutely the best cup of tea I have ever had! I somehow know she's the right person, so I offered her the job and she's accepted."

Seeing Tansy and Marigold, Vi took their hands and asked, "Did you like playing with Polly?"

"Yes, she's very nice and sweet," Tansy said.

"She knew all about sharing and saying 'thank you' when I gave her my dolly. I liked her," Marigold confirmed with a grin. "Will she come back to play?"

"Tomorrow, she and her mother are coming here to live with us," Vi replied. She was happy to see the girls' faces light up with anticipation.

"Our Lord has been very good to us today," she said, looking happily at all her friends. Then she quoted from Psalm 118: " '…the LORD has done this, and it is marvelous in our eyes. This is the day the LORD has made; let us rejoice and be glad in it.' "

Still holding the girls' hands, Vi danced a few more steps, and the girls broke into giggles.

Vi looked down at them, and with mock sternness, she asked, "Are you laughing at the way I dance?"

"We never saw you dance before," Marigold said with another giggle.

"It makes us happy to see you so happy," Tansy explained.

"Well, I am happy," Vi affirmed as she led them down the stairs. "Samaritan House has a new cook. You two girls have a new friend. And when I was at the door just now, I saw the sun coming out from behind the clouds. After lunch, I propose we take a walk and be glad in this happy day our Lord has made."

CHAPTER

15

A Sorrowful Message from Afar

*Blessed are those who
mourn, for they will
be comforted.*

MATTHEW 5:4

*A*s November moved toward its close, the number of people visiting Samaritan House increased. The clinic was busy every day, and with Mrs. Appleton's skills, the "mission ladies" were soon serving an afternoon meal to anyone who needed food. After each meal, Vi held a brief devotional service. Though no one was compelled to attend, many did, and they seemed to draw comfort from the Bible readings and prayers. Some people, like the old couple to whom Emily had given the basket of food, came regularly, while others appeared only once or twice, but the doors of Samaritan House were open to all.

Christine's duties as housekeeper now became increasingly demanding, so Mrs. O'Flaherty took over minding the children: Tansy and Marigold, baby Jacob, and Polly Appleton. Other children were added to the group when their parents came to the clinic, and Tansy proved herself an excellent assistant to Mrs. O when extra help was needed.

Vi was engaged almost from dawn to dusk in the many tasks necessary for the running of the mission. But as the date of the ball drew near, she found herself spending more time with Mrs. Lansing. The invitations had been sent, and replies began to arrive. Vi was most impressed by the number of important people who accepted: the mayor and several other politicians, a number of leading businessmen, the president of India Bay University, and quite a few of the city's best-known physicians, lawyers, and bankers — and their wives. There would also be a large contingent of Vi's family members, and she took great comfort in knowing they would be there to support her.

Following Mrs. Lansing's advice, Vi had been working on her speech — finding the words that expressed what was in her heart. She consulted with Dr. and Mrs. Lansing about some of the facts she wanted to include, particularly about the history of the Wildwood area and the extent of poverty within the city. In the end, she found the speech was much easier to compose than she expected, though she experienced bouts of nerves whenever she thought about delivering it to so many people. When she confessed her fears to Elsie on one of her visits to the city, Vi received an insight into her mother's own steadfast demeanor and composure in any group.

"I remember the first time I had to address our bankers and lawyers in New Orleans," Elsie said. "It was the summer after your Papa died, when we were all staying at Viamede. I knew what I wanted to say, but I was afraid the words just wouldn't come out. So I shared my fears with your grandfather, and he asked if I was ever nervous when I talked with the Lord. 'Do your hands quake with fear when you pray to your Father in Heaven? Do you feel tongue-tied and self-conscious when you tell Him your thoughts?' he asked.

"I said that I always felt at peace when I prayed and shared my feelings with God," Elsie continued, "for in Him is perfect peace and infinite understanding. And Papa said that if I felt such peace with Him who is the 'King of kings and the Lord of lords,' I should feel no fear in speaking with mere mortals like myself. When I thought over what Papa had said, I realized that I had no cause for fear. It's true that my hands did shake a little when I first began to speak to all those men, but that is normal, I believe. The point, my dear, is that our Heavenly Father will be there with you. Speak what is in your heart. He will never fail you."

Vi took her mother's story to heart. *I shall think of my speech as a conversation with my Heavenly Friend*, she told herself, and her thoughts became a prayer. *I can say anything to You, Lord, and my speech at the ball is for You above all. Grant me the confidence to speak*

for Your great glory. And please open the hearts of all who hear my words, that they may be inspired to support Your work at the mission.

Three days prior to the ball, Vi arrived at the Lansings' home for a last meeting before the big event. She had expected to review the guest list one last time and determine the seating for supper. But when she was shown into the parlor, where Mrs. Lansing was waiting, Vi instantly saw her dear friend's troubled expression.

"I have received a letter from Mr. Bartleby," Mrs. Lansing said as Vi sat down beside her.

"It is not good, my dear," Mrs. Lansing said, taking Vi's hand. "He has learned that the children's mother, Mrs. Evans, has died."

Vi gasped. The news went through her like a blade, and she could not speak at first, for her thoughts were too confused for words.

Mrs. Lansing went on gently, "Apparently Mrs. Evans was more ill than she told her girls, and I believe that is why she was so anxious to arrange their trip to the North. Mr. Bartleby thinks she died the very week that the girls left. She was buried at the Greer plantation, but no one beyond the farm knew of her passing until one of Mr. Greer's servants mentioned it to a storekeeper in the town of Bethel."

Vi's voice trembled as she said, "All this time we thought . . ." She was unable to complete her sentence, for a knot of sadness in her throat choked off her words.

"I know, I know," Mrs. Lansing soothed. "We all prayed that Mrs. Evans and the girls would be reunited. And they will be someday, in our Heavenly Father's house. But for now, we must focus on the children and their needs."

Vi hurriedly took a handkerchief from her purse. She wiped away the tears that had fallen from her eyes. Then she sat up straight and squared her shoulders.

"You're right, Mrs. Lansing," she said.

Vi sniffed quickly and said, "My aunt and uncle in Philadelphia have written that the effort to locate Tansy and Marigold's grandparents is going slowly. Evans is a common name, and records are sometimes poorly kept in small towns and villages. Aunt Adelaide assures me that they won't give up, but for now, we are the only family that Tansy and Marigold have."

Mrs. Lansing squeezed Vi's hand gently and said, "Until their relatives are found, the girls have a home at Samaritan House and loving friends to help them through their sorrow. The Lord has called their mother to Him, and He has given the girls into your care."

"But how can I tell them?" Vi asked, and tears trembled in her eyes again. "They have been through so much. Oh, and they are so excited about the ball! Though they will not be there, they have plans to help me dress, and they have made Mrs. O'Flaherty teach them how to waltz. They've made paper dolls in fine dresses and—and…"

"It might be kindest to delay telling them until after the party," Mrs. Lansing counseled. "I think that is what their own mother would have done. Allow them a few more days of happiness."

"Did Mr. Bartleby know anything else?" Vi asked.

"Yes, there is something," Mrs. Lansing said. "He says that his friend, the judge in Bethel, has been unable to find old Mrs. Greer's will. It should be in the public record, but it is not there. Now Mr. Bartleby himself plans to go to Bethel and conduct a thorough search of the records. He mentioned that someone is assisting him with the investigation—one of his law clerks I presume. They believe that finding the will is very important. I wrote to Mr. Bartleby after you told me about your frightful confrontation with Mr. Greer. Mr. Bartleby says that he cannot understand it unless there is some legal connection between the girls and Mrs. Greer—a small inheritance perhaps."

Vi's mind flashed back to the afternoon in the hotel parlor. She could picture Mr. Greer's red, angry face. "He knew!" she exclaimed. "Mr. Greer knew that Mrs. Evans was dead, yet he told me that she was sick. He used that to justify his claim on the girls. Why should he want to take the girls back to South Carolina if their mother was no longer alive? It makes no sense—none at all."

"We must leave it to Mr. Bartleby and his assistant to solve the mystery," Mrs. Lansing responded. "Your responsibility is to those orphaned children, Vi. They need you more than ever. Do not worry yourself about the preparations for the ball, for I have everything ready. Your mother and I will handle any last-minute necessities. She and your grandparents will be staying with us, and you will also have guests, I hear."

"Yes, my sister Rosemary and my friend Zoe Love will stay at Samaritan House," Vi said.

"Then let young Tansy and Marigold enjoy taking part in all your preparations," Mrs. Lansing said, repeating her earlier advice. "Let them have these next few days. There is 'a time to be silent and a time to speak,' as we are told in Ecclesiastes. You can give those children a few more hours of carefree joy, for their time of mourning will come soon enough."

Vi said softly, "I've never had to tell anyone such news before."

"You have Mrs. O'Flaherty and Miss Clayton to help you," Mrs. Lansing wisely reminded her young friend. "Draw on the Lord and strengthen one another, so you can be strong for those dear children. Faith will guide you and the girls through this."

Vi drove home in deep thought that day, but by the time she reached Samaritan House, she was full of determination to give Tansy and Marigold their time of happiness. It was not as difficult as she supposed, for the girls' excitement about the ball was like a tonic. Their bright, smiling faces when they greeted her at the front door of the mission told Vi that Mrs. Lansing had been correct.

"Your ball gown has been delivered, Miss Vi," Tansy said importantly, "and Mrs. O put the box in your bedroom."

"She says you should try it on right away," Marigold bubbled gaily. "Can we help you, Miss Vi? We want so much to see how beautiful you'll be at the ball. Oh, you'll be the beautiful-est lady there! I just know it."

Vi removed her hat and cloak and hung them on the rack in the entry. "If the dress is here, I think I should try it on. And you can be a big help to me," she said. "You can tell me how it really looks."

"I already know that," Marigold giggled. "You'll look pretty as a princess."

"Well, let's go to my room, and we'll soon know if you're right," Vi said. She took their hands, and they were all laughing as she led them up the stairs.

Zoe came to the mission early the next morning. Vi opened the door and rushed out to meet her. It had been two weeks since they had seen one another, and as they hugged, Zoe realized how much she'd missed seeing her friend.

"I'm here to help," she declared. "Put me to work, Vi, at whatever needs doing."

"Are you sure you mean that?" Vi asked.

"You know I can scrub floors and make beds and polish furniture. Whatever you need, I am ready to do it."

"I take you at your word," Vi said with a wry smile. She took her friend's arm and as they entered the house, she said, "I want to introduce you to Mrs. Appleton. She's preparing a beef stew for our afternoon meal, and she has a basket of potatoes that need peeling."

"Then lead me to the potatoes," Zoe laughed. "Today I peel potatoes—tomorrow I dance!"

"I'm so glad you've come," Vi said. "I need a dose of your good cheer."

"You're not still worried about your speech?" Zoe said in surprise. "You'll be wonderful. That's because you really *believe* in what you're saying. You believe in Samaritan House and the people of Wildwood. My Papa always said that every great speech is grounded in faith and truth. Think of our Lord's sermon on the mount—the words so simple, yet the meaning so profound."

Vi hadn't really been thinking about her speech, but it buoyed her spirits to hear Zoe's confident assurances. *How You have blessed me, Lord*, she thought as she led Zoe to the kitchen. *How many good friends I have to support me and the mission. To have friends who are loyal and true in times of need—dear Lord, it is a shower of blessing.*

Vi had already confided the news about Mrs. Evans to Mrs. O'Flaherty and Emily, and both readily agreed with Mrs. Lansing's advice. For the little girls' sakes, they set aside their own sorrow and determined to make the days leading to the ball as happy as possible. As soon as they had a private moment, Vi would tell Zoe, and she hoped her friend could stay on for the next week. The ball, Vi thought, merely delayed the coming of grief to Samaritan House. Difficult times lay ahead, and Vi needed to gather her strong and compassionate friends in a circle of love that would enfold the children as they faced the greatest trial yet.

CHAPTER

16

At the Ball

Let them praise his name with dancing and make music to him with tambourine and harp.

PSALM 149:3

At the Ball

Vi was almost late leaving for the ball. The Travilla carriage was sent to get the ladies of Samaritan House, which this night consisted of Vi, Mrs. O'Flaherty, Zoe, and Rosemary. They were all dressed in their finest, and the night was chilly but clear, so there was no rain to endanger their warm velvet cloaks and beautiful gowns. As the driver handed them into the closed vehicle, a small but rather raucous crowd was gathered to see them off. The well-wishers included Tansy, Marigold, and Polly Appleton, Christine and Enoch, and even little Jacob, who was having great fun clapping his chubby hands and saying "bye-bye" over and over.

After the driver closed the carriage door, he rose to his seat and began guiding the matched pair of horses to the gate. But at an outcry from the house, he reined the horses to a halt.

"Wait! Wait!" Enoch was calling.

Vi looked out her window and saw Mary Appleton running toward the carriage. She was waving something above her head. Vi opened the carriage door, and as Mary drew near, Vi saw what she was holding.

"My speech notes!" Vi exclaimed.

Mary reached the carriage and pushed the sheets of paper into Vi's outstretched hand.

"I was afraid you might forget these, so I checked your desk to be sure," Mary said. "And there they were. These too," she added with a cheerful laugh as she handed Vi a pair of wire-framed eyeglasses. "Can't read that speech without your spectacles."

"Thank you so much," Vi responded with a guilty smile. "I'd lose my head if it weren't attached."

"You're gonna make us all proud, I know," Mary said, returning Vi's smile.

"I'll do my best," Vi replied.

Seeing that Mary was safely out of the way, the driver cracked the reins, and the carriage drove off into the night.

"Don't any of you laugh at me," Vi said as she tucked the notes and her glasses into her purse. "You are all sworn to secrecy—especially you, Rosemary. If Ed or the twins hear that I forgot my spectacles, they will tease me all night."

"Why *especially* me?" Rosemary asked in a tone that she hoped sounded both haughty and hurt.

"Because you are most likely to think it funny," Vi replied with a little laugh.

"I don't think it at all funny that you're so forgetful," Rosemary said in a deep tone. Then she added, "I *spec* I can keep a secret as well as anybody," and burst into giggles.

The Lansing home looked splendid. The large main parlor and adjoining dining room had been cleared of their furniture, save for numerous comfortable chairs and sofas set about the walls, to create a spacious ballroom. The musicians had already set up their stands at the far end of the room and were tuning their instruments when Vi and her friends arrived. She caught sight of a smallish platform rising about a foot above the floor in front of the band. Realizing that it was where she would stand when she delivered her speech, she felt a little shiver run up her spine, but quickly dismissed it.

The second parlor and sitting room contained small tables for supper, and a large buffet was already covered with plates of delectable foods. A separate table held a large crystal punch bowl and matching punch cups.

Since it was the first Friday of December, Mrs. Lansing had decided on a wintry theme for her decorations. All four rooms and the entry were hung with garlands and sprays of winter greenery, and the cool aroma of freshly cut evergreens permeated the air. Vases of white roses were placed on every mantel, and a beautiful flower arrangement in a silver urn sat at the center of the buffet table.

The library door stood open so that guests might gather there if they wished to escape the music. And Vi noticed that seating had also been arranged in the large entry hall.

Mrs. Lansing, Elsie, and Rose Dinsmore were there to greet Vi and her companions. Vi apologized for being a few minutes late, but since the guests had not yet begun to arrive, it was not a problem. Mrs. Lansing and Elsie gave Vi and the others a quick tour of the party rooms, and Mrs. Lansing asked if the décor met their approval.

"Everything is absolutely beautiful," Vi declared. "I cannot thank you enough for doing this, Mrs. Lansing."

"You're most welcome, my dear," Mrs. Lansing replied with a jolly smile. "But the house pales in comparison to the splendor of you three young ladies." She complimented Zoe's and Rosemary's dresses. Then she said to Vi, "You look exquisite, my dear. I have never seen you wear lavender before, but it is a brilliant color for you. Turn around now, and let me see your dress in full."

Vi made a shy turn, and the silk of her gown rustled softly. The dress was truly beautiful—the lavender fabric was embroidered with tiny violets in a deeper shade and artfully bustled at the rear. The scooped neckline and capped sleeves displayed Vi's graceful neck and slim arms to perfection.

"Tansy and Marigold helped me select the material," Vi confided. "I hadn't intended to get a new gown, but they insisted."

"And right they were," Mrs. Lansing said, "for you will dazzle tonight."

Mrs. Lansing then reviewed the schedule for the evening. She expected all the guests to be on hand by nine o'clock.

That was when Dr. Lansing would formally greet everyone. He was to say a few words about the purpose of the evening and introduce the Lansings' minister, who would offer a prayer, and then Vi. After her remarks, Dr. Lansing would call the guests to the floor, and the mayor and his wife would lead the grand march to start the dance.

"Will there be a receiving line?" Elsie asked.

"It's traditional, but I decided to forgo it," Mrs. Lansing replied. "I think it better to mingle with our guests and acquaint them with the needs of Samaritan House in normal conversation."

"A very good idea, Naomi," Elsie agreed.

Soon the guests began to come, and while Dr. and Mrs. Lansing were greeting each new arrival, Elsie escorted Vi and Mrs. O'Flaherty around the room, introducing them to many people whom Vi had heard of or perhaps met at Ion when she was younger. She was happy to tell anyone who asked — and a surprising number of people did — about her work in Wildwood. Some expressed surprise that a young lady of her position would take on such a challenge. A few were politely doubtful of the value of a mission in such a "degenerate" area of the city. But most people seemed genuinely interested.

The house was soon filled with happy guests, and Vi was enjoying herself so much that she didn't notice the time until Dr. Lansing came to her and said, "Our moment has arrived, dear girl."

She took his arm, and they proceeded to the platform. At the doctor's signal, the musicians, who had been playing softly, laid down their instruments. Vi and the minister stood to the side, and the doctor mounted the platform.

His greeting to his guests was both gracious and humorous, and he thanked everyone in the room for coming to his home. Then the minister stepped up, and heads were bowed as he offered a prayer, thanking God for bringing so many people together. He asked for the Lord's grace so that everyone might open their minds and their hearts to their Heavenly Father's love for all mankind. Then he prayed that each person there might remember Christ's words to the disciples in John 15:12: " 'My command is this: Love each other as I have loved you.' " He closed his prayer with the words of Psalm 113: 5-7: " 'Who is like the LORD our God, the One who sits enthroned on high, who stoops down to look on the heavens and the earth? He raises the poor from the dust and lifts the needy from the ash heap.' "

Throughout the room, Vi heard the soft whispering of many people's amens. With her notes and her spectacles clutched tightly in her hand, she stepped up onto the platform and looked out on her audience. In an instant, her eyes swept the room and her mind registered the faces of her loved ones—her grandparents and Zoe, Mrs. O'Flaherty flanked by the twins. At one side of the room she saw her cousins Cal and Arthur Conley and their mother, Aunt Louise, who stood beside Aunt Lora and Uncle Charles Howard. Near them, she spotted Dr. Bowman, Emily, and a small, elderly woman whom Vi took to be Emily's aunt. Close to the platform, Vi saw her dear, smiling mother arm in arm with Mrs. Lansing. Then she caught sight of Rosemary, whose mouth was forming silent words: "Good luck, Vi. God's with you."

Vi smiled and started to speak. She began by telling the people about a woman she had met in a mission in New Orleans—an older woman who had very few material possessions but who, with her husband, was raising her young grandchildren. In spite of her many responsibilities and her own poverty, this woman, Vi said, came every day to the New Orleans mission to work with the poor children there and enrich their lives.

"Meeting her and others like her helped me understand how fortunate I am," Vi said next. "God has blessed me with a loving family and with a life of privilege. He has also blessed me with opportunities to see how fortunate I am in comparison to others. In New Orleans, in Europe, and then in New York, I have seen the misery and the scope of poverty in some of the world's greatest cities…and the courage of people who must live each day with so little. Now, I see that same courage here in India Bay—in the place we call Wildwood. If you have never been there, it is not what you may think.

"You have doubtless heard of the crime in Wildwood, the gambling and drunkenness that blight the poor neighborhood. But I have seen other things that you probably haven't heard about. I cannot begin to describe how many times each day I am moved by the kindness and generosity of the good people who live there. I have benefited from the bravery of people who put the needs of others above their own personal safety and welfare. I'm learning from the people of Wildwood much more than I could ever teach them. And perhaps the greatest lesson is that they are no different at heart from any of us here. I wish you could meet the people in my neighborhood. I hope some of you will.

"My purpose tonight is to tell you briefly about Samaritan House. It's a mission open to all. Our goal is to serve the residents of Wildwood. Our method is not to tell people what we will do for them, but to listen to them and do our best to respond with services that meet genuine needs."

At this point, Vi put on her spectacles and consulted her notes. She quickly described the services the mission offered or would soon offer—the medical clinic, the school, the daily meals. She mentioned anticipated needs: a day nursery where working parents might bring their babies and small children and be assured of their safety; home visits for the elderly who could not come to the clinic. She made a point of telling her listeners how many of the poor of Wildwood were men disabled in the Civil War—veterans who were denied any compensation for the sacrifices they made on the battlefields.

Vi removed her glasses and looked about the room. Then she continued, "I could list a hundred improvements that would help Wildwood: A streetcar service that would allow people to get to their jobs without having to walk two miles to the nearest streetcar line. Paved roads and the same water system that brings fresh, disease-free water to the rest of the city. Sidewalks so people can walk safely on the streets and children might play without fear of being trampled by carts and horses. I know that none of this can be accomplished overnight. But I hope Samaritan House will be a place to begin.

"You're here for a reason, and I greatly appreciate your willingness to listen. You may be surprised to know that I am not begging for your money—at least, not yet." (This earned a good laugh and some nods of approval from the guests.)

"All I am asking is that you consider what can be accomplished—for Wildwood and for everyone in India Bay—if you, the people who are able to create change, will open your hearts to those who lack such power. I think you will discover, as I have, that those who cannot change the *conditions* of their lives are nonetheless blessed with wisdom and strengths that will benefit us all. A great city will be judged, as each of us will, by what it does for the most defenseless of its citizens. We all want India Bay to be a great city, but can it shine like a city on the hill when so many of its people suffer?"

Vi paused for a moment and looked about the room before she went on.

"When I began to think about what I would say tonight, our gracious hostess, Mrs. Lansing, recommended that I study the example of our late President Abraham Lincoln. Speak from the heart, and speak briefly, she said. Following her advice, I want to remind you of his words. They were written for his second inauguration. Our country was then in a time of war and division, but to me, President Lincoln's words are as fitting today as they were in 1865."

Violet's Bold Mission

Vi put on her eyeglasses again and read: " 'With malice toward none, with charity for all, with firmness in the right as God gives us to see the right, let us strive to finish the work we are in, to bind up the nation's wounds, to care for him who shall have borne the battle and for his widow and his orphan, to do all which may achieve and cherish a just and lasting peace among ourselves and with all nations.' "

Looking up, she said, "The division is no longer between North and South. It's between those of us who have and those who have not. But our Lord has challenged us all alike—rich and poor, fortunate and unfortunate—to love one another as He loves us. He has told us the truth, that whatever we do for the least among us, we do for Him. To feed the hungry and clothe the ragged. To care for the sick and those imprisoned by their poverty. To teach the children and give hope to the helpless. To love our neighbors as ourselves. Perhaps in Samaritan House, all can meet in unity of purpose, generosity of spirit, and the shared conviction that in all things God works for the good of those who love Him. In Samaritan House, we have planted a seed. Your love and support will water it. And God will make it grow."

Her final words—a heartfelt thank-you—were lost in the applause. It was not what Vi expected, particularly since she had decided to quote Abraham Lincoln to people who still nursed wounds from the South's defeat in the Civil War. At best, she thought she might earn a polite hand, but this? She was overwhelmed.

Dr. Lansing stepped up beside her. He held up his hands to still the guests, and then he addressed the room: "My good wife and I want you all to enjoy yourselves this evening. But we hope that you will also think about the message you have just heard and what each of you might do to help the work of Samaritan House. Consider the man from whom the mission takes its name—the Good Samaritan who could not pass by a stranger in need as he traveled along the road to Jericho."

At the Ball

He paused for a few seconds, then said, "And now, ladies and gentlemen, it is time to dance. If you will take your partners, our esteemed Mayor Aldrich and Mrs. Aldrich will initiate the festivities by leading the grand march."

Another round of applause went up as the mayor and his wife came forward. The guests began to clear the floor, and couples formed their line behind the leaders. Vi had just left the platform when the mayor motioned to her. She went to him, and he said, "I want to hear more about this effort of yours, Miss Travilla. The problems of Wildwood are never far from my mind, and I think I can benefit from your ideas. Perhaps you can come see me someday soon."

"Why, yes, Mr. Mayor," Vi said, her face flushing. "I would be happy to meet whenever it is convenient for you."

The mayor smiled, "I'm a busy man, but perhaps not as busy as you. I will contact you next week, and we shall set an appointment."

Before Vi could reply, the musicians struck up a lively march tune, and the mayor and his wife moved off to lead the parade of fashionable dancers.

Vi hurried to the side of the room where her mother, Mrs. O'Flaherty, and Rosemary stood. She hardly had a moment to receive Elsie's warm hug before they were surrounded by guests who wanted to congratulate Vi and compliment her speech. She was amazed and gratified by the outpouring of good wishes.

The grand march and the first waltz were completed and the first set of dances was in full swing before Vi had a moment to take her breath.

Ed came to her and said, "That was a grand speech, sister, I'm really proud of you. I wish I could do half so well."

"It wasn't too preachy, was it?" she asked in a whisper. "I don't want people to think I was telling them how they should feel."

"Not preachy at all," Ed replied. "People knew you were speaking from your own heart. I'm a tough critic, and I tell you honestly that you struck all the right notes. I just overheard some gentlemen discussing the disgrace of allowing war veterans and their families to suffer so. They sounded serious about doing something to help."

"That would be wonderful, wouldn't it?" Vi replied.

"Let's go into the buffet room. It will be easier to talk there," Ed suggested.

Their mother and Mrs. O'Flaherty were engaged in conversation with a group of ladies, and Rosemary was dancing with her cousin Dr. Conley. Zoe was also on the dance floor, partnered by one of the twins. As Ed and Vi wound their way around the ballroom, they were stopped repeatedly by guests who wanted to know more about Samaritan House. It took almost a half hour to reach the buffet, where Vi gratefully accepted Ed's offer of a cup of punch. They sat at one of the tables, and Vi was telling her brother about her brief conversation with Mayor Aldrich.

"Excuse me, Miss Travilla, but I believe you forgot these," said a voice that Vi instantly recognized.

She looked up into the smiling face of Mark Raymond.

"Your eyeglasses, Miss Travilla," he said. "I found them on a sideboard in the parlor and knew they were yours."

"Th-thank you, Professor Raymond," Vi stammered as she took the spectacles from his hand. "But how—why are you here?"

"Your brother asked me," the professor replied.

Vi quickly turned to Ed, her expression so puzzled that it was almost comical.

"Mark arrived today, and he has some news for you," Ed explained. "Mrs. Lansing said we could go to the little sunroom for privacy. If you're through with that punch, we can go there now."

Vi had risen before he finished speaking.

"Don't forget your glasses," the professor said, and Vi grabbed them up from the table.

Heavy drapes had been drawn across the many windows in the sunroom, and a fire burned brightly in the fireplace. The room, though not much used in cold weather, was warm and cozy. Vi took a seat on a small wicker settee, for in truth, she felt a little light-headed—perhaps as an aftereffect of her performance that evening or possibly because of the sudden appearance of the professor. Seeing the paleness of her face, Ed took his seat beside her.

"I thought you were in Boston with your children," she said to Professor Raymond.

"I was, but being with my own children, I could not stop thinking about the two little girls you have taken under your wing," he said. "I told my youngsters about Tansy and Marigold, and they agreed that the girls needed help. So after ten days, I left Boston and traveled south, to Columbia. There I met with Mr. Bartleby—and thank you for sending me his address. When I explained my mission and showed him my credentials, he agreed to let me assist him."

"Then it was you!" Vi exclaimed. "We thought his assistant was a law clerk."

"I asked him not to mention my name, in case my efforts proved fruitless," the professor said. "As a scholar in archeology, I am never shy of putting my name to my research. But I was not so sure of my abilities as an investigator of a modern-day mystery."

"Mrs. Lansing received Mr. Bartleby's letter, and we know of Mrs. Evans's death," Vi said, lowering her gaze. "But we haven't yet told the children."

"I'm glad of that," the professor said. "I asked Mr. Bartleby to delay writing to Mrs. Lansing until we knew more about the girls' situation. The news I bring will not lessen their grief, but perhaps it will give them new hope for the future."

Vi looked up, and the professor read the questions in her beautiful eyes.

"I believe we have solved the mystery of Greer's determination to take the girls," the professor said. He took a straight-backed chair and placed it so he could sit just opposite Vi and Ed. He leaned forward, and his eyes shone.

"Tansy and Marigold are heiresses, Miss Travilla," he said. "Not of money but of very valuable property."

Vi drew in a deep breath, and exhaled slowly. She said, "You must have found Mrs. Greer's will."

"We did, after a great deal of looking," the professor replied. "I have visited many dusty courthouses in the last few weeks. I searched Bethel high and low and the surrounding county seats, and I could find nothing. But I heard of a judge in a neighboring county who knew Mrs. Greer well, and I sought him out. He told me that her lawyer lived in Columbia. I went back to the capital city and located this lawyer. He's retired now but sharp as a tack, and he knew all about Mrs. Greer's will. It was filed in the court in Columbia, where she also owned some property. It's there now, but the lawyer gave me a copy which he had kept."

The professor reached into his coat pocket and pulled forth a legal document.

"Mrs. Greer did leave her plantation to her son," he went on. "But there were several hundred acres—highly valuable acres it turns out—which she was selling to Mr. Evans, the girls' father. Her lawyer said that when she signed the agreement to sell the land, she also revised her will. If she should die before the sale of the farm was completed, then Mr. Evans and his wife would receive the deed without further payments. She didn't want Mr. and Mrs. Evans to know of this arrangement. Her lawyer remembered her exact words: 'Mr. Evans is a free man and a proud man. He should not feel beholden during my life-time.' The lawyer is sure that she wanted to protect the Evans family from her son, whose greedy nature grieved her greatly. When Mr. Evans died, Mrs. Greer altered her will again. The farm was to go to the girls' mother at Mrs. Greer's death. Mrs. Evans and the girls moved in with Mrs. Greer, who paid her generously to be head housekeeper. And the Evans farm was kept up by a man whom Mrs. Greer hired."

"Mrs. Evans didn't know that the farm would be hers?" Vi questioned.

"Apparently not," the professor said. "I don't know why, but I can guess that Mrs. Greer did not want Mrs. Evans to feel financially responsible for the farm's upkeep. Mrs. Greer's thinking was complicated, and it took us some time to piece the story together. But as I said before, we believe she was trying to protect the Evanses, including the children, from her son."

"But there is no doubt now that the girls will inherit their family's farm, is there?" Ed asked.

"They will inherit, through their mother. The law is clear on that point," the professor affirmed. "I said they didn't inherit money, but that is not quite accurate. Mrs. Greer's will also provided a direct bequest to be put in trust for Tansy and Marigold's education. It's to be paid from the estate, and the amount is not huge but substantial enough to lessen Mr. Greer's income—a kind of justice for the man who made Mrs. Evans spend the last year of her life working for no wages."

"She must have used the last of her savings in her attempt to send the children to their family in Pennsylvania," Vi noted sadly.

"Poor Mrs. Evans never knew of Mrs. Greer's generosity," the professor said. "Mrs. Greer's lawyer informed her son of her will's provisions, and the will was duly filed in Columbia. But Greer took advantage of the poor communication between that city and the rural towns. He hired a shyster lawyer in Bethel, had a second will forged, and that will was presented in the court of Bethel. Sometime later, it mysteriously disappeared. But based on the false will, Mr. Greer claimed the Evanses' farm as his. As you know, Mrs. Evans was head housekeeper for Mrs. Greer, but the son made her work as a housemaid. Mrs. Evans and the girls were moved from Mrs. Greer's home and given only a one-room shack in the old slave quarters."

"You have evidence of all this?" Vi asked.

"We have the will and the testimony of the Bethel lawyer who filed the forged will. He's a cowardly man. When Mr. Bartleby and I confronted him with Mrs. Greer's true will, he instantly quivered out his confession."

Ed wanted to know if Mr. Greer would be arrested and tried for his fraud and theft.

The professor laughed in a knowing way, "If they can find him," he said. "When he came back to Bethel from India Bay, he somehow got wind of Mr. Bartleby's queries, and I believe he had his bags packed even then. As soon as he learned that his lawyer had confessed the forgery, Greer left for parts unknown. He cannot return here, because he would be arrested for the assault on Enoch and the girls."

"But he still holds the bulk of the estate," Ed said. "Surely he will put up a defense."

The professor then told them the final part of the story. Mr. Greer had borrowed heavily against the estate to fund his gambling. Mrs. Greer's properties would soon belong to the banks. Except for the Evans farm, which belonged to the girls, all would soon be sold and used to repay Mr. Greer's loans.

"He wanted to get the girls back for fear someone might take an interest in them and uncover his fraud. A new railway line is being built through Bethel and will pass across the girls' property. The railroad is prepared to pay a great deal for the land, and Greer couldn't risk having anyone learn the truth. That sale was the only thing that could save him from absolute ruin."

At the Ball

"What of Tansy and Marigold's education trust?" Vi asked.

"It may take a while, but it will be used for their education once the plantation is sold and Greer's debts are paid," the professor assured her. "I've taken the liberty of suggesting that Mr. Bartleby represent the girls, and he will write to your mother of his desire to do so. He will be an ardent supporter of the girls' legal rights. I have another suggestion for your mother, and I hope you will agree with me. Until their family is located, the girls must have a temporary guardian, and I think your mother is the perfect choice. They could continue to live at Samaritan House, Miss Travilla, but your mother has an incomparable reputation even in the law courts of South Carolina. There will be little opposition to Mrs. Edward Travilla's guardianship."

"I know she will do it," Vi said. "She adores the children and would do anything for them. But do you think we have really seen the last of Mr. Clinch and his men? Do you think that the girls are entirely out of danger?"

"I do," the professor said with firmness. "The girls are no longer in harm's way, for Clinch had no personal interest in them. However, you will see him again, Miss Travilla. It is unavoidable, because he is a part of Wildwood. But I doubt he will cause you more problems. You've proved your determination and your courage, and a man like that cannot intimidate anyone who does not fear him."

"No, I'm not afraid of Mr. Clinch," Vi said in a low tone. "But I tremble at what I must do next."

At the professor's questioning look, she explained, "I have a terrible duty to perform tomorrow. It's time for the children to know the truth, and I must tell them of their mother's passing."

The professor leaned forward again, and without thinking, he took Vi's hand. "It is one of the saddest duties a person can have. But I can think of no one so capable as you, Miss Travilla, and the other ladies of Samaritan House, to do it with all the love and compassion those children will need. I wish there had been such kind people there for my own children when their mother died."

Vi looked into his eyes and saw tears. And she understood suddenly how painful his own experience must have been. Her heart went out to him.

"Thank you, Professor Raymond," she said softly. "I am deeply in your debt for everything you have done for us. I hope someday there will be a way I can repay your kindness."

He blinked several times, and the tears were gone. With a flush of embarrassment, he realized that he was still holding her hand, and he released it. He stood and went to the fireplace, gazing at the flames.

"You can do something for me," he said. "With your permission, I would like to talk to Tansy and Marigold once they know about their mother. Through my investigations, I learned a lot about Mrs. Greer and the Evans family. As one who is unfamiliar with the ways of the South, I was surprised and heartened by the great affection and esteem they had for each other, regardless of their differences in status and color. It might help the girls to learn what I heard from people who knew them all in happier times."

"It would be very kind of you," Vi said with a gentle smile that highlighted her dimple. "You will always be welcome at Samaritan House."

Ed had been observing this conversation, and he was thinking how far they had come since he'd first introduced his sister to his friend. Vi was so cold then, and the professor so aloof. After that first meeting at Ion, Ed had decided that Vi and Mark Raymond were simply oil and water, and he'd reluctantly accepted the apparent fact that they could not get along. But now he saw something different—a warmer Vi, a more humble Mark. He wasn't sure what it all meant, but it made him smile.

Ed was about to say something when the door of the sunroom flew open, and Rosemary rushed in.

"Mrs. Lansing said you might be here, and you can't hide from me," Rosemary declared in a teasing tone. Then she saw the third person in the room, and she exclaimed, "I didn't know you'd come to the party, Professor Raymond! Oh, this is splendid! Did you hear Vi's speech?"

The professor made a little bow in her direction and said, "I certainly did, Miss Rosemary. And I was very impressed."

Rosemary turned to Ed and said in her funny, demanding way, "You have to come now, big brother. You owe me a dance and then Zoe. You promised, and I want to dance every dance I can, for this is my very first ball, and I don't want to be a wallflower."

Ed stood and gave his hand to Vi, who also rose.

"No, there have never been any wallflowers in the Travilla family, and I can't let you be the first, you little pest," he said with a laugh that Rosemary knew well.

"You must come too, Professor Raymond," Rosemary said, her face glowing with merriment.

"How could I resist such an invitation?" he responded.

Then he looked at Vi and inquired, "Perhaps you will give me the pleasure of the next dance, Miss Travilla. I cannot claim to be light on my feet, but I shall do my best."

"It would be my pleasure, sir," Vi replied.

He extended his hand to her. She took it, and he drew her arm through his.

She looked up at this tall, generous man with his strong face and slightly lopsided smile. And she thought about all the unexpected things he had done for her, for the children, and for the mission. She'd never encountered anyone so unpredictable before, and she wanted to know more about him.

"I shall enjoy a dance with you, Professor Raymond," she said as they left the sunroom and headed in the direction of the music. "Indeed, I think I shall enjoy it very much."

Violet's Bold Mission

The music of the band and the sounds of people enjoying themselves escaped the Lansings' house and reached the ears of a man who sat in a buggy across the street. He had a good view of the brightly lighted house, though his buggy was hidden in deep shadows.

"Very impressive friends you have, Miss Travilla," Clinch said to himself. "The mayor, the police commissioner, all those stuffed-shirt politicians I've seen traipse inside tonight. And the tall man who came to my hotel. Is he your knight in shining armor? Are you telling all your fancy friends about your mission, Miss Travilla? Are you getting them all on your side tonight? Did you think I wouldn't hear about your party? You underestimate me then."

An ugly sneer curled his mouth. "I no longer underestimate you, Miss Travilla. I can't scare you off like those weaklings who came before you. And I can't wring your pretty neck," he said with a mirthless laugh. "But I'll find a way. In time, I'll find a way to make all of Wildwood mine again."

He snapped the reins fiercely, and his horse almost bolted into the street. With a silent curse on his lips, he drove off into the night.

232

What will happen to Tansy and Marigold?

What surprises are in store for Vi and the mission? Is more trouble ahead?

Violet's story continues in:

VIOLET'S PERPLEXING PUZZLE

Book Five of the *A Life of Faith: Violet Travilla* Series

Collect all of our Elsie products!

A Life of Faith: Elsie Dinsmore

* Now Available as a Dramatized Audiobook!

Collect all of our Millie products!

A Life of Faith: Millie Keith Series

* Now Available as a Dramatized Audiobook!

Beloved Literary Characters
Come to Life!

Elsie Dinsmore and Millie Keith are now available as lovely designer dolls from Mission City Press.

Made of soft-molded vinyl, these beautiful, fully jointed 18¾" dolls come dressed in historically accurate clothing and accessories. They wonderfully reflect the biblical virtues that readers have come to know and love about Elsie and Millie.

For more information, visit www.alifeoffaith.com or check with your local Christian retailer.

A Life of Faith® Products from Mission City Press

It's like Having a Best Friend from Another Time

Check out
www.alifeoffaith.com!

WND Books
COLLECTOR'S EDITION

All the best

STOP THE PRESSES!

STOP THE PRESSES!

THE INSIDE STORY OF THE NEW MEDIA REVOLUTION

JOSEPH FARAH

WND Books

STOP THE PRESSES!
A WND Book
Published by World Ahead Media
Los Angeles, California

Copyright © 2007 by Joseph Farah

Cover Design by Linda Daly

WND Books are distributed to the trade by:

Midpoint Trade Books
27 West 20th Street, Suite 1102
New York, NY 10011

WND Books are available at special discounts for bulk purchases. World Ahead Media also publishes books in electronic formats. For more information call (310) 961-4170 or visit www.worldahead.com.

First Edition
ISBN 10-Digit 097904510X
ISBN 13-Digit 9780979045103
Library of Congress Control Number: 2006939631
Printed in the United States of America

10 9 8 7 6 5 4 3 2 1

DEDICATION

THIS MAY BE the only book for the press, about the press, and by a member of the press dedicated to Ronald Reagan.

Ronald Reagan changed the world more than any man in the twentieth century. Of that there is no doubt in my mind.

He ended the Cold War by challenging the Soviet Union. He popularized supply-side economics. He restored hope in Americans. He renewed the world's faith in our country as that "shining city on a hill."

But others can address more eloquently what Ronald Reagan meant to the nation and the world. I want to tell you what Ronald Reagan, the greatest president in my lifetime, meant to me—personally. How he not only changed the world, but changed my life.

And I never even met him.

I grew up in a second-generation American home where Franklin D. Roosevelt was an icon and voting Democratic was an article of faith.

Amid the cynicism of the Watergate scandal and the national demoralization that came in its wake, I was naturally inspired by the presidential candidacy of a man who seemed like a nonpolitician from Georgia in 1976—a man named Jimmy Carter. But after four years of official ineptitude, even Jimmy Carter could see America was mired in a national malaise. He just didn't know he was as responsible as anyone.

Along came Ronald Reagan.

He was upbeat. He smiled. He was confident. He had faith in the country. He recognized the enemy. He rallied Americans to a common goal of expanding freedom here and abroad. He had a clear vision of where he wanted to lead the country, and most Americans recognized and embraced it.

I did not. I was a slow learner. As a young member of the media elite, I was still trapped in an old mindset. I feared that Ronald Reagan, as his adversaries and most of my colleagues warned, would "blow up the world."

I'm somewhat ashamed to say today I voted again for Jimmy Carter in 1980.

Ronald Reagan's landslide victory in 1980 helped awaken me. I wanted to know why I was so out of touch with the rest of the country. I began reading more about Reagan's ideas, about his philosophy. I read Whittaker Chambers's *Witness*. I read other books that had impacted the new president. And, lo and behold, they began to make sense to me.

At the same time, I took notice of the fact that our hostages in Iran, taken during Jimmy Carter's presidency, were immediately released as Reagan was sworn into office. It seemed to me the Islamofascists in Tehran were afraid of this new cowboy in the White House—and that was a good thing for the hundreds of Americans trapped in our embassy for more than a year.

Over the next year or two, I saw something happen in America. When President Reagan would seek reelection in 1984, he would characterize it as "morning in America." It was a new dawn. It was a new day. The whole nation felt better about itself. We knew who we were as Americans again, thanks to the leadership of Ronald Reagan.

And I finally started to get it too.

Ronald Reagan taught me about freedom—what it really means.

My best chance to meet Ronald Reagan came in 1990 when he made a return visit to the California Capitol in Sacramento. I was the editor of the *Sacramento Union*, the historic daily in town and the oldest west of the Mississippi. I asked Speaker Willie Brown for accreditation to come hear the former president speak—and maybe get a chance to shake his hand.

In true partisan style, Willie Brown denied me that chance—probably out of spite for characterizing him as the crook he was and knew himself to be.

So I missed my last chance for a face-to-face, in-person encounter with Ronald Reagan. Yet I do not exaggerate today when I say that much of what I have since accomplished in my life, with God's help, would not have been achieved without Ronald Reagan's influence and inspiration.

There would be no *WorldNetDaily*.

There would be no daily column.

There would be no nationally syndicated newspaper column.

There would be no *Taking America Back*.

There would be no WND Books.

There would be no *Whistleblower* magazine.

There would be no *G2 Bulletin*.

There would be no *Stop the Presses*.

And that's just Ronald Reagan's impact on one person. Think of all the ways he has affected the lives of hundreds of millions of Americans and others around the world. It's truly amazing how God can use one man to help transform the lives of so many others.

It was a wonderful life, indeed. I just wanted to acknowledge it right here. Not only did he bring down the Berlin Wall and end the Cold War, he inspired the hunger for freedom that is still today transforming the vital institution of the free press.

They say Ronald Reagan achieved what he did by going over the heads of the establishment media that was so hostile to him and his message. I witnessed that. And in witnessing how effectively it could be done, I was inspired to try it myself. Today, a whole generation of New Media personalities, big and small, is doing just that.

Thank you, Ronald Reagan, for showing us the way. Thank you for showing *me* the way.

CONTENTS

INTRODUCTION

"STOP the presses!"

You've seen newspaper editors shout that phrase in old movies when a big story was breaking.

I'm not sure, but Lou Grant may have said it in the old TV series about a newspaper city editor in Los Angeles.

I never was a newspaper editor on television or in the movies, but I did play one in real life.

I'm one of only a handful of people in the United States who have actually said "Stop the presses!" and meant it. I was fortunate enough to have served as a top daily newspaper editor in the old days when breaking news meant just that—stopping the presses, replating, and getting the latest stories out to people on newsprint.

I'm talking about the old days, before newsrooms even had computers. I remember that—working with typewriters, pencils, scissors, and glue pots.

In fact, I even helped coach actor Ed Asner and the rest of the cast of the TV show *Lou Grant* on what it was like working in a real-life big-city newspaper.

It's all different today. It's a new world for the media. Few people anywhere get newspapers for breaking news. We get breaking news from television, radio, and the Internet. Newspapers can still provide context, details, analysis, features, enterprise reporting, investigative reporting, etc., but even today's newspaper executives would agree that the place to break news is on their Internet sites. That's where people turn for the latest news.

Occasionally I still read the old newspaper trade journals when I need some light entertainment. They are literally filled with articles about the Internet and how to adapt to this brave new world that threatens the very existence of the media landscape in which I toiled for so many years.

INTRODUCTION

Back in 1997, I threw my lot in with the Internet. I saw in this new medium the chance to reinvent the American news media, to reform it, to do the job right, to recapture the spirit and purpose and ideals of the free press, to utilize the new technology to reinvigorate and revitalize the role of the free press as a guardian of liberty, an exponent of truth and justice, an uncompromising disseminator of news.

I believed—and still believe—that the "mainstream," corporate, establishment press lost its vision, lost its way. It no longer understood its historic, unique, and still-vital mission.

What is the purpose of a free press in a free society?

Had I asked that question of the grizzled, veteran newsmen I knew when I began my professional career in newspapers thirty years ago, I believe many of them could have answered the question correctly. And, yes, there is a correct answer—just one.

"The central mission of a free press in a free society is to serve as a watchdog on government."

That's why the founding fathers of this great nation included special protections for the free press in the First Amendment. They understood the vital role the free flow of information plays in an open, self-governing society.

The founders believed in checks and balances on the potentially tyrannical power of government. They were all too familiar with the heavy hand of unaccountable government and they wanted no part of creating a new one.

The free press, they understood, was another layer of the checks and balances they had devised in the new government. That's why the American press is still often referred to as the Fourth Estate. The separation of powers between the executive branch, the legislative branch, and the judicial branch of government was to keep the federal government off balance so its terrible power could not be concentrated in one man or one group of men. And the press, an independent, nongovernment "estate," would be there to watchdog the first three estates.

But this well-conceived, well-devised system got broken—as many of the founders expected it would as time went by. As the nation grew and power became more concentrated in Washington, the free press acted less like a watchdog and more like a lap-dog of government.

I saw this happen in my lifetime. I witnessed it up close and personal.

And just as political power became more concentrated in Washington, media power became more concentrated in the hands of a few major corporations—corporations that sought the favor of government at least as often as they sought to check its power. In a very real sense, the nation's political, cultural, and spiritual health came under the spell of a strange new beast the founders could never have envisioned—the government-media complex.

Rather than functioning as natural adversaries, the press began to act more like a public relations arm of the government—promoting big-government solutions to problems real and imaginary.

It was with the recognition of this fundamental flaw in the institution of the press that I set out to correct the course of the news media—not by criticizing my colleagues, not by throwing stones, not by educating them through seminars, not by complaining about bias, but by doing the job better—leading by example.

This is my story. It's a drama that is still playing out. But the handwriting is on the wall for the Old Media. The revolution is underway. It's a development as big as the invention of the printing press was in Gutenberg's day. It is a story that is impacting the lives of everyone around the world. It is shaking the very foundations of the power-hungry elitists who want to control the flow of information and thus control the people.

It's nothing short of a miracle for freedom-lovers and news junkies.

And it's a story that, until now, has never been told.

CHAPTER ONE

HOW THE
REVOLUTION STARTED

*"How beautiful upon the mountains are the feet of him that bringeth
good tidings, that publisheth peace; that bringeth good tidings of good,
that publisheth salvation; that saith unto Zion, Thy God reigneth!"*

—Isaiah 52:7

A S MY PLANE descended into Sacramento International Airport that June day in 1990, I gazed at the farmlands below
considering the challenge that lie ahead.

I had just been hired to be the newspaper "doctor" at the now
late, great *Sacramento Union*—then the oldest continuously published daily west of the Mississippi River, the paper where Mark
Twain started his career.

Turning this newspaper around—even giving it a chance to
survive—was not going to be an easy task. The *Union* was a distant and fading number two paper in a relatively small market in
a country with only about a half-dozen cities supporting competing dailies. The *Union* was owned by a couple of real estate de-
velopers who had no other media holdings from which synergies
could be drawn. While it was once the big morning paper in
town, a series of ownership changes, neglect, and failed experiments had drained its resources and left it with just sixty thousand paid readers.

On the other hand, the McClatchy chain's flagship paper, the
Sacramento Bee, dominated the marketplace with close to four
times the circulation of the *Union*.

I could see immediately from the landscape on that approach to the airport that the Sacramento-area population of about one million was extremely spread out. That posed problems for any newspaper, but especially for a struggling number two. It meant that even when you found willing new subscribers, it was frequently not worth the time, effort, and expense to deliver it to them. The odds were not on our side.

In other words, we needed a miracle.

So, I did something that would be considered foolish and superstitious by most of my media colleagues. I prayed.

We didn't have much time to fool around in Sacramento. I needed to make some fast changes that would have a major positive impact to offset declining circulation and advertising trends.

I had learned from my years in the business that successful newspapers had personalities. And those personalities were shaped by the personalities of those involved in the creative process—editors, reporters, columnists, marketing people.

Since I was a stranger in this town, I was searching in particular for one personality who captured the imagination of this marketplace.

One autumn day in 1990, I was walking down L Street a few blocks from Sacramento's beautiful Capitol Building, an architectural replica, in many ways, of the U.S. Capitol. It was a beautiful day and traffic was backed up on the one-way street. Most of the cars had their windows open. I could hear the Rush Limbaugh radio program coming from the open windows. It seemed everyone in that traffic jam was listening.

As I continued to walk up the street, I could listen to the program without interruption from all the car windows. All of the drivers, it seemed, were tuned in to KFBK and listening to Rush Limbaugh. It was amazing.

As Rush liked to say: "I own Sacramento." He wasn't kidding.

One name dominated all others in Sacramento—Rush Limbaugh. In fact, he was beginning to dominate nationwide.

A year or two earlier, Rush had left Sacramento, where he was an extremely popular local talk-show host on KFBK, and headed off for national superstardom in New York.

My mind started reeling. How could I get Rush Limbaugh involved in the *Sacramento Union*? What were the chances?

I didn't know Rush Limbaugh in 1990, but I was desperate. I was a man on a mission. So I did something brazen. I cold-called him.

Well, you'd be surprised who you can get on the phone when you're the editor of the *Sacramento Union*.

Rush often talks about his special love for Sacramento. And he means it. Why else would he agree to write a column for the struggling *Sacramento Union*, giving us a quick shot in the arm? Not only did he agree to write a column, he agreed to write a *daily* column— one we would feature on the front page. And he also graciously agreed to record local spots for us promoting the *Sacramento Union* as the alternative voice to the liberal elite *Sacramento Bee* to run before, during, and after his show.

Do you want to know how politically and culturally near-sighted my colleagues in the media were before 1990?

It turns out that before he left Sacramento, Rush had asked my predecessors at what was considered to be a "conservative" daily newspaper if they would publish columns by him. They turned him down.

That should give you a pretty good idea of just how defiantly arrogant the establishment media are in this country. Is there any newspaper in the country today that could not benefit in readership from publishing exclusive works by Rush Limbaugh? I guess we can all see that today. But back in 1989, not even the "conservative" paper in Rush's adopted hometown recognized what he had to offer.

I did. The response to the Rush Limbaugh daily columns on the front page of the new *Sacramento Union* was amazing. We published those columns and we aired his spots and the phones rang off the hook at the *Union*.

Why did Rush take a chance on us? What was so important about trying to save the *Sacramento Union*? How was our effort different from any other attempt to save a struggling newspaper?

Long before there was a *WorldNetDaily.com*—seven years before, in fact—there was this bold journalistic experiment of a similar kind taking place in the capital of California. I was just thirty-five when I took that first flight into Sacramento in 1990 and began the effort to revive the historic paper against all odds.

To that point in my life, though, it was certainly the culmination of a long career in daily newspapering—one, I believe, God had his hand on from the beginning.

I don't want to sound like some Holy Joe, but years earlier I had dedicated my life to Jesus Christ. He became my best friend, my Savior, my Lord, my Compass. The Bible had become my bearings, my moral foundation, my spiritual nourishment.

About the same time, I read another little book that inspired me. It was called *In His Steps* by Charles Sheldon. It was a novel written around the turn of the twentieth century about people who make all the important decisions in their lives based on the principle of "What would Jesus do?"

The book was wildly popular. In fact, *In His Steps* sold more copies than any other book in America between 1880 and 1935— millions and millions. One of the stories in that book was about a local newspaper editor. And after reading *In His Steps*, I tried to be that newspaper editor.

You want to know what was different about the *Sacramento Union* than any daily newspaper you've ever read? That was it. It was edited, from the top, by a Christian executive who wasn't ashamed or bashful or timid about using his Christian worldview and his Christian convictions as the guideposts for doing his job as a newspaperman.

But don't mistake what we did in Sacramento for some church newsletter. The hallmark of the paper was hard-hitting investigative reporting into fraud, waste, abuse, and corruption in government—of which, I assure you, there was plenty in the capital of California.

In the short term we had for this renaissance in Sacramento, we did manage, among other things, to get the state superintendent of schools indicted, convicted, and sentenced on a felony conflict-of-interest charge through our intrepid and dogged reports. This was no low-level flunkie. He was considering a run for the governorship and was also a prospect to be Bill Clinton's secretary of education.

But after our reports, his name, Bill Honig, is little more than a historical footnote.

The *Sacramento Union* stood for something. It was a tough, no-nonsense, investigative seven-day-a-week newspaper that challenged the status quo, championed the little guy, had no sacred cows, and developed some real personality during my tenure as editor.

I think that's what Rush Limbaugh saw in it, too. I think that's what our loyal readers and advertisers saw in it. And I think that's why we enjoyed at least a temporary rebirth as a journalistic institution.

It could have been a fairy-tale ending in which the handsome prince (me) lives happily ever after. But as much as we all enjoy fairy tales, God's got a much bigger agenda.

Sure, we located many thousands of people who wanted to subscribe to this new *Sacramento Union*. As I said, the phones were ringing off the hook. But the problem was that many of those new would-be subscribers lived far out from the city—meaning it would not be profitable to send trucks and cars out to deliver those papers.

There were lots of people who wanted the exciting new product we had put together—hard-hitting investigative reporting on government corruption, fraud, waste, and abuse in the capital of the largest state in the country; bold commentary; a strong Christian perspective; and…Rush Limbaugh. Unfortunately, we were still operating in the paradigm of the Old Media.

In the Old Media, we gathered the news, we prepared our stories, we set them in type, we made plates, we ran massive presses and barrels of ink, and we bundled those newspapers and delivered them in trucks and cars for hundreds of square miles. By the time the papers arrived at homes and businesses, it was already time for a new edition. It was a tough distribution system—one the *Sacramento Union* and other struggling number two papers probably would not be able to overcome.

I wracked my brain for a solution. I was not the only one. The man who hired me, James H. Smith, a virtual living legend in the newspaper business, was thinking long and hard about the problem, too. He had been hired a few months earlier to be publisher of the *Sacramento Union*—and we would become fast friends and partners in our aggressive, desperate, quixotic effort to turn the paper around.

Smith had been the president of the *Washington Star* during its heyday—having worked with my newspaper mentor, Jim Bellows, the former *New York Herald Tribune* editor who went on to run the *Los Angeles Herald Examiner*, where he hired me. Smith had also served as general manager of the *Sacramento Bee*, so he certainly knew the competition.

When I took the job at the *Union*, I got a call from Bellows— then working at *TV Guide*, I believe.

He asked, "Is that Jim Smith—from the *Washington Star*?"

"Yes, it is," I said.

I couldn't tell from Bellows's non-reply whether he thought that was a good thing or a bad thing. But clearly he had a different kind of relationship with Smith than I did.

But my experience with Jim Smith was nothing but good. Here was a newspaperman's newspaperman. He had an "aw shucks" Jimmy Stewart persona, but he could be as tough as nails when he needed to be. And we needed to act fast if there was going to be a *Sacramento Union*. Neither of us wanted to be the guys remembered for killing the oldest newspaper in the West.

One day Smith told me about a new friend he made in Silicon Valley, just ninety minutes or so to the west. He was a computer engineer by the name of Bob Evans, who had developed some seemingly fantastic technologies and applications for electronic distribution of text.

Now, keep in mind, this is quite a few years before the Internet was even invented. I'm not even sure Al Gore was working on it yet. However, what Jim Smith and I saw in Silicon Valley in the summer of 1990 convinced me that there was a New Media coming. I didn't know if it would come soon enough to help me save the *Sacramento Union,* but I knew it was coming soon and that it would herald an age of new competition in the media.

The technology we saw utilized unused bandwidth on television signals to transfer potentially massive amounts of data—mostly text, in this case. We wondered if we could possibly har-

Jim Smith and I sit atop the newsprint rolls at the *Sacramento Union,* circa 1990.

ness this technology to take the *Sacramento Union* to people we couldn't reach with newsprint. Unfortunately, this particular technology required users investing in a little converter box that would sit on their TV. Unless there was a lot more programming available, it was unlikely we could persuade tens of thousands to buy little boxes so they could read a newspaper on their TV.

Had the Internet not come along when it did, some other technology like Bob Evans's experiments in teletext surely would have. But it would be another five years, really, before the Internet was a word on anyone's lips—too late for the *Sacramento Union*.

Jim Smith left first, and I followed shortly after in 1992. We realized we could not turn the paper around with the resources the owners could provide. Before we tossed in the towel, we even spent a year trying to find new owners for the paper— people better suited to the challenges involved in saving a dying paper. We were unsuccessful. Two years after I left, I watched the sad spectacle of the *Sacramento Union* die a rather undignified and torturous death.

With no Internet, no New Media, no meaningful press alternatives yet on the horizon, I wasn't ready to give up on the Old Media. I couldn't imagine what God had in store for me. Once again, Jim Smith and I teamed up, this time to form a nonprofit, tax-exempt corporation called the Western Journalism Center. The idea was to encourage more of the kind of independent, muckraking investigative reporting we did at the *Union*.

And, of course, there was plenty of work to do for truly independent, muckraking investigative reporters: Bill Clinton had just been elected president of the United States. Increasingly, I turned my sights away from the capital of California and toward the capital of the United States.

As I was toiling away establishing the Western Journalism Center, dissecting the Clinton administration, and dreaming about a media revolution that still seemed far from reality, I got a phone call from, well, let's call him the godfather of the New Media.

Because, while Rush Limbaugh couldn't help save the *Sacramento Union*, he accomplished something much greater. He saved AM radio. He certainly had set off a communications revolution.

He certainly did give voice and hope to millions of politically disfranchised Americans. He certainly paved the way for hundreds
of other radio talk-show hosts—not only of his own political persuasion but for those from the left, right, and middle.

Think about it. In the late 1980s, broadcast experts were predicting the demise of AM radio. It was good for nothing, they said.
FM was where it was at; the clarity of the signal and stereo sound
made it the choice for music formats—which were all the rage.
There was no talk radio to speak of. There were a few local
shows—no politically challenging national perspectives.

Then along came the man I call "The Great One."

Honestly, Rush Limbaugh could have done whatever he
wanted with his career. The man is a great entertainer. He com-
bines the humor and performance ability of Jackie Gleason with
the political insight and convictions of Ronald Reagan. A lot of
people cringe when he says it, but let me tell you, his talent really
is on loan from God.

I told you about my cold-call to Rush back in 1990. This time,
in 1993, it was Rush Limbaugh calling me.

Actually, Rush had called me frequently during my *Sacramento
Union* days. He liked to check in and find out what was going on
with his friends in his adopted hometown—and what better way
than to talk to the editor of the daily newspaper? We'd also talk
about the day's news, conspire a little over politics—just friendly
banter and chitchat. I was always pleasantly surprised when the
phone rang at night and it was Rush calling. Soon he would be far
too busy for those kinds of chats with anyone.

But in 1993, it was all business. His brother, David, had called
first. I had gotten to know David through our deal on the newspaper column. David Limbaugh, now an author and columnist in his
own right, served then as his big brother's lawyer, agent, and con-
fidante. This time David wanted to know if I could help Rush.

A year before, Rush's *The Way Things Ought to Be* was a number one bestseller. Rush had stunned the publishing world with
the immense success of the book—just like he stunned the world
with his unprecedented success in radio syndication. Now he was
facing another book deadline. He needed a collaborator.

I don't even remember whether Rush and David knew at the time, but I had some considerable experience with book collaborations in the past—having worked with other bestselling authors on a half-dozen titles. Even while toiling away in the newspaper business over the preceding fifteen years, I had loved books and had worked on many as a quiet collaborator.

None before or since, of course, would be as big as *See, I Told You So*. It had an initial printing of two million copies—unprecedented and unrepeated, to my knowledge, in the publishing business. But even more striking is the fact that those first two million copies sold out in the first eight weeks of release.

I spent the spring and summer of 1993 working on the book that would rival even Rush's first book, *The Way Things Ought to Be*. I got to work closely with the man—talk to him whenever I needed. It was a special time. I enjoyed total access.

Whenever people find out about my relationship to Rush Limbaugh, they always want to know: "What is he really like?"

That's easy. Rush Limbaugh is generous, funny, encouraging, kind, and insightful—probably all the things his listeners imagine him to be. I actually found him to be a little more reserved than his radio persona, maybe even a little shy. But working closely with Rush Limbaugh on his bestselling book was a treat for me and a memory I will always cherish.

Later that year, I helped his publisher organize perhaps the most amazing book party I have ever seen. The Beverly Hills Hotel was the scene and the guests included as diverse a group of interesting people as you could ever imagine—from Star Parker and Thomas Sowell to Judith Regan, Arianna Huffington, and the late Brandon Tartikoff.

They understood, along with the hundreds of other guests there that night, that Rush Limbaugh represented and personified the focal point of a new and formidable challenge to the media status quo.

Rush had demonstrated he could pull phenomenal ratings on radio, sell hundreds of thousands of subscriptions to his newsletter, launch a successful syndicated television show, sell out personal appearances, and sell millions and millions of books. More important, he showed he could change the political culture of the country.

The New Media Revolution was already birthed. All we were waiting for now was the new medium, the Internet, to arrive.

That's me at Rush's book party in Beverly Hills with the late Brandon Tartikoff and Scott Kaufer, then a top Warner Brothers executive.

CHAPTER TWO

HILLARY'S NIGHTMARE BECOMES A REALITY

"Congress shall make no law respecting an establishment of religion, or prohibiting the free exercise thereof; or abridging the freedom of speech, or of the press; or the right of the people peaceably to assemble, and to petition the government for a redress of grievances."

—First Amendment of the U.S. Constitution

A T SOME POINT in 1995, Bill and Hillary Clinton had what I describe as "a prophetic nightmare."

You probably remember Hillary talking about this bad dream in a television interview in which she explained that her husband's problems were all manufactured by "a vast right-wing conspiracy."

What you might not know is how this nightmare was actually chronicled in a 331-page report copublished and distributed, at taxpayer expense, by the Democratic National Committee and the White House counsel's office. The report was titled, "The Communication Stream of Conspiracy Commerce."

This was a report distributed to select U.S. reporters in an effort to discredit a new breed of investigative reporting into what was already emerging as the most scandal-plagued administration in the history of the United States.

Let me quote from the opening lines of the report: "'The Communication Stream of Conspiracy Commerce' refers to the mode of communication employed by the right wing to convey their fringe stories into legitimate subjects of coverage by the mainstream media. This is how the stream works. First, well-funded right-wing think tanks and individuals underwrite conservative newsletters and newspapers such as the Western Journalism Center, the *American Spectator,* and the *Pittsburgh Tribune-Review.* Next, the stories are reprinted on the Internet where they are bounced all over the world. From the Internet, the stories are bounced into the mainstream media through one of two ways: 1) The story will be picked up by the British tabloids and covered as a major story, from which the American right-of-center mainstream media (i.e., the *Wall Street Journal, Washington Times,* and *New York Post*) will then pick the story up; or 2) The story will be bounced directly from the Internet to the right-of-center mainstream American media. After the mainstream right-of-center American media covers the story, congressional committees will look into the story. After Congress looks into the story, the story now has the legitimacy to be covered by the remainder of the American mainstream press as a 'real' story."

Now, remember that the White House was having this bad dream back in 1995. This was long before anyone had ever heard of Matt Drudge. It was long before *WorldNetDaily.com* was even on the drawing board. To keep things in perspective, I think Monica Lewinsky was a teenage undergraduate student at the time.

What was I doing? I was directing the Western Journalism Center, which was giving the Clinton administration fits through its investigative projects. But our connection to the Internet was tenuous at best. By 1995, that little investigative-reporting center I founded with Jim Smith was indeed already experimenting with the Internet. The Western Journalism Center Web site was called "etruth.com" (which is now the domain of the Elkhart, Indiana, local newspaper—*The Truth*).

I called Western Journalism Center "little." That is an understatement because, throughout its history, it never operated with an annual budget of more than $500,000. Yet clearly the White House report, other documents obtained later, and the attacks on the center by the Clinton administration show it was perceived as its number one threat in the media.

The full story of the Communication Stream of Conspiracy Commerce has never really been told—until now. Think about this document—and what it says about the power of a handful of dedicated, intrepid reporters who pursue the truth no matter what the consequences.

Hundreds of copies of the report were distributed throughout the 1996 presidential election year by the White House counsel's office and prepared, according to the administration, by a staffer there. Why would what was clearly a political document, designed only to boost Bill Clinton's personal standing by attacking critics, be subsidized by American taxpayers? Who received the report? My colleagues in the big media—select reporters who, the administration hoped, would deflect stories about the administration by refocusing attention on the handful of "evildoers" who were exposing the White House's misdeeds.

To my knowledge, not one of the "reporters" who received the handout from the White House ever bothered to ask why the president was keeping files on private citizens and using taxpayer dollars to smear them publicly. That should give you an idea of just how sad the state of American journalism was in 1996.

Imagine another president trying this. What if, say, Richard Nixon had kept files on pesky reporters? What if he probed into their religious affiliations? What if he used taxpayer dollars to undercut their credibility—the very lifeblood of a journalist—and distributed the files selectively to those in the media he trusted?

What if George W. Bush tried it?

I can tell you one thing. I would condemn it if it ever happened again—no matter who the president was. And I am certain the entire press establishment would be up in arms.

Remember Nixon's enemies list? Do you recall what a badge of honor it was for any reporter to find he or she was listed on it? Do you recall how much national and international attention Nixon's enemies list received?

Perhaps you don't know—few do—that Bill Clinton maintained a media enemies list of his own. But there was one difference between Nixon's list and Clinton's. Those who found themselves on Clinton's list—people like me—faced real harassment at the hands of the government. On the other hand, those on Nixon's list just didn't get invited to White House parties.

I've been trying to tell this story now for more than a decade. I've been trying to call attention to it so we can avoid a repeat of this ugly history.

Here's how it all started. In the summer of 1994, my nonprofit news organization, the Western Journalism Center, began an investigation into various Clinton administration scandals. By December of that year, our work had made it onto the White House's radar screen and we were officially listed on the first known "enemies list"—a fourteen-page memo written by Associate White House Counsel Jane Sherburne.

Of course, I didn't know that then. I didn't find out until years later, when the document showed up among thousands subpoenaed by congressional investigators.

In other words, as early as 1994, the White House was keeping tabs, gathering information, and compiling files on me and my group.

A year later, the Communication Stream of Conspiracy Commerce was being distributed to select journalists by the White House counsel's office, showing the Clinton administration was involved in a pattern of illegally maintaining and distributing for its own political purposes dossiers on private citizens.

The 331-page report focused on three news organizations at the nexus of this "conspiracy" against Clinton—the conservative magazine *American Spectator*, the Richard Scaife–owned *Pittsburgh Tribune-Review,* and my own Western Journalism Center. The report contained a full-blown, five-page biography on only one journalist—me.

Where in the Constitution is the president granted the power to maintain dossiers on private citizens for political gain? By the way, we will perhaps never know the full extent of this illegal spying operation inside the Clinton White House because the White House is exempt from requests under the Freedom of Information Act.

So, to make this crystal clear, the Clinton White House collected data on private citizens, used it for political purposes, and kept those files secret with impunity to this day. You would think journalists would rise up en masse to protest such civil liberties abuses. Yet I couldn't get the time of day from most of my colleagues, and the American Civil Liberties Union wouldn't touch it with a ten-foot pole.

Interestingly, when you read the Communication Stream report, you find that the White House never actually contests a single fact reported by me or the Western Journalism Center. Instead, the report attempted only to tarnish our reputations—to "kill the messenger," so to speak. Our motives were questioned. Our associations impugned. Our character maligned. But nowhere were our facts challenged.

The opening paragraph of the report, for instance, characterizes the center as a "well-funded, right-wing think tank." That one phrase is wrong on three counts. The center operated on a budget of no more than a half-million dollars a year, most of it raised from small contributions of $25 or less. The center's mission was not ideological. Instead, it sponsored investigative reporting that focused on government fraud, waste, secrecy, corruption, and abuse. If that's a right-wing agenda, then take it up with Thomas Jefferson, James Madison, and the framers of the Constitution. Being a watchdog on government is supposed to be the central role of a free press in a free society. Lastly, the center was never a think tank. It was a nonprofit news agency.

I founded the center—and later *WorldNetDaily*—to fill a growing void in my industry's commitment to investigative reporting, especially the kind that holds government accountable to the people and the Constitution. I believed—and still believe—that the watchdog role of the press had become obscured during my lifetime—that journalists had lost sight of their most important task. But my mission was not about criticizing my colleagues. It was to lead by example—to do the kind of reporting that others were missing. The Clinton White House overreaction to our work is testimony, I believe, to the importance of such investigative reporting and its effectiveness.

The Clinton White House resorted to name-calling and guilt-by-association tactics in its report on its media enemies. It claimed—straining credulity—that I and my organization had been deftly manipulating the mainstream media's news coverage of the many scandals that plagued the president. Not only was I credited with setting the editorial agenda for the *New York Times* and *Washington Post*, but the White House suggested I was actually controlling the flow of information to the entire Western world through the clever use of the Internet and international press contacts.

Oh, how I only wish I was so powerful and smart—then or now.

As I mentioned, in concocting this vast media conspiracy, the White House report profiled just one journalist—me. Now, I don't tell you this to boast. I tell you to illustrate the absurdity of the Clinton fantasy. My White House rap sheet extended a full six pages—longer even than Dick Scaife's. How is it, I wondered, that a media conspiracy could exist with only one journalist involved?

What got the White House so worked up was the very first major national investigative project the center undertook. It was an examination of the death of White House Deputy Counsel Vincent W. Foster. As a direct result of the news reports resulting from this investigation, Whitewater Special Counsel Robert Fiske was fired by a three-judge oversight panel, hearings on Foster's death resumed in the House and Senate, and public-opinion surveys showed two-thirds of the American people doubted the official findings of simple suicide.

But it wasn't just the Foster probe that concerned the White House. The report also included other articles of concern—a story about the president and an internationally notorious Russian suspected of smuggling nuclear arms and a story about the Lippo Group's connection to Clinton's massive land grab in Utah.

But the biggest story we ever broke—though it never got the traction it deserved—was the one involving the Clinton administration's favored method of punishing those who crossed it.

It was in 1996 that an Internal Revenue Service investigator showed up at my offices to announce the center was being audited and in danger of losing its tax-exempt status. Why? Because the center had done critical reporting of the president in an election year.

That's what the agent told us.

I'm not kidding.

Imagine reporters investigating the president during an election year! You can't do that in America, the IRS told us—at least not as a tax-exempt news organization. Just as a reminder, the largest news-gathering organization in the world—the Associated Press—is tax-exempt. National Public Radio is tax-exempt. PBS is tax-exempt. Do you suspect that these phantom rules about tax-exempt news organizations were being applied rather selectively during the Clinton years?

I should point out, of course, that there are no restrictions on what tax-exempt news organizations can report—during election years or nonelection years. But this was the claim that justified a nine-month audit of my news service in 1996—one in which IRS agents literally stationed themselves in my office from 9 a.m. to 5 p.m., poring through our financial records and correspondence.

Additionally, if there was any remaining doubt about the motives behind this audit, field agent Thomas Cederquist told our accountant that "this is a political case and the decision will be made at the national level."

On October 22, 1996, I broke the story of this illegal audit and a pattern of other IRS scrutiny of other Clinton enemies in the pages of the *Wall Street Journal*. A firestorm erupted—at least momentarily. There was wide media coverage. IRS Commissioner Margaret Milner Richardson resigned. A congressional probe was launched.

The audit was concluded in May of the following year. Our organization was nearly broke as a result. Employees were laid off. Publications closed down. Major donors had been scared off. Legal and accounting bills had risen. Staff time was eaten up by the process.

I decided to pursue justice nonetheless. I filed Freedom of Information Act requests in vain. The government stalled us—even refusing to turn over our case file as is required under the "Taxpayer's Bill of Rights."

Later, with the help of Judicial Watch's Larry Klayman, we filed a ten-million-dollar lawsuit against the IRS agents and other officials we deemed responsible. We filed a Freedom of Information lawsuit too, still trying to secure the documents that would prove we were targeted for political reasons.

In July 1999, the Treasury Department finally responded with some documents it had been withholding for years—including a secret internal report on an investigation of our audit. The report concluded that the audit of the Western Journalism Center began when the White House sent a letter of complaint to the IRS Exempt Organizations Division.

It seems a Clinton donor in Los Angeles was incensed at the reporting of the center. He clipped a full-page ad we had taken out in the *Los Angeles Times* and sent it to the president with a suggestion to audit us. The White House dutifully sent the request over the IRS and bingo.

Did you catch that? Clinton's own Treasury Department concluded that this was a political audit—that it was triggered when that letter from the White House arrived at the IRS.

The *Wall Street Journal* story described a much bigger story than the audit of my news organization. It showed our audit was part of a wider pattern of political audits directed by the White House against any individual, any business, or any organization it deemed an enemy. The list of those audited eventually included Paula Jones, the Heritage Foundation, Concerned Women for America, the National Rifle Association, Oliver North's organization, and dozens and dozens of other individuals and organizations that crossed the administration or threatened to do so.

This was a *real* enemies list—an enemies list of people who endured real pain because of Clinton's targeting. And I'm proud to say that I was near the top. I wear that distinction like a badge of honor.

When Nixon was threatened with impeachment in the 1970s, one of the articles drawn up against him was for using the IRS to go after political enemies. As it turned out, Nixon resigned before he could be impeached. We learned later that while Nixon attempted to pursue political enemies with the IRS, he never succeeded. His IRS commissioner told him to go jump in a lake. And that was the end of it.

This was not the case in the 1990s when Clinton was in charge. He successfully targeted enemies using the IRS. He got away with it. Not only was there no talk of impeachment for this offense, his buddies in the establishment press largely ignored the story altogether.

So, today, occasionally, you will still hear members of my profession bemoaning Nixon's alleged use of the IRS to go after political enemies, but you will rarely if ever hear what actually happened during the Clinton years. It was widespread. It had real effects on real people. It had a chilling effect on free speech in this country.

Contrast Clinton's abuse of the IRS with Nixon's. I recall seeing one of Nixon's most virulent critics, Noam Chomsky, on C-SPAN in January 1998. It was part of a panel discussion on "Race, Gender, and Class."

Chomsky is an avowed and leading theoretician of the left. He's a linguist who chooses his words carefully. Here's what he said about being on Nixon's enemies list: "Nixon's enemies list was nothing. We hear so much about it today. I was on Nixon's enemies list. They never even audited my taxes."[1]

Having Bill Clinton for an enemy, I was not so fortunate. Neither were dozens of other high-profile individuals and organizations that crossed him during his two terms in office. But nobody ever held Clinton accountable. And today, the widespread use of political audits during the Clinton regime is a forgotten crime.

I was eventually permitted to brief some congressional staff members for former Representative Bill Archer (R-TX) in January 1998. But nothing was ever done. No blistering reports were ever issued. No indictments were forthcoming. Amazingly, even though Clinton was impeached, his use of political audits was not among the charges.

Quietly, some members of Congress told me they, too, were afraid of speaking out too forcefully for fear they would get the same treatment—or worse—from the IRS.

What does it mean when such abuses go unpunished and unrecognized? It means they will be repeated in future administrations—maybe even by a future Hillary Clinton administration.

Think about this. There is no federal agency more feared by the American people than the IRS—and with good reason. The power to tax is the power to destroy. More than any other administration in history, the Clinton regime harnessed all the terror of that agency and directed it against its political enemies.

In a very real way, the IRS served as Clinton's secret police agency—the go-to guys when no other punishment would do.

I mentioned earlier that Larry Klayman's Judicial Watch came to our legal aid over the IRS abuse with the filing of two lawsuits. Guess what happened when Judicial Watch filed the lawsuit? That organization was also audited—and one of its representatives was told: "What did you think would happen when you sue the president of the United States?"

Clinton didn't use just the IRS, by the way. He used other agencies as well—including, in my case, his own Energy Department secretary, Hazel O'Leary.

Back in her days in the Clinton Cabinet, O'Leary would abuse her office by offering government contracts for those who would play political ball with her boss—and threaten those who got out of line with cutting off the gravy train.

My own personal experience with O'Leary came in 1995 when she personally applied the most heavy-handed political pressure imaginable to a donor to my nonprofit investigative reporting center. She told the contributor, someone whose company relied on federal contracts for millions in revenue every year, that if he gave any more money to the Western Journalism Center, those contracts would be in jeopardy.

Why was O'Leary concerned about the center? Because it was involved in a long-term, high-profile investigation of Clinton administration corruption—including the president's untoward personal and political connections to hostile foreign intelligence agents.

O'Leary should have been booted out of office for that kind of abuse. She should have been tried and convicted of abusing her authority. But the Clinton administration had a great record at one thing—keeping its political hatchet men and women from paying any price for breaking the law.

While Clinton may have escaped justice for these crimes, there were consequences for his actions. The Clintons' paranoia birthed their own worst nightmare—"the New Media."

Back then, no one was calling what we did the New Media. Hardly. It was clear the Internet had great potential. Yet few were exploiting it in 1995 and 1996.

What we were doing that got the attention of the White House was good, old-fashioned investigative reporting. If no one else would publish the fruits of that labor, we published it ourselves in newsletters and posted it on our Web site. We discussed it on talk radio. Hosts like Rush Limbaugh brought the work to the attention of millions. Indeed, as Hillary pointed out in the Communication Stream of Conspiracy Commerce, sometimes we were fortunate enough to get our work picked up by foreign papers. And sometimes that work ended up being picked up by a handful of American newspapers. When it wasn't, we were sometimes forced to purchase ads in daily newspapers to bring attention to the work.

Likewise, Matt Drudge had already begun his now-ubiquitous *DrudgeReport.com*, but it was hardly the powerhouse it would become after the Lewinsky scandal. (Notice Hillary's early nightmare about the Internet makes no reference to the *Drudge Report!*)

So why was Hillary so nervous? What would have caused her way back in 1995 to issue a report so fearful of the Internet? Was it indeed a premonition of things to come? Remember, this was an administration doomed to scandal exposed by the Internet—the one form of mass communication its partisans in the old establishment press couldn't seem to control. And already, by early 1995, the White House could see the handwriting on the wall. Here's some more from that 331-page White House report on the Internet:

"The Internet has become one of the major and most dynamic modes of communication. The Internet can link people, groups, and organizations together instantly. Moreover, it allows an extraordinary amount of *unregulated* [emphasis added] data and information to be located in one area and available to all. The right wing has seized upon the Internet as a means of communicating its ideas to people. Moreover, evidence exists that Republican staffers surf the Internet, interacting with extremists in order to exchange ideas and information."

It doesn't take a PhD in computer science to recognize that the Clintons and their political allies were scared of the Internet—deathly scared. They were clearly dying to get their hands on it—not for their own creative use, mind you, but for the purposes of control, for stifling free expression by others.

A few years later, in 1998, Hillary was asked by reporters if she favored curbs on Internet expression, which, by that time, had played a key role in breaking news about the president's scandals.

Here's what she said: "We are all going to have to rethink how we deal with this, because there are all these competing values." According to a Reuters report, she deplored the fact that the Internet lacks "any kind of editing function or gatekeeping function."[2]

WorldNetDaily had not yet celebrated its first birthday when Hillary made that statement. The *Drudge Report* was barely a toddler.

And think about this: in 1995, when she had that first nightmare, there were only about one million computers connected to the Internet. By the end of 1998, there were fifty million. Today, there are in excess of a billion connections. To put that in perspective, after the invention of television, it took more than ten years before there were fifty million sets in the world. The same rise on the Internet took less than three years.

I probably don't have to tell you why Hillary was so anxious about the power of the Internet. She and her husband and much of the rest of the political and cultural establishment intuitively understood what this new medium could mean—the end of the hammerlock control of the media by a certain worldview.

What *was* that worldview? What *is* that worldview? That's a story for another chapter.

CHAPTER THREE

HOW THE PRESS GOT THIS WAY

"And ye shall know the truth, and the truth shall make you free."

—John 8:32

IT WAS the best of times. It was the worst of times. Can I use that famous line? Back in the early 1980s, I was a young journalist on the fast track.

I had been fortunate enough to get hired into the world of big-time daily newspapering by a living legend—James Bellows, the former *Washington Star* top editor and the former city editor who groomed Jimmy Breslin, Tom Wolfe, Dick Schaap, and dozens of other gifted writers.

Now Bellows was running the *Los Angeles Herald Examiner* and trying to give his old paper, the *L.A. Times*, a run for its money. He hired aggressive, hungry young journalists from the New York area—people like me—to take on the tired, stuffy, staid big morning paper.

To give you an idea of what an uphill challenge this was going to be, when I got to the *Herald Examiner* in 1979, it did not yet have computers. We worked with old-fashioned upright manual typewriters, pencils, paper, scissors, and glue pots.

The Hearst daily was still an afternoon paper in a country that had soundly rejected afternoon papers about ten years earlier. The *Herald Examiner*, once the big paper in town, had never recovered from a union effort at a shutdown—one of the bloodiest strikes in the history of the newspaper industry. People were shot. People died. It went on for years. Circulation plummeted.

But for me, a twenty-four-year-old working-class kid from New Jersey, this represented the chance of a lifetime. I made the most of it. I absorbed everything I could from Bellows and my colleagues. Three years later, I was running the newsroom.

By the standards of what I had expected in terms of goals from my professional journalism career, I had achieved everything. Life was good. Friendships were abundant. I loved LA.

In addition to all the fun at work, there was plenty of fun outside, too. It was during my years at the *Herald Examiner* that my friend Scott Kaufer, then the top editor at *California Magazine*, and I started what became one of the most famous media softball leagues in Hollywood history.

The players included Brandon Tartikoff, the late *wunderkind* of NBC Entertainment and Paramount Studios; Chris Carter, who would go on to create *The X-Files*; Tony Dennison, the actor who would play John Gotti and other famous mobsters; and many other top studio and network execs, actors, and writers.

None of that really impressed me. But as a lifelong baseball fanatic, what I will always remember is the season I got to play with and manage Hall of Famer Ernie Banks—the famous Cubs shortstop and first baseman who coined the phrase: "It's a beautiful day. Let's play two."

During one of our weekly twelve-inning marathon games, I noticed an older gentleman watching from the sidelines.

"You like baseball?" I asked.

"Sure do," he said, probably thinking he wasn't actually seeing any played before him on this day.

After some more idle chitchat, it became clear that this man was one of the greatest baseball players in the history of the game. It was Ernie Banks—a man who clubbed 512 career major league homeruns.

Sheepishly, I asked if he would like play with us. Startlingly, he said he would. That's how Ernie Banks became my first baseman. I got to manage him and play shortstop with this living legend who started his career as one of the greatest shortstops.

This was typical of life in Los Angeles in the 1980s. Everywhere you went there were stars. Life was good—at work and at play.

One day I sat at my desk in the center of the hustle and bustle of the newsroom and looked around. Somehow I was beginning to feel oddly out of place in this environment—like a fish out of water. I loved the work. I thrived on the deadlines. I flourished under the stress and excitement.

As I observed my colleagues shuffling papers and typing their stories, it hit me. Of the approximately two hundred journalists I had come to know, it occurred to me I was probably the only one who went to church on Sunday.

Think about that.

In the United States, about 44 percent of people attend religious services at least weekly.[1] Most of those are Christians. That's a higher percentage of churchgoing than any other Western country.

Yet that wasn't reflected at all in America's newsrooms. There was a huge gulf between the lifestyle of the average American and the average journalist. And that gulf had been long in the making.

During my twenty-five years of doing everything you can do in the newspaper business—from reporting to copyediting to top editorial management, I actually witnessed what I believe could accurately be characterized as the takeover of America's newsrooms by ideologically motivated extremists.

A coup took place. America's newsrooms, from coast to coast, were hijacked. The old rules were swept away like chaff falling off the presses. And in came the brave new world of propaganda disguised as news, intolerance disguised as tolerance, control disguised as pluralism.

I saw it happen. It happened in my lifetime. Let me tell you what I saw.

To understand what I witnessed, you need to understand me. Because I truly believe that we all see through the lens of who we are and what we believe. It's very important to understand this concept of "worldview." This is not a simple story of liberal bias in the media. This is not a simple story about Democratic Party activists infiltrating the press and dominating it. This is not a simple story about anti-Christian bigotry in America's cultural institutions.

There is some truth in all those observations, but they each miss the mark if we are to diagnose the real illness plaguing the press in America.

Who am I?

I am, first and foremost, a follower of Jesus Christ. After that I am a husband, father, journalist, businessman, etc.

That's my lens.

We all have lenses—not just Christians.

There are a lot of people out there who try to exclude Christians from being involved in the world because they would "impose their morality on the rest of us."

You've heard it over and over again, haven't you? "He is imposing his religious views on the rest of us. He is putting religion ahead of science."

Now, I happen to be quite honest about my opinion on this subject. I am opposed to murder, theft, adultery, lying, idolatry, and other things because the Bible tells me they are wrong. I believe we live in a world governed, ultimately, by God. I believe there is accountability for what we do. I believe that without the immutable laws handed down by God—not just those etched in stone by Moses, but those etched on our hearts—we wouldn't have a clue about right and wrong.

In fact, I will go further. Without God, right and wrong would be meaningless. There would be no such thing—just various opinions.

I'm also honest about the fact that my faith in God shapes everything I do—from my politics to my business decisions to the way I treat my dog. I am hardly alone in this way. Christians are hardly alone in this way. Everyone operates in the same way. We all do what we do based on our beliefs.

You see, everyone is religious—even the atheist. Everyone worships at the altar of something—whether it's science or money or power or a golden calf.

Everyone has a worldview—a lens through which they see the world and make decisions about it.

Whether it's Ted Kennedy or John Kerry or Nancy Pelosi or Barney Frank or Arlen Specter—they've all got a religion. It may be a bad religion. It may be a false religion. It may be a perverted religion. It may be an evil religion. But everyone has one—whether they believe in the God of the Bible or not.

Some of these people, however, like to pretend they don't. Others like to pretend they have a religion but it doesn't affect what they do, the decisions they make every day. Others like to pretend that they don't make any effort to impose their religious values on others.

In fact, if you think about it, every single effort to pass a new law is an effort to impose somebody's sense of morality on others. Imposition of moral values is a two-way street. The only question is whether good values or bad values will prevail. Whether we walk in the light or in the darkness. Whether we speak the truth or accept a lie.

This is true not just in the area of public policy debates but in our everyday lives—no matter what we do. Even if we are journalists. Perhaps especially if we are journalists.

Some critics have actually suggested I might be disqualified from being a journalist because of my faith. It would "compromise my objectivity," they say.

These are people who have lost touch with the real mission of the free press.

My faith calls me to seek the truth. "And ye shall know the truth, and the truth shall make you free."[2]

Truth is the real mission of the free press—or it should be. It's not objectivity. It's not impartiality. It's not neutrality. It's not "fair and balanced."

Think about how the noble profession of journalism was subverted in America. The founders understood that the free press was an institution critical to the establishment and maintenance of a free country. They set in place a number of checks and balances in the system of government they created—

including three branches of government under the rule of law and the will of the people.

But the First Amendment also guaranteed special protections to the press, because the founders understood that without a vital and free press acting as yet another check and balance on the corrupting power of government, their great experiment in liberty would not long endure.

That is why today we still refer to the press as the "Fourth Estate"—another independent counterweight to the three branches of government.

It all worked pretty well and kept America free. There was, of course, a bloody conflict between the states. There were other major tests of the Constitution. But the free republic survived largely intact through two centuries.

However, a radical shift of power began to take place about fifty years ago. In the 1960s, America's cultural institutions—the press included—were taken over by a new way of looking at the world, a new religion, if you will.

To put a face on it, consider Walter Cronkite. He was not only "America's most trusted man" in the 1960s, he was not only the CBS news anchor, he was the managing editor of the most important source of information for the American people.

We were told he was the newsman's newsman. He was the picture of objectivity. He had been a correspondent for United Press International during World War II, then joined CBS television in 1950 as a reporter before becoming the evening news anchor in 1962.

"That's the way it is..." was his signature line in signing off his broadcasts for nearly twenty years.

But who was this man really?

Only years after his retirement did we find out that Cronkite was, well, how do I put this delicately? Cronkite was a crock. Cronkite was a crackpot. Cronkite was an extremist—apparently carefully shrouding his wacky worldview, well out of the realm of mainstream American opinion, while cultivating an image of trust, sobriety, and patriotism and defining for a generation what television news was all about.

He was like a grandfatherly institution in the early days of TV. People believed him. *Uncle Walter wouldn't lie to us*, America believed.

Thus, when he gave his opinions, they had impact. One example was his report on the Tet offensive in Vietnam, which is credited with swinging the tide of opinion against the war.

Isn't it important to know how this man got such an important job? Did you ever wonder about that? It's a lesson in the way the establishment media work. It illustrates the revolving door between the press and politics in America.

The July 10, 2000, issue of the far-left socialist magazine the *Nation* reported on the death of Blair Clark, who served as editor of the *Nation* from 1976 through 1978: "Whether it was calling on Philip Roth to recommend a *Nation* literary editor or persuading CBS News President Richard Salant to make Walter Cronkite anchor of *CBS Evening News*, Blair had a gift for the recognition and recruitment of excellence."

Clark was not only the editor of the Marxist *Nation*, he was also heir to the Clark thread fortune, a Harvard classmate and friend of John F. Kennedy, a buddy of *Washington Post* editor Ben Bradlee, and the manager of Eugene McCarthy's 1968 campaign for the Democratic Party presidential nomination.

He veered back and forth between politics and journalism seamlessly (no pun intended, given his family's connection to the thread industry)—as an associate publisher of the *New York Post*, a reporter for the *St. Louis Post-Dispatch*, vice president and general manager of CBS News, and yet remaining a fixture in Democratic Party politics throughout his career.

Clearly, Clark wasn't the kind of man who would promote Walter Cronkite for the most visible job in journalism because of his press accomplishments alone.

Even more telling is Cronkite's political activism since leaving his anchor job—outspokenness that more than suggests this has always been a man with a strong political agenda.

In 1989, Cronkite spoke to a dinner organized by People for the American Way, a group founded by Norman Lear. His candid politics surprised even that audience.

"I know liberalism isn't dead in this country," he said. "It simply has, temporarily we hope, lost its voice.

"About the Democratic loss in this election...it was not just a campaign strategy built on a defensive philosophy. It was not just an opposition that conducted one of the most sophisticated and cynical campaigns ever. ... It was the fault of too many who found their voices stilled by subtle ideological intimidation.

"We know that unilateral action in Grenada and Tripoli was wrong. We know that Star Wars means uncontrollable escalation of the arms race. We know that the real threat to democracy is half a nation in poverty. ... We know that religious beliefs cannot define patriotism. ... God Almighty, we've got to shout these truths in which we believe from the housetops. Like that scene in the movie *Network*, we've got to throw open our windows and shout these truths to the streets and the heavens. And I bet we'll find more windows are thrown open to join the chorus than we'd ever dreamed possible."[3]

Cronkite prides himself on being the consummate newsman. Yet in his retirement years, he's become little more than a poster boy and PR man for a new global political order—one that even he admits would deprive Americans of their sovereign rights and independence.

For instance, he has come out firmly, boldly, explicitly—and stupidly—for the formulation of a global government at the expense of U.S. national sovereignty. On October 19, 1999, Cronkite accepted the Norman Cousins Global Governance Award from the World Federalists Association at the United Nations in New York.

He told those assembled, including Hillary Rodham Clinton, that, as a newsman for CBS, he once had to keep his views on such matters to himself. The first step toward achieving a one-world government, he said, is to strengthen the United Nations.

"It seems to many of us that if we are to avoid the eventual catastrophic world conflict, we must strengthen the United Nations as a first step toward a world government patterned after our own government with a legislature, executive, and judiciary, and police to enforce its international laws and keep the peace," he said. "To do that, of course, we Americans will have to yield up some of our sovereignty. That would be a bitter pill. It would take a lot of courage, a lot of faith in the new order."[4]

He warned, "We cannot defer this responsibility to posterity. Time will not wait. Democracy, civilization itself, is at stake. Within the next few years, we must change the basic structure of our global community from the present anarchic system of war and ever more destructive weaponry to a new system governed by a democratic U.N. federation."

And just in case it wasn't entirely clear what he was advocating, Cronkite said, "Today the notion of unlimited national sovereignty means international anarchy."

This is the real Cronkite—the one who was disguised all those years as the neutral, nonpartisan newsman. He said there were three immediate steps necessary to move the world toward this goal of globalization of authority: give the U.N. more money, ratify all of the treaties negotiated by supra-national bodies pending before the U.S. Senate, and democratizing the U.N.

Cronkite said the U.S. has failed to ratify treaties for only one reason—the influence of the "Christian Coalition and the rest of the religious right wing."

"Their leader, Pat Robertson, has written that we should have a world government but only when the messiah arrives," he said. "Any attempt to achieve world order before that time must be the work of the Devil. This small but well-organized group has intimidated both the Republican Party and the Clinton administration. It has attacked each of our presidents since FDR for supporting the United Nations. Robertson explains that these presidents were and are unwitting agents of Lucifer."

In 2000, in an interview with the BBC, Cronkite was even more blatant in his plea for world government. The BBC's Tim Sebastian asked Cronkite if the United Nations had lived up to his earlier dreams for a "Parliament of Nations." Here's what he said in response: "I wouldn't give up on the U.N. yet. I think we are realizing that we are going to have to have an international rule of law. We need not only an executive to make international law, but we need the military forces to enforce that law and the judicial system to bring the criminals to justice before they have the opportunity to build military forces that use these horrid weapons that rogue nations and movements can get hold of—germs and atomic weapons."[5]

Note that Cronkite advocates having "an executive" make international law. That's the way it works, I guess, in places like Cuba and other totalitarian hellholes around the world. Is that what Cronkite has in mind? And this executive—presumably unelected and unaccountable—would be backed by a global military monopoly that would hunt down rebels even before they armed themselves or committed any "international crime." So now the "newsman" was advocating the creation of global thought police.

But it gets worse.

"American people are going to begin to realize they are going to have to yield some sovereignty to an international body to enforce world law, and I think that's going to come to other people as well," he said. "It's a fair distance to get there, but we are not ever going to get there unless we keep trying to push ourselves onto the road."[6]

Most people do not take such talk seriously. They say, "Oh, Cronkite's just an old dreamer. There's no real threat of world government on the horizon. Why are you spending so much time worrying about Cronkite, Farah? Get over it."

Please understand why I bring this information to your attention. It's not because Cronkite is *different* from his colleagues. It's because he's the *same*. I could spend chapters writing similar profiles of the other icons of the Old Media. But Cronkite epitomized trust, honesty, candor, and, most important of all, *objectivity*, more than any of his colleagues. He was the one who stole America's hearts and minds with his grandfatherly face and charm.

Cronkite is merely a symptom of the disease. Think about what you have read here: a so-called "newsman" promoting the ultimate form of centralized, all-powerful government. It's incongruous. It's mind-boggling. It's...betrayal.

Thomas Jefferson, who told us that the government that governs best governs least, must be rolling over in his grave. Jefferson, one of America's most important founding fathers, had this to say: "Were it left to me to decide whether we should have a government without newspapers, or newspapers without a government, I should not hesitate a moment to prefer the latter." That's always been my attitude. It certainly ought to be the attitude of real newspeople the world over.

Hey, Walter! The central role of the free press is to serve as a watchdog on government. The founding fathers knew this. It's certainly not to help lay the groundwork for the most tyrannical and powerful system of government the world has ever known. That's what you're doing, Walter. It's time to turn in your press credentials—permanently.

Do you feel manipulated? Are you still going to put your trust in the dinosaur establishment press? Or are you going to be more selective and discerning in your information choices? Of course you are. That's why you are reading this book. That's why you have, in all likelihood, already begun getting your news from alternative sources—the New Media.

And with good reason. Because the truth is that Walter Cronkite's views are not at all out of line with most of his colleagues. It's just that he now feels free to be more honest and up front about those views than he did when he was "the most trusted man in America."

And that's why I have taken time to offer this powerful illustration. I could do the same thing with many other journalistic institutions—from the *New York Times* to the Associated Press to Time Warner.

They are all operating under a belief system quite at odds with mainstream America. That's why I hate it when people refer to these institutions as "the mainstream press." They are anything but mainstream. You are mainstream. I am mainstream. We hold the values that made America the shining city on a hill that it is—or was.

What is this belief system that holds most of my colleagues under its spell? In its simplest terms, you could characterize it as "moral relativism." While America has been perceived throughout most of its history as a nation operating within a Judeo-Christian framework, those values came under heavy and sustained attack beginning in the 1960s. But the challenge began long before the 1960s.

It all started many years ago, around the turn of the last century, when an Italian Communist by the name of Antonio Gramsci came up with a strategic spin on accomplishing the political objectives of socialism. Gramsci argued that the road to victory wasn't necessarily found in armed, violent clashes, but rather in a long-term struggle for the hearts and minds of the people.

He advocated a long march through the cultural institutions—education, academia, the press, the entertainment industry, the foundations, even the churches. If you take over the key cultural institutions, he explained, the political establishment will fall into your hands like the last domino.

Think of it this way: the culture is the Ho Chi Minh trail to political power. That's what Gramsci's disciples figured out. The enemies of freedom, the advocates of state control and socialism, have been following Gramsci's cue around the world for at least the last seventy-five years.

They have thoroughly succeeded in sacking America's cultural institutions—and today the political establishment is sitting there like an overripe plum just waiting to be harvested.

In fact, as I have been telling people for at least the last fifteen years, America has drifted so far from its founding principles there is no chance it can be returned simply by electing the right people to office. The political system is broken not because the Constitution failed. It is broken because the hearts and minds of the people have been corrupted by the morally relativistic indoctrination of America's subverted cultural institutions.

The only way America can be returned to greatness is by taking back the cultural institutions that shape the way Americans think.

That's how a "Culture War" is waged. The only way the ill effects of the long march through institutions can be reversed is for responsible, freedom-loving people to fight back on all fronts, to stop surrendering in the Culture War, to reclaim and redeem those lost cultural institutions, to begin their own long march.

I've dedicated my life to restoring the uniquely American principles of the free press. I never believed this could be accomplished by exposing the problems and biases of the press. The only way it could be accomplished was by establishing new models, new competition, by lighting candles rather than cursing the darkness.

That was the vision that inspired me as a newspaper editor. It was the vision that inspired me to create the Western Journalism Center. It was the vision that inspired me to launch *WorldNetDaily*. It was the vision that inspired me to found WND Books, an enterprise that created another mini-revolution in the publishing world. It was the vision that inspired me to write my last book, *Taking America Back*, and this book you are holding in your hands now.

For the press, the Internet has proven to be a great equalizer. Matt Drudge, sitting in his Florida home with his laptop computer, makes more of an impact on the day's news than most of the biggest daily newspapers in the country. *WorldNetDaily*, meanwhile, is read by more people each day than the audience that watches Larry King.

Isn't it time we stop complaining about the bias of the establishment media? I mean, look at the facts. This is a battle we are winning. The press is one cultural institution where a counter-revolution is well underway. There is more competition than ever before. The networks and the newspaper monopolies are going down like T-Rexes.

I don't understand why there is still so much hand-wringing going on about the press. The press will never be the same.

In other words, the free market, working through the Internet, is solving long-standing institutional problems in the media, as well as exposing fraud, waste, corruption, and abuse at the highest levels of government. Imagine that!

Now, if we can just keep Hillary's grubby, power-hungry little hands off it.

CHAPTER FOUR

A BRIEF HISTORY
OF THE FREE PRESS

"There is nothing so fretting and vexatious, nothing so terrible to tyrants, and their tools and abettors, as a free press."

—Samuel Adams

THIS CHAPTER is titled, "A Brief History of the Free Press." There's a reason for that—the history of the free press is brief indeed.

Most people don't know that. And that's why I'm chronicling it here.

By the same token, the history of freedom itself is rather short. I often point out how America's successful, but still brief, experiment with freedom runs counter to much of the world's history.

Few Americans get it. I'm not sure very many non-Americans comprehend it either.

July 4, 1776, wasn't just the birth date of American freedom. It was, quite literally, the birth date of freedom around the world. That's why the French called George Washington not just the founding father of the American Revolution, but "the father of freedom." He was truly the inspiration for freedom fighters everywhere.

Likewise, the notion of freedom of the press—a notion we take for granted today, though it is still unobserved and unrecognized by most of the world's population—could be said to have been birthed at the same time, in America's not-too-distant revolutionary past.

For perhaps the first time in the world's history, two governments in 1776 enshrined in their constitutions unalienable protections for freedom of the press. They were both American governments.

That year, the Virginia Assembly adopted its Declaration of Rights. Article XIV stated: "That the freedom of the press is one of the great bulwarks of liberty and can never be restrained by despotic government."

If only it were so. If freedom is fleeting, freedom of the press is downright ephemeral. The sad truth is that despots frequently restrain it—even crush it.

But unless men visualize goals and enumerate rights, mankind is unlikely to recognize and realize them. And it is quite true that America's founding fathers first saw an inextricable connection between a shackled government and an unshackled press.

In the same year America's Declaration of Independence was being signed and distributed, the Pennsylvania Constitution was also enshrining the first official protections of freedom of the press. "That the people have a right to freedom of speech, and of writing, and publishing their sentiments; therefore, the freedom of the press ought not to be restrained," it read.

Shortly after, in 1780, another former British colony, the Commonwealth of Massachusetts, put it this way in Article XVI of its Declaration of Rights: "The liberty of the press is essential to the security of freedom in a state; it ought not, therefore, to be restricted in this commonwealth."

A few years later, when the Bill of Rights was approved, a special word of protection for the press was included amid the rights of religious freedom, freedom of speech, and the right to gather and petition elected officials. "Congress shall make no law respecting an establishment of religion or prohibiting the free exercise thereof; or abridging the freedom of speech, or of the press; or the right of the people peaceably to assemble, and to petition the government for a redress of grievances," reads the First Amendment.

That's how basic the founders considered the role of the free press to a free society. To say this notion was revolutionary in the history of mankind would be an understatement. Nowhere previously had a government acknowledged it had no business messing with the free press.

And honestly, I don't think it has been done since—at least not with the same sense of purpose, meaning, and clarity that it had in eighteenth-century America. The founders meant what they said. We know because of the sometimes spirited debates they conducted over such issues.

Let me underscore what I am saying about this breakthrough. The First Amendment, while often hailed and often imitated, has never been replicated anywhere else in the world—even 230 years later! No other government—anywhere, anytime—has articulated the concept that journalists have an inherent, God-given right to do what they do. Nor has any other group of governors honestly determined that it is actually in their own best interest to be examined, studied, investigated, audited, inspected, interrogated, observed, reviewed, scrutinized, watched, castigated, chided, criticized, condemned, and clobbered by citizen-journalists.

I have traveled around the world. Nowhere—not even in the so-called advanced twenty-first century—do I see any country governed by any constitutional provision as sharp and unambiguous in its protections of the free press as the eighteenth-century American First Amendment.

My colleagues once knew this. They once appreciated what a breakthrough in freedom occurred uniquely here in America. They once acknowledged that the vital mission they fulfill isn't possible in anything but a free society like the one established by our founders.

It wasn't that long ago that my colleagues said it as plainly as I am saying it right here.

"A free press was born when America was born," explained Jerry W. Friedman, executive vice president of the American Newspaper Publishers Association Foundation just two decades ago. "It was not handed down or inherited. The concept of press freedom was deliberately constructed by the framers of our Constitution to instill the spirit of independence as an absolute, crucial ingredient in the creation, existence, and survival of a free society."[1]

The founders were, of course, inspired by others. They were avid readers of *Blackstone's Commentaries*, published in 1765, which explained: "The liberty of the press is indeed essential to the nature of a free state; but this consists in laying no previous restraints upon publications, and not in freedom from censure for criminal matter when published. Every free man has an undoubted right to lay what sentiments he pleases before the public; to forbid this is to destroy the freedom of the press; but if he publishes what is improper, mischievous, or illegal, he must take the consequences of his own temerity."

Yes, freedom of the press is a uniquely American heritage. But that hardly means America "has it made" when it comes to matters of a free press.

Exactly one year before September 11, 2001, *WorldNetDaily* announced the findings of a scientific public opinion survey we commissioned to find out what Americans believed about the First Amendment and the press. What that survey found was fairly shocking.[2]

About 30 percent of 1,000 respondents, all likely voters, said the most vital function of the press is to inform consumers about risks they face in the marketplace. Another 18 percent said they were not sure. About 15 percent said the main job of the press is to chronicle crimes and fires. More than 7 percent believe the main job of the press is to entertain the public, according to the survey. More than 4 percent said the most important role of the press is to shape public opinion. Nearly 2 percent said the main role of the press is to "give people something to talk about."

Fewer than 20 percent indicated they understood the central role—and traditional role—of a free press in a free society is to serve as a watchdog on government.

While there have been many polls conducted in recent years measuring public views of the performance of the press, this survey was unique in examining public opinions about what the press is supposed to do.

The survey also found that just 5.5 percent of the U.S. public believes the national news media are doing an excellent job. Just over 21 percent rate press performance as good, while nearly 38 percent rate them fair, and nearly 34 percent give them poor marks.

The survey illustrates the U.S. public is losing—or maybe has already lost—its understanding of the important role the free press has always played in safeguarding liberty and checking state power.

Again, that's why the founding fathers enshrined in the First Amendment specific, inalienable rights for the press. They understood the absolutely vital role the press was required to play to maintain liberty in the face of encroaching government.

When specifically asked to rate the importance of the "government watchdog role of the press," respondents overwhelmingly said it was "very important" (61.7 percent). Another 28.9 percent rated it "somewhat important."

Not surprisingly, Democrats generally give the press much higher marks than do Republicans and independents. Democrats are also slightly less likely to recognize the importance of the government watchdog role. Back then, in 2000, those leaning toward voting for Green Party presidential candidate Ralph Nader were most likely to cite the watchdog role of the press as vital (40.6 percent)—even over informing consumers of risks (19.2 percent). Pat Buchanan supporters were the next most likely to recognize the traditional watchdog role of the press.[3]

What's the lesson here?

Coupled with another poll showing only 45 percent of the American public believes they have the right to assemble and protest peacefully in public, it's clear we have a problem in the hearts and minds of the body politic.

The press and the schools are clearly not communicating basic civics lessons to the public. *WorldNetDaily*'s slogan, "A Free Press for a Free People," is not a collection of empty words. There is simply no way a free society can remain free without a vigorous, independent, vigilant free press that holds government accountable for its abuses.

In other words, it doesn't matter what the Constitution says if the American people don't embrace the values behind it.

I really believe this stuff. *WorldNetDaily* really believes this stuff. And I believe that belief comes through in our work. I know it is the secret to our success—something that cannot be successfully imitated without that core belief.

One of the reasons *WorldNetDaily* has been alone in doing what it does for ten years now is because precious few journalists—the only people capable of doing what we do—get it, and share our core belief that the central role of a free press in a free society is serving as a watchdog on government, exposing corruption, fraud, waste, and abuse wherever and whenever it is found, no matter who is perpetrating it.

If not many journalists understand the importance and mission of their profession, how many Americans should we expect to get it?

The history of the free press in our world is brief and littered with failed experiments. Yet we take it for granted in America and the Western world that this institution will always be there for us—that it will always serve its purpose, whatever that might be.

To understand how vital the information stream to the people is in creating or maintaining a free society, one simply needs to revisit the past.

There's an old saying: "Journalism is the first draft of history." And while the ancient Hebrews didn't practice journalism as we know it today, they did the best job of any people in recording their history. They also provided, through God's providence, the moral light that was needed to free people from tyranny and oppression.

Through their history, we can see that liberty was precious because it was rare and fleeting.

"It is remarkable that so few men and so weak a people could have exerted such an influence on mankind's quest for freedom because freedom, for much of the history of ancient Israel, was little more than a vision," wrote Columbia University journalism professor John Hohenberg in his book, *Free Press, Free People: The Best Cause*.[4]

It is a testimony not only to their God, but to what that God told all of us in the scriptures. "In the beginning was the Word, and the Word was with God, and the Word was God."[5]

How important is the word? All important. We're told in the Bible that God literally spoke the world into existence. We're told that God *is*, in fact, his Word. And his Word is him.

It was this knowledge that caused the Hebrews to revere the written word like no other people before them. It was what those words said that made them understand freedom, which is inextricably tied to right and wrong, to personal responsibility, to accountability to the Creator.

"There was good reason for the Israelites to revere such prophets as Isaiah, Amos, and Jeremiah and keep alive their words and their hopes in the years of captivity," explains Hohenberg. "Out of the later blossoming of Judeo-Christian civilization that they helped to create came an overwhelming urge toward individual freedom that has profoundly influenced all peoples. With the invention of the printing press, that influence was so magnified that the doctrine of freedom became an ideal in lands where it had never before existed."[6]

The printing press was invented in 1440 by Johann Gutenberg of Mainz, Germany. It is, of course, the printing press that gives us the very word we use synonymously with journalism—"press." The printing press was called a press because it was first fashioned out of a wine press. And why did Gutenberg feel compelled to invent it?

Because he wanted to print copies of the Bible. It's almost comical to think about today's journalists owing their very jobs—their livelihoods—to a process inspired by man's love of God's Word.

It was not until 1505—sixty-five years after the invention of the printing press—that someone got the idea of producing a "newspaper," albeit a primitive one. The first such effort is credited to Austrian printer Erhard Oeglin, hardly a household name in my industry, who announced the discovery of Brazil. The idea of printing news, however, did not turn the world upside down for more than two hundred years. Meanwhile, Gutenberg, whose Bibles today sell for millions, died in obscurity and poverty in 1468.

Slowly, a press ethic began to emerge. It wasn't "fair and balanced." It wasn't "all the news that's fit to print." It wasn't "infotainment." The important early pioneers of European journalism held a commitment to truth.

"In one thing only will I yield to nobody—I mean in my endeavor to get at the truth," wrote Dr. Théophraste Renaudot, editor of the *Gazette de France*, the first official French newspaper, in 1631. "At the same time, I do not always guarantee it, being convinced that among five hundred dispatches written in haste from all countries, it is impossible to escape passing something from one correspondent to another that will require correction from Father Time."[7]

Already, the idea of journalism being the first draft of history was taking shape. However, it didn't take long for ruling authorities to be concerned about this effort to seek out truth. Early news pioneers were often jailed for exposing corruption in high places. But a new ideal was being shaped in the hearts and minds of people striving for freedom and truth.

About this time, John Milton famously wrote these words: "Give me the liberty to know, to utter, and to argue freely according to conscience, above all liberties."

And, again, in his *Areopagitica* in 1644: "Though all the winds of doctrine were let loose to play upon the earth, so truth be in the field, we do injuriously by licensing and prohibiting, to misdoubt her strength. Let her and falsehood grapple; whoever knew truth put to the worse, in a free and open encounter?"

It would still take another century in a New World for an appreciation of the vital role of a free press in a free society to take shape. The concept was truly American.

In fact, I can be more specific. The concept was uniquely Christian-American.

We all remember Increase Mather from our history books. He was the most well-known Puritan minister of seventeenth-century New England. But did you know he was also a pioneer in early American journalism?

"The best-known Massachusetts minister of the late-seventeenth century, Increase Mather, also became its leading journalist," explains author and editor Marvin Olasky.[8] Mather, Olasky says, developed what might be called the "news sermon," a form of communication that was often published after it was delivered from the pulpit.

Olasky continues: "Printers moved naturally from the publication of Bible commentaries to the publication of theological treatises and sermons to the publication of news sermons and pamphlets on current events."

This not only represented the humble beginnings of an American free press, it was truly the advent of a free press in the world.

The first regular newspaper in colonial America was launched in 1690 by Benjamin Harris—again, a devout Christian. Harris had tried publishing an independent newspaper, *Domestick Intelligence*, in London. He was quickly thrown in jail. So he came to America and launched *Publick Occurrences Both Foreign and Domestick*.

While the publication was popular in Puritan New England, once again Harris found criticizing government officials in the colonies was no more profitable than it had been in England. Just four days after it was published, Harris was told he would be jailed if any more issues were printed and distributed.[9]

It would be forty years before another American publisher dared to use newsprint to criticize the government. This is where most journalism history books begin—with the story of John Peter Zenger. Zenger was the thirty-six-year-old printer-publisher of the *New York Weekly Journal*, a struggling newspaper that first appeared in 1733 to challenge the semi-official *New York Weekly Gazette*.

Zenger's criticisms of local officials soon made the paper required reading in New York—resulting in an official inquiry by the new chief justice of the province, James Delancey. He asked a grand jury to investigate Zenger and his publication for "seditious libel." Zenger was thrown into jail in November 1734—a year after his paper was launched—and remained there until August 1735.[10]

But the paper didn't die during his imprisonment. James Alexander, a former attorney general in New Jersey, continued to publish it in Zenger's absence. And ultimately the grand jury refused to indict Zenger.

That's the history that most journalism students learn about the Zenger case. What they don't generally hear or read is that Zenger too was motivated primarily by his strong Christian faith. Even his defense attorney, Andrew Hamilton, drew strong biblical allusions in making his case that truth was an absolute defense against the charge of libel.

"If a libel is understood in the large and unlimited sense urged by Mr. Attorney, there is scarce a writing I know that may not be called a libel, or scarce any person safe from being called to account as a libeler: for Moses, meek as he was, libeled Cain; and who is it that has not libeled the devil?" he said.[11]

By the middle of the eighteenth century, a new style of bold, independent journalism was spreading through the colonies. It would play a significant role in the coming War of Independence.

One of the principal players in this historical drama was Samuel Adams. No, he was not a brewer. No, he was not a pub owner. He was a pioneering American journalist. Today, Samuel Adams would be caricatured by journalists as a flame-throwing, right-wing Christian zealot. But it was Adams, writing as a columnist under a variety of pseudonyms for the *Boston Gazette*, who boldly challenged the Crown with his writings.

Olasky observes: "Adams emphasized investigative reporting more vigorously than any American journalist before him had: He did so because 'Publick Liberty will not long survive the Loss of publick Virtue.'"[12]

How important was this budding free press in the American colonies to the future of the new nation?

"The twenty-three small newspapers in colonial America scarcely seemed to be a formidable enemy for the British empire ten years before the first volley at Concord bridge," wrote Hohenberg. "Nevertheless, these few printing shops became the forge of American liberty."[13]

And after the revolution? Early nineteenth-century American journalism was characterized by a Christian worldview. This is (until Olasky's *Prodigal Press*) one of the great untold, covered-up stories of all time. Who would believe in today's secular world of American journalism that their predecessors—the very people who gave us the legacy of a free press in America—were mainly a bunch of "fundamentalist Christians"?

New York City alone had fifty-two magazines and newspapers that called themselves Christian in this time period. Between 1825 and 1845, more than a hundred cities and towns in America had Christian newspapers. As Olasky writes: "In the early nineteenth century, American journalism often was Christian journalism."[14]

But here's the real shocker. Did you know that the *New York Times*, today the bible of secular liberalism, was founded as a crusading antiabortion Christian newspaper in 1851? That's right. You probably won't read that in the official history sponsored by Pinch Sulzberger. Nevertheless, it's true. The *New York Times* is one more cultural institution that was subverted from its original mission, hijacked from its founding purpose, derailed from its guiding principles.

Henry Raymond, the founder of the *New York Times*, was a Bible-believing Christian. Under his leadership the paper became known for accurate news coverage. Though abortion was illegal in New York at the time, the practice was widespread—until the barbaric underground business was exposed by *Times* reporter Augustus St. Clair in a story called "The Evil of the Age."[15]

"Thousands of human beings are murdered before they have seen the light of this world, and thousands upon thousands more adults are irremediably robbed in constitution, health, and happiness," the story began.[16]

It left nothing to the imagination. Graphic images of human flesh decomposing in barrels of lime and acids. The names of abortionists and their political connections. The affluent lifestyle of the abortionists.

As a result of what became a series of stories in the *Times*, "New Yorkers would bury the abortion business for several generations," as Olasky tells it.[17] Indeed, it would not become a political issue again until the 1960s. By that time, of course, the *New York Times* had switched sides in the debate—and there was little vestige of the once dominant Christian press in America.

How far we've come in such a short time. How far we've fallen. The *New York Times* hasn't just abandoned its Christian heritage, it has declared all-out war on it.

That's not to say the *Times* hates Christians. That would be unfair. But it would be fair to say the *Times* despises what it sees as "right-wing" Christians.

Occasionally you will see the *Times* single out for praise those Christians who buck the trend—especially those who don't condemn such sins as abortion and homosexuality, two of the sacraments of the modern *Times* newsroom.

A good example is a piece about an evangelical megachurch pastor from Minnesota, Rev. Gregory A. Boyd. Boyd has some interesting ideas—given that he claims to base his beliefs on the same Bible I read.

But let's start with abortion and homosexuality. While Boyd claims to oppose abortion, he doesn't advocate that believers do anything to stop it. While he thinks homosexuality is not God's ideal, he opposes standing in the gap and opposing its strident political agenda.[18]

Many think the Bible is silent on abortion. I don't. In fact, I think it is the Judeo-Christian ethical teachings alone that kept abortion relegated to a few back alleys in America until 1973, when killing babies instantly became a constitutional right by proclamation of the high priests in black robes on the U.S. Supreme Court.

The Bible shows us what happens when those among us worship other gods. Recall the children sacrificed on the fiery altars of Baal. Did God allow for any compromise with that evil?

The Bible tells us that unborn babies had consciousness and that John the Baptist leapt in his own mother's womb in the presence of the pregnant Mary.

But let's cut to the chase on the abortion issue: what would Jesus do? Can anyone imagine Jesus walking by an abortion clinic without comment? Without action? With all that we know about the character of Jesus, can someone really suggest to me that he would not condemn such barbarism—that he would not do what he could to stop it and heal those involved with the sinful practice?

Trust me on this, when Jesus returns, he's not going to tell women it's their choice to kill their unborn babies.

Now what about homosexuality? What would Jesus have said? What would Jesus have done?

On this one, less speculation and guesswork is required. Because Jesus spoke openly and clearly on God's order for man and woman. Matthew 19:4–6 says: "And he answered and said unto them, Have ye not read, that he which made them at the beginning made them male and female, And said, For this cause shall a man leave father and mother, and shall cleave to his wife: and they twain shall be one flesh? Wherefore they are no more twain, but one flesh. What therefore God hath joined together, let not man put asunder."

It's even more clear-cut elsewhere in the Bible. It begins in Leviticus 18:22: "Thou shalt not lie with mankind, as with womankind: it is abomination."

That seems pretty clear to me. Not a lot of ambiguity there. The chapter goes on to state that people who commit these acts, and other acts God considers abominations, causes the land itself to be defiled. That's a reason for everyone to be concerned about homosexuality—especially the brand of open, in-your-face gay pride variety. Then, in the New Testament, Paul writes in Romans 1:22–27: "Professing themselves to be wise, they became fools, And changed the glory of the uncorruptible God into an image made like to corruptible man, and to birds, and four-footed beasts, and creeping things. Wherefore God also gave them up to uncleanness through the lusts of their own hearts, to dishonour their own bodies between themselves: Who changed the truth of God into a lie, and worshipped and served the creature more than the Creator, who is blessed for ever. Amen.

"For this cause God gave them up unto vile affections: for even their women did change the natural use into that which is against nature: And likewise also the men, leaving the natural use of the woman, burned in their lust one toward another; men with men working that which is unseemly, and receiving in themselves that recompence of their error which was meet."

It's also suggested in the Bible that homosexuals will not inherit the kingdom of God. Therefore, it's hard to imagine why someone who claims to be an evangelical would not want to let homosexuals know their behavior blocks them from eternal life. Some day, I suspect, Gregory Boyd will have to answer that question for himself.

He says Jesus never moralized about sex. But as you can see from Jesus's simple but eloquent statement about God's plan for men and women, he certainly did. He also shocked the Samaritan woman into changing her life. He told the accused harlot to go and sin no more. You have to ignore a lot of Bible to think Jesus didn't care about illicit sex.

Boyd reads the Constitution about as clearly and astutely as he reads the Bible, concluding that it says something about "separation of church and state," which it does not.

But despite all that, he's a favorite of the *New York Times*. If anyone at today's *New York Times* went to church, I'm sure it would be a church just like Boyd's.

You might think the *doyens* of the press establishment would have some respect for Christians, Christianity, and the Bible, given the critical role they played in shaping the history of the institution in which they operate and prosper today. But you would be wrong if you thought that.

Whether it is ignorance of the history we have just reviewed or contempt for a worldview they don't share, the "tolerant," "pluralistic," "open-minded," "liberal" journalistic community—and particularly those in elite positions of power—think anyone who believes the Bible is some kind of dangerous rube.

For example, take Bill Moyers (please, as Henny Youngman would say). Bill Moyers is the political activist who made a fortune and influenced millions in recent years pretending to be a journalist—a serious journalist. He generally makes his living, though, on PBS or some other publicly funded program. Why? Because no one would watch him otherwise. That's not a barrier to a show on PBS, because the network is underwritten by the government and fat-cat corporations and foundations whose directors think they are donating to charity when they give to PBS.

But I digress. I was watching a rambling interview Moyers did with Tim Russert on CNBC a couple years ago. He started by telling Russert that his latest show would try "to bring voices to the air that don't get heard usually. We're trying to tell stories that others overlook, or don't see, or don't think of as important as we do. And so we're just trying to provide, like public television should do, an alternative to mainstream journalism."[19]

These were the topics Moyers laid out as overlooked stories:

- Enron

- George Bush's links to big business

- Global warming

Does that sound like an alternative to you? Isn't this just what we hear if we torture ourselves by listening to CNN, ABC, CBS, and NBC? What's different? I'll tell you what's different. Moyers lets it all hang out. He is brutally honest in his partisanship, in his extremism, in his hatred of the values that made America great.

Is hatred too strong a term?

Not at all. This man is a Christian-basher—and a Jew-basher. If a Christian or Jew takes his or her religion seriously, he or she is seen as a threat to Bill Moyers. He equates such people with Osama bin Laden, the Taliban, Timothy McVeigh.

At the same time, he said he saw Muslims caught up in a "possibly quite hopeful inner debate."

"Fundamentalist Muslims believe like fundamentalist Christians that the law should reflect the faith and that religious people should govern the morals of society by legislative and political control," he explained. "Thomas Friedman of the *New York Times* says we're going to have to choose between the Muslims who pray to a god of hate and Muslims who pray to a god of love. Well, that's a choice Muslims are making, have made. I mean, the militant fundamentalists represent—what?—10 percent, 15 percent of Islam in the same way that the extremist Christians in this country, the Christian Identity crowd, the Christian militia crowd, represent 3 percent, 4 percent, 5 percent of Christianity."[20]

The "Christian Identity" crowd Moyers refers to here is a racist, xenophobic movement that Moyers and his ilk imagine represents the thinking of real Christians, when, in fact, they represent only a tiny minority—a perversion of Christianity.

Moyers then added some slurs against believing Jews. "Within all of the great Abrahamic traditions there is a violent tendency, a violent strain," he says.[21]

How do you deal with such nonsense, such pap, such tripe? Well, you can turn it off—which most people do, as I mentioned. Nobody takes Moyers seriously except the crowd at the *Nation*. But he still gets the free ride from the taxpayers and the big foundations. Ratings don't matter to them. They want to give us our media medicine—like it or not.

Here are the facts: Christians who believed very sincerely in the Bible—people who would, by today's standards, certainly be considered "fundamentalists" by Moyers—founded this nation, fought for its independence, wrote the greatest Constitution ever devised by men, set the wheels in motion for true self-government for the first time in history, *and* established the very institution of the free press that people like Moyers pretend to revere.

They drew their inspiration largely from the Christian and Hebrew scriptures. Some of them even wanted Hebrew to be the official language of the new nation. Most of them—from Washington to Adams to Madison—clearly believed in a quite literal interpretation of the Bible.

Were they haters? Were they Christian militia? Were they Christian Identity followers?

No, but they were revolutionaries. And if they had any notion of the way their vision of freedom had been perverted to coerce citizens to subsidize Bill Moyers's style of propaganda, they would undoubtedly be spinning in their hallowed graves.

Thankfully, however, Bill Moyers's worldview is being challenged today as never before. And it is being challenged because of new pioneers of the free press. At least some of these pioneers have a much different worldview than the one that has dominated the establishment press for a generation.

CHAPTER FIVE

A FREE PRESS FOR A FREE PEOPLE

IT'S MORE THAN WORLDNETDAILY'S SLOGAN: IT'S A GRAND TRADITION OF AMERICAN JOURNALISM

"I read the news today, oh boy..."

—John Lennon and Paul McCartney

I CHECKED OUT of the local supermarket recently wearing a *WorldNetDaily* baseball cap. The young man at the register noticed the cap and asked me about it.

"What's that, like an independent news site or something?" he asked.

"Yes," I said, somewhat surprised. "That's exactly what it is."

"Great, I'll check it out," he said. "I'm getting pretty tired of MSNBC."

Wow!

From the very beginning, the most important word in defining *WorldNetDaily* has been *independent*. Sometimes I think maybe people don't really appreciate that independence. Sometimes they seem more comfortable with the predictable labels than with the unpredictability of a truly independent news source.

So I was glad to hear the reaction from this young man who knew what he was looking for.

That's the essence of the *WorldNetDaily* difference.

I'm also pleased when I run into people like the store clerk who haven't discovered *WorldNetDaily*. There are a lot of them. I meet them everywhere. Sure, there are eight million people who read *WND* every month, but I am convinced the only reason more don't is because they haven't yet discovered it—which leaves us plenty of room for growth.

But what does it mean to be the leading independent news source on the Internet? What does that key word *independent* mean in this context? Why is it so critical to our success? And what do we mean when we characterize what we do as "fiercely independent"?

I love that word *independent*. And it has several meanings—all of which help define *WND*.

Firstly, of all the news agencies on the Net that were created specifically for the Internet, *WND* is the biggest. Oh, sure, *CNN.com* is bigger. But CNN is part of a monster, multinational, media conglomerate known as Time Warner. *CNN.com*—like *MSNBC.com, ABCNews.com, CBSNews.com,* and *FoxNews.com*—started as a television news network and added an Internet component. It used its cablecast network—and still does—to bolster the visibility of its Internet sites.

WND doesn't have a television network. Maybe it will someday. But it was started as an Internet news agency. *WND* does not have an offline newspaper associated with it. Maybe it will someday. *WND* does not have a radio network. Maybe it will someday. *WND* started on the Internet, for the Internet, with no help from media resources off the Internet.

In fact, believe it or not, *WND* started in my bedroom one evening.

I had been fooling around with the Internet, as I mentioned, since 1995—about the time I first discovered the *Drudge Report*. In the course of a week or so, several people mentioned the *Drudge Report*, persuading me to go check it out for myself.

There was some interesting content there for sure. But I sat there staring at it trying to figure out why seemingly so many people had "discovered" it and made it one of their primary stops on the Internet. It finally hit me.

What was revolutionary about this Web site was the fact that you could so quickly jump off to other news destinations and stories. Matt Drudge, the Internet pioneer I would later befriend, had inspired me. The *Drudge Report* was beautiful in its simplicity. I don't mean beautiful to look at—hardly. But what this visionary had seen before anyone else was that news judgment was not proprietary.

Matt Drudge sat there, at that time in his LA-area apartment, with his laptop computer and an Internet connection, and had at his disposal—like any of us do today—more information at his fingertips than I had years earlier as a powerful and influential member of the media elite running daily newspapers. He could quickly scan what all the major news services were reporting on a given day and bring his readers the best of it with a few clicks of the mouse.

He brought attention to the stories he thought were important—even though he didn't consider himself a newsman like I did. In a sense, he was like the person we called "the wire editor" in the old daily newsroom. He was the person who looked at what everyone else was reporting to help us make our news presentation complete the next day. Except Matt Drudge was doing it in real time—with hundreds more news sources available to him than any wire editor could ever dream.

This was a revelation to me. It was as if I had just discovered the light bulb—as if I had just found my destiny in life.

Flash back with me to 1990. There I was trying to save the *Sacramento Union*, the oldest daily in the West, from the inevitable extinction so many other number two papers had faced. During my time as editor-in-chief at that venerable institution, I traveled with my publisher, Jim Smith, to the nearby Silicon Valley to check out the new emerging technologies.

Jim Smith and I shared a dream of harnessing these new technologies and putting them to use for the profession we loved—the news business. We both saw that newspapers were dinosaurs. We loved them, but we were realistic. We had ink flowing in our veins, but we knew that technology was as old as Gutenberg. Things change, we recognized. And the news business had to change if we were to maintain any semblance of competition in our business.

And we saw something in the Silicon Valley that gave us hope.

Keep in mind, this was 1990. There was no Internet. It's hard to remember those days, even though it wasn't all that long ago. It was a different communications world altogether. An engineer by the name of Bob Evans—he would later become a key player in the life of *WND*—showed us something he invented. It was a "teletext" service that utilized unused bandwidth on television signals. All you needed was a little box you attached to your television and you could be flooded with, at that time, more news and information than anyone could imagine.

Evans had created a beta program in his own backyard in Palo Alto. He sold the boxes to customers and provided the information services for a small subscription fee.

We wondered if this could be the ticket to saving the *Sacramento Union*. Remember our problem. We had lots of demand for a fine alternative newspaper—statewide, even national demand—for what we produced. But we could not cost-effectively deliver that old-fashioned newsprint product to the many customers who wanted it.

We brainstormed over the possibilities. We researched it. And we concluded that persuading the public to buy into this new technology was probably a bigger "mission impossible" than saving the *Sacramento Union* in its then archaic form.

But these trips to Silicon Valley served a purpose for me. They convinced me—beyond any shadow of a doubt—that a new technology was coming soon that would revolutionize the news business that I loved so much.

You see, I dreamed of one day editing and operating an "electronic newspaper"—free of the constraints of newsprint and concerns about distribution.

And that was the flashback I had that first day I looked at the *Drudge Report*. Drudge had not created an electronic newspaper. But he had opened my eyes to the suddenly realistic possibilities of doing so with the new Internet technology that was rapidly catching fire. It's a good thing we didn't invest too much time and resources in that teletext experiment, because the Internet was about to arrive—just four or five years later.

When it did, I quickly began creating a Web site for my non-profit Western Journalism Center—the one with which Hillary and Bill had become so preoccupied. It wasn't an electronic newspaper yet, but it was the progenitor. Even the most dedicated Internet trivia buffs will surely be stumped to recall e-truth.com—now even difficult to find on the Wayback Machine. When you arrived at the opening page of e-truth.com, you were greeted by the following scrolling messages: "By visiting this Web site...you may be conspiring against the White House," and "Are you part of the Media Food Chain?" (a reference to Hillary's "Communication Stream of Conspiracy Commerce" report that had targeted my center for scrutiny).

You could learn all about our ongoing battle with the IRS and the White House, get a copy of the White House's "conspiracy" report, and read the latest news scoops from our very own small team of investigative reporters.

The name of the Web site was explained—because the "E" prefix had not yet become commonplace in the popular culture: "E-TRUTH: (a derivation of e-mail)—the dissemination of information, resulting from a tenacious desire to expose the truth, i.e., INVESTIGATIVE REPORTING, through an electronic medium, i.e., the INTERNET..."

Too many "i.e.'s" for me now. But that's what it said.

So, one evening I thought I would show off the e-truth site to Elizabeth on the home computer in our bedroom/office. It took an eternity to load. In fact, this was her introduction to the Internet. I think she said something in exasperation like, "Well, this will never go anywhere!"

But later it was Elizabeth, my wife and the cofounder of *WND*, who told me point-blank: "It's time for you to do what you've been dreaming about. It's time for you to invent your electronic newspaper."

In other words, *Get off your duff, Farah, take a chance, stop complaining about the media and go fix it!* She was more polite than that. But that was the essence of what she said.

So I did. I spent a few days mocking up on paper what I had been envisioning in my head for so long. I took the best of what

I had learned in all those years toiling away at newspapers—being inspired by great editors and great publishers and great reporters. There is something in *WND* that I borrowed from my experiences at the *Los Angeles Herald Examiner*. There is something I borrowed from my experiences at the *Sacramento Union*. There is something I borrowed from my experiences at other stops along the way.

I believed then and now that a great newspaper—newsprint or electronic—must have a personality of its own. And I did my best to infuse *WND* with that trait. It needed to be informative. It needed to be entertaining. It needed to be lively. It needed to be serious. And it needed to be fun.

You might also note that, more than any other Internet news source, *WND* kind of resembles a newspaper. That was intentional from day one. Not only were newspapers what I knew, but I believed that people would need to transition from the Old Media to the New Media. It made sense to me to make that transition as smooth as possible by providing something that looked familiar to them. *WND*, as much was as practical, borrowed many elements from newspapers. Many of those original transitional elements can still be found on the site today.

On May 5, 1997, the very first edition of *WorldNetDaily.com* went live. We had no way to publicize it. We had no budget for promotion. We just figured we would low-key it as we learned the ropes of this new medium. It was a historic, if inauspicious, debut.

Elizabeth and I had grand aspirations from the start. But we didn't have confidence that others would share our enthusiasm for a news service that pulled no punches, blazed new trails, recaptured the watchdog spirit of the American press, and fearlessly skewered sacred cows.

Ten years ago, my wife was the self-taught webmaster and high-tech guru and I was the editorial staff. The whole thing was cooked up nightly in our bedroom/office—mostly after we put the kids to sleep.

We started without fanfare because, truthfully, we had no idea what we were doing. Nobody had done it before. We were creating a nightly electronic newspaper every day—just the two of us.

Elizabeth and Joseph Farah, co-founders of WorldNetDaily.

In the beginning, *WorldNetDaily* was primarily a place to go to get a picture of what was going on around the world through links. We always had a few original news stories and my daily column. Occasionally Elizabeth would write a column too. She still does.

However, it didn't take long for us to see that we were on to something with the simple *WND* formula. Almost immediately, thousands of people discovered us. I don't know how, other than to say that we got a lot of help from hundreds of Internet links and talk-radio hosts from coast to coast.

In fact, we have heard from hundreds of talk-show hosts—some big names and other local radio personalities—who say *WorldNetDaily* is an essential component of their show prep.

Anyway, within a month or two, we couldn't help but notice we had thousands of people checking out *WND* every day. So it inevitably became a bigger part of our lives each and every day for the next five years.

By the summer of 1997, we were adding other original columns. Alan Keyes and the late David Hackworth were early signups. We also began running news stories by a handful of staff writers and freelancers.

I did make a phone call, though, shortly before or shortly after that first edition of *WND*. I can't remember for sure. I called Matt Drudge. I told him who I was and what I had in mind. I told him in no uncertain terms that he was my inspiration. But I also explained that we would be starting something much, much different from the *Drudge Report*.

And I asked him if I could hire him to come along for the ride.

That's right. I tried to hire Drudge. I think I offered him $50,000 a year—which was probably more than I could have afforded to pay him. All I wanted from him was a daily column for *WND* and a link to our new site from his.

My recollection is that he turned down my offer politely, but if I'm not mistaken, not without a little consideration. Remember, this is 1997! But we did agree to cooperate with one another in any way we could. And Drudge soon provided the first of what would be many permanent links to *WND*.

Without Drudge—along with dozens of radio talk-show hosts, including Rush Limbaugh, Dr. Laura, Michael Savage, and Sean Hannity—few would have discovered *WND* in those early days. *WND* also benefited immensely from its early presence on the Internet when there wasn't as much noise and competition for eyeballs. The Internet is and was a viral medium. And what *WND* did in 1997 was very new and very exciting. There just wasn't anything else like it—and there still isn't.

And that brings me to the second definition of *independent*.

WND is independent editorially. We don't tow anyone's party line. We don't even tow anyone's ideological line. We just do what I learned to do so many years ago in my years toiling in the press. We seek the truth—no matter who it benefits or who it hurts. That's our job, and we take it seriously.

I cannot overstate the importance of this independence. There are several copycats on the Internet today—other "news" sites that tried to emulate what they perceived to be the *WND* distinction. But they all failed the independence test. They all brought some political baggage with them. None of them brought with them the years of professional experience working in the Old Media world. None of them brought with them the standards and practices our staff developed from the beginning.

Those content sites imitating *WND* don't really understand what it is we do. And even if they did, they wouldn't be able to duplicate it. That's why I feel so secure telling you our industry secrets. I'd welcome others out there trying to replicate *WND*'s combination of professionalism, commitment to ethics, and independent stance. But I don't believe we will ever see it.

What we do see, instead, are ideological sites on the left and right attempting to deliver the news but failing the test because of their own biases, errors, and lack of professionalism.

Some of those who have learned the wrong lessons from *WND* are the "conservative" news sites. Those who read *WND* regularly, especially my column and my books, know I detest, abhor, reject, hate, abominate, loathe, scorn, despise, and recoil from the label "conservative."

It's not that I don't like conservatives. I really do. I love them. I just don't happen to be one of them for a variety of reasons that are very important.

First of all, I don't like labels. Back in the spring of 2005, a book came out called *South Park Conservatives*. I didn't read it, but *WorldNetDaily* was right there on the cover along with Arnold Schwarzenegger, my old friend Mickey Kaus, and other "heroes" of the New Media supposedly challenging "liberal media bias."

I can't tell you how much fun it is seeing your life's work reduced to a cartoon caricature. And what strange bedfellows! How did my news service wind up pigeonholed and stereotyped in such a way?

First of all, I have never seen the animated show *South Park*. Second of all, it would never be watched in my household. Thirdly, I consider the whole genre of coarse, vulgar cartoons anathema to our culture and think of the producers of such trash as irresponsible reprobates. Fourth, more different people tune into *WND* every month than the entire network that airs *South Park*.

But forget all that.

Let's deal with the other objectionable label—"conservative." I've said it before and I guess I have to say it again: I am not a conservative. Since I founded *WND*, it's difficult for me to understand how my creation could be so simplistically and erroneously mislabeled as conservative.

In fact, why is it that our entire national debate has to be reduced to terms like "liberal," "moderate," and "conservative"? Now, don't take offense if you proudly consider yourself a conservative, moderate, or liberal. Some of my best friends do. But I don't. In fact, I am offended when I am labeled like this. I'm offended when the fruit of my hard labors is reduced to a bumpersticker slogan. And I think it is important to raise the level of the national dialogue.

We have come to view politics in America through this prism of right versus left, conservative versus liberal, Republican versus Democrat—as if that's all there ever was, as if that's all there is, as if that's all there ever will be. It's not true.

These terms are misleading. They mean different things to different people at different times. When I hear hard-line totalitarians in China referred to as conservatives, I know I never want to be confused with them. When I hear George W. Bush call himself a compassionate conservative, I know I never want to be confused with his political philosophy. When I hear the Nazis described as right-wingers, I know I never want to be confused with them.

Frankly, if these labels represented the totality of the political spectrum, it would represent no choice at all.

I've been a newsman my whole adult life. This is what I do. Yes, I have strong personal opinions that I share freely and openly on a daily basis in *WND* and in books and a weekly syndicated column. But my main occupation has been, is, and always will be newsman.

I believe the proper role of a newsman is to seek the truth without fear or favor. Unlike many of my colleagues in the press, I have avoided political parties, organizations, and associations that could compromise my integrity.

My worldview undoubtedly shapes the way I see the world, just as the worldview of all other newsmen shapes their perceptions. But my worldview is hardly conservative.

By definition, conservatives seek to "conserve" something from the status quo. In other words, they constantly are on defense—busy holding on to turf rather than taking new ground.

That strikes me as a recipe for failure, defeat, retreat, compromise. I don't believe we live in a time for defensiveness—not for people who want to seek truth, spread justice, and expand freedom.

I'm not a conservative because I see precious little left in this world worth conserving. Playing defense, it seems to me, can only forestall an inevitable slide into tyranny. If we're not seeking truth, spreading justice, and expanding freedom, we are losing ground. There are no holding actions—not for long. My goal is to restore the dream that was America.

And that dream was, is, and always will be radical.

Was George Washington a conservative? No. He was a revolutionary. He was known throughout the world as "the father of freedom."

Today, as I pointed out in my last book, *Taking America Back*, those who stand for truth, justice, freedom, the rule of law, self-government, and the moral principles of the Bible are not part of the establishment. We're the rebels, the radicals, the revolutionaries. By the world's standards, we're the renegades.

Ten years ago, my wife Elizabeth and I founded *WorldNetDaily* with a very specific mission: "*WorldNetDaily.com* is an independent news site created to capitalize on new media technology, to reinvigorate and revitalize the role of the free press as a guardian of liberty, an exponent of truth and justice, an uncompromising disseminator of news.

"*WorldNetDaily.com* performs this function by remaining faithful to the central role of a free press in a free society: as a watchdog exposing government waste, fraud, corruption, and abuse of power—the mission envisioned by our founders and protected in the First Amendment of the Constitution."

To my knowledge, no other news agency in the world shares a similar mission—one that has been slightly revised over the years yet still retains our clear focus. If I were a conservative, I would proudly tell you. I am not. If *WND* were a conservative Web site, I would tell you and probably reap greater economic rewards as a result. But we are not.

I am not one to hide what I believe. I am not one to pull punches. I let it all hang out there for people to see. I have no reason to tell you one thing and do another. I am sincere in my efforts to explain what I see are critical shortcomings in the agenda of conservatism.

Yet with the advent of the Internet, other people get to have their say, too. And there are plenty who spend much of their time critiquing me and *WorldNetDaily*. It never fails that whenever I distance myself from conservatives, the twisted ideologues at Media Matters, founded by the ignominious David Brock, get their panties in a bunch.

One only needs to examine the mission of Media Matters and compare it with the mission of *WND*: "Media Matters for America is a Web-based, not-for-profit progressive research and information center dedicated to comprehensively monitoring, analyzing, and correcting conservative misinformation in the U.S. media. Conservative misinformation is defined as news or commentary presented in the media that is not accurate, reliable, or credible and that forwards the conservative agenda."

Which mission do you suppose serves a loftier and more meaningful purpose? Which represents a nobler endeavor? Which better serves the public? Which one seems more ideologically driven? Which one seems more obsessed and fanatical? Which one seems more one-sided and biased? Take a look at the staff bios and you will find that most have backgrounds in Democratic Party politics. They are not journalists. They are activists.

On the other hand, I have spent thirty years doing one thing—gathering the news and presenting it to people as accurately as I can. I did this for twenty years as a daily newspaperman—doing everything one can do in such an operation, from reporting to running editorial operations to serving as publisher. Then I founded *WorldNetDaily* because I saw that my colleagues had lost their way, their purpose, their sense of mission.

I'm not a conservative. I'm a newsman. I'm a news analyst.

WorldNetDaily is not conservative. It is a pioneering news agency. And, as even a cursory glance will demonstrate, it serves as a forum for a broad spectrum of opinion—even positions the ignominious David Brock and the activist staff of Media Matters might appreciate.

Why is it a big deal to me that I might be misidentified as a conservative?

Because it's not accurate. Because it's not true. And at *WorldNetDaily*, we actually value accuracy and truth.

And because, I believe, the national debate is being short-changed by reliance on these bumper-sticker labels, which are increasingly misleading and inaccurate.

There's another reason I think it's important for conservatives themselves to think about this label. Conservatives, by definition, seek to conserve something from the past—institutions, cultural mores, values, political beliefs, traditions. In other words, they are constantly on defense—busy holding on to turf rather than taking new ground.

From my experience, few conservatives have the stomach for fighting—the kind of fighting it takes to restore real freedom to America. It's not a time for timidity or compromise. It's not a time for defensiveness and conciliation. It's time to take the offensive in this struggle.

I'm not a conservative because I see precious little left in this world worth conserving. Conservatives, from my experience, do not make good freedom fighters. They seem to think a victory is holding back attacks on liberty or minimizing them. They are forever on the defensive—trying to conserve or preserve an apple that is rotten to the core.

What is the rotten apple? You can see it in the government schools that dumb down American kids. You can see it in the universities that pervert the concepts of knowledge and wisdom. You can see it in the federalization and militarization of law enforcement. You can see it in the proliferation of nonconstitutional government. You can see it in the real "trickle-down economics" of confiscatory taxes. You can see it in the unaccountable authorities that give us global treaties. You can see it in the relentless attacks on marriage and the family. You can see it in euthanasia, population control, and the phony "right" to abortion on demand. You can see it in the surrender of our national security.

Conservatives, it seems to me, only forestall the inevitable slide into tyranny. I don't want to forestall it. I want to prevent it. I want to reverse that slide. I want to restore the dream that was America.

Professor Friedrich von Hayek, author of *The Road to Serfdom*, is a hero to many conservatives. Yet he too rejected the label—not only for him, but for his mentor, professor Ludwig von Mises, as well.

"I cannot help smiling when I hear Professor Mises described as a conservative," he wrote. "Indeed, in this country and at this time, his views may appeal to people of conservative minds. But when he began advocating them, there was no conservative group which he could support. There couldn't have been anything more revolutionary, more radical, than his appeal for reliance on freedom. To me, Professor Mises is and remains, above all, a great radical, an intelligent and rational radical but, nonetheless, a radical on the right lines."[1]

I agree. That's what I want to be.

I'm concerned about the way my colleagues hurl these labels like pseudo-journalistic epithets. Whatever happened to the good old days when reporters reported?

Did those days really exist? Or are they just phantom images of a faulty memory?

Back in early 2000, there were a number of periodicals trying to figure out what *WND* was all about. Often they came to the easy and incorrect conclusion that it was conservative. One example was a generally very positive story in an online publication for journalists and publishers called *Content Exchange*.

The headline on Steve Outing's story was: "*WorldNetDaily.com*: Where Investigative Reporting Rules." I liked that.[2]

"*WorldNetDaily.com* seems to be an up-and-coming Internet news venture," he wrote. "With an average of 200,000 unique users visiting the site each day, the two-and-a-half-year-old online publication rivals some significant print publications in circulation."

It started out nice. But then the political labeling began: "What started out as a nonprofit, conservative-oriented online news and commentary enterprise in 1997 last year was spun off into a for-profit entity...." Not true. I invented *WorldNetDaily*. I should know how it started, what it is, and how it is oriented. Not only have I never used the term *conservative* to describe it, I think I have made it clear by now in this chapter that I detest the label. I reject it. I despise it. What more do I need to say?

I write a daily column for the whole world to see. My words speak for themselves. Why do others feel they must put words in my mouth and pigeonhole me with labels I don't like? I'll just never understand this practice.

When I asked Outing to correct this statement, he refused—suggesting instead that I write a letter to the editor, which he would publish. In other words, I wasn't qualified to *correct* the record about what I really believed. I was only qualified to *comment on* what I believed. "Among his favorite types of stories are those that report on corruption, abusive government, and government threats to individual liberties," Outing wrote. "(In other words, politically conservative themes.)"

Did you catch that? "Corruption, abusive government, and government threats to individual liberties" are "conservative themes." No wonder press people don't cover this stuff any more. They don't want to be labeled conservative.

When I asked Outing where he got this "conservative" notion, he said: "Well, in looking over the site I got a strong sense that it took a consistently politically conservative point of view. So then I did a Dow Jones Publication Library search and found a bunch of articles that mention you and *WorldNetDaily* from many sources. They all consistently call you a 'conservative' news site."

Unfortunately, this is how reporting works these days. But let me ask you a few questions: If every single newspaper in the world regurgitated a statement, does that make it accurate? Does it make it true? Does it make it correct? It's kind of like the question your mother used to ask you: if all your friends jumped off a bridge, would you?

I have been mislabeled a conservative so often now in print that it no longer seems to matter what I say or how I characterize myself. What I say about myself and my publication is my "opinion"—relegated to the letters to the editor section—while reporters who don't know me are free to make judgments about me and my work based on purely derivative journalism.

But remember, we're not here to dwell on the problems of the media. We're here to celebrate the birth of the New Media—to tell how it happened. We're here for a glimpse at a media revolution that is now a decade old. We're here to talk about one of the most exciting cultural developments of the last century.

And I like to think that *WorldNetDaily* is and was at the center of this revolution. I've mentioned what I believe sets us apart from the pack. It's not our political ideology. It's our journalistic creed. We still believe, like most of our colleagues once believed, that the central role of a free press in a free society is to serve as a watchdog on government.

Back in the summer of 2003, much to my surprise, the Pew Research Center for the People and the Press conducted a wide-ranging survey that found Americans support the idea of the media's role as a political watchdog.[3]

The findings were interesting. It seems Americans still believe the central role of a free press in a free society is to serve as a watchdog on government. But people in the press have lost their understanding of the mission. Just as I suspected.

The survey found Americans largely supportive of the media's role as a political watchdog. Most people—54 percent—said that by criticizing political leaders, news organizations most often prevent them from doing wrong. Just 29 percent said media criticism gets in the way of political leaders doing their jobs.

Interestingly, Republicans, who claim to support smaller government, are less likely than Democrats to support the watchdog role of the press. Back in 1999, when Democrats were running most of the federal government, they were less likely to recognize the important watchdog role of the press, according to the study.

But what about the reporters? Why don't they stick to the mission? Most reporters who cover government cover it like they would cover an old friend—or worse. The late Warren Brookes of the *Detroit News* suggested reporters who covered government had a vested interest in seeing government grow. When it grew, the reporters themselves grew in relative importance.

That is a frightening thought. Yet I think there is all too much truth in his observation.

I've said it for a long time, the answer to the institutional problems in the press is not more "fair and balanced" reporting. It's not more "conservative" media. The answer is to return journalism to its roots—to reawaken the press to its vital role in a free society.

It's time we remembered who we in the press are. We're watchdogs. Or at least we're supposed to be.

Back in May 1997 when we launched *WorldNetDaily*, there were already millions of Web sites around.

I wasn't sure how we would distinguish this new effort amid all the clatter. We didn't have money to promote the site, brand the name, or advertise our slogans. So we just did our best to produce a high-quality electronic news service with a unique mission—to serve as a true watchdog on government.

The rest, as they say, is history.

Of course there are tens of millions of other Web sites that have come online since 1997, but *WorldNetDaily*'s growth has continued—even while many other similar endeavors, some with far more investor support and others with far more existing media resources, failed.

WorldNetDaily really is different. It has a different mission—a clear and focused one. It employs professional, seasoned reporters and editors who actually think differently than those in other news organizations. Our people believe in doing New Media journalism the old-fashioned way—exposing waste, fraud, abuse, and corruption wherever we find it.

And that difference is being recognized in the marketplace—and rewarded with higher and higher traffic.

We see journalism as a search for the truth. That sounds simple—maybe even trite. But sadly, that's not the way it is practiced in America anymore—with a few exceptions.

Too often, the highest ideal in the American press today is for "fairness" and "balance." Is there a difference between "truth" and "balance"? You bet there is.

Remember Iraqi information minister Mohammed Saeed al-Sahhaf? His impromptu press conferences at the beginning of the Iraq war were a sight to behold. They offered up some real comic relief during the tense moments of the war in Iraq.

He was the Iraqi flack who contended with a straight face that U.S. forces were committing suicide at the walls of Baghdad, while coalition tanks were actually seen roaring past him. He asserted that no U.S. forces were in Saddam International Airport even after it had been secured by troops. He warned us of a big "unconventional" surprise that never came.

But there's a serious lesson in his bizarre assertions. Those kind of wild, baseless claims are not unusual in the Middle East.

In fact, they are the norm for Arab officials and spokesmen in times of crisis.

In the 1967 Six-Day War, Syrian officials claimed they had shot down most of the Israeli air force, when in fact they hadn't destroyed a single plane. Egyptian strongman Gamal abdel-Nasser told his people of great advances his troops were making in that conflict, even while they were running for their lives.

The Middle East is a region known for exaggeration, wild claims, myth-making, and bald-faced lies. It's part of the landscape, part of the culture, part of the fabric of life.

But in a world where "fairness" and "balance" are the highest ideals, those claims get equal treatment with accurate descriptions and depictions of real-world events. In other words, outrageous, laughable claims are taken seriously.

This is where modern American journalism is making a grave mistake—a potentially fatal error that is turning much of the media into an irrelevancy, a bad joke.

They say the hardest lie to overcome is the biggest one. Hitler and Goebbels knew it. And the modern tyrants and propaganda artists of the Middle East know it.

It's time for American journalism to return to its roots, its foundations, its principles. It's time, once again, to start seeking the truth.

Is the world a better place because of the media competition created by *WorldNetDaily*? Is America a better country because of the competition we have introduced? Does anyone really think we would all be better off with fewer media choices?

We have helped introduce a more lively and vigorous debate in the world. We were able to do it because people recognized what we had to offer was truly different.

We've come a long way since then. We've got a bigger staff. We have more original content. We have launched a half-dozen *WND* columnists into national syndication—including Bill O'Reilly, David Limbaugh, and myself. We now maintain a twenty-four-hour, seven-day-a-week Internet news site that literally millions depend upon as their main source of news.

From those humble beginnings in 1997, here are some of our accomplishments:

- *WorldNetDaily* was voted the most popular Web site in the world for nearly a hundred weeks in a row;

- *WorldNetDaily* is consistently ranked as the "stickiest" news site on the Internet—meaning readers average more time on it than any other;

- *WorldNetDaily* draws around five million "unique visitors" (meaning different people) every month;

- *WorldNetDaily* attracts between fifty million and sixty million page views per month;

- *WorldNetDaily* is consistently ranked first among all news sites in page views per visitor;

- *WorldNetDaily* is the leading independent news site on the Internet—meaning it's number one among all news agencies specifically created for the Net;

- *WorldNetDaily* became the first content site on the Internet to launch its own book publishing imprint—WND Books; and

- *WorldNetDaily* was the first Internet company to produce number one *New York Times* bestsellers.

Today, of course, *WorldNetDaily* is leading the information revolution. I don't think I exaggerate when I say this. It is read in two hundred nations around the world daily. It is read by the most influential newsmakers and by those in the media who report on them. But it is also the primary source of news for a growing number of regular people, particularly in the United States.

O'Reilly was an interesting story in our history. Though he is no longer a columnist for *WorldNetDaily,* having decided a few years ago to start his own Web site, our relationship with him is illustrative of the power of the New Media.

In the summer of 2000, O'Reilly's Fox News show was quickly gaining popularity. But it was not yet number one. He had not yet written his first nonfiction book. And he had not yet begun writing his weekly column for *WND*.

I didn't know O'Reilly, but I was intrigued with him. On a whim, I called his office and made an appointment to see him in New York. We compared notes. He was immediately attracted to the fact that we were so independent—and that we used that word to market *WND*.

"I'm independent too," he said.

In our first meeting, Elizabeth and I asked him what his personal goals were.

"I want my show to be the number one cable show," he said. "I want to write a bestselling book. And I want to launch a nationally syndicated newspaper column."

Just like that. Say what you will about O'Reilly, he knew what he wanted. He had goals. I suggested to him that a partnership with *WorldNetDaily* could help him achieve those goals. He agreed. It was that simple.

By the time his column debuted in September, I had already locked up an agreement for it to be syndicated nationally, which it is to this day. When his first book came out later that fall, it quickly shot to number one, thanks in part to tremendous promotions on *WND*, which alone sold some twenty-five thousand copies. And O'Reilly's TV show was a beneficiary of the synergy, too. Within a few weeks of launching his column on *WND*, O'Reilly had achieved all three of his goals.

I didn't have to remind him. He reminded me. He thanked me profusely.

I tell you this story to illustrate the power of the New Media—not to glorify my own work. I don't want to sound overly spiritual here, but let me risk it. Ultimately, I believe *WND* succeeded—and continues to succeed today—not because I'm so smart, but because we've been blessed by God with a clear vision—and he's had his hand on us ever since, guiding us, bailing us out of troubles we couldn't foresee, and keeping us alive and growing when the whole Internet world was turned upside down.

I like to think that the unusual set of experiences I had in the news media was no coincidence. I like to think that God had prepared me for a specific mission. I like to think that mission is realized—at least partially—in *WorldNetDaily*.

There's no question about it. We were in the right place at the right time.

WorldNetDaily still may not be a household word in most homes in America. It may not be uttered by the media elite as often as the *Drudge Report*. But its exploding audience makes it virtually incomparable—unparalleled. For hundreds of thousands of Americans and people living in about 185 foreign nations, *WorldNetDaily* is the standard by which news is now measured.

What makes them come? It's not bells and whistles. It's not a slick, multi-million-dollar marketing campaign. No. It's content. *WorldNetDaily* is substantively different from any other news enterprise on the planet.

The biggest difference is our commitment to traditional principles of American journalism. Even though we work in the New Media, we do journalism the old-fashioned way—we work hard and get our hands dirty. We make the extra phone call. We do the primary research. And we focus our efforts on performing the long-forgotten central role of a free press in a free society—to serve as a watchdog on government.

Exposing government fraud and waste is our bread, and laying bare official corruption and abuse is our butter. This is the way it used to be at American newspapers. This is the way it is supposed to be at American newspapers. This is not the way it is today at American newspapers.

People apparently appreciate our unique commitment to this simple mission. They like the fact that we skewer the sacred cows of the corporate-establishment-government-media complex. This is a commodity they can't get anywhere else. *WorldNetDaily* is, thus, habit-forming.

They come from the left and the right and the center—all skeptical of what the experts in big government and big business have in mind for them. *WorldNetDaily* is the meeting place for establishment media refugees who flock to cyberspace seeking truth like boat people fleeing some God-forsaken, tyrannical hell-hole in search of freedom.

Meanwhile, as our boat rises, the aircraft carrier representing the Old Media is listing.

The dinosaur media started to get the picture around 2001. In August of that year, the Associated Press Managing Editors, the Pew Center for Civic Journalism, and the National Conference of Editorial Writers released the results of a study they commissioned titled, "New Attitudes, Tools, and Techniques Change Journalism's Landscapes."

Here were the big conclusions:

Nine out of ten editors believed the future health of the newspaper industry depends on more interactivity with readers;

A majority of the editors admitted they were spending less time focused on what was once American journalism's primary role—covering government; and

Few in charge of the newsrooms viewed their role as simply disseminators of facts.

Back in the good old days of the Old Media, newspaper editors didn't rely on focus groups, public opinion surveys, and pseudo-scientific studies to determine what they should be doing with their time and what it was the public wanted. They knew what they were supposed to do and assumed there would be a market for it.

Those were the days when journalists understood intuitively that the central role of a free press in a free society is to serve as a watchdog on government. Oh, sure, newspapers always did other things—publish wedding announcements, run classified ads, watch the police blotter. But believe it or not, my friends, I remember the day—not that long ago—when my colleagues would agree that the main function of a free press is to expose government fraud, waste, abuse, and corruption.

That is no longer the case. And this study documents just how far the press has fallen and how fast and how my colleagues have lost their moorings.

Want to know what newspaper editors now think their number one role is?

In the study, ranked far and above all other job descriptions was the role of "news explainer." Do you believe that? In other words, newspaper editors don't think their job is to report the news. They believe their job is to explain it to their stupid readers.

Here are some other ideas they have about the role of the press. Some suggested that the newspaper should be a "catalyst for community conversation" or a "community steward." More editors believed in those values than in the "investigative watch-dog" role.

In fact, only 16 percent of the editors even cited the "watch-dog" role.

"Unprompted answers that could be grouped under the rubric of 'opinion leader and agenda setter' topped the list along with those grouped under the general category of 'community leader or good corporate citizen,'" explained the study.

Why am I not surprised that Old Media newspeople see themselves as "agenda setters" and "opinion leaders"?

The editors also mentioned they are spending more time covering issues such as health care, personal fitness, personal finance, the environment, diversity, and lifestyle than they are covering government.

Here are some sample quotes from the editors:

"The newspaper should help set the agenda and be an agent for positive change."

"The newspaper is an emotional, not an informational, experience."

"We should help build community by making people feel connected and by providing editorial and news leadership on important community lines."[4]

Gobbledygook. Psychobabble. New Age newspeak. This is why the Old Media are losing their grip. This is why circulation at daily newspapers has plummeted at the rate of between 0.5 and 1 percent every year for the last decade, with no signs of rebounding or even leveling off.

But it's good news for *WorldNetDaily* and the New Media. The field is wide open for competition now. The Old Guard still doesn't even see what's coming for them.

Contrast the meaninglessness of what those newspapers say about their role with our cohesive, succinct, and precise mission statement here at *WorldNetDaily*: "*WorldNetDaily.com*, Inc. is an independent news company dedicated to uncompromising journalism, seeking truth and justice, and revitalizing the role of the free press as a guardian of liberty. We remain faithful to the traditional and central role of a free press in a free society—as a light exposing wrongdoing, corruption, and abuse of power.

"We also seek to stimulate a free and open debate about the great moral and political ideas facing the world and to promote freedom and self-government by encouraging personal virtue and good character."

Which vision better suits your needs?

CHAPTER SIX

HOW WATERGATE INSPIRED ME

*"Were it left to me to decide whether we should have a government
without newspapers, or newspapers without a government,
I should not hesitate a moment to prefer the latter."*

—Thomas Jefferson

SOME PEOPLE just know what they want to do with their lives from the time they are little kids.

I was one of those people.

That doesn't mean I knew I wanted to start the biggest independent Internet news company. It doesn't mean I knew I wanted to be a media revolutionary, an entrepreneur, or an Internet pioneer. What it means is I knew I wanted to work with words.

I even knew I wanted to work in the print medium, because print is the basis of all serious communication. Not only was I fascinated with expressing myself in words, I also loved the idea of printing. I bought mimeograph machines and printed my own "underground" newspapers. I wrote short stories—not for class projects, but for fun. Even when I was eight or nine years old, I dreamed about working in a print shop. There was just something about the process that intrigued me. You might say I had printer's ink in my blood.

Well, I may not get to work much with ink anymore, but I do get to work with words. And I had plenty of experience with ink.

I may not believe in evolution, but I do believe in adaptation. I do believe you need to learn from your mistakes—and can. I do believe in change.

I am living proof that people can change—and change dramatically.

When I was in high school, the Vietnam War was raging—not only in the jungles of Southeast Asia, but in the streets of America. Like so many young people my age, facing the possibility of being drafted into the military and being shipped off to fight a war we thought—wrongly—was immoral, I got caught up in this movement.

People who know me understand I seldom do things halfway. And my activism against the war and for the causes of left-wing radical extremism in general was no exception.

Let me give you an example. The date was May 1, 1971; the location, Washington, D.C. The circumstances surrounded a massive act of antiwar civil disobedience. In my misguided youth, I was convinced the Viet Cong were the good guys and the U.S. soldiers fighting Communism were on the side of evil.

In an effort to "bring the war home," my companions and I overturned cars, set bonfires in the streets of the nation's capital, and generally created a nuisance intended to "shut the government down."

Somewhere in Dupont Circle, the law caught up with me. I was locked up on a charge of disorderly conduct along with thousands of other miscreants, first in a prison yard and later in a juvenile cell. I was sixteen years old.

For the record, I still think the Vietnam War was a huge mistake for the United States, but for entirely different reasons. My gripe now is that the politicians in Washington had no intention of allowing our troops on the ground to win the war and liberate Vietnam from the oppression under which it still lives today.

Back then, the thought never occurred to me that the good guys could really be the bad guys and vice versa. I did my time for the crime. I spent three days incarcerated. Later, I was told by the court that there would be no record of my arrest—even though, in my case, it was a righteous bust.

What had happened will sound all too familiar to Americans today. The American Civil Liberties Union sued the U.S. government over the mass arrest totaling about eighteen thousand in the streets of the Capitol over a three-day period. The ACLU demanded successfully that none of the thousands of arrests made during the May Day demonstrations of 1971 would be part of the criminal records of the participants.

In fact, many of the adult rioters actually got monetary settlements from the lawsuit.

What a country!

How radical was I back then?

The older I get, the more I realize how little I knew when I was young.

To put it in perspective, I thought John Kerry was a hero.

Thank goodness I grew up. The amazing thing is he didn't. He hasn't learned a bloody thing since 1971 when he brought shame on himself by trying to bring it on America and the men still fighting in Vietnam.

I once thought Jimmy Carter would be a good president. I was so fooled I voted for him twice—even though he had practically ruined the country in his first four years in office.

I once feared Ronald Reagan. Today I can't imagine any sensible person, any moral person, fearing this gentle human being who only tried to stand up for what's right—the greatest president of my lifetime.

I once voted for George McGovern. That's how crazy I was. What's worse is I didn't think his ideas were radical enough. I was a walking, talking argument against allowing eighteen-year-olds to vote.

I once believed that socialism was a humane and just economic system. The fact that it killed hundreds of millions of people only meant it wasn't being practiced by the right people.

I once thought America's founders were just a bunch of dead, white slave owners. That's what I was taught.

I once believed America was relatively safe from attack by foreign enemies. What a dope!

I once seriously considered the idea that Israel was the cause of unrest in the Middle East, dismissing the wars that ravaged the region before Israel came into existence in 1948 and the fact that the bloodiest wars fought in the region since have had nothing to do with the Jewish state.

I once thought that poverty caused crime. Only later did I learn that during the Great Depression, the crime rate actually dropped.

I once actually bought into the lie that there was no basic difference between men and women—that it was all just a matter of societal conditioning.

I once thought the Bible was great literature—and only great literature. I didn't know it was also the best history book ever written, the best science book ever written, the best law book ever written and, most importantly, an actual love letter from the One True Living God.

I once thought God was too big and too impersonal to care about me and you. I've learned that's just not true.

I once thought I had all the answers. Only now am I beginning to ask the right questions.

I was so radical in my high school years—and our country's cultural and academic establishment had degenerated so far by the early 1970s—that I was actually recruited by some of the most prestigious colleges and universities *because* of my political activism. But I was such a rebel; I saw this effort as some kind of seduction into the world of the establishment. It would not be for me. I chose to attend a state commuter school with what Marx would call "the *lumpenproletariat*."

This proved to be the right choice for a guy whose only real passionate interest was in politics and writing.

In my freshman year in college, the Watergate scandal was breaking wide open. I was so fascinated by the intricacies of the story unfolding before the nation's eyes that I decided to take a leave of absence from school, get a part-time job, and set myself in front of a television so I could watch every minute of the Senate Watergate hearings.

We were watching a U.S. president go down in flames. And it did not elude my attention that a pair of lowly *Washington Post* reporters—Bob Woodward and Carl Bernstein—had started the ball rolling with their investigative reports.

This was the job for me!

Again, I was hardly alone in this epiphany. If you look at graphs of enrollments in journalism schools, you see a major upward surge coinciding with the Watergate scandal. Every long-haired, idealistic punk who wanted to "change the world" had the same idea. They would do it through journalism.

When people ask me why the old-establishment, dinosaur media are so biased, this is the number one reason. It's the people in the newsroom. It's about their motivations for being there in the first place. People attracted to the profession of journalism tend to be people who want to change the world by changing people's perceptions of the world in which they live.

That was how I, too, got started. I admit it. Most of my colleagues won't. I will leave it to you to judge who is more honest.

The real clincher for me, of course, was seeing the movie, *All the President's Men*, Woodward and Bernstein's book adapted for the big screen—starring Robert Redford and Dustin Hoffman. If I ever had any doubts about what I was going to do with my life— which I didn't, they were dispelled with the Hollywood portrayal of the two hero reporters, risking life and limb to tell the whole, sordid truth about their government.

I took what I learned about investigative reporting—the inspiration from the popular culture and the technique from the classroom—and put it to use first right in my own college. When I became editor of the William Paterson College weekly, the *Beacon*, we had our own little Watergate.

First, we investigated the college president's inclination to over-enroll the school as a way of increasing his budget. Then we made a discovery so shocking (I hope), so unusual (I think), that publication of the story resulted in his immediate resignation.

What was the shocker?

I got a tip that the president was actually serving as president of another college in another state—double-dipping with two full-time jobs hundreds of miles apart. How he got away with it even for a few months is beyond me. But he did.

I remember picking up the phone a few hours before putting the story to bed, dialing the number for the president's office at this faraway school and hearing them announce his name.

This was one for the books!

When you break a story like that, no matter what the venue—big-city daily, worldwide Internet audience, local weekly or college paper—there is a sense of immense satisfaction that is hard to describe. I wanted that feeling—again and again and again.

And I got it—in all those venues.

Even while working at the college paper, I landed a part-time job at a local daily newspaper. During the day, I would prowl around campus for stories. At night, I would prowl around various city council and school board meetings looking for my next Watergate.

Woodward and Bernstein weren't my only heroes back then. This may come as a shock to some of you, but I actually came of age idolizing Dan Rather.

In 1973, he stood up to Richard Nixon and asked tough questions in a press conference when the Watergate scandal was unfolding. Nixon tried to deflect the query by saying: "Are you running for something?"

Rather's brilliant retort: "No, Mr. President, are you?"

This is when Rather was the White House correspondent for CBS. He had not yet ascended to the anchor job, where he would soon displace Walter Cronkite. This was the kind of reporter I wanted to be at the age of nineteen. I read Rather's book. And I set out to be a courageous investigative reporter.

But there was a problem.

To do this kind of work honestly, you've got to be tough on all politicians—left, right, Democrat, Republican. And I soon learned that my hero—Dan Rather—was one of those journalists who, for whatever reason, was only tough on Republicans. In other words, he had a political ax to grind. It was true of "Woodstein," as Ben Bradlee referred to his Watergate dynamic duo, too.

It certainly wasn't a bad thing to want to hold government accountable. It certainly wasn't a bad thing for reporters to go toe to toe with the most powerful man in the world and not blink. It certainly wasn't a bad thing that reporters were skeptical about those in high places back in the early 1970s.

The problem was that many of those reporters would let down their guard when a new regime from a different political party took power.

Rather, it turned out, was a partisan political activist—not a journalist. It's what we will always remember about Rather. It would be his undoing. Later, the aging network news anchor would end his multi-generational career with a bang—by claiming to have in his hands smoking-gun documents that proved President George Bush didn't fulfill his National Guard duty thirty years earlier.

Rather made the mistake of accepting at face value bogus documents from an anonymous source and peddling them like they were the Dead Sea Scrolls. But then he made an ever bigger mistake—one that allowed him to get caught.

He permitted those papers to be posted on the network's Web site, where they could be inspected by three hundred million Americans far more discerning than Rather and his producers.

They looked bogus. They smelled bogus. And within hours, experts and amateur sleuths on the Internet—with far fewer resources than Rather's fact-checking staff—were poking holes in them. Big holes. Monster holes.

Rather was exposed as a fraud—at least to any discerning American who cared to examine the facts rationally. Like Cronkite before him, he'd always been a fraud. He had no integrity. He was a partisan shill. And I'll prove it to you.

Do you remember him cooing with Bill and Hillary Clinton in those love fests that passed for interviews during eight years of that regime? It was sickening. He was a sycophant. He loved them, and it showed.

Several years ago, Rather spoke at a fund-raiser for the Texas Democratic Party. A fund-raiser!

He later apologized and said it was the biggest mistake he ever made in his career. But what Rather really meant was that getting caught was the biggest mistake he ever made.

He's been doing the partisan work of Democrats ever since he's been in the business. The only time he was honest about it was when he spoke to that fund-raiser.

This was no mistake. You can't tell me that after thirty-five years in the business, Dan Rather just forgot that newsmen weren't supposed to dabble in partisan politics. He thought he could get away with it. He thought he was bigger than life. He thought the rules that applied to mere mortal journalists no longer applied to him.

When challenged about this partisanship, Rather denied it. And he offered as proof his opposition to President Lyndon Johnson's conduct of the Vietnam War.

Well, Dan, I've got news for you. Lots of other Democrats objected to Johnson's conduct of the war, too.

Maybe you're saying, *Well, what about you, Farah? You idolized Rather and chose to go into journalism with the same motivations as your colleagues. What made you different?*

It turns out that what I really loved about Watergate was the fact that we lived in a country in which the most powerful man in the world could be dethroned by two lowly reporters. I don't want to debate the ethics of Woodward and Bernstein here. I don't want to debate whether they, too, along with their newspaper, had axes to grind. It's beside the point, really.

Ultimately, what I took away from Watergate was healthy. And I have tried to apply that ideal throughout my news career. President Nixon was corrupt. Whether he was the most corrupt president of our time is beside the point, too. I personally would make the case that dishonor belonged to William Jefferson Clinton. But the idea of holding presidents and other politicians accountable is a high American ideal. It's like I say over and over again, the central role of a free press in a free society is to serve as a watchdog on government.

But there's a danger in having such an attitude today—even in the media. If you do, many people will confuse what you do with some kind of political agenda. It's why *WorldNetDaily* is often pigeonholed as a conservative news outlet.

The truth is, we're just doing our jobs—as real journalists. This is the way newspeople are supposed to act. We're supposed to be skeptical of government—maybe even cynical.

We are supposed to root out government fraud, waste, abuse, and corruption at every turn.

That's what we do at *WorldNetDaily.com*. That's our philosophy. That's our credo. That's our mission. We specialize in exposing government fraud, waste, abuse, and corruption wherever we find it and whomever is responsible for it.

This simple formula—a basic assumption of the American journalistic tradition for two hundred years—taken to the New Media a decade ago has resulted in an unparalleled commercial and popular success.

How is this possible? How could such a simple idea resonate to such an extent?

It's only possible because the old media—the corporate-statist-dominated government-media complex—has lost its way.

These folks literally do not even remember why they are in the news business. They have no sense of mission. And it shows all over their work.

But I'm here to tell you that one of the main reasons the federal government has been getting bigger and bigger is because of the propaganda dished out by the Old Media.

Think about it. When you read the front page of the *New York Times* or listen to Katie Couric or one of the other celebrity talking heads, think about how they present the news. Usually the formula is something like this: They present a problem—real or imagined. They hype it into a crisis. And then they offer an implied solution—almost always a government solution—higher taxes, more regulation, more freedom-restricting legislation.

That's the formula for news in the Old Media today. And while it has been successful at helping the state grab power, it is turning people off in bigger numbers all the time. People are hungry for real alternatives because they sense they are being manipulated.

They respond very enthusiastically to the truth.

CHAPTER SEVEN

STORMING THE TEMPLE

THE HUMBLE BGINNINGS OF A NEW KIND
OF NEWS ORGANIZATION

*"Nothing could be more irrational than to give the people power,
and to withhold from them information without which power is abused.
A people who mean to be their own governors must arm
themselves with power which knowledge gives."*

—President James Madison, "Notes on Virginia"

TECHNOLOGY can enslave us or help us find our way back to freedom.

Just as the printing press represented a boon to the dissemination and accumulation of popular information and real knowledge, the New Media can create a similar—even greater—knowledge explosion.

I remember that feeling I had when I sat in my office presiding over the editorial departments of newspapers in the 1980s and 1990s. It was a feeling of being plugged in—really having a handle on what was going on in the world.

I got that feeling—and I'm sure many other old-time newspaper editors can relate—because I had at my disposal lots of information. It came in the form of the Associated Press wire and other supplemental news services like the *New York Times*. Of course, we had our own staff reporters, bureaus, freelancers, and other sources of information to add to the sense of being on top of things.

Here's how much our world has changed since then. Today, anyone with a computer and an Internet connection has at his fingertips more information than I had back then, more than the editor of the *New York Times* had back then. In fact, if you're online today, you have exponentially more information than they had back then—and just as much as they have now.

The Internet is the great equalizer when it comes to communications and knowledge.

Let's face it. It's hard to even remember how we did research before the Net. It often meant going to a library and wading through reference books—many of which can be found today with a click of the mouse.

I toiled in the world of big-league journalism for nearly thirty years. I have run daily newspapers in major markets. I have been an investigative reporter. I have taught journalism in major universities.

With all that experience, I thought I had seen it all as far as the news business is concerned—until, that is, I founded the most successful and largest independent news service on the Internet.

Empires don't die easily. It will be a while before we see new institutions like *WorldNetDaily* take on the stature and influence of their predecessors. But if you look carefully, you can see the cracks appearing in the walls. The dam has been breached.

Remember how Bill and Hillary Clinton tried to demonize the work of a few determined reporters by creating the myth of an elaborate conspiracy in which stories were created, bounced around the Internet, found their way into a few newspapers, then forced their way into the mainstream?

It didn't take long for the so-called "mainstream media" to adapt this conspiracy theory as their own when they found themselves getting clobbered and scooped by those of us storming their holy temples of news-gathering. Who could blame them? There had to be some excuse for small groups of ragtag media entrepreneurs beating up on the Goliaths of the corporate media.

Let's take a case study.

On February 27, 2000, the *Washington Post* magazine published a column by Mar Fisher headlined "When Barbarella Met Jesus."

I'll pick up the story about actress Jane Fonda where it gets interesting.

"Not only has Fonda split up with Ted Turner, but she has supposedly, reportedly, perhaps, or maybe definitely found Jesus," Fisher writes. "The couple's separation was 'prompted in part by Fonda's stunning embrace of born-again evangelical Christianity,' said the story on *WorldNetDaily.com*. This is one of those Internet specials, a report that originated on a wacky Web site and found its way onto page one of the *Washington Times* before flying all over the infotainment universe."

Notice the way we are disparaged for breaking news. How dare we! This is the exclusive purview of the professional media class—the people who work inside the newsrooms of the corporate media elite.

When we broke news that had to be reported later by the establishment media, they made it look like some kind of a fluke.

Remember, this is coming in 2000. This is long after "one of those Internet specials"—in the form of the *Drudge Report*—got the president of the United States impeached. And this is before the advent of the blogging revolution that empowered everyone with a computer and Internet connection to become citizen journalists.

Notice also that writing well after the initial reports in *WND*, the *Washington Post* columnist did not challenge any of the facts of the story. He just challenged the integrity of those who delivered it—without so much as providing a single reason to do so.

Wacky Web site?

What was wacky about it? He didn't offer. Maybe he didn't like the color scheme? Who knows?

Just like the conspiracy theory woven by the Clintons years earlier, the conspiracy theories woven by the establishment media in covering up their own incompetence, laziness, and the successes of their new competitors were often based on errors, misstatements, and exaggerations.

The story of Jane Fonda's "conversion" was indeed broken in *WorldNetDaily*. It was then immediately picked up by the Associated Press, the largest newsgathering organization in the world, which disseminated the story to hundreds of news outlets throughout the world. Only then did the *Washington Times* follow up with a front-page story.

Here's where we go next. Fisher asks why Jane Fonda still raises such passions. And he accurately quotes me with the answer: "'It has something to do with her always seeming driven by her emotions,' suggests Joseph Farah, the online reporter who broke the conversion story. 'She always seems to be in the center of things: Hollywood star, Vietnam protester, wife of Tom Hayden, positioning herself to be at his side if he got to the White House. And you can't underestimate the impact of seeing her sitting on that anti-aircraft gun. She's looking through the sights and she's laughing. Vets can't get past that.'"

An accurate quote. That's what I said. But from there, the *Washington Post* magazine veers off into the realm of psychoanalysis—of me! He concludes, amazingly, that that my criticism of Fonda is based not on her betrayal of the U.S. and American prisoners of war but, rather, on some imaginary, deep-seated, spurned "love."

"Well, fine, I said to Joe, but I think there's something else going on here," Fisher writes. "The guys—and it is overwhelmingly men who populate the hate-Jane Web sites ('I'm not Fonda Jane') and talk shows—work so hard to keep up their antipathy toward Fonda because once upon a time, they fell for her. I don't want to say that Farah bought my theory immediately, but suffice it to say that before I'd finished that sentence, he interrupted: 'For me, it was Barbarella.'"

Here's the problem: the reporter never even asked me that question. He never said anything like that at all. He flat-out made it up for his column. I wouldn't even know what he was talking about had he asked me anything like that question. What anti-Jane Web sites? I've never heard of such a thing. And I never said I hated Jane. And I certainly never had to work at maintaining any antipathy toward her.

Now get this from Marc Fisher: "Farah was a teenager when he went for Fonda," Fisher writes. "Spurned love, even from a celebrity a guy has never actually seen in person, tends to flip people out. Add the emotional wallop of Vietnam, and Fonda's power starts to come into focus."

Why is this so outrageous? Because it is a complete fabrication. Even though this "journalist" had interviewed me, he made up "facts" to help him make his case.

Had Fisher asked me if I ever met Jane Fonda, he would have found out that I surely did. Not only did I meet her, I actually served as one of her bodyguards during her "Indochina Peace Campaign" swing through the Northeast in 1972. I'm not proud of that fact. But it is the truth.

While the big media continue to pummel the New Media for not getting the story straight, it is my humble observation that the Old Media is getting it increasingly wrong.

Sometimes it's palpable and the motivations for the distortion are obvious. And, again, let's use the Jane Fonda story as an illustration.

Before Fisher and the *Washington Post* had their say, the *Washington Times* spun its own version of the story first broken by *WND*.

"News of her conversion…leaped from Internet gossip to mainstream newspapers following the disclosure last week that she and her husband, Ted Turner, have separated," reported Robert Stacy McCain of the *Washington Times*.[1]

Internet gossip? Do you see the way the establishment press likes to make those little digs at the new kids on the block? Have you ever known *WorldNetDaily* to disseminate Internet gossip? If anything, *WND* has been known for hoax-busting on the Internet. But this is the way the Old Media try to put themselves on a higher plateau than us—even when they are making excuses for not having a story first.

For the record, *WorldNetDaily* is not, never has been, and never will be in the Internet gossip business. We reported the Fonda story factually and none of the details of the story have been questioned or refuted in any way. In fact, it took weeks or months before any other original reporting by anyone else had increased our understanding of the actress's spiritual experience.

But here's the point. I started *WorldNetDaily* as a responsible Internet news service with journalistic standards every bit as high as those at the *Washington Times*. Higher, I would say. *WorldNet-*

Daily is owned, mostly, by a lifelong journalist—one who has done everything you can do in the news business, from reporting to editing to directing the news operation to publishing. The *Washington Times*, need I remind, is owned by the Rev. Sun Myung Moon, a cult leader who declared himself the messiah in my presence in Seoul, South Korea, in 1992.

Which foundation would you say is stronger and more credible? How is it that my work as a journalist is judged by newspeople employed for a cult?

I'm not just picking on the *Washington Times* here. I could ask the same questions of those who work for the multinational corporations that produce much of the news in this country. Why are they credible? What do they do that makes them credible? How have they earned their credibility? What have any of them done in the news business that I haven't done—or that others at *WND* haven't done?

I spent decades in the newspaper business, and ran daily newspapers in major markets for much of that time. I have testified in major First Amendment trials as an expert in newspaper standards and practices. I have taught journalism at the university level. I have written for the *Los Angeles Times*, *Wall Street Journal*, *San Francisco Chronicle*, the *Jerusalem Post*, and dozens of other major establishment newspapers. So one must wonder why suddenly, when I began to devote my energies to Internet journalism, that what I did would no longer be taken seriously by elitists trapped in the Old Media world.

Answer? One word: jealousy.

Your consumer choice for news basically comes down to an independent New Media outlet such as *WorldNetDaily* or the Monopoly News Network—a corporate-establishment hybrid of highly filtered, slickly managed, tightly controlled information.

Take your pick. It's that simple.

I really don't like to criticize the work of my colleagues in the press. I prefer to do the job better. There are plenty of media critics around. What *WND* has done, uniquely, is to do their job better and let the results speak for themselves. It's a powerful weapon against "media bias."

Let me give you a more recent example—a small one, but illustrative of how *WND* performs this unique service.

Here's the way CNN, the number one Internet news service in the world, covered a poll on Iraqi public opinion September 27, 2006, under the headline "Poll: Most Iraqis favor U.S. pullout in a year":

> Seventy-one percent of Iraqis responding to a new survey favor a commitment by U.S.-led forces in Iraq to withdraw in a year.
>
> The majority of respondents to the University of Maryland poll said that "they would like the Iraqi government to ask for U.S.-led forces to be withdrawn from Iraq within a year or less," according to the survey's summary.
>
> Given four options, 37 percent take the position that they would like U.S.-led forces withdrawn "within six months," while another 34 percent opt for "gradually withdraw(ing) U.S.-led forces according to a one-year timeline." (Watch why one analyst says U.S. strategy is flawed—1:45.)
>
> Twenty percent favor a two-year timeline and just 9 percent favor "only reduc(ing) U.S.-led forces as the security situation improves in Iraq."
>
> The month's poll came in the midst of a turbulent year marked by increased Sunni-Shiite sectarian violence in Baghdad and elsewhere in the nation.
>
> A U.S. commander said Wednesday that suicide attacks in Iraq are rising as the Islamic holy month of Ramadan gets under way.
>
> The poll's summary also suggests that most Iraqis think the American presence is doing more harm than good.
>
> "An overwhelming majority believes that the U.S. military presence in Iraq is provoking more conflict than it is preventing and there is growing confidence in the Iraqi army," the summary said. If the U.S. made a commitment to withdraw, a majority believes that this would strengthen the Iraqi government.
>
> Support for attacks on U.S.-led forces has grown to a majority position—now 6 in 10. Support appears to be related to a widespread perception, held by all ethnic groups, that the U.S. government plans to have permanent military bases in Iraq.

The WorldPublicOpinion.org poll was conducted September 1–4 by the Program on International Policy Attitudes at the University of Maryland. It was fielded by KA Research Ltd./D3 Systems Inc. Questions were asked of a nationwide representative sample of 1,150 Iraqi adults.

The poll comes as lawmakers in Washington wrangle over a bleak National Intelligence Estimate that concludes the Iraq war has become a "cause célèbre" for jihadists, who are growing in number and geographic reach.

The intelligence analysts who authored the report said the Iraq insurgency against U.S.-led forces was an "underlying factor" fueling the spread of Islamic radicalism.

That's the report—in its entirety. It certainly sounded like bad news for the United States and its military coalition partners in Iraq. But what the report didn't tell you was, perhaps, just as important as what it did tell us.

Here, for the purposes of contrast, is the *WND* report—same day—on the very same poll, under a much different headline, "Bin Laden loses Iraqi hearts, minds: Silver linings in 'bad news' poll on U.S. occupation":

WASHINGTON—A poll of Iraqi public opinion, sponsored by a group with strong Democratic Party connections, is being portrayed by major news services as extremely bad news for the continuing U.S. occupation.

News accounts highlight negative findings such as:

About 6 in 10 Iraqis approve of attacks on U.S.-led forces.

About 7 in 10 want their government to ask U.S. troops to leave within a year.

Almost 80 percent say the U.S. military force in Iraq provokes more violence than it prevents.

Indeed, those were some of the findings of the poll and they are certainly not good news for the Pentagon and White House.

But there are some silver linings getting little attention in the poll conducted earlier this month for University of Maryland's Program on International Policy Attitudes. And many of those behind the organization conducting it have ties to past Democratic administrations and think-tanks known for opposing the war.

Overall 94 percent have an unfavorable view of al-Qaida, with 82 percent expressing a very unfavorable view. Of all organizations and individuals assessed in the poll, Osama bin Laden's terrorist organization received the most negative ratings.

Antipathy toward bin Laden's terrorists is near unanimous among Shiites (95 percent) and Kurds (93 percent). Even among his fellow Sunnis, 77 percent express unfavorable views of al-Qaida.

When the personality of bin Laden is measured, he doesn't do much better.

In addition, the new Iraqi army gets higher marks. One of the driving forces for wanting an early departure of U.S. troops may have to do with increasing confidence in Iraqi army forces—trained by Americans.

Pro-American leaders in Iraq fare better than those opposing American policy. Ayatollah Sistani, who has rejected Iranian meddling in Iraq, is supported by 95 percent of Shiites. Prime Minister Nouri Al Maliki runs a strong second with 86 percent. But Muqtada al Sadr, the Iranian-backed militia leader, gets only 51 percent support.

Asked whether Iran is having a mostly positive or negative influence on the situation in Iraq, just 45 percent of Shiites say it is having a positive influence. Kurds and Sunnis are overwhelming negative about Iran.

Syria is also seen as a problem in Iraq. Most Shiites (68 percent) think Syria is having a negative influence. Most Kurds agree (63 percent). Sunnis are only slightly more positive, with 41 percent having a favorable view.

The board of advisers for the Program on International Policy Attitudes, which conducted the poll, includes Anthony Lake, national security adviser to President Clinton; I. M. Destler, formerly a senior associate at the liberal Carnegie Endowment for International Peace and at the liberal Brookings Institution; Alan Kay, a board member of the progressive Center for Defense Information and a commissioner of the Global Commission to Fund the United Nations; Gloria Duffy, U.S. deputy assistant secretary of defense and special coordinator for cooperative threat reduction in the Clinton administration; Bill Frenzel of the liberal Brookings Institution and a special adviser to Clinton on NAFTA; and Catherine Kelleher, a deputy assistant secretary of defense under Clinton who served on President Carter's national security council staff and a former senior fellow at the Brookings Institution.

Among other studies the program has conducted was an October 2003 report showing how viewers of U.S. media—especially Fox News—hold "misperceptions about American foreign policy." Some of those "misperceptions," however, turned out to be, at the very least, debatable—such as whether there were weapons of mass destruction in Iraq and whether Saddam Hussein had links to al-Qaida.

Try to imagine a poll being commissioned by a group dominated by members of previous Republican administration taking aim at Democratic Party policies. Is there even a remote chance this would be "overlooked" by CNN and other establishment press types? I don't think so.

But I want to be clear on this: I am not telling you that the problems of the establishment press are limited to bias toward Democrats. I am not telling you the problems of the establishment press are limited to a commitment to liberal social notions. I am not telling you the problems of the establishment press are limited to anti-Bush sentiments or antiwar nostrums.

The institutional problems with my industry go far deeper than that. The real problem—and it's insidious—is that the establishment press is, just that, "establishment." The press, whose real value to a free society depends on its commitment to "comfort the afflicted and afflict the comfortable," has stood that value on its head. Today, the press goes along to get along. Rather than hold an inclination to challenge the status quo, to challenge centers of power, it does the opposite.

Now maybe it seems like this *WND* story was defending Fox News. It was not. It was defending accuracy. And Fox certainly has no monopoly on accuracy.

In fact, I've got plenty of bones to pick with Fox—which has been assumed by too many to be *the* alternative news source, *the* place for "fair and balanced" reporting, *the* source for unbiased news.

While Fox News has executed a clever marketing formula to persuade Americans it is all that, in my humble opinion, as a lifelong journalist committed to pursuing truth, I would have to tell you there's not a dime's worth of difference between Fox and CNN.

Honestly, sometimes I watch the cable news shows and find myself laughing out loud. I get confused between some of them and *The Daily Show* on Comedy Central.

One quiet Saturday in the fall of 2003, I found myself watching *Fox News Watch*. I don't think I've been back since.

It started with Jane Hall of American University saying the following in explaining why she thought the U.S. press was pro-war with regard to Iraq: "There's a point about balance, but I would like to say, you know, what about—is there any complicity on the part of people who said this is going to be a—quote—'cakewalk,' who said we know what we're doing and who have no plans for getting out of there. I mean did they bear any responsibility or are we just going to blame the media?"

I don't know who told Jane Hall the war was going to be a "cakewalk." I'm sure someone did. And I'm certain they deserve to be spanked. But I have searched endlessly through LexisNexis for even one responsible elected official or member of the press who used the term and could find nary a one.

That's always the tip-off. If they don't name names, that's because there are none to name.

While I couldn't find anyone who actually predicted a cakewalk in either Iraq or Afghanistan, I did, however, find dozens of people, like Jane Hall, denouncing those unnamed, disembodied yokels who predicted a cakewalk.

Jane Hall, I take it, is supposed to be one of the left-leaning members of the "fair and balanced" model on this media show about the media. But she was topped by right-wing conservative Cal Thomas who offered this whopper in a little history lesson on terrorism and the media.

"We know that Osama bin Laden watched the movie *Blackhawk Down*," asserted Thomas. "That had some influence on him in his belief that Americans would cut and run. So the media plays a game for and against both sides. It can be used by our enemies if they portray that the American will is crumbling to stiffen their backbone."

Hmmm. Interesting idea that bin Laden watched *Blackhawk Down*.

I wonder which Afghan cave bin Laden watched it from.

Thomas made this statement so confidently that one would be tempted to believe there must be at least some truth in it. There's just one little problem, however: *Blackhawk Down* was released December 2001. It could hardly have factored into bin Laden's terrorist plans September 11, 2001—unless he managed to get a very early preview.

Of course, what Thomas actually meant was that bin Laden, as has been well-chronicled with the terrorist leader's own words, was that he observed the "Blackhawk Down" incident in Somalia and concluded American soldiers were, as he put it, "paper tigers."

I don't mean to pick on Fox or Hall or Thomas. The truth is they all do it. It's nothing but a bunch of hot air on these talking-head shows. Many words are offered on each of these shows— they just don't mean all that much. I hope Marshall McLuhan was right and the medium *is* the message, because there's no *other* message in the medium, as far as I can tell.

Am I being too hard on TV news? Not at all. If it had any substance, I might. It's very difficult to hit Jell-O solidly.

Television is good when there's breaking news that requires visual imagery, when cameras are present. What the age of twenty-four-hour cable has taught us is that those times are actually few and far between. The rest of the time, we watch a bunch of chattering magpies.

Except that magpies make more sense.

And that's why we need real reporting. It all starts in print— the written word. Most of what they babble about on cable TV began as written words. There is no shortage of babble in our society. But there still is a distinct shortage of real, honest, intrepid, old-fashioned, principled reporting in the great tradition of American journalism.

Meanwhile, professional meddlers—the academic class—want American journalism to become more like the foreign variety. Take, for example, what Margaret T. Gordon, a professor of news media and public policy at the Evans School of Public Affairs at the University of Washington and formerly the dean, had to say in an opinion piece in the *Seattle Times*.[2]

"Most Americans who are still paying attention to these matters [Iraq war] feel they are getting spun continuously, and almost jokingly offer up facts and arguments they've read or heard—and their opposites," she wrote. "Citizens are asking journalists and media critics why the media don't 'do something' to discover and publish 'the truth.' Why don't journalists seem to be trying to get to the bottom of this?"

Gordon goes on to explain that the profit motive is to blame.

"As a loyal American trained as a journalist some forty-five years ago, I am convinced that journalists in the U.S. feel increasingly trapped between their professional values and the marketing/profits mentality so evident now everywhere in the news industry," she wrote. "The old professional values urge them to dig, investigate, and bring to the light of day the relevant facts and issues, while the market/profit mentality asks, 'Is it worth it? Do enough people care?'"

She continues: "It seems clear enough that the market/profit mentality has won out, especially in electronic news, and to a considerable extent in the print media. While it is impossible to ascertain a cause-and-effect relationship, there does seem to be at least correlation between the media coverage—or lack of it—of government and citizen attitudes toward both government and the media. Trust in both seems to be nearly gone. Meanwhile, the push for corporate profit margins much higher than those of average American businesses goes on—with 40 to 100 percent in the electronic media and 12 to 45 percent in the print media common during 2003."

The answer? Create a BBC-type channel or two, a fully supported National Public Radio, and "methods for supporting and rewarding courageous, high-quality and responsible print media."

In other words, let the government do it.

I have a better suggestion. And it's what we have tried to do with *WND*: let's get back to the basics of good, old-fashioned American-style journalism.

Gordon has been in the classroom too long. She's been involved in the media in the theoretical realm and been thinking about it too much. All it will really take for the American press to get back on track is to rediscover its historic mission as a government watchdog—exposing corruption, fraud, waste, and abuse and reclaiming its Fourth Estate role.

It can't do that with government funding. It can't do that if it's part of the problem. It can't do that if it is not truly independent of government.

If Gordon worries that government is no longer accountable to the people, how can she possibly believe the answer is make the media part of government?

And I have no doubts that Gordon is not alone among media academics and even real-world media practitioners. They know the government is unaccountable—and they want to get in on the action and be unaccountable, too.

They know if there is any attempt by the people to rein in government-supported media that journalists will be able to cry censorship. While the corporate media may have lost its sense of mission, ultimately it is still accountable to the people because it needs to sell its products. That's what bugs Gordon. She and others like her hate capitalism. They don't trust the marketplace. They do trust government—and that's the problem.

I've been saying it for years. The American news media have lost their way.

That's why we stormed the barricades when we did a decade ago with *WND*. As I've said, I believed—and still do—the press had lost its sense of mission. I've been very clear about what that mission is. But I doubt 1 percent of reporters and editors in this country have any clue about the primary role of a free press in a free society.

It's not just journalism professors who believe government control is the best way to achieve a free press in America. Add to the list a guy you may have thought was "antiestablishment"—Michael Moore. Listen to what he told *Murmurs.com* back in 2001:

"We're in the dark ages in this country right now. We're the only country in the whole world without dominant state-controlled media. In a democracy, the state is supposed to be the people. So if it's truly the people, I'd rather run the risk of a government truly run by the people than a corporation doing it."[3]

Unbelievable. Stunning. Stalinesque. It's rare that someone like Moore, as outspoken as he is, actually comes right out and says what he thinks about the First Amendment, about free expression, about the role of government in our lives.

Moore also makes it clear in his interview that his real beef is his own inability to make the kinds of movies and shows he wants to make by operating in the free-enterprise system.

"All my stuff lately has been funded from Europe," he says. "The TV show was from the BBC and Channel 4. The film I'm working on is from a German studio. Canadians funded the last season of *The Awful Truth*. ... Other cultures that haven't had the Moral Majority suppression have moved their culture forward. We haven't."

Such arrogance. Such candor. Nothing I have seen or read better exemplifies the totalitarian instincts of those who would ramrod their ideas down the throats of Americans if only they had the chance.

I know what some of you are thinking, *Farah, if you had the chance, you'd do the same thing. Wouldn't you like to get a government grant to support* WorldNetDaily?

The answer to that question is an unequivocal no.

WorldNetDaily never has and never will allow itself to be co-opted by government or special interests. We never have and never will seek to force others to listen to our news reports or our opinions. We never have and never will coerce others to support our endeavor to renew and reinvigorate the free press in America. I hope I speak for others in the New Media—but I have no idea whether that is the case.

The trouble with the establishment media in this country is just the opposite of what Moore suggests. The press and the pop culture are tied inextricably to the wants and wishes of government. The partnership is just too close. The skepticism of raw government power is too weak. Big corporations that run the media elite know all too well where their bread is buttered—in the form of licenses and political favors. They have forgotten what the principal role of a free press in a free society is—to serve as a watchdog on government.

The biggest threat to freedom in America or any society is and always is from government. Don't forget that.

Let's tell it the way it is: Michael Moore is a spoiled little would-be despot. He wants you to support his little enterprises under the threat of violence, pure and simple. That's the way the government—even the U.S. government—works.

Think about it. Do you feel good about the taxes you spend now? Do you think the money collected by the Internal Revenue Service is really supporting the people's will? Would you like to be on the hook for even more? Would you like it if Washington were calling all the shots with regard to what you see and hear and read?

That's what Michael Moore and his ilk want.

What I want are more choices, more attention on government fraud, waste, abuse, and corruption, more watchdogging, more voices, more investigative digging. Can you imagine that happening if the press in America becomes even more controlled? Can you imagine that happening if we rely on government to investigate itself? Can you fathom that there are people like Michael Moore who believe the government simply doesn't have enough power over our lives, our thoughts, our opinions, and the flow of information?

The only thing the free press should have to do with government is exposing it. How can you do that when you're on the payroll? Government is getting a pass from the press even now. There's empirical data to show it.

The Council for Excellence in Government published findings of a mammoth study, "Government: In and Out of the News." The study found there is far less news about the federal government than there used to be on the evening news broadcasts, as well as on the front pages of the national and regional newspapers. In addition, news reporting on the federal government tends, the study found, to be focused on the executive branch.

The report examined more than 400 hours of airtime on the three major television network evening news shows and more than 13,000 front-page stories during the first year of three presidential administrations—Reagan, Clinton, and George W. Bush. The number of stories touching on the federal government dropped by 31 percent on TV news, by 12 percent in the national print press (*New York Times* and *Washington Post*), and by 39 percent in the four regional newspapers analyzed (*Austin American Statesman, Des Moines Register, San Jose Mercury*, and the *St. Petersburg Times.*)

The drop in government coverage would have been even more profound if it were not for the September 11 terrorist attacks. Before September 11, 2001, the report notes, the media were on track to produce more than 40 percent less government coverage than they carried twenty years ago.[4]

How sick is it that the big media are now giving big government a pass? Well, it's even sicker than that.

Don't forget how some major news organizations have accommodated the requirements of brutal totalitarian governments—just so they wouldn't lose the privilege of broadcasting meaningless video from those nations.

CNN's former chief news executive Eason Jordan finally was forced to disclose that his network withheld shocking news about Iraq because reporting it would have jeopardized its bureau privileges in Baghdad. Jordan wrote in the *New York Times* how one of CNN's Iraqi cameramen was abducted and tortured for weeks.

He told how Saddam Hussein's son Uday told him in 1995 that he intended to murder two of his brothers-in-law who had defected and Jordan's King Hussein who gave them asylum. While Eason Jordan said he felt compelled to warn the king, he made no mention of an attempt to warn the brothers-in-law, who were lured back to Iraq and murdered a few months later.[5]

All of this, of course, raises the question of what good is a news bureau in a totalitarian country if you can't reveal the evil that goes on inside? In fact, it would seem, based on Jordan's account that the CNN bureau's presence in Baghdad was actually an obstacle to reporting the news from Iraq.

Worse than that, CNN's presence in Iraq provided cover for Saddam Hussein. Since CNN was not permitted to report the atrocities taking place there, the world was given the false impression that conditions in Iraq weren't really that bad. After all, how bad could Iraq be if it permitted a CNN news bureau in its capital?

Maintaining the facade of a news bureau, when in fact that bureau was officially muzzled, was a grave journalistic disservice by CNN. If you can't report the news honestly, don't pretend you can.

Why has CNN fallen from the coveted number one perch in cable news ratings? I would submit that is was CNN's statist, pro-establishment, pro-globalist bias that hurt the network. It has only itself and its own narrow vision of news—not Fox News Network—to blame for its fall.

I need to make very clear at this point that there is a danger the New Media will fall prey to the same temptations that seduced the Old Media. In fact, it has happened already to an extent. The bigger the corporation, the more willing they are to sell their soul to the devil.

For instance, it didn't take Yahoo! long to pull a CNN. Way back in 2002—just a few years after the company was born—the Internet search engine signed a pledge to purge its Chinese Web site of material that China's control-freak dictatorship might deem subversive. In other words, Yahoo! began self-censoring its Internet content to win friends and influence the totalitarian elite in Beijing.[6]

According to the agreement, Yahoo! promised to avoid "producing, posting, or disseminating pernicious information that may jeopardize state security and disrupt social stability." It agreed to monitor information posted by users and to "remove the harmful information promptly." Further, it would avoid linking to sites whose content might not be "healthy."

Not to put too fine a point on it, Yahoo! pledged to become part of the repressive Chinese government's thought police.

China, of course, wants the benefits of the Internet, the potential for commercial rewards, but wants no part of the inherent freedom it brings with uncensored information. Yahoo!—and later Google—thus allowed China to have its cake and eat it, too.

What was Yahoo!'s excuse? The company claims it is only following local law. The truth is that companies like Yahoo!—like the Chinese government—are trying to have the best of both worlds.

Just two years earlier, a group of anti-Nazi activists in France sued Yahoo! for selling Nazi paraphernalia—a violation of French law. At that time, Yahoo! management claimed the Internet was borderless and could not be held accountable to local laws—a sensible position in most respects.

Why would Yahoo! cooperate more closely with the Chinese dictatorship—one of the most brutal regimes in the world—while fighting the local claims of a free European nation?

I think you know the answer. China represents the biggest untapped marketplace in the world. Yahoo! sees great potential for commercial rewards in China—just as clearly as China sees it. If it takes compromising with basic human rights to position the company with the Beijing leadership, Yahoo! will do what it needs to do. So will Google. So will CNN. So will the *New York Times*.

Do you really want to know how easy it is to buy influence in the big media?

Think back to just after September 11, 2001. Do you remember when Saudi Prince Alwaleed bin Talal attempted to donate $10 million to New York Mayor Rudolph Giuliani for costs associated with the terror attack on the city?

Giuliani rightly told the prince to take his check and stick it where the sun don't shine.

Why? Because of highly inappropriate remarks the prince made while making the contribution. He suggested the terror attack was a result of America's role in attempting to resolve the Mideast conflict.

"This untended sore will fester, spread," the eighth richest man in the world said. "The reality is that until the Israeli-Palestinian situation is resolved, the world remains at risk."

Nonsense. And Giuliani recognized it as such. This was money that was coming with strings attached. The prince was trying to buy influence, goodwill, even sympathy for his cause of spreading fanatical Islam—the kind that prohibits Bibles in his own country, that prohibits Christian prayer, that prohibits "infidels" even from entering their "holy city" of Mecca.

But while he was told to go packing by Giuliani, the prince was more than successful at buying influence in the financial world and particularly with the Western media that big business controls.

For instance, the prince now owns a whopping $2.05 billion worth of AOL stock. AOL/Time-Warner, as you know, controls, among many other media enterprises, CNN, the influential global news network. He also owns at least $50 million worth of Disney stock, the company that controls, among other media enterprises, ABC. He also controls at least 3 percent of News Corporation, the parent company of the *New York Post*, Fox News Channel, the *London Times*, and many other media outlets around the world.

He also has large holdings in such American corporate names as Compaq, Kodak, Xerox, Amazon, eBay, Internet Capital Group, Infospace, DoubleClick, Coke, Pepsi, Ford, McDonald's, Gillette, and Procter & Gamble.

Guess how much stock he owns in *WND*? Nada, zip, zilch, bupkus.

Here's a guy who wants influence and has demonstrated his desire to use it. How will that influence be manifested in Western media holdings? Here's an indication—from the horse's mouth: The prince told the *London Times* he frequently makes calls to bosses of the companies in which he is invested.

"I am always in close touch with them, but I don't play an active role," he said. "If I feel very strongly about something, I convey a message directly to the chairman or the chief executive."

Think about this: the Saudis are the principal sponsors of the brainwashing camps they call Islamic schools in Afghanistan and Pakistan—the indoctrination centers that produce new bin Ladens and new leaders for the Taliban. They are also the principal sponsors of fanatical Wahabbi Islam preached in 70 percent of the mosques right here in the United States.

Saudi Arabia, far from being the moderate state most Americans have believed, is a brutal totalitarian police state—one that persecutes Christians and recognizes no rights to free speech, free press, or freedom of religion. There's not a single church in all of Saudi Arabia, and Christians have been jailed and executed for worshipping in the privacy of their own homes.

How can we allow them to sink their tentacles into our media institutions?

You might think that the bigger the media enterprise, the more invulnerable they are to economic pressures. The reverse seems to be the case.

The bigger they are, the easier they fall.

CHAPTER EIGHT

GOOGLE THIS!

"The organization of our press has truly been a success. Our law concerning the press is such that divergences of opinion between members of the government are no longer an occasion for public exhibitions, which are not the newspapers' business. We've eliminated that conception of political freedom which holds that everybody has the right to say whatever comes into his head."

—Adolf Hitler

WHY a chapter on Google?

Google isn't really in the news business. Google disseminates news gathered by many other news organizations, but, until now, Google has not been known as a content provider.

So why would I devote a whole chapter of this book to the ubiquitous mother of all search engines?

There's a good reason.

This book, in case you haven't noticed yet, is not just about the press. It's about the New Media. It's about how the press is changing. It's about how technology is breaking the hammerlock of control on information held for so long by a few mega-corporations.

And it's about the dangers ahead for the New Media as well as the opportunities.

This is where Google comes into the picture.

What can you say about a company that that refuses to give the U.S. government the time of day, but is only too happy to cave in to the demands of the tyrannical, repressive dictators in Beijing?

About all you can say is "Google."

What can you say about a company that reminds users of Halloween and Earth Day, but forgets Memorial Day?

About all you can say is "Google."

What can you say about a company that refuses to link to some news sources that are critical of radical Islam, but hosts blogs containing homosexual pornography?

About all you can say is "Google."

What can you say about a company that hosts blogs promoting "boy love," sexual relationships between men and adolescents, but refuses to run ads from a Christian ministry to homosexuals?

About all you can say is "Google."

What can you say about a company whose top executive presides over a business that makes it easy to find out anything about anyone, but who protests when people use his service to find out about him?

About all you can say is "Google."

What would you say about a company that blocks anti-Clinton ads, but not anti-DeLay ads?

About all you can say is "Google."

What would you say about a company so determined to kiss up to the totalitarians in China that it has already wiped Taiwan, an independent and free island nation claimed by Beijing, off the face of its Internet maps?

About all you can say is "Google."

What would you say about a company that is one of the great free enterprise success stories of the decade, but gives nearly all of its political donations to those who seek to rein in and regulate capitalism?

These are a few of the reasons I hate Google. I admit it. I despise it. I resent it. I think it is immoral. I think it is evil. And yet I use it hundreds of times a day. I even allow Google ads to run on *WND*.

Am I a hypocrite?

Maybe.

I mean, what can you say about a guy who hates Google, but uses it constantly? Everybody does. As of this writing, 49 percent of Internet searches are conducted on Google. As of this reading, I'm sure it's more.

I guess you'd have to conclude that I am human.

Google has become so pervasive since it came on the scene in the last five years that it is clearly a force with which to be reckoned. And that's another reason for this exploration—something no one else has yet attempted in the company's short history.

I became passionate about Google in January 2006 when the company refused to hand over data on search patterns to the U.S. Justice Department in an investigation into child pornography.

Google cited the privacy of its users.

But understand that the U.S. government was not looking for details about personal usage—only for search *patterns* that would show the effectiveness of anti-porn filters. The government was trying to prove that minors could stumble on to child-porn Web sites by accident by entering quite innocent search terms. Its lawyers say that for its case to be tested, it needs a sample of actual searches.

Yahoo!, Microsoft's MSN, and America Online all agreed to cooperate, insisting they would not hand over data that identified individual users. But Google, whose name has become synonymous with searches, refused.

Now, I find it very, very difficult to rationalize that bad decision at Google. But let's give the Google guys a break and imagine that they are trying to stand up against big government in some principled way. Let's say that they resent centralized authority in general and believe it is dangerous to cave into its demands.

There's a little problem.

If that were Google's position, it went out the window a week later.

When the Chinese government, a totalitarian force unrivaled in the world today for brutality, harshness, and freakish control asked Google to censor its search results in China in exchange for more access to the world's fastest-growing Internet market, the search giant caved in without protest.

Google agreed to create a unique address for China to ensure Beijing's subjects would not get access to information the government deemed threatening. You can be sure no one in China will be able to Google the content of, say, *WorldNetDaily.com.*

To get the Chinese license, Google agreed to omit Web content that the country's government finds objectionable. Incredibly, Google will base its censorship decisions on guidance provided by Chinese government officials.

In other words, in case you don't yet see the point, Google flouts reasonable government requests designed to protect children from the emotional and spiritual ravages of porn, but accedes without protest to the demands of dictators only interested in denying their people information.

Just so you know, as I'm writing these words, I am getting so angry, I'm on the verge of my own personal boycott.

Think about this. Thanks to Google's appeasement of the totalitarians, Chinese Internet users will continue to be sheltered from reading about subjects such as Taiwan's independence movement, 1989's Tiananmen Square massacre, and the forced abortion policies of Beijing.

Google officials, who once adopted as a company motto, "Don't be evil," say they "agonized" over the decision. That suggests they know they did something wrong. When you struggle with your own conscience like that, there's a reason. But the bottom line and the continuing appeal of communism with weak-minded "progressives" like those who run the company, won the day. No wonder Google hasn't been using the "Don't be evil" slogan much: they can't live by it, and they know it.

How do Google executives justify their actions?

"We firmly believe, with our culture of innovation, Google can make meaningful and positive contributions to the already impressive pace of development in China," said Andrew McLaughlin, Google's senior policy counsel.[1] Translation? *We need this marketplace—at all costs. While we will never pay a price for fighting the U.S. government's reasonable requests, we know there will be a huge economic impact for refusing Beijing's demands.*

"This is a real shame," said Julien Pain, head of Reporters Without Borders's Internet desk. "When a search engine collaborates with the government like this, it makes it much easier for the Chinese government to control what is being said on the Internet."[2]

When Google censors results in China, it intends to post notifications alerting users that some content has been removed—to comply with local laws. The company provides similar alerts in Germany and France when, to comply with national laws, it censors results to remove references to Nazi paraphernalia. Imagine the hoops through which Google would jump to please Hitler if he were still around.

Google has clearly chosen sides in the struggle for freedom in the world. It has chosen the side of slavery—and higher profits.

It's despicable. It's evil. It's immoral.

But what should we expect from a search engine whose maps, until October 2005, already showed the free and independent republic of Taiwan as part of China?[3]

They were surprised in Taiwan to learn from Google that their island was already under the rule of Beijing—since it has never been in the history of Earth. Angry officials protested the demarcation of Taiwan as a "province of China" on its online map service.

"Taiwan is an independent, sovereign state. Taiwan is not part of China," said David Huang, whip for the Taiwan Solidarity Union legislative caucus. "Taiwan has never been ruled by China, nor has the Chinese government deployed any government functionaries or armed forces here."[4]

The caucus asked the Taiwan government to lodge a formal protest and urged the public to lobby Google.

Guess what? It worked. While Google may be immoral, while it may not be able to discern right from wrong, while it may be led by holier-than-thou, hypocritical executives, it turns out Google is a "paper tiger," in the words of their inspirational hero Mao Tse-tung. But maybe that moniker should be updated. Google isn't a paper tiger. It's an electronic tiger.

Following a few days of protest—not only in Taiwan, but in the United States as well—Google scrapped the notation on the Taiwan map. Naturally, the thugs in China actually had the audacity to protest the correction![5]

As far as Google goes, that would be enough for me. The fact that it caved in—lock, stock, and barrel—to China, just so it could do business with its one billion subjects tells me everything I need to know about the character of the people at the top of the company.

But we actually have learned quite a bit more about Google in its short and meteoric rise as the search engine of choice. What we have learned should be alarming, especially when you consider how pervasive, how omnipresent it is in the so-called New Media. Let's face it, even though Google is not in the business of gathering news, it is very much in the business of disseminating it.

In some respect, Google may be the gatekeeper Hillary Clinton was looking for. There's little doubt Google will be sending her millions for her campaign for the presidency—along with lots of other politicians, nearly all Democrats.

What is the definition of irony? A company that gives all its money to the Democratic Party but bans searches of the word "democracy" in countries that don't permit it.

When I say Google gives nearly all of its political contributions to one party, I am not exaggerating. As I reported in 2005, in the three previous election cycles, Google employee contributions went to the Democrats to the tune of $463,500, with a paltry $5,000 going to the Republicans.[6]

Why did I track the money? Way back in the Watergate era we were always told to follow the money. It says so much about motivations. You can tell where people's hearts are by watching their pocketbooks. And, if that saying is true, the hearts of Google employees—from the lowest level to the highest level—belong in the Democratic Party.

Of approximately two hundred individual Google employee political contributions to political candidates in 2004, 2002, and 2000, all but six went to Democrats, Democratic Party organizations, and Democrat-supporting organizations such as MoveOn.org. One $250 contribution went to Ralph Nader, one went to President Bush's campaign, and three went to Utah Republican Sen. Orrin Hatch's campaigns.

Google Chairman and Chief Executive Officer Eric Schmidt was by far the biggest benefactor, giving $100,000 to the Democratic National Committee in 2000, $25,000 to the Democratic Congressional Campaign Committee in 2004, as well as maximum $2,000 contributions to 2004 Democratic presidential candidates Senators John Kerry and Joe Lieberman, Gov. Howard Dean, and Rep. Richard Gephardt.

Schmidt also gave $11,000 to the Democratic Senatorial Campaign Committee in 2000, according to records of the FEC, as well as tens of thousands more to a variety of other Democratic candidates including Sen. Hillary Rodham Clinton of New York.

Besides his cash contributions to Kerry in 2004, Schmidt formally endorsed the Democratic candidate for president after he got the party's nomination.

Google products manager Laura A. Debonis was another big giver to the Democratic cause, offering up $25,000 to the DNC in 2004 and another $10,000 to the New Hampshire Democratic State Committee, though she lives in San Francisco.

David Drummond, a Google executive, also gave $23,000 to the DNC in 2004.[7]

But the most striking thing about the list of Google political activists is the one-sided nature of the giving. From programmers to engineers to scientists to business development staff to general managers, there is near unanimity in support of Democrats and Democrat organizations.

Now, should it surprise us when we see Google's political values reflected in its content? I believe when you see that kind of rigid political regimentation and unity in a company, it should surprise you if you *don't* see it.

And see it we do with Google.

Maybe the most stunning example of this bias creeping into Google's advertising policies is one involving Eric Jackson, chief executive officer of World Ahead Publishing, my friend and colleague in the publishing venture that brings you this book.

Jackson's company attempted to take out Google ads for one of its titles, *Their Lives: The Women Targeted by the Clinton Machine*, by Candice E. Jackson (no relation). The publisher said his ads for this anti-Clinton book were rejected by Google without explanation other than "unacceptable content."

Jackson says Google's online ad guidelines make no mention of political content being disallowed. He points out that while ads for the anti-Clinton book—which featured images of the book's cover and pictures of the former first couple—were deemed offensive, the company continues to run ads for overtly liberal advertisers with headlines such as "Hate Bush? So Do We," and "George W. Bush fart doll."[8]

Was this an aberration? It doesn't appear to be. Just a month earlier, Google rejected political ads targeting House Minority Leader Nancy Pelosi by the group RightMarch.com. The group had designed its Google ad campaign based on one it observed already running on the company's site with the only difference being that it was directed against then-House Majority Leader Tom DeLay.

When its ads were rejected, RightMarch.com pointed out that a nearly identical campaign was already running on Google. The company assured that those ads targeting the Republican politician would be removed, just as the ads opposing a Democratic politician were rejected.

When questioned about the apparent double standard by *WorldNetDaily*, Mike Mayzel, spokesman for Google, said both the anti-Pelosi ad and the anti-DeLay ad were pulled.

"Both ads were taken down," he said. "Any assertion to the contrary is false. As soon as an ad is reviewed and found to be in violation of our policies, we take it down as soon as possible. Any suggestion we would leave some ads up longer than others for reasons of political bias is false."

But they weren't taken down.

A search of Google's site the same day Mayzel was making that statement showed at least three more anti-DeLay ads still running.[9]

Could it get any worse? Could the Google boys show any poorer judgment? Have I already blown my wad in this anti-Google screed?

Stay with me. You ain't seen nothin' yet.

A marriage and family therapist intern is trying to convince Google to drop a Web site from its popular free blog host that promotes "boy love," sexual relationships between men and adolescents.

Stacy L. Harp of Orange, California, told *WorldNetDaily* one of the readers of her Weblog pointed out the site, called "Paiderastia: The Boy Love Revival." Right at the top of its homepage, the site explains it's all about "erotic/mentor/spiritual love between adolescents and adults."[10]

While Google claims to prohibit pornography from its sites, it clearly seems more concerned about banning "hate speech" and ideas with which its employees find repugnant. For instance, *WorldNetDaily* found Google permitted advertising for homosexual videos featuring explicit anal sex.

Protesting such a decision by Google can get you in trouble. Because Google also banned an advertisement from a Christian organization, Stand to Reason, because the group's Web site contains articles opposing homosexuality. That was determined by Google's thought police as "hate speech."

An e-mail from Google to Stand to Reason explained: "Google AdWords policy never permits ads or keywords promoting hate, violence, or crimes toward any organization, person, or group protected by law," including those distinguished by their "sexual orientation/gender identity."

AdWords is a program on Google in which ads are listed in the right-hand margin of search results when key words an advertiser submits match those put in by a Net user. The company says it does not restrict actual search results that come up, only the advertisements that accompany them.

After reading the *WorldNetDaily* story about Google's policy regarding the Christian site, a reader forwarded a letter he wrote to the search-engine firm:

"You will not allow ads that lead to Web sites advocating against homosexuality, but typing 'a-- f---ing sex' in Google leads to sidebar ads for 'awesome anal videos,' et al. The incredible double standard displayed by you and the Left in general is at the root of the rot in this country. Of course, the right to free speech protects [anal sex], but not the belief that homosexuality is a sin. That is truly amazing, don't you agree?"

Indeed, a *WorldNetDaily* investigation showed using the readers' criteria yielded several ads for videos and pornographic Web sites. When the word *gay* is added, the theme of the ads switches to homosexual porn.[11]

Google seems to like homosexuals almost as much as it likes the jackbooted thugs who oppress a billion Chinese people. What it doesn't like are Christian groups seeking to restore godly values to government.

ChristianExodus.org, a group looking to have like-minded people move to one state to help restore godly values to government, says it too has been rejected by Google's ad censors.

An e-mail from Google cited "sensitive content" as the reason for the rejection, though it was not specific in what was considered sensitive.

"After reviewing your application, our program specialists have found that it does not comply with our policies," the Google AdSense Team wrote. "We have reviewed your site and found that many of the ads that would appear on your site would not be relevant to your site's content. As the ads would not provide a valuable experience for your site's users or our advertisers, we feel that your site isn't a good fit for the AdSense program at this time."[12]

Google provided two pages outlining policies, but neither mentions the word *sensitive*.

Under the content section, some preclusions listed include:

- Excessive profanity;

- Violence, racial intolerance, or advocate against any individual, group, or organization;

- Hacking/cracking content;

- Illicit drugs and drug paraphernalia;

- Pornography, adult, or mature content; and

- Gambling or casino-related content, etc.

While Google suggests its highest calling is not offending anyone, some Americans have been ticked off at its failure to mark Memorial Day, the holiday in which the country honors its fallen heroes.

"Google's habit of celebrating holidays like New Year's, Halloween, Christmas, and Thanksgiving by altering its logo to match the season's theme has been extended in the past to honor the birthdays of famous inventors, scientists, artists, and musicians, as well as Earth Day and the Persian New Year, but on the day Americans honor those who died serving their country, it's business as usual at the Internet-search giant," said the *World-NetDaily* story.[13]

The story explained Memorial Day visitors to Google found the company's standard logo—no mention of Memorial Day. Since 1999, Google has redesigned its logo for major holidays like Christmas and Thanksgiving, as well as minor ones like Ground Hog Day and St. Patrick's Day. It's even honored artists like Picasso, Monet, and Andy Warhol as well as Earth Day and the Burning Man festival.

Another blatant example of Google exerting its own warped worldview into its content decisions came when the company cut off its news relationship with a number of Internet content sites that are critical of radical Islam or link it with terrorism.[14]

Huh? Doesn't everyone link radical Islam with terror?

What else is Google rejecting because of its corporate likes and dislikes?

Gun ads.

Surprise, surprise. For years now Google has refused to sell advertising to firearms dealers or companies that sell gun parts or knives.[15]

Despite all this political correctness run amok, most Americans still don't have a clue about Google's bias. Daily, I would say, I get e-mails from people who tell me they are suspicious about Google because of what I call the "miserable failure" test.

It is hardly a secret that when you type the phrase "miserable failure" into the Google search engine that the first entry to pop up is the official White House biography of President Bush. But here

I've got to give Google a pass. This is *not* evidence of Google bias. This is a result of a phenomenon known as "Google bombing."

As the target of an organized Google bombing campaign, I know all about it.

Basically, to make this as simple as possible, it works like this: computer users post a phrase on web pages and link it to another web page—such as the Bush biography.

Bush wasn't the first Google bomb victim. Nor was he the last. One of the first Google bombs was discovered in 1999 when someone got the bright idea to search the phrase "more evil than Satan" and Microsoft's home page came up.

But the term wasn't even coined until two years later in 2001 by Adam Mathes.

Only later did Internet users discover the "miserable failure" test. Then again during the 2004 presidential campaign, it was found that searching the term "waffles" brought you to the official John Kerry Web site. As of this writing, it still does. Kerry had been Google bombed. And I wouldn't be a bit surprised if he claimed his fourth Purple Heart for the attack.

Then came my turn.

Introducing the "Google Bomb Project," an endeavor apparently launched in 2005 and whose goal is "exposing the hard right through Google bombing." Naturally, I was the first target, followed quickly thereafter by radio talker Tammy Bruce and then Karl Rove. (I guess we know who rates on the Internet.)

Don't worry, it doesn't hurt. I didn't feel a thing, in fact. I didn't even know it happened until an e-mailer brought it to my attention. The site responsible, apparently organized by blogger Scoobie Davis (not to be confused with Scoobie Doo), led to a host of inaccurate reports about me and those with whom I am accused of conspiring.

Scoobie announced breathlessly January 6, 2005: "I finally started working on the Google Bomb Project site. My first target is Scaife monkey-boy and the head of *WorldNetDaily*, Joseph Farah. Google bombing is a cheap, easy method of media hacking. Let's help Internet researchers with the truth about Farah."

Perhaps the most interesting aspect of this Google bomb attack is not in the words used—but in "the art." It was only through my exploration of the Google bomb phenomenon that I learned of a massive acrylic-on-canvas mural painstakingly painted by Joel Pelletier of AmericanFundamentalists.com. It is eight feet, four inches by fourteen feet, one and a half inches—a knockoff of an 1888 Ensor original.

Pelletier admits it took him six months to study and paint this band of conspirators, which includes yours truly, as well as George W. Bush, Rush Limbaugh, Rupert Murdoch, Ann Coulter, and close to 120 others.

Why?

Because "all Americans need to know what is going on—the vast right-wing conspiracy that Hillary Clinton warned about is real, they think they can do no wrong with God on their side, and they are here on this painting," the artist hyperventilates.

Yes, promoting this conspiracy is part of the Google bomb attack on me. Now when people search my name, they will see me linked with other famous "fundamentalists"—like Bill O'Reilly and Sun Myung Moon.

Scratch just under the surface of some of the other links used in this particular Google bomb effort and you will see the dark underbelly of the impotent, extremist American Left—a sick and seething anti-Semitism so virulent it would make Josef Goebbels blush.

In an open letter written to me, one of the Google bomb conspirators charges: "Jewish power is pushing us to the eve of destruction, and...you are a liar and a hypocrite and just as unethical in your own way as the media you seek to supersede."

It just warms my heart that people like this detest me so that they would make me their number one Google bomb target in 2005.

But again, in the interest of truth and justice—always my highest callings—you can't blame Google for Google bombing.

You can blame Google for plenty more, however. What is the definition of a hypocrite? I hereby nominate for the award of hypocrite of the decade, Google CEO Eric Schmidt.

I mean everybody knows how easy it is to collect information on virtually any subject at Google. That's how the company makes money. But you should have seen the company squawk when a reporter getting information about Schmidt, googled his name.

CNET News reporter Elinor Mills used the search engine to find out data about Schmidt, bits of which included:

- Schmidt's shares in Google were worth $1.5 billion

- He's a resident of Atherton, California.

- He hosted a $10,000-a-plate fundraiser for Al Gore's presidential campaign.

- He was a pilot.

According to the *New York Times*, David Krane, Google's director of public relations, called CNET editors to complain once it published the facts.

"They were unhappy about the fact we used Schmidt's private information in our story," Jai Singh, editor in chief of *CNETNews.com*, told the *Times*. "Our view is what we published was all public information, and we actually used their own product to find it."

Singh said Krane called back to say Google would not speak to any reporter from CNET for an entire year.[16]

That's my case against Google. And, if I do say so myself, I think it is a pretty compelling one. But there's another reason I detest Google.

It is a traitor to the New Media. Google is a sellout to the Old Media world. It is part of the media elite—and not just because of its size and quick success.

In 2005, Google announced plans to begin giving preference to such establishment news agencies as CNN and the BBC in searches over new independent media enterprises like *WorldNetDaily*. As Google explained it, the rankings will be "according to quality rather than simply the date and relevance to search terms."[17]

Needless to say, I take this personally.

Prior to this reorganization, the company's search engine responds with thousands of hits in response to simple entries such as "Iraq," which lead to news Web sites. These are ranked either in order of relevance or by date, so that the most recent or most focused appear at the top of the huge list.

"This means that articles carrying more authority, say from CNN or the BBC, can be ousted from the first page of results, simply because they are not as recent or as relevant to the keyword entered in the search line," explains a news account in the *New Scientist*. "Now Google, whose name has become synonymous with Internet searching, plans to build a database that will compare the track record and credibility of all news sources around the world, and adjust the ranking of any search results accordingly."[18]

In other words, Google is going to be making value judgments about which news organizations are more credible.

I have to wonder what kind of expertise Google has setting such parameters. But given their example—CNN and BBC—it's clear Google's own prejudice is for the same old biases of the establishment press.

According to the report, the parameters used will include:

- Average story length;

- Number of stories with bylines;

- Number of bureaus cited;

- How long the company has been in business;

- Number of staffers employed by the agency;

- Volume of Internet traffic attracted to the site; and

- Number of countries accessing the site.

"Google will take all these parameters, weight them according to formulae it is constructing, and distill them down to create a single value," says the report. "This number will then be used to rank the results of any news search."[19]

While *WND* may do very well in some of these categories—for instance, in Internet traffic and number of countries accessing the site—it cannot, of course, begin to compete with news agencies such as the Associated Press with its thirty thousand employees worldwide.

Yet this is the beauty of the New Media, where a handful of guerrilla journalists have not only broken big stories ignored or overlooked by the big media, but helped expose the biases of those organizations.

This raises some serious questions:

Is Google trying to win credibility itself with the Old Media?

Is Google taking sides with the Old Media against the New Media?

Whatever happened to the idea of unfair trade practices?

In the United States, we have a tradition of leveling the playing field and fostering competition in business. It seems now that Google has emerged as something of a dominant search engine it is preparing to help well-established global news agencies hang on to their dominance—even as they appear most vulnerable to a media revolution sparked on the Internet.

I don't like it.

And, if you haven't figured it out yet, I don't like Google, either.

CHAPTER NINE

THE DRUDGE EFFECT

"A journalist is a grumbler, a censurer, a giver of advice, a regent of sovereigns, a tutor of nations. Four hostile newspapers are more to be feared than a thousand bayonets."

—Napoleon Bonaparte

HE DEFEATS presidential candidates with a stroke of his keyboard.

He makes bestsellers with a click of his mouse.

He drives the national debate with his choice of headlines.

Those are some of the supernatural powers that have been attributed to Matt Drudge. And, if you've been watching his work at the famed *Drudge Report* for as long and as closely as I have, you would probably agree there is more than a little truth behind them.

I'll tell you what I think of Drudge in a minute. But here's what others are saying about the guy who has become ubiquitous in our new world of New Media.

Mark McKinnon, one of President Bush's top campaign consultants, said he checks the site thirty to forty times per day: "When there's a siren, that's a three-alarm news deal."[1]

Democratic strategist Chris Lehane: "Literally, it goes up on Drudge and the phones start ringing."[2]

"Today Matt Drudge can influence the news like Walter Cronkite did," says Mark Halperin, author of *The Way to Win: Taking the White House in 2008*. "If Drudge says something, it may not lead everybody instantly in the same direction, but it gets people thinking about what Matt Drudge wants them to think about."[3]

"Our largest driver of traffic is Matt Drudge," says *Washington Post* editor Leonard Downie.[4]

We all know the role Matt Drudge played in what ultimately led to the impeachment of President Bill Clinton. It was the story of the "stained blue dress" that stuck amid an encyclopedia of administration scandals. More recently, some have attributed the defeat of Sen. John Kerry in 2004 to the erstwhile Drudgester.

John F. Harris and Halperin, in *The Way to Win*, say that although Kerry beat himself and was outfoxed by a better politician in George W. Bush, Drudge was a major factor.

"Here is another nominee for who beat John Forbes Kerry: Matthew Drudge," they write.[5]

Maybe you never heard him called "Matthew" before. In fact, Drudge is so pervasive in our culture today that we seldom hear any first name. It's just Drudge. And everyone knows who you are talking about as surely as if you said "Cher" or "Madonna."

"If you are reading this book, you probably know who Matt Drudge is," they continue. "It is a guarantee that most of the reporters, editors, producers, and talk-show bookers who serve up the daily national buffet of news recently have checked out his eponymous Web site, and that www.drudgereport.com is bookmarked on their computers. That is one reason Drudge is the single most influential purveyor of information about American politics."

And keep in mind this is coming from two people who don't like Drudge very much.

"Drudge, with his droll Dickensian name, was not the only media or political agent whose actions led to John Kerry's defeat," write Harris and Halperin. "But his role placed him at the center of the game—a New Media World Order in which Drudge was the most potent player in the process and a personification of the dynamics that did Kerry in. Drudge and his ilk made Kerry toxic—and unelectable."[6]

There is no better illustration of the power of Drudge than what happened July 28, 2004, and thereafter leading right up to Election Day. In the day before Kerry "reported for duty" and accepted the Democratic presidential nomination, Drudge blared some of the findings of new book, *Unfit for Command: Swift Boat Veterans Speak Out Against John Kerry*.

Before the report, the book was languishing at number 1,318 on Amazon. Within twenty-four hours it was number two, and within forty-eight, number one. So numerous are his New Media triumphs that many are just forgotten—like the fact that he scooped the establishment news media on Bob Dole's selection of Jack Kemp as his running mate and Connie Chung's ouster at CBS.

This is Matt Drudge—the guy who got one president impeached and played a significant role in the election of another.

The impact of this man can hardly be overstated. It's like Doug Harbrecht, the man who introduced him at the National Press Club in 1998, said: "So why is Matt Drudge here? He's on the cutting edge of a revolution in our business and everyone in our business knows it. And like it or not, he's a newsmaker."

And how did he do it? I'll let Drudge tell his own story—as told to that Press Club audience:

"I swung into another clerk job, this time at CBS. I folded T-shirts in the gift shop, dusted off *60 Minutes* mugs. Occasionally after hours I had conversations with the ghost of Bill Paley. It was during one of these wee-hour chats that he reminded me the first step in good reporting is good snooping.

"Inspired, I went out of my way to service the executive suites. I remember I delivered sweatshirts to Jeff Sagansky, at the time president of CBS.

"Overhearing, listening to careful conversations, intercepting the occasional memo, I would volunteer in the mail room from time to time. I hit pay dirt when I discovered that the trash cans in the Xerox room at Television City were stuffed each morning with overnight Nielsen ratings, information gold. I don't know what I did with it; I guess we, me and my friends, knew *Dallas* had got a thirty-five-share over *Falcon Crest*, but we thought we were plugged in.

"I was on the move—at least I thought so. But my father worried I was in a giant stall. And in a parental panic he overcame his fear of flying and dropped in for a visit. At the end of his stay, during the drive to the airport, sensing some action was called for, he dragged me into a blown-out strip on Sunset Boulevard and found a Circuit City store. 'Come on,' he said desperately, 'I'm getting you a computer.' 'Oh, yeah, and what am I doing to do with that?' I laughed.

"And as they say at CBS studios: Cut, two months later. Having found a way to post things on the Internet—it was a quick learn—Internet news groups were very good to me early on—I moved on to scoops from the sound stages I had heard, Jerry Seinfeld asking for a million dollars an episode, to scoop after scoop of political things I had heard from some friends back here.

"I collected a few e-mail addresses of interest. People had suggested I start a mailing list, so I collected the e-mails and set up a list called the *Drudge Report.* One reader turned into five, then turned into a hundred. And faster than you could say 'I never had sex with that woman' it was one thousand, five thousand, a hundred thousand people. The ensuing Web site practically launched itself."

Only in America! But the story of Drudge's success is not just a story of the realization of the American dream for one funny, insightful, and hardworking guy. The truth is that America needed entrepreneur Drudge as much as Drudge needed the entrepreneurial opportunities that America afforded.

Within two years of his launch, there were new, more traditional media launches inspired by it. First came the Fox News Channel in 1996 and then *WorldNetDaily.com* in 1997.

I don't know whether Rupert Murdoch will admit to being inspired by Drudge, but I do. Here are some facts to consider:

- There would be no WorldNetDaily.com today without the inspiration of Drudge.

- There would be no "blogosphere" today without the inspiration of Drudge.

- There would be no talk radio as we know it today without the inspiration of Drudge.

Americans—indeed, people all over the world—are getting their news in new ways today because of this Internet pioneer. He led the way.

Today, the Internet is where TV producers look for their news budget—not the *New York Times*.

Today, the Internet is where radio talk-show hosts get their talking points—not the *Washington Post*.

Today, the Internet breaks the news, and the rest of the media world talk about what is broken there.

Thank Matt Drudge for that breakthrough. Thank Matt Drudge for the new competition we have in the media. Thank Matt Drudge for breaking the media monopoly.

How? Why? What happened? Again, let Drudge provide the answers from that famous address to the Press Club skeptics:

"Well, clearly there is a hunger for unedited information, absent corporate considerations. ... We have entered an era vibrating with the din of small voices. Every citizen can be a reporter, can take on the powers that be. The difference between the Internet, television and radio, magazines, newspapers is the two-way communication. The Net gives as much voice to a thirteen-year-old computer geek like me as to a CEO or Speaker of the House. We all become equal.

"And you would be amazed what the ordinary guy knows.

"From a little corner in my Hollywood apartment, in the company of nothing more than my 486 computer and my six-toed cat, I have consistently been able to break big stories, thanks to this network of ordinary guys. The *Drudge Report*, first to name the vice-presidential nominee on the Republican ticket last election; first to announce to an American audience that Princess Diana had tragically died; first to tell the sad, sad story of Kathleen Willey; first every weekend with box-office results that even studio executives, some of them, admit they get from me. A new cable network is forming. I was first to announce the unholy alliance between Microsoft and NBC.

"I've written thousands of stories, started hundreds of news cycles. My readers can follow earthquakes, weather patterns, read Frank Rich on Saturday, Maureen Dowd on Sunday, from my site link to Bob Novak on Monday; dozens of other media spectrums, from Molly Ivins; track the world's newswires minute to minute.

"And this is something new. This marks the first time that an individual has access to the newswires outside of the newsroom. You get to read all the news from the Associated Press, UPI, Reuters, to the more arcane Agence France Presse and the Xinhau. I'm a personal fan of the Xinhua Press.

"And time was only newsrooms had access to the full pictures of the day's events, but now any citizen does. We get to see the kinds of cuts that are made for all kinds of reasons; endless layers of editors with endless agendas changing bits and pieces, so by the time the newspaper hits your welcome mat, it had no meaning.

"Now, with a modem, anyone can follow the world and report on the world—no middleman, no big brother. And I guess this changes everything."

But Drudge created as much jealousy as excitement—as much anxiety as hope. We'd been here before. And Drudge noticed.

"I was here last night looking over the Press Club, and I noticed a room dedicated to one of—someone I can relate to, John Peter Zenger. And there's a plaque outside the room. And I think he could relate to some of the heat I've been getting. To honor members of the newspaper industry, this room commemorates the achievements of John Peter Zenger two hundred and fifty years ago, whose courage in publishing political criticism helped establish the precedent of press freedom in colonial America.

"He was born in Germany. Zenger was a publisher in 1734 when he was imprisoned on charges of criminal libel for articles in his newspaper criticizing the royal governor. Risking his business and possible life, Zenger stood fast and was acquitted in a jury trial after a brilliant defense of press liberty by his lawyer, at that time Andrew Hamilton.

"It got me thinking that really what we're looking at here is history repeating. When radio lost out to television, there was anxiety. The people in the radio industry were absolutely anxious and demanded government stop the upcoming television wave. Television was very nervous about other mediums coming forward; cable. The movies didn't want sitcoms to be taped at movie studios for fear it would take away from the movies.

"No, television saved the movies. The Internet is going to save the news business. I envision a future where there'll be three hundred million reporters, where anyone from anywhere can report for any reason. It's freedom of participation absolutely realized."

Of course, Hillary didn't see it that way. Drudge recalled her dire warning about "the gatekeeping function" being lost with the rise of the Internet and how that can lead to "all kinds of bad outcomes." To which Drudge responded: "Would she have said the same thing about Ben Franklin or Thomas Edison or Henry Ford or Einstein? They all leapt so far ahead out that they shook the balance. No, I say to these people, faster, not slower. Create. Let your mind flow. Let the imagination take over. And if technology has finally caught up with individual liberty, why would anyone who loves freedom want to rethink that?"

When I look over that speech Drudge gave to the Press Club, I realize again how far ahead of his time he was. Do you see what he was predicting with accuracy years before it happened? He was predicting the blogosphere. It didn't exist in 1998.

It's worth noting that Drudge was greeted at that event with a series of rude, self-righteous questions from the beltway media establishment. Immediately after his address, Harbrecht posed this incredibly insipid query: "How does it advance the cause of democracy and of social good to report unfounded allegations about individuals and Nielsen ratings?"

The cause of democracy? The social good? That's what these guys *think* they are doing. Who do these guys think they are? Martin Luther King? Florence Nightingale? They think they are making society better. They think they are improving our political system. They think they are, in effect, miracle workers. What they are clearly not doing, however, is their jobs—serving as watchdogs on corruption, fraud, waste, and abuse in government and other centers of power.

But I digress. The point is that the media police were confronting Drudge on reporting "unfounded allegations." To say Drudge hit the ball out of the park would be an understatement.

"Well, that's a good question. ... One of my competitors is *Salon Magazine Online*, which I understand is the president's favorite Web site. And there's a reporter there, Jonathan Broder. He was fired for plagiarism from the *Chicago Tribune*. And I read that in the *Weekly Standard*. But do I believe it? Because, as much as I love the *Weekly Standard*, they have had to settle a big one with Deepak Chopra, if I recall. I heard that from CNN. But hold on. Didn't CNN have the little problem with Richard Jewell? I think Tom Brokaw told me that, and then I think Tom Brokaw also had to settle with Richard Jewell. I read that in the *Wall Street Journal*. But didn't the *Wall Street Journal* just lose a huge libel case down in Texas, a record ... $200 million? I tell you, it's creative enough for an in-depth piece in the *New Republic*. But I fear people would think it was made up."

Even the hostile audience at the National Press Club had to laugh at that one. Drudge's point was simple. Mistakes are made in the establishment press all the time. In fact, I would say, many more poor judgments are made in the traditional press than are made in online journalism. So where do these guys get off vilifying Drudge, *WorldNetDaily*, and the handful of other Internet news pioneers who are actually doing what journalists are supposed to do—watchdogging government, exposing high-level corruption, challenging the status quo?

Drudge's words were indeed prophetic. Within a week, the largest news-gathering organization in the world, the Associated Press, made one of the biggest goofs you can possibly make in media. This behemoth of a news agency, with some thirty thousand employees worldwide, which prides itself on fact-checking, editing, and being "responsible," reported on its Web site that Bob Hope had died.

Now, for the record, Bob Hope eventually did die—as we all do. But it wasn't in 1998. It was five years later on July 27, 2003.

When the AP made this gaffe, within minutes a congressman was announcing it on the floor of the House of Representatives, and ABC News was reporting it on radio nationwide.

How did this happen? With all the wonderful checks and balances built into the establishment press's infallible systems, how could such a crucial and embarrassing mistake be made? Where were those corporate gatekeepers? Doesn't ABC have editors? Doesn't the AP double-check reports before cybercasting them on the Internet? Where were their sources? Why didn't anyone pick up the phone and call Bob Hope's home to learn he was quietly eating breakfast with his wife and that, in the memorable words of Mark Twain, rumors of his death were greatly exaggerated?

Drudge may not have had any journalistic credentials when he entered the world of the Internet. But I sure did—more than twenty years' worth. Yet I admit I am subject to human error as much as the next guy. All the training and experience in the world doesn't make you immune.

I think one of the biggest differences between the new Internet journalism and the Old Media is that practitioners of the former are willing to admit their human frailties and correct their errors. The general public finds that lack of arrogance refreshing—which explains why the Old Media is so jealous of people like Matt Drudge.

Following within a week of AP's muffed Bob Hope obit came an establishment media scandal of historic proportions. CNN and *Time* magazine teamed up on one of the greatest frauds in the history of American journalism—an investigative report claiming that U.S. troops had used deadly nerve gas during the Vietnam War and had purposely set out on missions to kill defectors. There was zero credible evidence for any such allegation. Nada. Zip. Zilch.

Later, the *Time*-CNN report was criticized in news stories in the major media, discredited in an op-ed piece in the *New York Times*, subject to an investigation by the magazine itself. Eventually CNN was forced to retract the entire report.

During the fallout, one fact was conspicuously downplayed in all the establishment press coverage: the problems with the CNN exposé were first exposed on the Internet—specifically in *WorldNetDaily*, and, more to the point, by yours truly.

Yet not one account in the AP, *Washington Times,* or any other print or broadcast news media has bothered to mention that fact, or to give credit where credit is due. Some talk-radio hosts noted it. My point is not to try to grab some credit for a story broken nine years ago. I point this out primarily to illustrate how self-conscious the establishment press is—how insecure, how defensive, how pathetic.

Even back then, just about a year after we got started at *WND*, with the new medium still in its infancy, we had the big boys on the run. They were scared, threatened, jealous, and protecting their turf in the only way they knew how.

Having spent twenty years working in the establishment press, running daily newspapers in major markets, I think I'm in a pretty good position to understand the mentality, to see both sides, to have some perspective.

Just like the exponential growth Drudge noted in his talk to the Press Club, in the span of one year, *WorldNetDaily* exploded from nothing—little more than a vague concept in my head—to an Internet force to be reckoned with. And today, ten years later, it is serving nearly ten million *different* people every thirty days.

One of the nice things about reaching so many people in a medium like the Internet is that you hear from so many of them. There is immediate feedback—and lots of it. I hear from thousands of people a day through e-mail. Many of them are breathless in their praise for what we are doing. They are grateful beyond words for this alternative. They are eager to tell their friends and relatives about this unique site.

I cannot begin to tell you how much that means to me. It is one of my greatest motivations for continuing the hard work day after day.

While my ego might lead me to believe this enthusiasm is due to my creative genius, my sensibilities tell me it's much more complicated than that. *WND* and Drudge have filled a great void in the lives of Americans.

It wasn't that long ago that CNN was the new kid on the block. People laughed at Ted Turner for dreaming up the idea that an all-news cable network could actually find a niche in the marketplace. Now CNN is part of the media establishment—part of a huge multinational media conglomerate. And CNN was toppled as the number one cable TV network by Fox News.

There are fewer and fewer conventional newspapers in the land. When you travel around this country from city to city, you see very little difference between the papers. They all run the same stories, follow the same script, take their cues from the same sources. This is a prescription for disaster, yet few in the industry seem to notice. They hold conferences and seminars with one another and reinforce each other's prejudices and ignorance. They blame falling circulation and ratings on all the wrong causes.

I used to be frustrated by what I saw in my industry. Now I'm grateful. It's as if God put blinders on my colleagues, and at the same time opened up incredible opportunities in a revolutionary new medium for me, positioning me perfectly to use all the tricks of the trade I learned from the Old Media.

I always believed the institutional problems of the news media could only be solved through competition, rather than kvetching and complaining. But it took the new technology to level the playing field so those opportunities could be created.

Think about it. Think about what Drudge did. Newspaper companies had spent hundreds of millions of dollars—perhaps billions—researching ways of effectively and efficiently distributing their information electronically. The experiments, focus groups, and text-marketing campaigns had continued for a decade before anyone had ever heard of the *Drudge Report*. Then, Matt Drudge, with no resources at all, set up shop with a computer in his Hollywood apartment and showed them all up. And he did it based on gut instincts—not market research, focus groups, and demographic surveys.

With his brilliant use of links, he gave us an easy way to compare and contrast news accounts from all over the United States. Most people have probably forgotten how controversial that was ten years ago. It scared the establishment press as much as Drudge's critical reports scared Hillary at the White House.

Did you know that the *Washington Post*, CNN, and other big news organizations actually resorted to lawsuits to try to prevent the kinds of news links provided by Drudge and *WorldNetDaily*? Do you know what their excuse was? They didn't like the idea of ordinary consumers being able to compare their news accounts to those of other news organizations.

Later, as Len Downie of the *Washington Post* noted, they figured out how much traffic was coming to their Web sites from the *Drudge Report* and *WorldNetDaily*. All was forgiven. And the big news agencies began courting our links. Personally, I hate to provide them. But an insider at the *Washington Post* told me that Drudge is their number one referrer, while *WND* is number two.

I have often speculated that if Matt Drudge and *WND* operated like a cartel and cut off their hyperlinks to certain large news agencies, we could actually do them serious harm. But why bother? The big media are imploding from their own dead weight.

Since the earlier press scandals I mentioned, there have been many more—even more prominent. Think Jayson Blair and Dan Rather. Even today, though, you will still hear about the irresponsibility of the New Media. You will hear how you can't trust independent Internet journalists. You will hear how only the big media have standards.

And who will you hear this from? Why, as a matter of fact, you hear it from the self-proclaimed gatekeepers of the truth—the arrogant establishment media.

You will notice I never refer to the establishment media or big media as "mainstream." I shudder when I hear that reference.

Personally, I don't think there is anything mainstream about the Old Media. They may have been mainstream once, but all the surveys show the general public is seeing them differently.

People are getting their news from alternative sources. They are turning in droves to Internet news sources that have broken the hammerlock of control over the flow of information.

That's why the "mainstream media" are no longer mainstream. I prefer to call them the "downstream media" or the "lamestream media."

The New Media are not infallible, but the Old Media no longer have any grounds for their arrogance, for their phony claims to superior standards. The charade is over.

Think of the success of this media revolution born in the last ten years. It is a paradigm shift so dramatic it boggles the mind.

Anything is possible.

Take your hat off to Matt Drudge.

CHAPTER TEN

HOW *WND* DEFEATED GORE IN 2000

"Why should freedom of speech and freedom of the press be allowed? Why should a government which is doing what it believes to be right allow itself to be criticized? It would not allow opposition by lethal weapons. Ideas are much more fatal things than guns. Why should any man be allowed to buy a printing press and disseminate pernicious opinion calculated to embarrass the government?"

—Nikolai Lenin, 1920

WHEN *WND* investigates Democrats, Republicans cheer. But when *WND* investigates Republicans, you ought to hear them whine.

It works the other way around, too.

Yet that is the nature of a watchdog press. You can't be truly independent, fearless, and credible as a news agency, unless you are ready, willing, and able to ferret out waste, abuse, fraud, and corruption wherever and whenever it is found.

I received an e-mail from a nice Republican, Christian lady recently. She thought I was being too tough on President Bush.

"I do believe you are a Christian," she said. "Check out Job sometime to see what the Lord has to say about 'friends' who judged Job! How easy for you to criticize. Where is your gratitude for the president's service?"

Job?

I've read Job. But I fail to see the parallel. Job was judged by his friends as sinful because of the afflictions he endured.

How is criticizing the most powerful man in the world akin to judging those who are suffering?

Nothing bad is happening to Bush. He hasn't lost his home and family. He doesn't have sores on his skin. He hasn't lost all his wealth. On the contrary, when it comes to Bush, we are exposing the bad things he is doing and has done to the country.

When people did bad things to the country in ancient Israel, the prophets called them on it—even kings. The prophet Nathan pointed the finger at David. Did he judge him? You bet he did.

Holding leaders accountable is a very biblical thing to do. Suggesting that all we should do is pray for them and hold them in high regard is anything but biblical—as the founding fathers clearly understood from poring over the Scriptures in English, Greek, and Hebrew.

So that's how I responded to this nice Republican, Christian lady who questioned my faith and called me hateful and arrogant because I held Bush accountable to his oath of office.

She wrote back and explained: "These are difficult times—especially for Israel. I believe that the Lord sent us a leader at such a time as this who would stand up to the enemies of Israel—His beloved. Say what you want about GWB, he is firm in his convictions and support for Israel—much more than any other president we have had. Imagine, Joseph, what would have happened had John Kerry or Al Gore been in command!"

"It doesn't seem to be 'good' for our country to have you 'pile on' with less than constructive criticism during these troubled and dangerous times," she added. "If you are comfortable answering to the Lord about your judgment, who am I to question you?"

What would have happened had John Kerry or Al Gore been in command?

It's a good question to ponder.

Certainly, the country would not have been better off. I take a backseat to no one in my contempt for these demagogues.

But let me remind readers that, in all likelihood, Al Gore would have been elected president of the United States in 2000 had it not been for the intrepid investigative reporting of *WND*—

reporting, by the way, that has been extremely costly to my company.

It's very likely you don't even know what I am talking about. Just as Drudge has been credited with being a major factor in the defeat of John Kerry in 2004, it was *WND* that was credited in 2000, by many who understand what happened in that election year, with the defeat of Al Gore.

You may recall that Gore lost the election because he did not win his home state of Tennessee. And, although the establishment press has accurately reported that Tennessee's eleven electoral votes would have put Gore at 271 and thereby made him the next president of the United States, most have missed the reason Gore suffered his first-ever political defeat in that state.

In his first run for Congress in Tennessee, Gore won an overwhelming 94 percent of the vote. His dominance was such that he ran unopposed for his next two House terms. And when he ran for his second term in the Senate, Gore became the first statewide candidate in Tennessee's history to take all ninety-five counties.

So why did Gore lose Tennessee on November 7, 2000—the first time a presidential candidate has failed to win his own state since George McGovern lost his native South Dakota in 1972?

The usual press analysis is that Tennessee's demographics had changed, sending the once-Democratic stronghold tipping to the Republican Party. There's probably some truth to that conventional wisdom. Yet the answer is far more fundamental than that.

"It was the character issue," says popular Nashville radio talk host Phil Valentine. "Thanks to talk radio and sources like *WorldNetDaily* getting out the truth, I believe it tipped the state to Bush."[1]

It was Valentine who initially broke a story on Gore's ties to alleged criminal figures in Wilson County, Tennessee, next door to Gore's home county. Shortly after that, *WND* ran an exhaustive, eighteen-part series of investigative reports detailing Gore's involvement in and interference with criminal investigations linked to his uncle, retired Judge Whit LaFon, and top campaign fund-raisers like Clark Jones of Savannah, Tennessee. According to Valentine, it was stories like those that spelled Gore's defeat.

"They [the stories] stayed under the radar nationally," he said, "but around here they were on everyone's lips."

Charlotte Alexander, editor of the *Decatur County Chronicle* in Parsons, Tennessee, agrees.

"Absolutely, it was the integrity issue," she affirms. Alexander's paper republished the *WND* series of articles profiling Gore's seamy political dealings in Tennessee.

"We sold out of every edition that carried those stories. People literally drove in from hundreds of miles away to buy twenty-five, fifty, a hundred copies, whatever they could afford, to take back with them," she said. "We had well-known Democrats come in here after reading those stories and say out loud that they couldn't be associated with somebody that behaved as Gore had." Alexander even had additional copies printed, but the public soon gobbled those up as well.

"Those [*WorldNetDaily*] stories coming out about Gore involving himself in criminal investigations were just too much," says former Tennessee Bureau of Investigation agent Milton Bowling. "I'm a Democrat, but I couldn't get past that. I know plenty of people who felt the same way. It was never a matter of party in Tennessee; it was always about character and integrity. Gore flunked that test."[2]

There is little evidence Tennessee suddenly turned Republican. In fact, Tennesseans have been conservative politically for decades. Since 1968, Tennessee has been a swing state in presidential politics, usually voting Republican, but giving its electoral votes to Democrats such as Jimmy Carter in 1976 and Bill Clinton in 1996.

From the beginning, the Gore campaign was concerned about the influence of the *WND* stories. Doug Hattaway, one of Gore's primary campaign spokesmen, personally called media outlets across middle and west Tennessee in late September and early October, pleading with, and in some cases reportedly threatening, news directors to keep the stories off the air and out of print.

"Doug Hattaway called me," said freelance TV reporter Tommy Stafford. Stafford had produced a story for WMC-TV in Memphis on the Charles Thompson and Tony Hays articles in *WND*. "He hammered at me," said Stafford, "but I told him, 'Look,

I interviewed these guys. They're credible.'" Hattaway then turned his attention to the news director at the Memphis station and the story was put on indefinite hold. "It was that kind of arrogance, plus the credibility issues, that beat Gore in Tennessee," said Stafford. "Political parties didn't have anything to do with it."[3]

"It was an uphill battle against news sources like the *Tennessean*, who refused to tell the true story," said Valentine. "I think people began to question Gore's character and integrity here in Tennessee. I think the truth came back to bite Gore in Tennessee, and I find it ironic that, if Florida holds for Bush, it will be Tennessee that was Gore's downfall."

"Whether the mainstream media believed the *WorldNetDaily* stories were credible or not," said Alexander, "the voters did. I've never seen articles that attracted the kind of attention these did. They cost Gore the margin he needed in middle and west Tennessee. They cost Gore Tennessee's electoral votes. That's a fact."

I remember when we were running those eighteen stories in the last stages of the 2000 election. I was concerned and disappointed that they were not getting any "bounce" from my colleagues in the national press. But even I was not aware of what was happening in Tennessee. Those articles were reverberating. They were being reprinted in local newspapers. They were being talked about on radio. They were even covered by local television.

And that, as Paul Harvey would say, is the rest of the story about how *WND* defeated Gore in his home state in 2000, depriving him of the presidency. Had Gore won Tennessee, the disputed Florida vote would have been meaningless. He would have been sworn in as president.

Ironic, isn't it? Al Gore invented the Internet, and it may have turned out to be his undoing.

I tell you all this not simply to blow my own horn—though I have no problem doing that and no shortage of reasons. But I think it's important for people to understand the impact of the New Media on the political culture of the United States.

Right after Election Day, I was pummeled with criticism from George W. Bush supporters who stated emphatically that my own frequent and sometimes harsh criticism of the Texas governor during the campaign had negatively impacted an election that was, at that time, still too close to call. Reader after reader wrote blaming me for the stalemate. Hundreds of them said that had I simply done "the right thing" and endorsed Bush that I could have provided the margin of victory for him.

However, what these folks failed to realize is that our investigative reporting into the obvious corruption of Gore—in both his character and in his political life—had a far greater impact on the national election than my own principled agnosticism toward the Republican alternative.

But that was hardly the end of the story. Immediately following the election, a Tennessee auto dealer and Democratic Party activist, Clark Jones, began threatening *WND* with a defamation lawsuit. I have to tell you, at first it seemed like one of the many toothless threats we receive in the news business any time someone's feelings are hurt.

The retraction demands alleged *WND* reported things it hadn't reported. They disputed seemingly indisputable facts. Nevertheless, we addressed them seriously and forthrightly as we are trained to do in the news business.

Then, in April 2001, Clark Jones, Al Gore's top fund-raiser in Tennessee, filed a $165 million libel suit against *WND*, reporters Thompson and Hays, along with numerous other defendants— some of whom had little or nothing to do with the preparation and publication of the series.

Now, I have to tell you, a $165 million lawsuit is big no matter how you slice it. It is, in fact, one of the largest defamation lawsuits ever filed in the United States. And you would be hard-pressed to find any meaningful coverage of the case—now in its sixth year—anywhere else but *WND*. In fact, in the history of U.S. libel cases, this may be the biggest.

Normally, media colleagues rally around those hit with such suits. That has not been the case here.

Jones claims personal embarrassment and humiliation as a result of some of the articles, which said that he reportedly intervened in a Tennessee Bureau of Investigation probe into narcotics trafficking in Hardin County in 1999. In addition, the car dealer claims that the articles implicated him in the 1980 arson of his own business, the Jones Motor Company, and also pegged him as a suspected drug dealer. He claims business losses and health problems resulted from the series as well.

Hays's twenty-part series on drug trafficking in west Tennessee was primarily responsible for the *Courier of Savannah* winning the 2000 Public Service Award from the Tennessee Press Association. He has published numerous magazine and newspaper articles on Tennessee political corruption, and a history of the Savannah area, the last through a grant from the Tennessee Historical Commission.

Thompson, who started his journalism career in print media, soon moved to television, where he captured an Emmy for his investigative reporting as well as the Headliner's Award. He worked for a number of years as Mike Wallace's producer at CBS's *60 Minutes* and was a founding producer of ABC's *20/20*. His investigation into the explosion of "gun turret two" on the USS *Iowa* in 1989 resulted in a book, published by W. W. Norton in 1999 and a movie starring James Caan.

Where are the First Amendment activists in this case? So far, only one legal group has stepped up to the plate—the United States Justice Foundation. It joined the defense team representing the two freelance reporters.

Let me put it bluntly: this lawsuit is the legal equivalent of a drive-by shooting. I don't think it's an accident that the number one independent Internet news site was targeted by powerful and wealthy friends of the losing presidential candidate—and that the suit pertained to an investigative series that may well have cost that candidate the Electoral College votes he needed for victory. The fact that this disgraceful attack on the First Amendment has never been actively denounced by journalists and media activists from coast to coast is a sad commentary on the state of our industry.

This is not a case about the reputation of one man. It's clearly about revenge for Al Gore losing the presidency.

In a very tangible and real way, the *WND* "Tennessee Underworld" series impacted the presidential election. There is no doubt in my mind.

This is a very big lawsuit. Am I afraid? No. But defending ourselves in this nightmarish case has been expensive and distracting. And no lawsuit—especially one for $165 million—can ever be taken lightly. After all, we live in the age of O. J. Simpson. Juries can be quirky. Sometimes courts don't actually find justice. A spirited defense against this action is essential. And spirited defenses of high-profile lawsuits filed by wealthy, politically connected activists take time and money.

Getting sued—or being threatened with lawsuits—is an occupational hazard when you take journalism as seriously as we do. Just as coal miners risk cave-ins and police risk being shot, journalism organizations risk being sued. It goes with the territory. When people don't like what you report about them—even if your reporting is totally true—they can and often will sue you, or threaten to, if they have the means.

While the Jones-Gore case represents by far the biggest legal challenge in *WND*'s ten-year history, there have been plenty of threats. We kind of pride ourselves by the roster of "enemies" we've made over the years—including atheist-activist Michael Newdow and at least half a dozen radical Islamic groups that have issued retraction demands. Because of *WND*'s aggressive reporting on Islamic terrorism, several Muslim groups—both in the United States and overseas—have threatened to sue *WND*. So far, each attack has been successfully defused out of court by *WND*'s dedicated attorneys.

Attacking from another direction, atheist Newdow—who infamously sued to have the "Under God" phrase taken from the Pledge of Allegiance—turned his legal guns on *WND*, filing a $1 million libel lawsuit against the Internet news organization. *WND* quickly beat back Newdow's baseless attack.

These attacks forced *WND* to set up a legal defense fund to stave off the threats and help pay for the ongoing litigation. But it has cost us hundreds of hours. It has cost us hundreds of thousands of dollars.

But if Al Gore thinks he's going to be treated with kid gloves by me as a result of this kind of bullying tactic, he doesn't know who he's dealing with. As you already know, I did not cave in to the pressure tactics of the Clinton administration during eight years in the 1990s, and I have no intention of caving in to the pressure tactics of Gore—or anyone else—in the twenty-first century.

In fact, after six years of this kind of abuse, I haven't gone soft on Al Gore. Do you want to know what I think of him?

He's irresponsible.

He's a traitor to his country.

He's a congenital liar who wouldn't know the truth if it bit him on the backside.

He's an enemy of the American people.

He's unworthy of American citizenship, let alone the high offices he has held and aspired to hold.

He needs a keeper.

He's producing enough hot air to make his doomsday predictions about global warming a self-fulfilling prophecy.

He's one coconut short of a piña colada.

Honestly, he never ceases to amaze me.

It is incredible to me that the man can be taken seriously by millions of Americans.

No one in politics is more willing to revise history—and lie—than Al Gore. Let me give you some examples.

In March 2006, he gave a speech in Florida, accusing the Bush administration of deceiving Americans about weapons of mass destruction in Iraq and connections between Saddam Hussein and Osama bin Laden.

"I'm not calling it a lie," he said. "I'm not. I'm not. We got what turned out to be the false impression that Saddam Hussein had a lot to do with attacking our country on September 11. We got the impression that he was about to build an atomic bomb with uranium from Africa and give it to his buddy, Osama bin Laden."[4]

Of course, those were not the impressions the Bush administration gave to the American people at all—no matter how accurate or inaccurate such nonassertions may have been. But if the

American people got those impressions from anywhere, the Clinton-Gore administration was just as responsible as its successor.

Gore has been playing this game for a long time. And Americans need to recognize that's what it is—a despicable political game that has nothing to do with America's national security or protecting the lives of U.S. military servicemen.

It began for Gore on June 24, 2002, when he gave a speech at Georgetown University in which he accused Bush of "intentionally misleading the American people by continuing to aggressively and brazenly assert a linkage between al-Qaida and Saddam Hussein. If he is not lying, if he genuinely believes that, that makes them [sic] unfit in battle against al-Qaida. If they believe these flimsy scraps, then who would want them in charge?"[5]

He may be backtracking today, but changing his story is nothing new for Gore.

Four years earlier, it was President Clinton who was warning, on February 17, 1998, of "reckless acts of outlaw nations and an unholy axis of terrorists, drug traffickers, and organized international criminals." He said these "predators of the twenty-first century," who are America's enemies, "will be all the more lethal if we allow them to build arsenals of nuclear, chemical, and biological weapons and missiles to deliver them. We simply cannot allow that to happen. There is no more clear example of this threat than Saddam Hussein's Iraq."

Later that year, it was the Clinton-Gore administration that prepared an indictment of bin Laden, that read in part: "Al-Qaida reached an understanding with the government of Iraq that al-Qaida would not work against that government and that on particular projects, specifically including weapons development, al-Qaida would work cooperatively with the government of Iraq."

But Gore doesn't want you to remember any of that.

He wants you to think that Bush deceived Americans—presumably even himself, a guy with access to his administration's classified security briefings. Gore changed his mind, but he prefers you to think he knew better all the time. Would you call that a lie? Would you call that disingenuous?

Here's what Gore was saying as late as September 23, 2002, about the threat Iraq represented to the United States and the world:

"We know that he [Saddam Hussein] has stored secret supplies of biological and chemical weapons throughout his country."

"Iraq's search for weapons of mass destruction has proven impossible to deter and we should assume that it will continue for as long as Saddam is in power."

And what would you say about a former vice president of the United States, a candidate for the presidency, who lies about "terrible abuses" against Arabs by his country while addressing an audience in Saudi Arabia?

That's what Al Gore did. And he did it during a time in which the Arab and Muslim world is already enflamed against the United States and the West because of the Muhammad cartoons.

What would I say about Al Gore? How would I characterize him? Here's what I would say in a wholesome forum like this:

He's irresponsible.

He's a traitor to his country.

He's a congenital liar who wouldn't know the truth if it bit him on the backside.

He's an enemy of the American people.

He's unworthy of American citizenship, let alone the high offices he has held and aspired to hold.

He needs a keeper.

He's producing enough hot air to make his doomsday predictions about global warming a self-fulfilling prophecy.

He's one coconut short of a piña colada.

Gore actually claimed Arabs had been "indiscriminately rounded up" and held in "unforgivable" conditions following September 11.

"The thoughtless way in which visas are now handled, that is a mistake," Gore said during the Jiddah Economic Forum. "The worst thing we can possibly do is to cut off the channels of friendship and mutual understanding between Saudi Arabia and the United States."[6]

Gore told the largely Saudi audience, many of them educated at U.S. universities, that Arabs in the United States had been "indiscriminately rounded up, often on minor charges of overstaying a visa or not having a green card in proper order, and held in conditions that were just unforgivable."

"Unfortunately there have been terrible abuses and it's wrong," Gore said. "I do want you to know that it does not represent the desires or wishes or feelings of the majority of the citizens of my country."[7]

Despicable, treacherous, seditious—that's what Gore's speech was.

There is no excuse for what Al Gore did in Saudi Arabia. It's beyond shameful. It's beyond sedition. He is inciting more terrorist attacks on America—providing the very excuses and cover these animals welcome.

This man is not suitable or worthy to be a dogcatcher in America.

He is a disgrace to this wonderful, tolerant bastion of freedom and pluralism.

Imagine going to a foreign country where it is illegal for Christians and Jews to live and worship and decrying phantom human-rights abuses *in America!*

That's what Al Gore did.

Imagine going to a foreign country where it is illegal for women to drive and decrying phantom human-rights abuses *in America!*

That's what Al Gore did.

Imagine going to a foreign country that was responsible for most of the manpower used in the September 11 attack on America and decrying phantom human-rights abuses *in America!*

That's what Al Gore did.

Imagine going to a foreign country that provided much of the funding for the Taliban hosts of those who attacked American September 11 and decrying phantom human-rights abuses *in America.*

That's what Al Gore did.

Imagine gong to a foreign country that still, to this day, aids the worst Islamofascist terrorists in the world and decrying phantom human-rights abuses *in America!*

That's what Al Gore did.

Do you think I've gone soft on Al Gore?

And what is this menace to society up to now?

He has joined the New Media. That's right, this darling of the First Amendment has become a cable TV "entrepreneur."

Officially, the new television network is known as "Current."

I call it "Algorezeera."

When the former vice president embarked on his acquisition of a TV cable network, he assured the public there would be no partisanship, no ideological agenda behind the effort.

Is Al Gore really capable of programming a TV news network that is nonideological?

I really question that. In fact, I would question whether anyone can truly divorce themselves from their own worldview in the presentation of the news. I would question whether anyone should pretend they can do that.

I certainly question whether Al Gore can do it.

Whether the agenda is driven by the worldview of the Bible or the worldview of atheism, there is no escaping our worldview. Everybody's got one.

And Al Gore has one deeply rooted in religious fervor and fanaticism—much like his colleagues over at *Al-Jazeera*. If you doubt what I'm saying, check out his book, *Earth in the Balance*. In it, he says his vision of environmentalism must become "the central organizing principle for civilization."

"The prevailing ideology of belief in prehistoric Europe and much of the world was based on the worship of a single earth goddess, who was assumed to be the fount of all life and who radiated harmony among all living things," he writes. "The last vestige of organized goddess worship was eliminated by Christianity as late as the fifteenth century in Lithuania ... it seems obvious that a better understanding of [goddess worship] could offer us new insights into the nature of our human experience."[8]

Gore is a proponent of goddess worship. He believes this pagan idea is a better and more legitimate spiritual belief system than Christianity.

Still not convinced this man is one coconut short of a piña colada? Check this out: he actually can't decide which has more intrinsic value—the life of a human being or the life of a tree.

"The Pacific Yew can be cut down and processed to produce a potent chemical, taxol, which offers some promise of curing certain forms of lung, breast, and ovarian cancer in patients who would otherwise quickly die," he writes. "It seems an easy choice—sacrifice the tree for a human life—until one learns that three trees must be destroyed for each patient treated."[9]

Do you think someone with those kinds of extreme views is capable of keeping them out of his TV news programming?

I don't think so.

CHAPTER ELEVEN

THE OTHER SCOOPS THAT SHOOK THE WORLD

*"The job of the newspaper is to comfort the afflicted
and afflict the comfortable."*

—F. P. Dunne, journalist-humorist

I THOUGHT I was prepared for anything when we launched *WorldNetDaily*.

After all, I had served for years as one of the youngest top newspaper executives in the country. I had been around the block, witnessed the impact of good investigative reporting on public policy, and had high expectations about the role of the press in a free society.

But nothing could have prepared me for the immediate national and international impact *WND* made from the very start.

Just four months after our inauspicious—almost secret—debut, I was watching a C-SPAN interview with former secretary of state Alexander Haig when a caller from Las Vegas asked him about a story I had written, even referencing my name.

It had to do with China's involvement with the port of Long Beach on behalf of its state-owned COSCO shipping company and a plan called Sea Launch, in which Russia and China teamed up with Boeing to launch satellites from offshore in the same area.

Haig smirked his way through most of the comment and question, before responding: "Well, that's a wang-banger. Let me answer that, because it's all hogwash. And whoever wrote such claptrap ought to be put in jail for perjury. This is totally untrue.

The COSCO operation in Long Beach is no more than a taking over of a now-defunct naval port facility and bringing jobs and opportunities to the local community and opening up America and China together. This other talk that you mentioned is just plain hogwash. And I would be very, very skeptical of people running around accusing our president of some kind of disloyalty. Let me tell you, that's not the case."[1]

That's what he said.

On national television, Al Haig called for me to be arrested— summarily imprisoned. It was quite an exhilarating moment. This was, after all, the man who had claimed to be in charge of the whole country immediately after President Reagan was shot. Now he was calling for me to be jailed for perjury! (And I hadn't even testified under oath.)

Why was Haig so testy?

Because he was, and probably still is, a hired gun for the People's Republic of China. Henry Kissinger and Haig have made a fortune by opening doors in China for U.S. companies vying to get into that lucrative market. Haig has even collected directly from the Chinese at least once as a paid but unregistered adviser.

In other words, Haig was defending the actions of the Clinton administration because he was dipping into the same trough, drinking from the same polluted well.

RSC-Energia, a Russian company well connected with the GRU, the military-intelligence agency that succeeded the KGB, was, as I had reported, a partner with Boeing and others in the Long Beach–based operation called Sea Launch, that plans to begin launching satellites from offshore platforms. It was, among other reasons, the proximity of this high-tech venture of great strategic significance that was driving China's ambitions for a beachhead in Southern California. With the presence of COSCO, a company closely tied to the Chinese army and navy, it would serve, my sources said, as a key listening post for Beijing and Moscow.

While Haig was calling for me to be jailed for exposing this development, he was serving officially and publicly as a senior honorary adviser to COSCO, a People's Liberation Army front.

By the way, time usually tells who was telling the truth and who was lying. That is the case with COSCO and Sea Launch. Both projects are a reality today in the Long Beach port area. And the Democratic president that the Republican Haig defended got away with accepting hundreds of thousands of dollars in campaign cash from the Chinese in 1992 and 1996.

In the future, the New Media would prove it was not only an attention getter, but a proven force in changing the direction of public policy. One of those opportunities came less than a year later.

In June 1998, *WND* first exposed an executive order signed by President Clinton in the dark of night. It was called Executive Order 13083. It would have justified federal intervention in any issue for any reason. There is simply no other reasonable way of interpreting it. It would have reduced state and local government to, at best, advisory status. I say "at best" because Clinton didn't even bother to consult with state and local officials before issuing EO 13083.[2]

While visiting Birmingham, England, on May 14, President Clinton quietly signed a skillfully crafted executive order that would have fundamentally altered the relationship between Washington and the states and seriously eroded the balance of powers established by the Tenth Amendment.

Executive Order 13083 began innocently enough by restating the principles of federalism that limit the power and scope of the U.S. government under the Constitution. In fact, my reaction to reading the first two sections of the order was surprise that such principles would even be acknowledged by the Clinton administration, which typically acted as if there are no limits to the jurisdiction of the federal government.

That was the window dressing. The meat came in section 3, where the president attempted to establish all the exceptions to such principles.

"It is important to recognize the distinction between matters of national or multi-state scope (which may justify Federal action) and matters that are merely common to the States (which may not justify Federal action because individual States, acting individually or together, may effectively deal with them)," the order reads. It then lists nine kinds of issues that would justify unilateral federal action:

1. When the matter to be addressed by Federal action occurs interstate as opposed to being contained within one State's boundaries;

2. When the source of the matter to be addressed occurs in a State different from the State (or States) where a significant amount of the harm occurs;

3. When there is a need for uniform national standards;

4. When decentralization increases the costs of government thus imposing additional burdens on the taxpayer;

5. When States have not adequately protected individual rights and liberties;

6. When States would be reluctant to impose necessary regulations because of fears that regulated business activity will relocate to other States;

7. When placing regulatory authority at the State or local level would undermine regulatory goals because high costs or demands for specialized expertise will effectively place the regulatory matter beyond the resources of State authorities;

8. When the matter relates to Federally owned or managed property or natural resources, trust obligations, or international obligations; and

9. When the matter to be regulated significantly or uniquely affects Indian tribal governments.

In other words, under the provisions of Executive Order 13083, the federal government could do whatever it pleased any time it wanted. Let's face it; this list of exceptions could be interpreted as giving Washington the right to intercede in virtually any matter, anytime, anywhere. Think about it.

Health care? You bet. That's a matter that occurs interstate. Environmental standards? We can't leave an important matter like that to the states. Education? Well, we need national standards. Law enforcement? Crime occurs everywhere, doesn't it? Gun laws? Some states are not doing their part to protect people from firearms. Discrimination? Would you believe there are still some states that don't allow homosexuals to marry one another?

State and local government, in effect, would become advisory boards to Washington, more specifically, to the president—or, shall we say, dictator—of the United States of America. After all, this sweeping rewrite of the Constitution was accomplished by one official without consultation, advice, or consent of the Congress or judicial branch.

The executive order stated that the federal government would "permit elected officials and other representatives of State and local government to provide meaningful and timely input in the development of regulatory polices...." Forget about ordinary private citizens. They are mere subjects as far as Clinton is concerned.

With one stroke of the pen, while, perhaps fittingly, on foreign soil, President Clinton attempted to redefine the American system of government.

And not a word was written about it in the *Washington Post*, the *New York Times*, the Associated Press, or the *Wall Street Journal*. It wasn't until *WND* broke the story that nationwide opposition began to mount—and only then did other media begin to cover it, without, I might add, any reference to the news organization that broke the story and alerted the American people to the threat.

This would become a familiar patter for the future.

But make no mistake, the story of Executive Order 13083 and its fallout was a major early victory for the New Media.

Weeks after it was signed, nobody in Congress even seemed to know about the order. Those who took the time to read it simply didn't comprehend the threat it represented.

But then two congressmen—Reps. Ron Paul of Texas and Bob Barr of Georgia—sponsored legislation, HR 4197, the "State Sovereignty Act of 1998," declaring 13083 null and void.

"The head of each Federal department and each Federal agency shall ensure that each activity of the department or agency, respectively, is carried out in accordance with all provisions of Executive Order 12612 (as in effect on October 26, 1987) as apply to the activity under the terms of that Executive Order," the bill added.

Executive Order 12612 had been issued by President Reagan. EO 13083 repealed its provisions.

The second major encouraging development was the action taken by the "Big Seven" organizations of state and local governments—the National Governors Association, National Conference of State Legislatures, the Council of State Governments, the U.S. Conference of Mayors, the National League of Cities, the National Association of Counties, and the International City/County Management Association.

In an unexpected move, these organizations united to take issue with EO 13083. They drafted a letter to Clinton demanding he withdraw the executive order. They also sent representatives to meet with Mickey Ibarra, the chief of White House intergovernmental relations.

The conflict resulted in the first story about EO 13083 in the establishment press. The *Washington Post's* David Broder was forced to report on the controversy. But how did the controversy get started? The *Washington Post* couldn't say—because, besides *WorldNetDaily*, no other news organization had previously reported on the executive order. Rather than mention how national opposition was fomented, Broder just left the issue unaddressed.

WorldNetDaily carried the first significant story about the order June 17. That story and subsequent follow-ups were linked to and broadcast e-mailed all over the Internet. Talk-radio hosts from coast to coast, including Rush Limbaugh and Michael Reagan, picked up the story and warned of the order's unconstitutional implications.

You know what this was? This was the first real-life example of why Hillary Clinton had those Internet nightmares years earlier. This was an example of phantom "vast right-wing media conspiracy" in action. Only this time, when Clinton's deeds were exposed, there was as much opposition expressed from Democrats as Republicans, from liberals as conservatives.

As a result of the controversy, White House officials told the *Post* they had decided to recommend to the president that implementation of the order be delayed so that state and local officials could have their say.

Later, however, Executive Order 13083 would be officially revoked. It was something of a first. No president had ever issued an executive order and revoked in it such a short period of time.

Still, there was an even bigger story here. How did *WND* manage to scoop the rest of the press on 13083? Very simple. Until we came along, apparently no other news organization ever bothered to read executive orders. We decided we would look at all of them.

And it's a good thing we did. Because Clinton, we later learned, planned to use the power of executive orders to go over the heads of Congress and legislate from the executive branch.

At the very moment Americans were learning about EO 13083, the Clinton administration was rubbing its hands together plotting to amass "imperial powers" with even more orders.

As top White House aide Paul Begala arrogantly put it in a *New York Times* story on July 5, 1998, about the president's agenda for bypassing Congress with executive order power: "Stroke of the pen. Law of the land. Kinda cool."[3]

That line would come back to haunt Begala and his boss after *WND* put it in context for millions.

"He's ready to work with Congress if they work with him," explained Rahm Emanuel, senior policy adviser to the president in that same story. "But if they choose partisanship, he will choose progress."

Was Clinton within his rights as president to use the power of the executive order? There's no question other presidents abused the practice. But none more than Clinton.

Executive orders were originally intended to give presidents rule-making authority over the executive branch—to allow him to preside as the chief executive officer of the White House and its vast number of employees and departments. Clinton reinvented the executive order as a form of presidential law-making authority—something in direct contradiction to the Constitution.

Nevertheless, executive orders, unless challenged and overturned by Congress or revoked by presidents, have a way of becoming the law of the land, as Begala suggested.

I saw this as a pretty big deal, given one of Clinton's executive orders would empower him to declare a national emergency and set up the Federal Emergency Management Agency to direct federal, state, and local governments. The provision replicated the executive powers laid down in the 1933 War Powers Act and would allow FEMA to control all communication facilities (including, presumably, *WND* and the *Drudge Report*), power supplies, food supplies, airports, transportation of any kind, seaports, waterways, and highways. Congress would not even be able to debate the president's declaration for the first six months of totalitarian rule.

The president could have implemented this draconian plan under "any threat to national security, perceived or real." Would you trust Bill Clinton with that kind of authority? Apparently, the Republican-controlled Congress did. And so did the corporate media establishment. No one spoke out against the prospect of American fascism—not even the American Civil Liberties Union. I use that term "American fascism" advisedly because it was a similar arrangement under which Adolph Hitler suspended the German constitution by presidential decree.

Bill Clinton got away with a lot during his eight years in office, but he didn't get away with this broad daylight attempt to rip up the Constitution, thanks to our efforts at *WND*. Am I proud about that? You bet.

We had some other big successes too—some big stories that produced big results, convincing me that the New Media offered America real hope about reinvigorating the role of the free press in a still free society.

Long before the September 11, 2001, terrorist attacks, the federal government was already plotting new ways to snoop on ordinary American citizens. In 1998, we began investigating what was called the "Know Your Customer" banking plan of the Federal Deposit Insurance Corp.

According to the plan, which, again, had not been debated by anyone in Congress or reported on by any news organizations, banks would be asked to establish "profiles" of their customers and report any deviations from those profiles. Under certain circumstances, for instance, bank customers might find themselves explaining to the FBI, Internal Revenue Service, and Drug Enforcement Agency why they made a $15,000 deposit to their bank account.

Fortunately, the FDIC did provide for citizen comment prior to implementation of their "Know Your Customer" plan. And thanks to the reports in *WND*, they received some—171,268, to be exact, all before the deadline.

Our reporters learned that *WND* had become a household epithet in the halls of the FDIC. But at least they answered our phone calls. As a result of the hullabaloo started by the *WND* reports, the resonance they got in talk radio and other media, the U.S. Senate eventually voted 88–0 against implementing the plan that was previously on the fast track with no opposition.

Another big series of scoops offered up in the early days of *WND* was on the subject of what I referred to as "a domestic arms buildup." It turned out the Clinton administration wasn't really against guns. It was very much for them—as long as they were in the hands of federal law enforcement, which saw a massive increase in size in those eight years.

When Bill Clinton took power in 1993, there were 69,000 federal cops on the payroll. Five years later, *WND* discovered, there were 83,000.

What were they doing? Were they hunting for terrorists? Were they making city streets safe from violent predators? Were they bringing down the murder rate in Washington, D.C.? No. They weren't doing any of those things. And most of them were not even a part of agencies with familiar initials—like the FBI,

DEA (Drug Enforcement Administration), INS (Immigration and Naturalization Service), or the U.S. marshals service. Only 33,000 of that total figures into the ranks of those agencies.

If most of the growth took place outside of traditional law-enforcement agencies such as the FBI, who was carrying all the new guns? The answer was, simply, everyone from the postman to the Environmental Protection Agency field worker to agents of U.S. Fish and Wildlife Service and Army Corps of Engineers.

Sometimes I think about what the world would be like without *WND*. It would be a world where some of the biggest stories are never told. Like what? How about the deaths of 50 million people?

In the fall of 1998, we took a look at a World Health Organization report—one seen, I'm certain, by hundreds of other news organizations. But we saw something there no other news agency saw or was willing to report. It was a finding that should have prompted front-page headlines around the globe.

The report, released at WHO's Regional Committee for the Western Pacific, said more than fifty million women were estimated to be "missing" in China because of the institutionalized killing and neglect of girls due to Beijing's population control program that limits parents to one child.

Many of the girls were killed while still in the womb—the victims of ultrasound technology that revealed the baby's sex. Others, WHO said, were starved to death after birth, the victims of violence, or were not treated when they became ill.

The report's statistics showed that in 1994, 117 boys were born for every 100 girls in China. Though baby girls tend to have a higher survival rate than boys, that natural process has been dramatically reversed in China by infanticide, gross neglect, maltreatment, and malnutrition of females in a culture that regards boys as more desirable—especially when couples get only one chance at parenthood.

The trend transcended the infancy stage, too, the report showed. Girls were at higher risk than boys of dying before the age of five in China—despite their natural biological advantages.

"In many cases, mothers are more likely to bring their male children to health centers—particularly to private physicians—

and they may be treated at an earlier stage of disease than girls," the paper reported.

Just to put this story in perspective, WHO was documenting what can only be described as the biggest single holocaust in human history—and doing it in a surprisingly clinical and low-key fashion.

I even came up with a new name for this holocaust, and it stuck. I called it "gender-cide."

WND may not have broken the story about a stained blue dress, but I like to think we have broken some stories far more shocking and, in the big scheme of things, far more important. How about this one?

In 1998, *WND* first alerted the nation about the fact that, as governor of Arkansas, Bill Clinton knowingly oversaw the illicit sale of state prison blood to Canadian hemophiliacs and others—spreading AIDS and other deadly diseases to hundreds, perhaps thousands, in the 1980s. While this story has never quite made it into the *New York Times*—at least not in a form that would be understandable to people—the "blood trail" story has been turned into a major motion picture.

And I'm sure it's an exciting movie. In 1999, *WND* reported, in cooperation with the *Ottawa Citizen*, that two crimes occurred within hours of each other hundreds of miles apart that raised questions as to whether someone was attempting to silence those who tried to expose the scandal.

In Pine Bluff, Arkansas, someone firebombed a prosthetics clinic owned by Michael Galster, the author, under the nom de plume Michael Sullivan, of *Blood Trail*, a fictional account of the prison-blood scandal. Since writing his book, Galster was on an international campaign to expose the blood trail that led from the Arkansas prisons to the AIDS deaths in Canada.

Meanwhile, in Montreal, someone broke into the offices of the Quebec chapter of the Canadian Hemophilia Society, which had recently unearthed documents that showed Finance Minister Paul Martin was a board member of the corporation that owned Connaught Laboratories, the company that fractionated and distributed the Arkansas prison plasma in Canada. Officials at the Hemophilia Society said thieves stole a computer, telephones, and documents from a box labeled "Hepatitis C, Krever Commission, Reform of the blood system, HIV-AIDS." Executive Director Pierre Desmarais said it appears the thieves were looking for information rather than goods.

In 2005, the Canadian Red Cross pleaded guilty to distributing this tainted blood in a health disaster that killed more than 3,000—more than were killed on 9/11.

In 2005, filmmaker Kelly Duda released his documentary *Factor 8: The Arkansas Prison Blood Scandal*. It showed how senior figures in the state prison system altered prisoners' medical records to make it look like they were not carrying the deadly diseases.

In 2006, Scots infected with HIV protested Bill Clinton's appearance in Glasgow highlighting the former president's connection to the scandal in which tainted blood from high-risk Arkansas prisoners was used to treat thousands of people in Europe who later came down with AIDS and hepatitis.

Clinton may not yet have been held accountable for these crimes. But I'm confident he will be. If not in this life, certainly in the next.

Sometime, as in the case of the FDIC banking plan, results of good reporting are almost immediate. Such was the case with *WND*'s scoop on Citibank's policy of denying bank services to firearms businesses.

The strange policy was exposed by *WND* in 2000. It took all of three weeks for the corporate banking giant to reexamine its policies and determine that they were "inconsistent."

Here's another big, big story first broken by *WND*. And when you think about the extremely limited resources a news company like *WND* has versus the corporate giants, it really is a David and Goliath mismatch. Did you know that *WND* was the first news agency in the world to report the space shuttle Columbia disaster was likely the result of a problem with foam insulation breaking free from the external tank and slamming into the leading edge of the left wing?

When did *WND* report it? Not a month later. Not a week later. But one day later—February 2, 2003.

"Did environmentalism bring down Columbia?" was the headline on the report published at 5 p.m. that fateful weekend day. While most news organizations were waiting for the Associated Press to lead them, *WND* looked at the evidence available, compared it with the track record of similar problems at NASA, and did the necessary Internet research to come up with conclusions that would—only months and years later—be validated by the independent reporting of the *Washington Post* and other investigators.

The *WND* report made clear that the problem found to cause the Columbia disaster, in which seven crew members were killed, had been discovered and noted more than six years earlier. *WND* found the memo on NASA's own Web site. A NASA whistleblower, it turned out, had been repeatedly reprimanded for pointing out the recurrent problem.

Over and over again, big stories and small, *WND* reporting— I gotta tell you—has been leading the way, not just among New Media enterprises, but among all of them.

Whose investigative reporting led to the withdrawal of Supreme Court nominee Harriet Miers?

Whose investigative reporting led to the cancellation by NBC of the program *The Book of Daniel,* a series about a pill-popping Episcopal priest with a dysfunctional family and congregation and a show in which a "hip" Jesus character made a recurring role?

Whose investigative reporting first revealed Julian Bond, the chairman of the National Association for the Advancement of Colored People, gave a speech at Fayetteville State University in North Carolina in which he equated the Republican Party with the Nazis?

Whose investigative reporting first revealed the threat of electromagnetic pulse weapons to the security of the United States and specifically Iran's plans to use them?

Fun stories, serious stories, big stories, little stories—*WND* breaks an amazing number. And it does it daily—even hourly. All of these stories, by the way, are chronicled on the Web site, year by year, in narrative form under the heading "*WND* SCOOPS." Space in these pages does not permit me to even scratch the surface of the scoops legacy. But in cyberspace, there is no shortage of electrons.

Having said all that, there is one story that stands out head and shoulders above all the others as a defining investigation for *WND*. It is the story of Terri Schiavo.

Maybe you're thinking, *Farah, are you nuts? The whole world stopped to cover the death of Terri Schiavo.* And you'd be right. But what you may not know is that the whole world might never have known the name Terri Schiavo had it not been for three years of dogged, determined, relentless reporting on the brain-damaged woman—before any other national news organization touched it!

That's right. *WND* was there first—and, in this case, *WND* remained there, all alone, for what seemed like an eternity, before any of our colleagues finally waded in.

In the spring of 2005, the world was riveted to the harrowing story of a forty-one-year-old handicapped woman named Terri Schindler-Schiavo.

And let me break away from my dispassionate role as a reporter for a moment to tell you what I think happened to her. As the entire world watched, Terri was mercilessly killed by dehydration over a period of weeks. Those who attempted to bring her water were turned away—arrested if necessary.

She was denied water and food—not exactly extraordinary means of sustaining a life.

The only excuse for this barbaric behavior was a court order from a local county judge in Florida in support of Terri's husband's request to kill his wife by withholding sustenance. Michael Schiavo had claimed that, in a casual conversation twenty years earlier, Terri had said she didn't ever want to live "hooked up to machines."

The claim was specious because it was never more than hearsay evidence from the man most determined—for whatever his motivations—to see her die.

It was specious because it was consistently countered by many people who knew Terri better and longer than her husband, Michael Schiavo.

It was specious because Michael Schiavo had moved on with his life, found a new woman he referred to as his "fiancée," lived with her for ten years, and raised two children with her.

It was specious because Michael Schiavo not only had emotional reasons to deprive Terri of life, he had possible financial motivations.

It was irrelevant because Terri had never been hooked up to machines.

It was irrelevant because people's minds change about all kinds of things over twenty years—including issues of life and death.

The truth is Terri had no business ever being placed in a hospice—a place for terminally ill patients—and being shut off from light and stimulation and visitors, particularly a place partly owned by the very people trying to rob her of life.

It was a national disgrace that this woman was killed with the whole world watching.

It was a national disgrace that our political system failed her.

It was a national disgrace that our judicial system betrayed her and denied her justice.

That's what I came to believe about this case. But I had a little more time to think about it than most Americans. Because two intrepid *WND* reporters—Sarah Foster and Diana Lynne—covered the case when no one else did or would. Lynne ultimately wrote the book *Terri's Story: The Court-Ordered Death of an American Woman*, still the best piece of long-form journalism done on this remarkable story.

It's healthy to have more news coverage—especially the kind *WND* provides from a distinctly different perspective.

No longer does the arrogant viewpoint of elitists in New York, Washington, and Los Angeles dominate the national debate.

The impact of what news sources like *WND* have contributed to our society cannot be overstated.

This happens on a daily basis. And it is a development we have begun to take for granted in just the last decade.

For those of us old enough to remember what it was like when the *New York Times* and Associated Press—two news organizations—virtually dictated the news agenda for the country, this development represents a sea change, a revolution, a media palace coup.

Most Americans, however, have no idea how tenuous this development is. Most have no idea how precious few are the resources available to news organizations like *WND*. Most have no idea how we are being challenged and tested and attacked on a daily basis because of the impact we are having.

This is a plea to those who do understand—or who have an inkling or an imagination. Spread the word. Now is the time to come to the aid of this bold, independent media revolution.

CHAPTER TWELVE

STANDARDS AND PRACTICES

TAKING THE BEST OF OLD MEDIA TO THE NEW MEDIA

*"There is a great disposition in some quarters to say that the newspapers
ought to limit the amount of news they print; that certain kinds of news
ought not to be published. I do not know how that is. I am not
prepared to maintain any abstract position on that line; but
I have always felt that whatever the divine Providence permitted
to occur, I was not too proud to report."*

—Charles A. Dana, newspaper editor

THERE'S AN INDELICATE old newspaper saying that sum-
marizes succinctly the way the industry traditionally viewed
the issue of personal and journalistic conflicts of interest.

The curmudgeonly city editor would say to his reporter: "Hey,
I don't care if you sleep with elephants, just don't cover the circus."

That was the American journalistic standard for a long time—
right up until the 1970s. Today, I'm sorry to say, the circus is being covered by people sleeping in the elephant tent, the hyena
cage, the sheep exhibit, and the gerbil display.

We have witnessed in the last thirty years the transition of
American journalism from a profession of disinterested chroni-
clers to one more akin to a band of lobbyists using the press to
support activist causes.

Let me give you an example. Exhibit A is a group called the
National Lesbian and Gay Journalists Association.

Not only is the organization successful at working inside the media to ensure favorable coverage of homosexuals and their political agenda, it even persuades the corporate press barons to pay their freight! The Hearst Corporation, Knight Ridder, the *New York Times, Newsweek,* NBC News, *Time,* ABC, CBS News, CNN, Fox News Network, *Brill's Content,* and *Newsday* are among the big media companies that lend financial support to this cause. The Ford Foundation and American Airlines are two other major patrons.

Have you ever wondered why coverage of homosexuals and their cause is so universally positive? Now you know. NLGJA activists work at the *Dallas Morning News,* CNN, *Newsday,* the *New York Times, USA Today,* and virtually all the major corporate establishment news organizations.

How is it that I know so much about NLGJA? Okay, I have a confession to make. Year after year, I've been personally invited to the NLGJA's conventions. Why would they invite me? No, folks, it's not what you are thinking. I am not about to "come out." I assure you I am a hundred percent heterosexual and monogamous. I don't think they'll be asking me to make a keynote address.

No, the NLGJA will be looking for bigger names, more reliable names—people like Barbara Walters, Lesley Stahl, *New York Times* publisher Arthur Ochs Sulzberger, all of whom have participated in previous NLGJA events. Even Dan Rather and the late Peter Jennings have participated.

All of these heavyweights lend their support to this pressure campaign simply because it is chic. Try to imagine what would happen if a group of Christians in the news media got together to try to work toward "fairer and more accurate coverage" of their faith. Would the cause be underwritten by the press establishment? Would it be supported by the big names?

Of course not. And that's one of the reasons you don't get the "straight" story, pardon the pun, when you read the establishment press. The thought police are hard at work in the newsroom. They are busy filtering and spiking and spinning.

That's okay with me. I used to get upset about it. Now I realize it represents an opportunity for us, for me, for *WorldNet-*

Daily, for the New Media, for the truth, for old-fashioned journalistic standards.

Maybe you're thinking, *Well, Farah, you're not exactly a paragon of objectivity yourself. Where do you get off chastising those people with different viewpoints who work in your industry?*

Ah, that's the point. It's not about viewpoints. It's about organizations. It's about memberships. It's about loyalty to causes above one's loyalty to journalistic ethics.

You see, I don't belong to any organizations. I'm not even registered to a political party. That's how seriously I take my professional obligation to impartiality. Since I've been a journalist, I've never worked on a campaign, I've never worked in politics or government, and I've certainly never lobbied my colleagues for special kid-glove treatment of my pet causes.

Yes, I have pet causes. I have strong beliefs. And I think it's great to be open and honest about them. That is part of the great tradition of American journalism.

So let the establishment press cater to activists. Let it scrape and bow to an elite and narrow constituency hopelessly out of touch with mainstream American values. Let it throw its money and glamour behind pressure groups.

But let's expose it too, so the American people know what's going on.

Here's another example of the way political activists with an agenda work inside the big media. You might remember a little dust-up back in 2004 right around the election.

Sen. Arlen Specter (R-PA) was positioning himself to become the next chairman of the Senate Judiciary Committee, a powerful post that has much influence over judicial nominations by the president and whether those nominees will be confirmed by the upper house.

Specter gave an interview to an Associated Press reporter warning the president to avoid naming pro-life justices to the Supreme Court. He was quoted as saying: "When you talk about judges who would change the right of a woman to choose, overturn *Roe v. Wade*, I think that is unlikely. The president is well aware of what happened, when a number of his nominees were sent up, with the filibuster. ... And I would expect the president to be mindful of the considerations which I am mentioning."

I believe he said something very close to that, though he later denied it, saying he was misquoted. Maybe he was, maybe he wasn't. But what most people failed to see was that Specter wasn't the only one with an agenda in this interview. The reporter had one, too.

The reporter who broke the story had no business covering politics for the Associated Press, the largest news-gathering organization in the world and, without a doubt, the most influential. Her name was Lara Jakes Jordan and she has betrayed a partisan ideological agenda in stories over and over again. Years earlier, she had set up Specter's colleague, Rick Santorum, in an ambush interview. I'll state my case plainly: she is one of those undercover political activists disguised as a reporter.

Lara Jakes Jordan is married to veteran Democratic Party operative Jim Jordan, the former executive director of the Democratic Senatorial Campaign Committee and former manager of Sen. John Kerry's presidential bid.

Would you trust her political coverage if you knew that? And her political activism is not reserved exclusively to the news reports she writes for the AP.

In January 2003, Mrs. Jordan was one of the signatories on a letter to her bosses at the AP attacking the news organization for "rolling back diversity" by not extending benefits to domestic partners.

In a symbolic move, the signatories to the letter returned key chains AP management gave them to "celebrate" its corporate diversity. The key chains carried the slogan: "AP Diversity: Many Views, One Vision."

Do you get the picture?

"I don't care if you sleep with elephants as long as you don't cover the circus."

Mrs. Jordan violated that old newsroom ethic. She abdicated her right to cover the circus because she was sleeping with an elephant—or, in this case, a donkey.

Let's look at some other examples. The Old Media are loaded with them. They could easily fill a book by themselves.

When Dan Rather was caught red-handed passing off forged and fraudulent documents indicting the president of the United States for supposedly not fulfilling his National Guard obligations, he resorted to the Hillary Clinton defense.

One of his producers was quoted as saying: "All Dan could say was that this was an attack from the right-wing nuts, and that we should have expected this, given the stakes. He was terribly defensive and nervous."

Have you ever noticed the last refuge of scoundrels is not patriotism, as the old aphorism goes, but labeling—name-calling, reducing intelligent debate to bumper-sticker shouting.

I detest labels. Every time I use one myself, I cringe. It's not good reporting. It's not good analysis. It's not good debate to resort to using them.

Whatever happened to the good old days when reporters reported?

Did those days really exist? Or are they just phantom images of a faulty memory?

I have been mislabeled a conservative so often now in print that it no longer seems to matter what I say—how I characterize myself. What I say about myself and my publication is my "opinion"—relegated to the letters to the editor section—while reporters who don't know me are free to make judgments about me and my work based on purely derivative journalism.

But this isn't about me.

It's about truth. It's about real dialogue. It's about more than superficial discussion of important, vital national issues.

You might notice that I restrain myself from using labels in my work. It's very difficult. But it's very important to do so. Sometimes I slip. But even though I detest most of what constitutes the ideology of liberalism, I don't just hurl that label as an epithet.

Why? Because it is ineffective. It lowers the level of our debate and discussion. It's overly simplistic.

In news reporting, it is even more important to avoid that kind of political labeling—or stereotyping—of people and ideas.

177

This is especially true if the person being labeled doesn't agree with the label.

I should know whether I'm a conservative or not. I think I should have the right to decide what my worldview is. It is very offensive to me when others try to pigeonhole me—so I try not to do it to others.

What do these labels we hurl really mean anyway? They mean different things to different people. They have meant different things at different times in history. And they mean different things in different places.

For those old enough to remember the old Soviet Union, the hard-line communists were known by some in the media as conservatives. At the same time, their arch-nemesis in the world, Ronald Reagan, was also known as a conservative.

If dropped into today's world, Thomas Jefferson would be perceived as a right-wing Christian. In his time, he was known as a liberal.

This is another reason labels are so problematic—and I want no part of them, not for me and not by me.

So, understanding all that, how can we continue using these confusing labels so readily, so frequently, so cavalierly?

While I love talk radio, unfortunately, it is falling victim to this kind of bumper-sticker blame game.

I'm sure Dan Rather considers me one of the right-wing nuts who helped expose his journalistic sins.

Have you ever noticed, though, how the use of labels actually says more about those who use them than about those to whom they are directed?

You rarely hear a right-wing nut call someone else a right-wing nut. You rarely hear a left-wing nut call someone else a left-wing nut.

It's all a matter of perspective.

And that's what people like Dan Rather have lost—besides their jobs.

In the world of the Old Media, there has long been a revolving door through which political activists and so-called "journalists" travel. One day George Stephanopoulos is working as the most visible paid advocate of President Bill Clinton's policies, the next day he is running one of the most important "news" shows on ABC. That's the way the revolving door works.

Remember when Al Gore lost his bid for the presidency in 2000—because he didn't win his home state, because of a *WND* investigative series on his Tennessee underworld connections? What was the first thing he did? How did he land on his feet?

He invaded my world of journalism—landing, astonishingly, a job teaching the subject at a major American university

In his first class as a professor of Columbia University's Graduate School of Journalism, Gore taught his students the meaning of the phrase "off the record." Students were asked to sign a pledge of confidentiality with regard to what was taught— a strange request indeed for a journalism class.

But it got stranger in the second class. To prepare for it, students were sent an e-mail explaining that "the vast majority of the world's scientists have concluded that human beings are influencing global climatic patterns in ways that portend changes in the global climate system more disruptive than any seen in the last ten thousand years."

The students were told to prepare to critique media coverage of the global warming issue. After the class, students said Gore suggested it was a cop-out for journalists to include in news reports skeptical views about global warming.

In other words, Al Gore was not teaching journalism. He was teaching propaganda methods that would make Joseph Goebbels proud. And why should that surprise anyone? This man is a fanatic. He is a cleaned-up, publicly presentable version of the Unabomber, Ted Kaczynski.

I don't make that comparison lightly—especially since one of Kaczynski's victims was a personal friend and one of the early supporters of my own journalistic endeavors. The facts speak for themselves.

The Unabomber spent seventeen years killing and maiming complete strangers. He explained: "In order to get our message before the public with some chance of making a lasting impression, we've had to kill people."

Years ago, some enterprising person put together a now-famous "Gore-Unabomber Quiz" on the Internet that challenged readers to read a list of quotations and decide whether Gore made the statement or Kaczynski. When I took it, I scored 50 percent. I dare say that would be an average score because the quotes are indistinguishable from one another in both substance and style.

Here's a quote not on the quiz. You tell me who called the automobile "a mortal threat to the security of every nation that is more deadly than that of any military enemy we are ever again likely to confront"? That's right. That's our former vice president and the man who won the popular vote in the 2000 presidential election. Why he wasn't forced to eat those words during the campaign, I cannot explain.

But it gets worse. He also said in his 1993 screed, *Earth in the Balance,* that we ought "to establish a coordinated global program to accomplish the strategic goal of eliminating the internal combustion engine over, say, a twenty-five-year period." I will never understand how he won the state of Michigan having committed those words to print. And even tougher to understand is why his opponent, George W. Bush, never taunted Gore with that quote in Detroit or anywhere else.

However, I digress. The point is: Columbia Journalism School might just as well add Kaczynski to the faculty. From my personal experience as a news industry executive, Columbia has always been more of a mill for turning out political activists than journalists, but the hiring of Gore just made it official. We should be thankful for such moves. They blow the lid off the veneer of "objectivity" and "neutrality" and "fairness."

No, Mr. Gore, it's simply not true that the vast majority of scientists agree that mankind-induced global warming is a threat. It's patently false. Most scientists that have any expertise in the area say just the opposite—that it is, indeed, *unlikely* mankind could significantly impact global temperatures and that there is no compelling evidence that the planet is warming.

Nevertheless, committed as he is to his own fanatical ideological agenda, Gore teaches journalists they should ignore the scientists who disagree and all the evidence they have produced.

Think about that! That kind of madman extremism, that kind of blind zealotry, that kind of rabid dogmatism has nothing to do with journalism. It's the kind of evil obsession and misguided militancy that leads to the political terrorism of the Unabomber.

I can't tell the difference between their rhetoric. Can you?

Not too much later, Gore was back to politics again, not that he ever left, of course. This time he was playing the role of media critic. The reason he and his Democratic Party cronies were having such a tough time, he explained, was because of a vast right-wing media conspiracy against them.

No, he didn't use exactly those words, as Hillary Clinton had six or seven years ago. But his take is pretty close. Same play, new spin.

"The media is kind of weird these days on politics, and there are some major institutional voices that are, truthfully speaking, part and parcel of the Republican Party," he said. "Fox News Network, the *Washington Times*, Rush Limbaugh—there's a bunch of them, and some of them are financed by wealthy ultra-conservative billionaires who make political deals with Republican administrations and the rest of the media. ... Most of the media [has] been slow to recognize the pervasive impact of this fifth column in their ranks—that is, day after day, injecting daily Republican talking points into the definition of what's objective as stated by the news media as a whole."[1]

He said it. I'm not kidding. It's no joke.

Al Gore honestly believes that the media are stacked against the Democrats—against bigger government, against taxing and spending, against more Washington control over the people. At least he says it with a straight face. Who knows what he really believes?

If all this sounds similar to Hillary's old "vast right-wing media conspiracy" chatter, that's because it is. Listen as Gore explains how the "communication stream of conspiracy commerce," to borrow another Clinton phrase, worked in 2002:

"Something will start at the Republican National Committee, inside the building, and it will explode the next day on the right-wing talk-show network and on Fox News and in the newspapers that play this game, the *Washington Times* and the others," he says. "And then they'll create an echo chamber, and pretty soon they'll start baiting the mainstream media for allegedly ignoring the story they've been pushing into the zeitgeist. And then pretty soon the mainstream media goes out and disingenuously takes a so-called objective sampling, and lo and behold, these RNC talking points are woven into the fabric of the zeitgeist."[2]

No matter how much the deck is stacked in their favor, people like Gore will always claim it is the other way around—until they have total control. Gore went back to the media later—serving as the front man in the purchase of a major cable TV network where he assured his political views would not impact programming. You believe that?

The media are filled with political activists. And the world of politics is filled with people who can easily retreat into the world of media at the drop of a hat.

In an earlier chapter, I told you about Walter Cronkite and his charade. He finally let it all hang out after retiring from CBS News and his position as "most trusted man in America." Now he shills for the global government crowd at the World Federalist Association.

Then there's that wretch Helen Thomas, formerly of United Press International. After retiring as White House correspondent, the eighty-five-year-old has hit the college lecture circuit railing against the current resident of her old beat.

Here's what she told a crowd at the Massachusetts Institute of Technology: "I censored myself for fifty years when I was a reporter. Now I wake up and ask myself, 'Who do I hate today?'"[3]

Ah, what a life.

Among those she hates are President Bush, timid officeholders, a muffled press corps, and cowed citizens. Her number one beef? The liberation of Iraq.

"I have never covered a president who actually wanted to go to war," she said. "Bush's policy of preemptive war is immoral—such a policy would legitimize Pearl Harbor. It's as if they learned none of the lessons of Vietnam."

Now, I'm very tolerant of dissent. I welcome vigorous debates on national issues of great importance. As the editor of the leading independent news site on the Net, I publish all kinds of opinions, many with which I strongly disagree.

But Helen Thomas has crossed a line. Her comments equating the war in Iraq with the attack on Pearl Harbor are dangerously close to sedition.

"Where is the outrage?" she demanded. "Where is Congress? They're supine."[4]

She continued her seething rage: "Bush has held only six press conferences, the only forum in our society where a president can be questioned," she continued sputtering. "I'm on the phone to Ari Fleischer every day, asking will he ever hold another one? The international world is wondering what happened to America's great heart and soul."[5]

Huh? You mean if Bush holds more press conferences, it will restore America's heart and soul in the eyes of the world? Thomas has definitely spent way too much time in Washington. Her incoherence is surpassed only by her arrogance and self-importance.

Imagine getting up in the morning and asking yourself: "Whom do I hate today?" I have no doubt that people like Thomas do just that. Not surprisingly, nobody reads it. Her audience is nil. She writes for the Hearst Corporation, one of my former employers, which ought to be ashamed of itself for providing a forum for this tired old battle-ax. But nobody is beating down her door to read her diatribes.

Only the closed-minded universities throw open their doors to hear her rant and rave about hating the president and pretending to be something she wasn't for fifty years—an honest, fair, impartial reporter.

So why do I care?

I care because I'm a journalist. I care because I have spent thirty years working in the same industry as Helen Thomas. I care because I don't like to see traitors like this misrepresenting the legitimate role of a free press. I care because I believe in dissent, but not treason. I care because I still think America is the greatest nation in the world and I'm not ashamed to say it.

I also care because of what Helen Thomas and Walter Cronkite demonstrate about the nature of the big media in this country.

These people are not truth-seekers. They are partisan political activists masquerading as objective news professionals. They are dishonest hypocrites who hide their true agendas while they hold positions of power in the media—only to discover candor about their real motives when it benefits them on the speaking circuit in retirement.

And I care because I want people to understand the difference between good journalism and bad. If they can't discern the difference, all is lost—for my profession and for our nation's future.

I still think of journalism as an honorable profession—if it is practiced the way it is supposed to be practiced. We need to preserve the institution of the free press if we are to preserve and expand our own freedom.

I saw this problem a long time ago—while I was still immersed in the world of the Old Media. Just three months after I took over as editor of the *Sacramento Union*, then the oldest daily in the West, Howard Kurtz, the media critic of the *Washington Post* wrote the first column his paper had ever devoted to my paper in its 145-year history.

Kurtz's intentions were to sound the alarm on a dangerous development in California's state capital. It seemed a daily newspaper was marching to the beat of its own drummer—not playing by the rules established in elite and secret conclaves at Columbia University or in studies commissioned by the Gannett Foundation or the Pew Charitable Trusts.

One of Kurtz's biggest gripes with me was the fact that I banned the use of the term "assault weapon" from the pages of the *Sacramento Union*. Instead of this phrase, our reporters and editorial writers would be required to be more precise in their language. Did they mean semiautomatic weapons? Did they mean fully automatic weapons? Or were they simply referring to guns that looked real mean?

What this little anecdote illustrates is that the traditional role of the press as watchdog of government has been stood on its head. Today, the watchdogs of the press are more likely to be guarding their industry's own politically correct mythologies and pathologies.

The fact is that the establishment press in this country is constantly bombarding our senses with lies about guns. Even worse is the way it carefully and systematically censors real news that could actually end up saving the lives of Americans.

For instance, when was the last time you read a story in your local newspaper or saw a TV news report about someone who used a gun defensively and effectively? I can't remember the last time. Yet such incidents occur some 2.5 million times a year.

How often have you heard this argument against gun ownership? Friends or relatives are the most likely killers—or, more precisely, 58 percent of murder victims are killed by relatives or acquaintances.

According to the broad definition of "acquaintances" used in the FBI's reporting, most victims are indeed classified as knowing their killer. However, using such definitions, the FBI includes drug buyers killing drug dealers, cabdrivers killed by first-time customers, gang members killing other gang members, prostitutes killed by their clients, etc.

When such non-acquaintance killings are actually taken out of the equation, it turns out only 17 percent of murder victims were family members, friends, neighbors, or roommates. Who's cooking the numbers? And why?

The media have also whipped up a lot of hysteria about concealed handgun permits. The perception has been created that, if such permits were made more readily available, there would be shoot-'em-ups at every street corner in America.

The fact of the matter is that millions of people already have concealed handgun permits. Yet only one permit holder has ever been arrested for using a concealed handgun after a traffic accident and that case was ruled self-defense.

If you believe the major media, you would think that a household gun is more likely to kill you or a member of your family than an intruder. Once again, lies, damn lies, and statistics. Overwhelmingly, people killed in their homes are killed by intruders' guns, not their own. No more than 4 percent of gun-death victims can be attributed to the homeowner's gun.

We hear a lot from the news media about "rights"—both real and imagined. Yet one of America's actual, constitutionally guaranteed rights is under assault by the media as never before. The press responds to gun issues in Pavlovian-style, with semiautomatic, rapid-fire disinformation.

The government knows better, the media tell us. Individuals can't be trusted to make intelligent and mature decisions about protecting themselves, the press claims. We'd all be a lot safer if there were fewer guns around, they suggest.

It makes you wonder: why is a class of people who make their living under the protections of the First Amendment, so willing to give up our rights under the Second Amendment?

Some people read comic books for laughs. I read a newspaper trade journal called *Editor & Publisher*.

It's a habit I picked up during my nearly twenty years of experience running daily newspapers. *Editor & Publisher* is the only place to turn to find out which old newspeople have turned up dead or been arrested on morals charges. But mostly I read it for laughs.

Editor & Publisher is chronicling the suicide of an industry. And as much as I loved the Old Media while I was a part of it, it's gone now. It is a mere vestige of its former proud self. It is little more than a corpse that doesn't know it has died—that its time is past. *Editor & Publisher* presents the industry with first aid tips when what it really needs is electro-cardiopulmonary resuscitation.

Here's a recent example.

Under the headline "Making newspapers more open to minorities," *Editor & Publisher* lectured the industry about hiring practices.

"News organizations have had difficulty balancing the desire to have a diverse work force with the myth of equal opportunity," explains Keith Woods, an associate professor in ethics at the Poynter Institute for Media Studies. "They are constantly in this conflict with themselves, trying to do something that bolsters the hiring and employment numbers of racial and ethnic groups

while at the same time holding to the idea that this is a meritoc-
racy, and everybody should be treated equally."[6]

In other words, this pointy-headed racist suggests blacks and
other members of racial minorities can't compete on an even
playing field for jobs and promotions, so they need special treatment, kid-glove handling, affirmative action, racial preferences.

Woods, who I bet has never worked in a real, competitive
newsroom in his life, says newspapers have to stop thinking of
"diversity" as a luxury and begin considering it a basic journalistic necessity.

"The attitude that you don't need any other understanding of
your world beyond the one you have is asinine," Woods says.
"Every single day you are reporting on a diverse world. If you
don't have examples of that diversity in your world, then it is all
the more important to seek it out. … If you want to tell people the
truth, if you want to give them an authentic rendering of news,
then you must acknowledge the differences. You can't accomplish truth and accuracy without diversity."[7]

One more quote from this genius: "If you go to a minority job
fair and find that only three people measure up to your standards, then ask yourself, 'What's wrong with my standards?'"[8]

Now, to be honest, there's a grain of truth in what Woods and
his agenda-driven collaborators at *Editor & Publisher* have to say
about diversity. One of the reasons newspapers are dying is because they are not reflective of the communities or the nation they
cover. But it's not a question of having enough black or brown
faces in the newsroom. It's a question of philosophical and ideological diversity. There is none. In most newsrooms today, everyone thinks alike—white, brown, black, red, yellow, or mixed.

The only kind of affirmative action program that might have a
chance of succeeding in the modern corporate newsroom would be
one in which conservatives, libertarians, Christians, Republicans,
independents, and other endangered species in the media world
were actively and respectfully recruited. It will never happen. Most
news agencies would rather close down—and they will.

And look at the rest of this drivel from Woods: if you can't find
racial minority applicants that meet your standards, lower your

standards. What a patronizing, plantation viewpoint. This guy needs help to distinguish fact from fiction, truth from falsehood.

No wonder the Old Media are losing viewers and readers.

What does all this mean? It means the establishment press is headed the way of the dinosaurs. Reading the newspaper trade journals today is like reading the newsletter of the hospital's intensive care ward.

Everybody knows something is wrong, but every newspaper doctor has a different prescription. In my humble opinion, as a veteran of the business for twenty years, none of them have a clue.

Listen to what Bruce Krasnow, city editor of the *New Mexican* in Santa Fe and a journalism instructor, said: "There are some terrific writers in the journalism class I teach at a local college. But for some reason, writing for a newspaper is not on their list of career objectives."[9]

Incredible! A decade or two ago, there were hundreds of applicants for every entry-level job at major metropolitan papers and plenty for papers in smaller markets, too, as young journalists fought for any way in the door of what was the most exciting business in the world.

Morale in big-city newsrooms is more in tune with what you would expect in a funeral home than what we recall from the days of *The Front Page* or *All the President's Men*.

"Any editor who has tried to fill an editorial opening knows the reality: Newspapers and those who edit them are no longer sexy," writes Krasnow. "The Watergate era, which brought the profession into the public spotlight and helped inspire energetic young reporters, is long gone, replaced by C-SPAN and CNN images of a stodgy, aging Washington press corps whose reporters bicker among themselves to fill air time."[10]

Krasnow continues: "Students in their twenties weren't even born when President Nixon resigned in 1974. Now, Lou Grant and even Murphy Brown have given way to Matt Drudge and personal home pages. Newspapers are no longer seen as agents of social change, and even if they were, college students don't see that as an attraction."[11]

What seems like bad news—even terminal, perhaps—to the establishment press types is actually a sign of hope. We're witnessing a media revolution. I don't think you can fully appreciate the depths of it, the scale of it, the beauty of it, unless you have been in both worlds as I have been.

Millions of people across the United States and around the world simply don't get their news the way they once did. Sure, they may tune in to the television ever so casually to hear what Katie Couric has to say, but the networks don't pack the same punch.

The Internet is where it's at for the future. It's growing faster than TV did in its heyday. But it is far more interactive, entertaining, and informative.

But Marshall McLuhan didn't get it quite right. It's not the medium that is the message. The message is the message. People want real information. They hunger for it. People are realizing that they have been controlled for too long. The Internet gives them far more choices—not all good, but choices nonetheless.

I can see where this is all leading. The journalism schools and the major foundations have been trying to reinvent the press for the last decade. They have wanted to figure out a new winning formula that could pacify the restless public. They gave it their best shot.

I don't like to criticize the establishment press.

It's just too easy.

It's like shooting fish in a barrel.

I prefer bigger game.

And I prefer doing the job the press is supposed to do, rather than criticizing others for not doing it, or for doing it wrong.

But once in a while, it's just too tempting to avoid. And as I said, it's important to teach consumers to be discerning—so they can tell the good from the bad. Once in a while, I see a story written so poorly, I just want to scream about it. Once in a while, I have to point out why what we do in the New Media is so important.

For example, here's a verbatim story from the Associated Press dated February 17, 2002:

"South Arabia Man to Get 4,750 Lashes"

RIYADH, Saudi Arabia—A Saudi court has sentenced a man to six years in prison and 4,750 lashes for having sex with his wife's sister, a newspaper reported Sunday.

The woman involved in the case was sentenced to six months in jail and 65 lashes, the paper Al-Eqtisadiah reported, though the court found she had not consented to the relationship. She had also reported the affair to the police.

Having a relationship with one's in-law is considered a serious offense under the strict Islamic judicial code that Saudi Arabia follows.

The court, in the port city of Jiddah, ordered that the lashes be administered to the man at a rate of 95 at a time.

Lashes are often handed out by Saudi courts, although rarely in such large numbers.

The court also ruled he was not eligible for a pardon "because of the ugliness and seriousness of his crime."

Now here is how that same story was told at *WorldNetDaily* the next day:

"Raped woman to be jailed, lashed; Saudi court sentences victim as well as perpetrator"

RIYADH, Saudi Arabia—A Saudi court has sentenced a woman to six months in prison and 65 lashes for getting raped by her brother-in-law and reporting it to police.

The perpetrator of the crime received 4,750 lashes and six years in prison for the attack, reports the paper Al-Eqtisadiah.

The man's sentence was for having sex with his sister-in-law, not rape. The court found the sex was not consensual. The victim reported the attack to the police.

Having a relationship with one's in-law is considered a serious offense under the strict Islamic judicial code that Saudi Arabia follows.

The court, in the port city of Jiddah, ordered that the lashes be administered to the man at a rate of 95 at a time.

> Lashes are often handed out by Saudi courts, although rarely in such large numbers.

> The court also ruled he was not eligible for a pardon "because of the ugliness and seriousness of his crime."

Do you see the difference? The AP version was what we call in the news business a "dog-bites-man story." The brutal, totalitarian Saudis were beating a man for "having sex" with his sister-in-law. Big deal.

The real story, however, was that the Saudis were punishing the victim—a fact that would be lost on the average reader because of poor story construction.

Was this an oversight? Stupidity? Poor news judgment? Or is it an indication that the largest news-gathering organization in the world, the AP, is protecting the Saudis? Hard to tell.

But again, facts are facts. You can see the evidence for yourself. Sometimes how stories are told is just as important as which stories are told. A good story told badly might as well not be told at all. If readers have to work at making sense of a simple story, the impact—the news value—will be lost on most people.

Sometimes political correctness definitely plays a role in the way stories are told. When Canada's *National Post* changed a Reuters's news story to characterize the al-Aqsa Martyrs Brigades as a terrorist group, it warranted the attention of the *New York Times*, and the managing editor of Reuters actually had the audacity to offer some criticism of the action.

The original Reuters line said: "…the al-Aqsa Martyrs Brigades, which has been involved in a four-year-old revolt against Israeli occupation in Gaza and the West Bank."[12]

The *National Post* changed it to: "…the al-Aqsa Martyrs Brigades, a terrorist group that has been involved in a four-year-old campaign of violence against Israel."[13]

"Our editorial policy is that we don't use emotive words when labeling someone," David A. Schlesinger, Reuters's global managing editor told the *New York Times*. "Any paper can change copy and do whatever they want. But if a paper wants to change our copy that way, we would be more comfortable if they remove the byline. My goal is to protect our reporters and protect our editorial integrity."[14]

Integrity? Is that what they call moral blindness now?

I've got some emoting to do on this topic.

Reuters, and every other news agency in the world, uses labels all the time—even *WorldNetDaily* (though I would suggest we apply them more carefully than most).

Take Reuters, for instance. The editors don't like the word "terrorist" anymore. But what about other labels? What about "right-wing"? I did a quick search and found dozens and dozens of examples of the gratuitous use of this term—and only occasionally referring to the hockey position.

What about "far right"? Again, bingo—lots of hits.

What about a less inflammatory label—like "moderate"? You'll find Yasser Arafat and his successor Mahmoud Abbas constantly referred to with that label.

What about "hard-liner"? You'll find Ariel Sharon was the only hard-liner in the Middle East.

But I thought Reuters editors didn't believe in sticking labels on people—only in describing actions? That's their story and they're sticking to it. Guess what? No amount of evidence to the contrary will persuade them they are wrong.

They are wrong, however. They're wrong about the word terrorist, too. If civilized people—and that includes most reporters and editors I know—cannot agree that what happened September 11 was terrorism, we've got a real problem on our hands. What can we agree on, for heaven's sake?

And, believe it or not, Reuters's editors are even confused about that.

In fact, that's when this new emotive policy began—right after the September 11 attacks. Reuters's editors couldn't bring themselves to characterize the work of Osama bin Laden and al-Qaida as the work of terrorists.

Why are we mincing words? If anything, terrorism is not a strong enough term to describe this atrocity. This is ultra-terror, this is super-terror, this is hyper-terror. This is mass murder.

Lots of U.S. journalists are agreeing with these journalistic extremists.

"I'm not sure they (Reuters editors) are making a mistake," says Geneva Overholser, the former editor of the *Des Moines Register* and now a syndicated columnist. "Our professional strictures require us to give thoughtful consideration to matters that our fellow citizens would simply make an emotional decision on."[15]

Oh, give me a break. What professional strictures? Name them. Show them to me. I've been in this business thirty years and I've never seen such strictures—at least not rules that require us to forgo common sense and any judgment about right and wrong.

The day I do is the day I find a new line of work.

It's easy to hoodwink the Old Media—if the story you are peddling fits into their perverted worldview of "tolerance," "diversity," and "multiculturalism."

Here's a good example of that phenomenon. An extremist advocacy group called the Council on American Islamic Relations, released a report less than a year after 9/11 suggesting there had been a major upsurge in anti-Muslim discrimination in the United States.

The press reported the pseudo-scientific findings without any analysis of the data, without exploring the group's broader Islamic agenda and without criticism by dissenting experts.

In other words, reporters and editors did what we refer to in the business as a "rip and read" job with the group's press release.

Being an Arab-American journalist with a different point of view, I had the opportunity to debate one of the officials of CAIR on television. I explained that the report had all the meaning and substance of a peace promise by the late, not-so-great Yasser Arafat.

I did something few reporters evidently bothered to do. I actually read the fifty-page report by CAIR. The study, it turns out, is based on some fifteen hundred reports gathered by CAIR, which solicits such complaints on its Web site. Has CAIR received more complaints about supposed civil rights violations against Muslims since September 11? I have no doubts it has. CAIR has received wide exposure on television and in press accounts since the terrorist attack on the United States. Does it stand to reason that as CAIR gets more visibility it would collect more complaints from disgruntled Muslims? You bet. But so what?

After all, there are about four million Muslims in America. These complaints, even if valid, represent less than .04 percent of the U.S. Muslim population.

The biggest percentage of complaints has to do with alleged profiling of Muslims at U.S. airports. Now I know many non-Muslims who feel like they have been shaken down unfairly and unnecessarily at airports since September 11. I don't attribute this to discrimination. I attribute it to the fact that we are at war—a fact conveniently forgotten by CAIR, which seems to have sympathy for the adversaries in that conflict.

Only 1 percent of the fifteen hundred complaints had to do with even the threat of violence. In other words, I myself have received more threats of violence—from Muslims—than all of the respondents in this report allegedly received from non-Muslims. This is news?

Among the grievances CAIR cites in the report is the shutdown by the government of phony Muslim charities serving as front groups for terrorism—organizations like the Holy Land Foundation. That's hardly a civil rights issue. It's a matter of prudent, if belated, national security precautions.

Some of the other outrages cited by CAIR include nasty e-mails the group has received from ordinary Americans. By that standard, I am a victim of so many civil rights violations that I should be entitled to reparations from the U.S. government.

The real news of this cooked-up report is what it says about CAIR itself. There is not one nice word in the fifty-page report about America. You get the impression from reading this report that Americans are running out and lynching Muslims for the sheer sport of it, that official U.S. government policy is to avenge the September 11 terrorist attacks by targeting Muslims at random, that Americans are a hateful, spiteful group of sadists intent on scapegoating innocents.

Nothing could be further from the truth.

CAIR's report gives America no credit whatsoever.

It raises the question: if conditions for Muslims are so bad in America, why is Islam the fastest-growing religion in America, according to CAIR? Why do Muslims flock to the United States—this hideous concentration camp for Muslims?

I'll tell you why. Many Muslims have come here and continue to come here to escape the Islamofascism of places like Iran, Iraq, and Saudi Arabia—places about which CAIR never has a bad word to say.

CAIR was late to the party in condemning Osama bin Laden for the September 11 terror attacks. It finally got around to it three months after the fact. Don't expect anytime soon a sweeping condemnation of the latest suicide bombing by Hamas, which killed fifteen people in Israel. The founder of this organization is on record in support of the goals and tactics of Hamas.

How seriously can we take the charges of a group that called the conviction of the 1993 World Trade Center bombers "a travesty of justice"? How seriously can we take a group that called the conviction of Omar Abdel Rahman, who conspired to blow up New York City landmarks, a "hate crime"? How seriously should we take a group about which Steven Pomerantz, former FBI chief of counterterrorism, says: "CAIR, its leaders, and its activities effectively give aid to international terrorist groups"?

Very seriously.

The real goal of this group was made clear by its chairman, Omar M. Ahmad, who told a rally of California Muslims in 1998: "Islam isn't in America to be equal to any other faith, but to become dominant. The Koran should be the highest authority in America, and Islam the only accepted religion on earth."

But yet this group, CAIR, is treated with kid gloves by the big media. It is treated with deference and respect. The words of its leaders and reports are taken at face value—with not even the slightest effort at investigation or corroboration.

Now, I must say, many of the diseases of the Old Media have infected the New Media as well. Just because a so-called news organization operates on the Internet doesn't give it any more credibility. In fact, all of the Old Media institutions are scrambling to make their Internet presence known. And don't forget that the number one news site on the Net is still *CNN.com*. Even New Media consumers must learn the art of discernment. With all of the competition on the Net, it is more important than ever.

One of our competitors in the New Media, for instance, is *Salon.com*. *Salon* is well known for supporting—or at least excusing—virtually anything the Clinton administration ever did. Every issue during the Clinton reign contained at least one brazenly apologetic ode to the White House.

"White House allies sometimes tout *Salon* pieces to reporters before they are even posted on the Web," wrote Howard Kurtz of the *Washington Post*.[16] *Salon*'s long-time Washington correspondent Jonathan Broder and frequent contributor Joe Conason were close friends of White House attack-dog Sidney Blumenthal.

Not only is *Salon* a key component of a real, documented, bona fide "left-wing conspiracy," it is also a classic illustration of what I call the "government-media complex." *Salon*'s staff is a pathetic collection of privileged and coddled journalistic hacks serving not as watchdogs of government, but as lapdogs.

So who's behind *Salon*? While I have had many questions—and accusations—directed to me about who might be behind *WND*, nobody seems to be interested in who is behind *Salon*. Why don't the *Washington Post* and *New York Times* do investigative reports on the secret sugar daddies behind the government's mouthpieces? Here's the secret money trail you won't see explored on *60 Minutes*.

It turns out a major Democratic Party donor is one of the principal backers of *Salon*. His name is William Hambrecht, a cofounder of Hambrecht and Quist, a Silicon Valley investment banking firm. The company provided venture capital investments to both Adobe and Apple, computer businesses that also bankroll *Salon*. Hambrecht even serves on Adobe's board of directors.

Hambrecht has hosted $10,000-a-person fund-raising dinners at his San Francisco home for Democratic House candidates attended by President Clinton. Between 1991 and 1997, Hambrecht contributed more than $284,000 to Democratic candidates and organizations exclusively. John Warnock, the top executive of Adobe, contributed more than $18,000 to Democratic office seekers. Steve Jobs, head of Apple, gave $167,500 to the party's candidates.

Isn't it interesting to note how the White House is promoting favorite Internet sites—just as it once tried to recruit and push favored radio talk-show hosts? The old threat to exposing White House lies was talk radio. The new threat is the Internet. With *WorldNetDaily* and the *Drudge Report* becoming "the Rush Limbaughs of the Web," the Clintonistas did what they could do for their friends—finding investors, promoting sites, even handing out "exclusives" actually unearthed by political private investigators.

Standards—that's what it all comes down to. What I have tried to do in my New Media ventures is to take the very best of the Old Media standards and raise them higher.

It also comes down to another word—truth.

There are lots of debates taking place in our world today. People argue over the value of tolerance, diversity, pluralism, freedom, multiculturalism, rights, and justice.

They argue about politics, war, civil disobedience, revolution, pacifism.

They even argue about right and wrong.

But hardly anyone bothers to argue about truth.

Mention truth today in some quarters and you will hear the question that Jesus of Nazareth heard from Pontius Pilate: "What is truth?"

I think the reason people avoid discussing truth is because it raises other deep and, perhaps, troubling questions.

Is there such a thing as truth? Apart from God, can there be such a thing as truth? Or, as Pilate wondered when he stared Truth in the eye, is truth all relative?

If truth is relative, isn't morality relative as well? Can there be absolute morality or absolute truth without God? Can there be right and wrong without the Author of right and wrong?

Deep questions.

If only we could get rid of those nasty concepts of One True God, sin, and redemption. Everything would be so much better. This seems to me to be the fundamental dividing point in so many of today's conflicts—whether they are domestic political differences or international crises.

It's time for all of us to ask ourselves the ultimate questions:

Do you believe in truth?
Do you believe in right and wrong?
Do you believe in sin?
Do you believe in redemption?
What is the purpose of life?
What is the meaning of life?
Do you believe in God?
Where do your notions about these questions come from?
Is truth knowable?
If we know truth, must we hide it in the name of tolerance?
Is it possible to know truth without the Bible?
Is it possible to know right from wrong without the Bible?
What do right and wrong actually mean without a standard?

These are tough questions for most in the media today. But fundamentally, isn't real journalism about a search for the truth? Isn't that a higher calling than "fair and balanced"?

I think so. And that's why we carved into the mission statement of *WND* a very prominent—even central—focus on truth: "*WorldNetDaily.com*, Inc. is an independent news company dedicated to uncompromising journalism, seeking truth and justice, and revitalizing the role of the free press as a guardian of liberty. We remain faithful to the traditional and central role of a free press in a free society—as a light exposing wrongdoing, corruption, and abuse of power.

"We also seek to stimulate a free-and-open debate about the great moral and political ideas facing the world and to promote freedom and self-government by encouraging personal virtue and good character."

A mission statement like that might not be strikingly different from mission statements crafted by news organizations in the eighteenth and nineteenth centuries in America. But it stands out in its peculiarity in the twenty-first century.

I've always been sort of an odd duck in the press establishment.

Long before I left a twenty-five-year career in daily newspapers—as a reporter, editor, and top news executive—I was something of a fish out of water.

By that I mean there aren't many practicing, faithful Christian believers in the news world. For whatever reason, it's rare to find people of biblical faith in the media world. It is dominated, and has been for a long time, by those who worship at other altars.

It's inaccurate to say people in the media are not religious. I think everyone is religious—even the self-professed atheists, who, in my opinion, have to have more faith to believe what they believe than those who worship the God of Abraham, Isaac, and Jacob.

Some worship false deities—money, alternate lifestyles, hedonism, misguided cynicism, political correctness, pseudo-intellectualism, evolution, Mother Earth, you name it.

Some, remarkably, given their calling to a profession that is supposed to hold power in check, even worship government.

To these people, nothing is so quirky, so quaint, so foolish as the person who puts his faith in God rather than man.

Take, for example, an article disseminated in July 2006 by the United Press International.

It wasn't a big story. And it wasn't particularly written poorly or cynically. In fact, I think it was a very interesting story—well worth publishing. It was about the leaders of severely drought-stricken Lubbock, Texas, organizing a day to pray for rain.

"Nobody is going to tell God what to do and what not to do, but we are in a serious drought in West Texas, and since He is the man who controls the rain clouds, we're asking Him for His mercy and His help," Mayor David Miller was quoted as saying.[17] (The only difference between the quote shared by UPI and the one printed here is a matter of capitalization: in the original version, "He," "Him," and "His" were lowercased.)

The story went on to explain that the city council and the county commissioners were adopting resolutions and asking local residents to join them in prayer and fasting for rain.

199

Lubbock had received only about half its normal ten inches of rain that year. And, since June 1, the growing season for cotton, it had received less than one inch.

Officials recalled that previously such prayers were answered. In January 2004, after a year of drought, the city and county set aside a Sunday to pray for rain and got the second-wettest year since records were kept.

It makes sense to me to pray.

But oddly, or maybe not so oddly, this UPI story appeared under the newstrack heading "Quirks."

Evidently, some editors at UPI consider prayer quirky. I'm sure they have much in common with my colleagues in the big media at large. And it's one of the reasons, you might say, that the corporate establishment press doesn't have a prayer.

CHAPTER THIRTEEN

FROM JEFFERSON TO WASHINGTON

HOW *WND* CREATED AND MAINTAINED ITS UNIQUE MEDIA VOICE

"A free press is not a privilege but an organic necessity in a great society. Without criticism and reliable and intelligent reporting, the government cannot govern. For there is no adequate way in which it can keep itself informed about what the people of the country are thinking and doing and wanting."

—Walter Lippman, columnist and author

NOT MANY PEOPLE would think of rural southern Oregon— redwood country, Bigfoot country—as the ideal place to establish the next great news company.

But that's exactly what Elizabeth and I thought in 1999 as we had a chance to reinvent *WorldNetDaily*, to capitalize it, to hire more staff, to create a new corporate culture, to build something new from the ground up.

I told you how we started the company in 1997—on a wing and a prayer. First launched in connection with my nonprofit endeavors at the Western Journalism Center, we quickly realized we had made a big mistake. Because *WND* and the Internet were growing so fast, we would need to raise investment capital to continue to compete in this environment. That wouldn't be possible as a nonprofit.

So we began the long and expensive and arduous process of spinning off *WND* from the center. In doing so, we had a chance to restart the company from scratch. We could locate it anywhere we wanted. We could hire whoever we wanted. We could establish the kinds of policies we wanted.

While living in Northern California, Elizabeth and I and the girls had enjoyed frequent weekend trips to beautiful southern Oregon. One day we got a somewhat crazy notion: "Why not live up here? Why not start our company here?"

We made arrangements to lease a 250-acre ranch with cabins we converted into office space. We purchased a beautiful log cabin for our home on six acres directly across the road. And we invited all new staff members—particularly administrative, editorial, and technical—to join us in southern Oregon.

It was not as tough a sell as I thought. Staffers came from as far away as Florida. They came to work together with like-minded colleagues—perhaps for the first time in their lives.

We didn't choose southern Oregon as an out-of-the-way corporate headquarters just because we liked it. It was a place with few distractions other than beauty, serenity, and good fishing and hunting. If we were going to create a new corporate culture for a new kind of news company, this would be the ideal place. Not Washington. Not New York. Not Los Angeles. Those places represented part of the problem, I had found after twenty-plus years in the business.

WND was not going to become contaminated, seduced, distracted—at least not right away! We wanted a chance to establish our own unique identity far from the not-so-bright lights and conventional wisdom of the big media centers. In southern Oregon, we could hear ourselves think. We could see the world more clearly. That was the idea.

We all lived and worked together in the imaginary state of Jefferson. For those of you who don't know, many people in southern Oregon and northern California consider themselves residents of the free state of Jefferson. There have been movements since the 1940s to declare this largely rural area a separate, independent state valuing personal freedom—a concept virtually unknown in the more populated regions of California and Oregon.

In 1988, a young Farah meets a young Oliver North. After moving to Washington fifteen years later, I would have the honor of taking over North's syndicated radio program.

Southern Oregon is not Portland. And Northern California is not San Francisco. They are sparsely populated regions with a different lifestyle, open spaces, beautiful, massive redwoods, and mountains, lakes, and rivers.

This was a place where we could focus on the important things—God, family, mission.

And you know what? It worked. For three years, we lived with a little distance between ourselves and the busyness of the world. The miracle of the Internet still allowed us to stay plugged in. And, yes, we did have some correspondents who traveled around the world or who worked in the power centers like Washington.

In those three years, we did create that unique corporate culture. We did learn from each other. We did get to the point where we could anticipate what each other were thinking.

It was from this remote vantage point that we covered some of the biggest stories of our time—including September 11, 2001.

But our intention was never to keep our little family together forever in "the compound." Southern Oregon is beautiful, peaceful, quiet—but it's not for everyone. One by one our team members began relocating. They could go wherever they wanted, as long as they could get a good Internet connection.

As for me and Elizabeth, we knew where we had to go—where our company would grow in the future. Whether we liked it or not, we had to be in Washington, D.C.

A friend asked me why we decided to move to Washington.

My answer? That's where the bad guys are.

Another acquaintance suggested I would become corrupted by this city—that it would "eat me alive."

My response? He that is in me is greater than he that dominates this city.

Beginning in 2002, we entered a new stage of development. The demands of travel and public appearances were greater. The opportunities for media exposure increased.

It was time for *WND* to focus on building up our reporting resources—and where better to concentrate that effort than right in the belly of the beast?

That's right. I called our nation's capital the belly of the beast. I make no apologies for it. Concentrations of power are always dangerous to liberty. And never before in the history of the world has more power been concentrated in one city than it is today in Washington.

Even though we are involved in what I consider to be a righteous war against Islamist terrorism in all its many manifestations, the real, long-term danger to America's freedom begins right here in Washington, where every day more laws are created than the people could possibly read, let alone thoughtfully approve, let alone obey.

Bad decisions are being made about how to spend your money more frequently than ever before. Your personal freedoms are being compromised. Your heritage of liberty and self-government are being denied. Your rights to life, liberty, and property are being destroyed.

Never before in American history has a vigilant watchdog on government been more needed.

That's why we came. That's why we will make our stand here. That's why we will expand our base in Washington. This is the pressure point. This is the chokepoint. This is where we will shine the light.

Sure, I could have remained comfortable in the woods. My own freedom would be greater. My own safety would be more assured. But this is a time to challenge the status quo. This is a time for agitation. This is a time for hard work. This is a time for risks.

The *WND* mission has always been to serve as a watchdog on government—to expose fraud, waste, corruption, and abuse wherever we find it, to comfort the afflicted and afflict the comfortable. What better place to do that than Washington?

When I told my wife, who knows me best, that some people feared I might be co-opted by the pressures of the beltway, do you know what her reaction was?

She laughed.

"They don't know you, Farah," she said.

Those who do know me and *WND* know we will never compromise. We will never knuckle under. We will never give in to get along. We will never join the club. We will never sacrifice our commitment to our profession for comfort or security. We will never abandon our values because of peer pressure. We will not be bullied, intimidated, coerced, or tempted to yield one square inch in our battle to spread freedom and promote responsibility.

What can one small news agency do? That's what people asked five years ago when we got started. We've accomplished much since then. But it's just the beginning.

We may be in Washington, but we are not of it.

We are still outsiders in this culture and we will remain so as long as I have the strength to breathe the precious air of freedom and dream visions of a better way of life.

We arrived in D.C.—sometimes known as the District of Criminals—just in time to witness the area paralyzed in fear by the Beltway Snipers. I hadn't seen such palpable fear in a community since the days of the Night Stalker in LA.

Neither had I seen such political correctness run amok in a police investigation.

How do I put this delicately?

Was I surprised that a Muslim was arrested for questioning in the D.C. sniper case? No.

In fact, hours before the arrest of John Muhammad, I told *WND* editors that I believed authorities were only withholding the name of the wanted man "because it must be Muhammad." I even got the name right.

For three weeks, the government, the police, the FBI, and most of the media ignored the strong likelihood of a connection between Islamic terrorism and the assassinations in Maryland, Virginia, and Washington.

In fact, I know of only one news agency that vigorously pursued this angle from the beginning—*WND*.

Was it because we are so smart and the others are so stupid?

I don't think so.

It is simply that *WND*, unlike many other news agencies, is not afraid of the truth. We don't hide from it. We don't pretend the truth is a lie and vice versa. We don't allow political correctness to overcome common sense.

And that's all it really took to see a link between this heinous string of killings and Islamic terrorism—common sense.

Remember when the Egyptian Muslim shot up the El Al counter at Los Angeles International Airport on July 4, 2002? It took the FBI months to conclude the obvious—that the motivation behind the attack was the same motivation behind September 11. Initially, the U.S. government pretended the facts led elsewhere—defying common sense.

I have no doubts in the sniper case that government investigators hoped they would find a non-Muslim responsible. I have no doubts they would have preferred to pin the crimes on "Christian right-wing militiamen." I have no doubts that they may even have overlooked some evidence because of their prejudices, their biases, their preconceived ideas. And I have no doubts that most of my colleagues in the media were only too happy to play along with this charade.

We have seen this phenomenon before. We saw it in Oklahoma City. Evidence suggesting a conspiracy broader than Timothy McVeigh and Terry Nichols was ignored. Evidence suggesting a Middle East connection was deep-sixed. Evidence suggesting anything but a "Christian right-wing militiamen" explanation was overlooked—intentionally and deliberately. That's not justice.

We saw it again in the TWA Flight 800 shoot down. Yes, I said shoot down. It was not a spontaneous explosion of the center fuel tank that brought down the airliner. It was a missile. Who fired it remains a mystery—because government investigators chose to pretend that hundreds of witnesses didn't really see what they said they saw. They chose to overlook the forensic evidence that pointed to a missile. They chose to ignore any evidence that suggested anything except a spontaneous center fuel tank explosion. That's not justice.

We saw it again several years ago when the FBI launched its infamous Project Megiddo—a politically directed witch hunt against "Christian right-wing militiamen" whom the agency described as America's gravest threat. The FBI chose to profile a group with little track record in violence and ignore another group that was, even then, planning the most spectacular terrorist operation in the history of the world.

How did we miss it?

We were looking in all the wrong places.

And because we were looking in all the wrong places, we missed the real threat—which came home to roost in a big way September 11.

We're very fortunate we were able to arrest John Muhammad and his young illegal alien accomplice. Because, once again, we were looking in all the wrong places.

Even after the arrest of a Muslim convert and an illegal alien in the deadly crime spree, I was astonished at how long it took the news media to note that fact—to question what it meant, to admit that they were all wrong in their presuppositions about this case.

I'm still waiting for any of them to acknowledge that one news agency got it right. But I'm not holding my breath—especially when our colleagues here in Washington work at the *Washington Post*.

Let me ask you a question: should an American newsman be so "objective" he ceases to be an American? That is what has happened inside my profession—and the *Washington Post* offers a good illustration.

Washington Post managing editor Philip Bennett gave an interview to a "reporter" for China's official government paper, *People's Daily*, in which he stated: "I don't think the U.S. should be the leader of the world."[1]

He also said he tried to keep opinions out of the news columns of the *Post*. If that's true, why is it that most Americans reading the *Post* knew all along that the paper wants U.S. government officials to consult with foreign leaders and the United Nations before taking actions in the best interests of this country? It's not just because we read the editorials of the *Post*—which I don't and most Americans don't.

It's because we read the *Washington Post* news columns and because those news columns help set the agenda for so much of the establishment, corporate, "mainstream" media elite—which, Bennett admits, is losing its hammerlock of influence on the American people with the advent of the Internet.

For a newspaper that is not supposed to care much about opinions—just the news—this guy sure is opinionated.

He said, for instance, that he does not see much evidence that the U.S. is trying to spread freedom around the world.

He suggested strongly that the United States is really motivated by old-fashioned colonialism and imperialism.

He said that even in wartime, his paper takes great pride in telling the world about matters of national security.

He admitted that his paper and the rest of the elite media are out of touch with America's religious and patriotic values.

He seemed concerned that the "American people are more conservative, nationalistic, and religious and more closed off to foreign influence than the media."

He was quick to instruct his interviewer that his paper never characterizes totalitarian China as a dictatorship.[2]

Just what were Bennett and his paper hoping to achieve by sucking up to the brutes in Beijing, who, even as this interview was being published, were laying the "legal" foundation for a future invasion of Taiwan?

Are they hoping to replace the readership they are losing in the United States with readership in the largest marketplace in the world?

Are they hoping to secure better access to news in the closed society of China by sending a message of solidarity with the communists?

Not since Walter Duranty of the *New York Times* covered up the crimes against humanity of Josef Stalin in his Pulitzer Prize–winning reports from the old Soviet Union has an American journalist betrayed the aspirations of freedom-loving people on such a massive scale.

The truth is that 1.1 billion people in China are held in bondage and slavery by their military government. Yet Bennett suggests the situation in China is "complicated." Never before in the history of the world, he says, have so many people been lifted out of poverty so quickly. That claim sounds reminiscent of those of Duranty—those that overlooked the massive deaths in the gulags, the firing squads, the millions of people who got in the way of this economic "progress."

What was Bennett thinking when he gave this interview to a "reporter" who is actually a paid agent of the totalitarian regime in China?

Was that a service to his profession?

Does Bennett view his work as an American journalist as comparable with the propaganda program of the Chinese government? If so, he may not be that far off. In many ways they both serve the same masters.

If America was anything remotely like the America Bennett portrays in his interview with the Chinese government apparatchik posing as a reporter, the *Washington Post* editor would be summarily brought up on treason charges.

Of course, he wasn't.

Because America is nothing like China. America is nothing like the secretive, imperialistic, colonialistic monster he describes.

But just because Bennett and the paper he represents won't be charged with treason doesn't make them any less traitors for what they have done and what they do on a daily basis— twisting, distorting, and manipulating the news through their prism of moral relativism.

Now do you see why it's so important for me to be right here, in Washington, inside the belly of the beast?

CHAPTER FOURTEEN

STANDING UP TO THE PRESS POLICE

*"The function of the press is very high. It is almost holy.
It ought to serve as a forum for the people, through which
the people may know freely what is going on. To misstate or suppress
the news is a breach of trust."*

—Justice Louis D. Brandeis, U.S. Supreme Court

IMAGINE SPENDING your entire professional life working inside the press establishment as a respected member of the journalism community—a newspaper reporter, a newspaper editor, a top executive of major-market dailies.

Then, one day, a new medium comes along—the Internet. You take all you have learned during a twenty-five-year career in the Old Media and apply those standards and practices to the New Media.

But instead of being greeted as a media pioneer, someone who is helping to expand opportunities for journalists and who is keeping the flame of press freedom and real competition alive, you suddenly are faced with suspicion by your colleagues and denied access to the most vital institutions of government.

That's what happened to me and to *WND* beginning in 2001 when we applied—seemingly as a formality—for press credentials to cover the U.S. Capitol.

Today, it's an almost unbelievable story, given the way many of the biggest media institutions in the world—including the *New*

York Times—try to persuade *WND* daily to post links to their stories because they understand the power and reach of the independent news source.

But it wasn't always like this. And it's important to remember just how precarious our position was not too long ago. In fact, even today, some of our colleagues in the press don't know what to make of *WND*. It is sometimes referred to cavalierly as a "blog." It's no wonder really. *WND* was the first of its kind—and, quite frankly, I'm not sure there is anything else quite like it yet.

It's also worth reviewing how *WND* was denied the most important credentials you can have covering Washington because it illustrates just how fragile press freedom is even in America.

For a full year, we waited and politely answered questions in pursuit of our credentials. Each time we had interaction with staff of the Senate Press Gallery, it seemed that we were close to resolving any issues troubling those charged with providing the credentials.

Keep in mind, the Senate Press Gallery is not only the place to go for credentials to access the Capitol. It is also the required first step in getting credentialed at the Democratic and Republican party conventions.

We were patient because we understood the Internet was a new medium—little understood by bureaucrats and members of the press's old guard. I also understood the need for security in the Capitol in the post-9/11 world. As difficult as it was for me, I played the Mr. Nice Guy role. I answered every question I was asked. I explained the facts of life to the committee. And in the process, my news organization and I were insulted and degraded—treated as second-class journalists.

But then our little talks took a turn for the worse. My patience was exhausted.

What happened? I did a little research and found out the press police weren't really policing the press at all. The Senate Press Gallery, while denying—or at least stalling—our application, had already bestowed credentials to many representatives of the government-controlled "press" of totalitarian countries, at least some of which were pretty hostile to the United States.

These included: *Al-Ahram, Beijing Daily, China Press, China Youth Daily, China Times, Sing Tao Daily*, the Vietnam News Agency, and the Xinhua News Agency.

While we waited to be blessed by the august body known as the Standing Committee of Correspondents, those so-called news organizations, and many others like them, were already fully accredited members of the Washington press corps, with full access to congressional hearings, offices, press conferences, deliberations, and special sessions.

When I finally put on the full-court press for an end to the stall, *WND* was officially denied credentials. We were shocked.

What was the basis for the denial? I will list for you the various excuses we got in that first year.

WorldNetDaily is a nonprofit.

Well, no it was not—as we had been telling Joe Keenan, deputy director of the Senate Press Gallery, since day one. The confusion about this stemmed from the fact that *WND* was originally launched under the auspices of a nonprofit, the Western Journalism Center, in 1997. By 1999, it had been spun off as a for-profit operation and has been ever since.

WorldNetDaily is partly owned by a nonprofit.

There was some truth to this statement. Because of the nature of the spin off, Western Journalism Center retained some stock in the for-profit, though it was a minority percentage. But I'll tell you why this was merely an excuse—a smokescreen—for the committee.

There were no rules prohibiting neither nonprofit news agencies from accreditation nor companies partly owned by nonprofits. In fact, there were many of them among the roster of news agencies accredited in the Capitol—the *Christian Science Monitor*, the Associated Press, Religion News Service, and the *Washington Times*, which, like the *Christian Science Monitor*, is owned a hundred percent by a church, even though the newspaper may be set up as a for-profit operation.

It seemed a double standard was being applied to *WND*.

WorldNetDaily doesn't have enough original content.

Again, there was nothing in the rules about this, which shows the committee was winging it—making them up as it went along. But even in 2002, when we first heard this excuse, _WND_ had some 2.5 million readers every month who seemed to think we had something to offer. We already had tens of thousands of original _WND_ news stories and columns permanently archived on our Web site.

We were already breaking countless important national stories. Our material was frequently cited, with attribution, by many of those news organizations accredited by the Senate Press Gallery, such as the Associated Press and the _Washington Post_. But the czars of the Washington beltway journalistic establishment apparently still did not think these journalistic credentials were sufficiently worthy.

WorldNetDaily runs ads with the news.

No, I'm not kidding, people. This was the last line of explanation from Keenan when all the other excuses were shot down. Yes, I know, newspapers have been mixing ads with news for more than two hundred years in America. I didn't come up with this, the government-media cabal did. Of course, it was the very fact that we sell products and advertising that enables us to be a legitimate for-profit daily news organization, though, again, not that it should matter under the committee's stated rules.

I don't think I have ever been so shocked in my life. While this committee, made up of my colleagues in the press, was granting credentials to official government mouthpieces such as Egypt's _Al-Ahram_ and China's Xinhua News Agency, they were denying them to American citizens who had spent their lives in the news business.

How outrageous was this? Let's take a look at _Al-Ahram_— credentialed as a legitimate newspaper to cover the U.S. Congress. _Al-Ahram_ has reported that the perpetrators of the September 11 terrorist attacks on the United States were not carried out by Osama bin Laden's al-Qaida, but rather by Israel's Mossad.

"The Jews and the Israeli intelligence agency Mossad are behind this vicious attack on the United States," wrote Gamal Ali

Zahran in October 2001.[1] The writer reportedly repeated the unsubstantiated rumor that thousands of Jews who worked at the World Trade Center did not show up to the office September 11.

The editors of Egypt's three largest papers—including *Al-Ahram*—were then and continue today to be appointed by the government in Cairo and the government owns the newspaper printing presses in the country. Let's face it. By credentialing such "news organs" in Washington, the Senate Press Gallery is fostering this kind of hate speech and bestowing a recognition on government propaganda agents unfit to cover the U.S. Congress.

Yet *WND*, an independent voice relied on by millions of Americans for their news coverage, was denied such access.

Do you get the picture?

The more I looked into the collection of misfits and spies that had been credentialed by the Senate Press Gallery, I wasn't even sure I wanted to be a part of it anymore. Amazingly, the Senate Press Gallery has rules against representatives of the U.S. government being credentialed, but no rules against those representing hostile foreign governments.

Did these folks not understand that the governments of China, Vietnam, Egypt, and other despotic, authoritarian regimes do not send "correspondents" to Washington to report freely and fairly on the events of the day? They send them there to serve those governments.

Ironically, our Washington bureau chief at the time, Paul Sperry, had been a credentialed investigative reporter covering the Capitol for many years. Prior to joining the staff of *WND*, he served as Washington bureau chief for *Investor's Business Daily*. Yet because his reporting was now published on the Internet instead of paper, he was being blocked from the full access he previously had known for many years.

Things were starting to get tense in this titanic battle with the U.S. Senate Press Gallery. I found it ironic that in the center of this fight was William Roberts, chairman of the Standing Committee of Correspondents for the gallery and chairman of *Bloomberg News*.

Back in 1989, when *Bloomberg News* was the new kid on the block in the news business, guess who was denied press accreditation by the same Standing Committee of Correspondents of the daily press gallery?

That's right. *Bloomberg News.*

And was the boss ever steamed about it!

Matthew Winkler, the news service's first editor in chief, described the frustration of being turned down for Capitol press credentials by people with far less talent, far less experience, and far less savvy in their ability to act as gatekeepers for the government-media complex.

"I can't tell you how insulting it is to have someone from the Podunk Gazette tell someone who's written a jillion articles for the *Wall Street Journal* that he can't get his dog tags," Winkler said.[2]

Now the shoe was on the other foot. *Bloomberg News* had a decade or so to become part of the establishment and—judging from the hostility I detected from Roberts—the new gatekeeper planned on deadbolting the door to ensure no new access to other upstarts like *WND.*

Roberts called me in February 2002. Keenan was flooded with more than two thousand e-mails in one day protesting the decision to deny *WND* credentials.

"I request—no, I demand—that you remove Joe Keenan's e-mail address from your site," screamed the severely agitated Roberts. His demands were sandwiched between some rather, shall we say, unprofessional and unprovoked obscenities of the four-letter variety.

Things were getting ugly—leading up to a face-to-face showdown in Washington. On April 15, 2002, the Standing Committee of the U.S. Senate Daily Press Gallery held the appeal proceeding. Officially, *WND* had been denied for the following reasons:

WorldNetDaily does not provide "daily news with significant original reporting content."

WorldNetDaily is not separate and independent from the Western Journalism Center, a tax-exempt, nonprofit corporation also founded by me.

We saw the committee making up the rules as it went along—and specifically rewriting them to block *WND* from exercising its First Amendment rights.

The Congress of the United States has authorized the press gallery to limit admissions based on the following criteria only:

- When applicants represent advocacy groups;

- When applicants represent lobbying groups;

- When applicants fail to neutrally report news;

- When applicants are not bona fide journalists;

- When applicants would cause physical congestion within the galleries; and

- When applicants would importune members of the House or Senate.

Now the Senate Press Gallery had redefined its mission—excluding from accreditation the world's leading independent Internet news site.

Why was it happening? Why was the committee making excuses? Why was it grasping at straws in a determined effort to keep *WND* out? I had come to the conclusion it was more than the fact that we did our reporting on the Internet.

I had been persuaded that this was a matter of unlawful discrimination based on some prejudice by its members. Maybe they didn't like the hard-hitting, watchdog-style, investigative journalism for which *WND* had become known. Maybe they didn't like the New Media and saw *WND* as a threat to their own organizations—newspapers and offline news services. Maybe their own political biases skewed their view of *WND* and its mission. Maybe it was a combination of all these reasons and more.

Whatever the case, *WND* was being shut out. It had become a major inconvenience for us. The denial by the press gallery kept some of *WorldNetDaily*'s staff out of the 2000 national political conventions. The denial made Sperry's already difficult job more difficult. But most of all, the denial was an affront to all those who take the First Amendment seriously.

The government had no business blocking the free exercise of the press. And that is exactly what it had done in this case.

Here's what I told the committee when we convened to hear our appeal April 15, 2002:

> I have little hope today of persuading this committee to reverse itself on its rejection of WorldNetDaily for accreditation to the Senate Press Gallery.
>
> For fifteen months, my news organization, the largest independent news site on the Internet, has patiently waited, answered irrelevant and often insulting questions about our ownership, our associations, our content, and received the runaround as we have sought nothing more than to fulfill our obligation to our 2.5 million readers by covering the Congress on an even footing with our competitors.
>
> The ultimate insult from this committee came in the form of a formal rejection of accreditation—a blatant denial of our First Amendment rights by an arm of the U.S. Congress.
>
> It was a clearly discriminatory decision and one not based on the rules governing the gallery, as Mr. (Richard) Ackerman [WorldNetDaily's attorney] has already pointed out.
>
> While I have little hope of disabusing you of the prejudices and biases you have against me and my news organization, I come here today to set the stage for a legal challenge and a public relations offensive that will be successful. We will not give up. We will not roll over. We will never let this issue rest.
>
> Clearly, based on the committee's release of the documents it examined in rendering its decision, there is a political bias at work. Clearly, the focus on a few unflattering articles—many of which predate the very existence of my news organization—demonstrates the predisposition of the committee against WorldNetDaily. Clearly, many of the questions raised by Senate Press Gallery deputy director Joe Keenan over the last fifteen months show the committee grasping at straws to find a justification for denial—even when none exist under the rules governing the gallery.
>
> Double standards are being used to block WorldNetDaily's access to the Capitol.
>
> While the committee finds WorldNetDaily ineligible because of association with a nonprofit organization solely devoted to promoting investigative reporting, it approves other news organizations that are themselves nonprofits and others controlled and owned by nonprofits with political and religious agendas. It even approves

foreign "news" organizations completely under the control and domination of totalitarian governments.

While the committee finds WorldNetDaily ineligible because of a lack of original content, it approves other news organizations with far fewer resources and far less in the way of track records of achievement in breaking nationally and internationally significant news stories.

While the committee finds it objectionable that WorldNetDaily runs clearly labeled advertisements for books, videos, and other products and services with its news presentation, it apparently has no problem with U.S. newspapers, which typically devote 80 percent of their space to selling goods and services to the public.

Those are the objections cited in your rejection of our application. None of them stands the smell test. None of them is within the purview of this committee under the rules governing the gallery. All of them strongly suggest underlying motives, biases, and prejudices.

Let's deal with some facts:

WorldNetDaily's original investigative reports have been picked up and credited by the Associated Press, the Washington Post, the New York Times, the Jerusalem Post, the London Times, the Wall Street Journal, the South China Morning Post, United Press International, the Toronto Star, the Los Angeles Times, the Chicago Sun-Times, and dozens of other responsible papers across the nation and around the world.

Indeed, WorldNetDaily has been cited by all five of the news organizations represented by this committee—Reuters, Cox Newspapers, Knight Ridder, Bloomberg—even the Columbus Dispatch.

We're doing the job. We're just doing it with a handicap, as our access to the Capitol, to the White House, and to the major political conventions has been severely restricted by the actions of this committee and its staff.

Somewhere, somehow, this committee has concluded that WorldNetDaily is not a legitimate news agency. I can only guess—based on the improper and out-of-bounds questions its staff has asked and on the information released by the committee about its decision-making process—that this conclusion is based on political biases.

Indeed, WorldNetDaily marches to the beat of a very different drummer. Our mission has always been to provide aggressive, watchdog-style coverage of government fraud, waste, abuse, and corruption. This often makes government officials and bureaucrats wary of us. And it also makes our less aggressive colleagues nervous.

Some, because of their own biases, choose to stereotype World-NetDaily inaccurately as a "conservative" or "libertarian" news site. That, I believe, is exactly what this committee is doing. It is uncomfortable with our style of journalism, so it is making excuses to deny us access to the Congress. That is unconstitutional. And we will prove it.

I dare suggest to you that I have more daily news experience and accomplishments than anyone in this room.

Twenty years ago, when I was twenty-seven years old, I was running a newsroom of some two hundred in a major-market U.S. newspaper. A few years later I was serving as editor in chief of a group of dailies and weeklies. A few years later, I was serving as editor in chief of the oldest daily West of the Mississippi. I've been a reporter. I've been a city editor. I've done everything there is to do in a daily newsroom. And that's all I've done in my career. I've never crossed the line and worked for political candidates or government. I don't even register to vote with a political party to avoid the appearance of conflicts of interest.

Let me briefly talk about the man you denied accreditation. Paul Sperry was not only accredited previously as Washington bureau chief of Investor's Business Daily, but while in that position, he determined for the gallery which other IBD staffers would receive accreditation. Sperry is a fearless and incorruptible investigative reporter—for my money, the best in the city. That's why we hired him more than two years ago. But when he came to WorldNetDaily, suddenly, in the eyes of the gallery, he became a pariah.

What is this controversy all about? There have been hints revealed in some of the questions raised by the committee.

I was asked about WorldNetDaily's connections with Judicial Watch, a conservative nonprofit group. Judicial Watch has no connection with WorldNetDaily.com, Inc. The group is a source of news to WorldNetDaily just as it is a source of news to many other news organizations. The chairman of the group sometimes writes opinion pieces published by WorldNetDaily. But there is no connection. Yet the question itself is revealing. Why would this be a concern? I believe the committee's own political biases are affecting its judgment and its ability to fulfill its responsibilities to the Congress and the press.

As further evidence of this point, I was asked about WorldNetDaily's relationship with Richard Mellon Scaife, the man Hillary Clinton described as at the epicenter of the "vast right-wing media conspiracy." Again, WorldNetDaily has no relationship with Scaife, though he does reportedly invest in a competing news site and owns his own newspaper. Yet why is the question even asked? Because, clearly, the committee and/or staff has a political agenda of its own and is imposing certain litmus tests on applicants.

The committee's fixation on Western Journalism Center is another giveaway of this political bias. Though I founded WJC and ran it for years as a tax-exempt, 501(c)3 corporation specifically restricted from lobbying, the committee has suggested in its rejection of our application that the center is some kind of political front group. It is nothing more—and never has been—than a charity promoting independent investigative journalism. Yes, it makes some politicians and government officials nervous to have watchdogs looking over their shoulder. But that's what the free press is all about. And that's the only agenda at work in Western Journalism Center. Despite the contentions of this committee, Western Journalism Center does not advocate anything except good journalism.

There are, however, many accredited members of the gallery who advocate, lobby, even spy on the U.S. Congress. They are the official organs of totalitarian states that have no concept of a free press. This is what makes your decision about WorldNetDaily so remarkable, so flabbergasting, so unjust, so duplicitous, so immoral, so unconscionable.

After September 11, most ordinary, tax-paying Americans are severely restricted from access to their own U.S. Capitol. But you have bestowed upon these state-sponsored propagandists privileges and access ordinary Americans will never know. You have given them unfettered access to the U.S. government while denying WorldNetDaily.

With all of the new security procedures in place today at the Capitol, unfettered access by the legitimate press is more important than ever. The American people still have a right to know what is happening in Washington, and the press's role is more important than ever. At the same time, it is my personal opinion as an American taxpayer that spies and lobbyists representing foreign dictators while masquerading as "journalists" do not belong in our Capitol.

I look forward to addressing any and all of your questions today.

By the way, a week ago, I moved my entire family to the Washington, D.C., metro area because this is where we intend to build up our editorial resources in the coming years. The actions of this committee are adversely affecting my business and our ability to compete. I not only expect to get this situation with Paul Sperry resolved, I expect many more WorldNetDaily staffers to be accredited in the years ahead—and without this kind of unacceptable and unconstitutional hassle.

Boy was that fun.

I had to get that off my chest. A spirited discussion followed. When it was all over, we felt certain we had made progress—made our points effectively. We doubted that anyone could look at the facts we presented and decide against us.

For a month, though, we heard nothing.

Then, incredibly, we received a letter from the gallery, on the letterhead of the U.S. Congress, suggesting yet a new reason had been discovered for the continued stonewalling of our very simple, straightforward request to be treated equally with other press outlets covering Washington.

More than a year earlier, Sperry's press badge was seized by Capitol police because it had expired. It was the badge he had obtained when he served in the same capacity for *Investor's Business Daily*. This was no secret. The Senate Press Gallery has been aware of this for more than a year. Sperry discussed it openly at our appeal hearing. It was the event that triggered our quest for permanent credentials.

Now it appeared to be the sole remaining justification for denying our bid.

Have you ever played a game where the rules keep changing? It's very difficult to win. The target keeps moving. The sand beneath your feet keeps shifting.

In August 2000, the press cops raised the stakes. In a secret meeting, the Standing Committee of Correspondents, an official institution of Congress funded by tax dollars, banned *WND*'s Sperry from covering the Capitol. It was the ultimate act of spiteful arrogance that followed eighteen months of stalling and excuse-making by the committee, which has searched in vain for any legitimate reason to block *WND* from the accreditation process that would give the independent news site unfettered access to the Capitol.

Until then, the committee had simply refused to grant permanent accreditation to *WND*, but provided limited access through day passes. Now even the day passes had been revoked.

The latest reason for turning away *WND* from the Capitol? The attorney for the committee said the unprecedented action was meant as punishment for Sperry for allegedly making "factually inaccurate" statements at the appeals hearing last April. Accusing Sperry of misleading the committee was the latest in a long list of excuses used to deny *WND* unfettered access to Congress.

First, *WND* was told the committee had no rules governing Internet-based media. The next objection was *WorldNetDaily*'s association with the nonprofit Western Journalism Center, from which it was spun off three years earlier. Then came erroneous charges that *WND* takes money from businessman Richard Mellon Scaife, whom the Clinton administration alleged directed a vast right-wing media conspiracy. Then questions arose regarding *WorldNetDaily*'s nonexistent connections to Judicial Watch. In the end, the committee settled on an alleged shortage of "original content" on the news site as a main basis for denying *WND* accreditation.

Nevertheless, through the entire fishing expedition, Sperry was permitted access to the Capitol through the indignity and inconvenience of day passes. Then he was informed that he would no longer be welcome in the Capitol at all.

Believe it or not, it got worse. In August, the Stalinists in the Senate Press Gallery prohibiting *WND* began lying to members of Congress who were now asking questions about their actions with regard to *WND*. While at first they kept *WorldNetDaily* reporters from exercising their First Amendment rights, they also began lying to their bosses in the U.S. Congress about the reasons for the denial.

When a constituent of Sen. Maria Cantwell (D-Wash.) asked her about the denial of credentials to *WND*, she went to the Senate

Press Gallery for answers. Here's what she told her constituent based on what she was told:

"To be considered a correspondent with a bona fide news organization, the rules state that the applicant's publication must have at least a [sic] fifty percent original content," she wrote. "*WND* failed to meet this criterion. In addition, the Standing Committee is not allowed to grant a permanent pass to news organizations that are engaged in paid publicity or promotion work of lobby activities.

"Because *WND* Editor and CEO Joseph Farah's journalism center owns half of the publication, this is considered a special interest, one that could lead *WND* to engage in the aforementioned activities and therefore disqualifies *WND* for a permanent pass," she continues.[3]

Let's start with these lies before we move on to others.

There is no 50 percent original content requirement under the rules of the committee. If there were, few U.S. news organizations would qualify. Just read your own daily newspaper and tell me if 50 percent of the content is locally originated. Having run daily newspapers for twenty-five years, I can tell you that advertising constitutes roughly 70 percent of successful papers. Of the editorial content, most daily newspapers run between 75 percent and 90 percent newswire content, leaving only a tiny percentage—somewhere between 10 and 25 percent—of original content.

Ironically, even members of the Standing Committee of Correspondents represented news organizations that publish far less than 50 percent original content—though they may have been ignorant of this fact because none of them had served in executive positions for those publications. They were reporters who had no business experience in their industry let alone in the New Media.

Now, with regard to "paid publicity" or "promotion work" or "lobby activities," every single major news organization in the United States hires publicists to promote its work. Every single news organization in the United States promotes its work in various ways. So, clearly, if such a restriction existed and were applied uniformly, the press gallery would be empty. And how did the gallery and Sen. Cantwell define "lobby activities"?

I found it interesting that a U.S. senator was getting yet a different story about the denial.

The gallery changed positions once again within weeks to offer *WND* "provisional" approval—as long as Sperry wasn't representing the company.

I told them they could "provisional" approval and—pardon the expression—shove it. I informed the committee that all further cooperation with them would end. I would not be answering anymore insulting questions. I would not be defending my twenty-five-year history in the news-gathering business. I would not meet with them. I would not accept their phone calls. I would not encourage third parties to provide them any more information or documentation.

Enough is enough, I said. I can't believe I was so accommodating for so long. No more abuse. No more excuses. No more negotiations.

The committee was a disgrace. Despite its taxpayer funding, it was disorganized. It was not in compliance with the law. It didn't announce its meetings to interested parties—a practice abhorred by journalists when government does it. It doesn't announce the results of those meetings to interested parties. In fact, some committee members admitted they really didn't even meet when they said they met. Maybe some phone calls were made. Maybe members read each other's minds.

A group like this couldn't buy my association. I didn't want to join their club, personally. But I did want my reporters to have access to the Capitol.

We began investigating the operations of the gallery itself. Like any government agency, it was a scandal waiting to be exposed.

My first contact with the Senate Press Gallery came in infuriating phone conversations with a man I later came to learn was a well-compensated bureaucrat named Joe Keenan. It was Keenan who misled *WND* time and time again about the status of our seemingly routine application for credentials. It was Keenan who handed us one poor excuse after another for never-ending deliberations. It was Keenan who always seemed to have one more irrelevant question as First Amendment rights were put on hold for eighteen months.

Late in the game, we learned that Keenan, having played a pivotal role in stonewalling and bullying *WND*, was up for a promotion that would earn him $111,000 a year. What are Keenan's credentials for such a job? One of the requirements of the position is six years of news media experience. It turns out, by the strictest definition of the term, Keenan has none, zip, zilch, nada.

For the previous twenty-five years, he had toiled away in relative obscurity in the Senate Press Gallery—shuffling paper around, keeping the bulletin board up to date, sharpening No. 2 pencils, and rubbing elbows with the journalists who cover the Capitol every day. Before that, Keenan reluctantly admitted he worked for the *Tucson Citizen*.

Given that Keenan was sitting in judgment of my own journalistic credentials and those of veteran investigative reporter Sperry, we decided to check out some of his bylines, talk to a few of his peers in the newsroom, find out what kind of newsman Joe Keenan was twenty-five years earlier.

It turns out he wasn't a newsman at all. Apparently he was a circulation worker—a newspaper delivery guy.

Keenan's "news media experience" qualifying him as a shoo-in for the job as director of the Senate Press Gallery was time spent supervising which bundles of newspapers got on which trucks to be delivered to Tucson readers. This was the arbiter of which journalists are fit to cover the Capitol. This was the man assigned to investigate me and my news organization to determine whether we are worthy to report on the activities of the U.S. Congress. This was one of my "peers" who sat in judgment of me and my twenty-five-year career reporting, editing, and running daily newspapers.

We'd had enough. We'd given the process time. In September 2002, I instructed our attorneys to demand the credentials at the threat of a lawsuit against the institution of the committee as well as the individuals wielding this terrible power over us. We gave them ten days to produce the credentials or else.

We were prepared to file in federal court a lawsuit charging intentional violations of the First Amendment, intentional violations of the Ninth Amendment, business disparagement, defamation, intentional interference with economic advantage, antitrust violations, violations of "sunshine laws," invasion of privacy, and other unlawful conduct by the Standing Committee of Correspondents, which administers the Senate Press Gallery.

Within that ten-day time frame, the gallery had an epiphany.

It was a total victory. And that victory would not have been possible without the valiant aid and assistance of Richard Ackerman and Gary Kreep of the U.S. Justice Foundation. These men and this organization were heroic in their commitment to our cause and to the First Amendment. The American Civil Liberties Union wasn't there for us, but USJF was.

CHAPTER FIFTEEN

WHEN PERCEPTION BECOMES REALITY

THE MIDEAST AS A CASE STUDY IN MEDIA DISTORTION

"Given a free press, we may defy open or insidious enemies of liberty.
It instructs the public mind and animates the spirit of patriotism.
Its loud voice suppresses everything which would raise itself against the
public liberty, and its blasting rebuke causes
incipient despotism to perish in the bud."

—Daniel Webster

FROM 1903 through 1908, two young bicycle mechanics from Ohio repeatedly claimed to have built a flying machine. They demonstrated it over and over again to hundreds of people, obtained affidavits from prominent citizens who witnessed their efforts, and even produced photographs of their invention at work.

Nevertheless, Orville and Wilbur Wright were dismissed as frauds and hoaxers in the *Scientific American,* the *New York Herald,* and by the U.S. Army and many American scientists.

But as Richard Milton points out in his entertaining book *Alternative Science,* the real shocker is that even local newspapers in the Wrights' home town of Dayton ignored the story in their backyard for five years.

Despite the fact that witnesses repeatedly visited and wrote to the *Dayton Daily News* and *Dayton Journal* over those years asking about the young men in their flying machine, no reporters were dispatched. No photographers were assigned.

Asked in 1940 about his refusal to publish anything about the sensational accomplishments of the Wrights during those years, *Dayton Daily News* city editor Dan Kumler said: "We just didn't believe it. Of course, you remember that the Wrights at that time were terribly secretive."

When the interviewer pointed out that the Wrights were flying over an open field just outside of town for five years, Kumler grew more candid: "I guess the truth is we were just plain dumb."

If you want to know the truth, a lot of journalism stinks today as badly as it did in the day of Orville and Wilbur Wright. At its worst, the problem is that journalists have the wrong goals, the wrong mission statement, the wrong objectives and methodology.

Ask the average Columbia Journalism School graduate today what they try to do in their reporting and they'll probably tell you they want to be "fair and balanced."

"Fair and balanced." Where have I heard that before? I guess it has a nice ring to it. It is, after all, the marketing slogan that lifted Fox News Channel to the top of cable news ratings heap.

But does that make it good? Does that make it right? Does that make it the highest calling for the press in the twenty-first century?

I say no. And I want to say it unequivocally and more emphatically in this chapter than I have said it before. As anyone who has read this far in my book knows, I deeply respect and revere the institution of the American free press. I believe it is vital to the future survival of our country.

Please don't mistake me for one of those outside agitators who is content to find fault with the way the news media do their job. I see the problems, all right. But better yet, I see solutions where no one else does.

But to understand how to fix a problem, you've got to recognize not only that it exists, but why. How does it perpetuate itself? Why doesn't this problem go away by itself?

I can think of no better way to illustrate this point than with a look at the myths and perceptions of the Middle East and the role the international media have played in ensuring the conflict gets worse and worse.

But before we start, let me reintroduce myself. Throughout the this book, you've come to know me as a journalist. You have no doubt surmised that I am a Christian. I have another identity, though—one that often has me appearing on television as an analyst or speaking around the country and around the world.

I am an Arab-American. I would not normally identify myself as any kind of hyphenated American, except I got tired of seeing one professional Arab-American spokesman after another on television blaming Israel for all the problems in the Middle East. That's when I decided I would have to play the Arab heritage card too in order to get in on the debate.

I have another distinction that qualifies me to talk about the Middle East. I covered the region as a correspondent. And I have immersed myself in the subject for the last twenty-five years.

There are a few subjects I really know:

- Baseball

- Hollywood, which I also covered

- *The Honeymooners*

- Popular music of the 1960s

- The media

- The Middle East

Let's face it. There is just no demand out there for Joseph Farah to talk or write about baseball, Hollywood, *The Honeymooners,* or popular music of the 1960s. So, accordingly, this chapter will combine two areas of my solid expertise.

But don't take my word for it. Listen to what *Al-Jazeera* has to say about me: "Farah is the number one Zionist Arab in the world today."[1]

I guess that's supposed to be an insult. For Jew-haters, you can't get much lower than that. When an anti-Semite bigot calls you a Zionist, that's the insult of insults. As for me, as long as I'm number one, I'll accept the condemnation from *Al-Jazeera* as the highest form of flattery.

What is a Zionist, anyway? From my deep studies into this subject, I have come to the conclusion that a Zionist is anyone—Jew or non-Jew—who believes the Jews have a right and a duty to rebuild their ancestral homeland in the Middle East. If that's the definition, I can more than live with it.

But it certainly should mean that you support every single thing the nation of Israel does. Because I don't. In fact, I think one of Israel's biggest problems is they don't have enough Zionists in their own government.

However, I digress. I don't want to talk too much about the Middle East. We'll save that for my next book. We need to focus on this issue of the media like a laser beam—only using the Middle East as a reference point so we can all recognize the problem and work toward a solution. Diagnosis first, treatment second.

Let me ask you this: Do you think the world's news media give Israel a fair shake?

I'll prove to you it does not.

The largest, most powerful and influential news-gathering organization in the world is the Associated Press. I've mentioned its importance earlier. It is a cooperative of the newspaper industry and has become even more pervasive in the last twenty years as private, full-service news services like United Press International have shrunk in size and scope, becoming virtually irrelevant—leaving in their wake one gigantic media monopoly.

In November 2003, AP put together a list of "recent terror attacks around the world." Here is that list in its entirety:

August 5, 2003: A suicide bomber kills 12 people and injures 150 at the J. W. Marriott in Jakarta, Indonesia. Authorities blame Jemaah Islamiyah, a Southeast Asian group linked to al-Qaida.May 16, 2003: Bomb attacks in Morocco kill at least 28 people and injure more than 100. The government blames "international terrorism," and local militant groups linked to al-Qaida.

May 12, 2003: Four explosions rock Riyadh, the Saudi capital, in an attack on compounds housing Americans, other Westerners, and Saudis. Eight Americans are among those killed. In all, the attack kills 35 people, including 9 attackers.

The original Joseph Farah—my grandfather—who emigrated from Lebanon to America at the turn of the twentieth century.

May 11, 2003: A bomb explodes at a crowded market in the southern Philippines, killing at least 9 people and wounding 41. The military blames the Muslim separatist group Moro Islamic Liberation Front.

December 30, 2002: A gunman kills 3 American missionaries at a Southern Baptist hospital in Yemen. Yemeni officials say the gunman, sentenced to death in May, belonged to an al-Qaida cell.

November 28, 2002: Suicide bombers kill 12 people at an Israeli-owned beach hotel in Kenya and two missiles narrowly miss an airliner carrying Israelis.

October 12, 2002: Nearly 200 people, including 7 Americans, are killed in bombings in a nightclub district of the Indonesian island of Bali. Authorities blame Jemaah Islamiyah.

October 6, 2002: A small boat crashes into a French oil tanker off the coast of Yemen and explodes, killing one crewman.

October 2, 2002: Suspected Abu Sayyaf guerrillas detonate a bomb in Zamboanga, Philippines, killing 4 people, including an American Green Beret. Four more bomb attacks in October blamed on Abu Sayyaf, a group linked to al-Qaida, kill 16 people.

June 14, 2002: A suicide bomber blows up a truck at the U.S. Consulate in Karachi, Pakistan, killing 14 Pakistanis. Authorities say it is the work of Harkat-ul-Mujahedeen, linked to al-Qaida.

April 11, 2002: A suicide bombing with a gas truck at a historic Tunisian synagogue on the resort island of Djerba kills 21 people, mostly German tourists.

September 11, 2001: Hijackers slam jetliners into the World Trade Center and the Pentagon and a fourth hijacked jet crashes in a Pennsylvania field, killing nearly 3,000 people.

December 30, 2000: Explosions in Manila strike a train, a bus, the airport, a park near the U.S. Embassy, and a gas station, killing 22 people. Philippine and U.S. investigators link the attack to Jemaah Islamiyah.

October 12, 2000: Suicide attackers on an explosives-laden boat ram the destroyer USS Cole off Yemen, killing 17 American sailors.

August 7, 1998: Nearly simultaneous car bombings hit the U.S. Embassies in Dar es Salaam, Tanzania, and Nairobi, Kenya, killing 231 people, including 12 Americans.

Do you notice anything strange about this list? It notes Islamic terrorism all over the world since 1998, but completely disregards all such terrorism directed at the citizens of one country and one country only—Israel.

Worse yet, AP's worldview generally reflects the thinking—if you want to call it that—of the mainstream, establishment Western media. That's why hundreds of newspapers actually published this list without blinking an eye, registering a protest, or asking any questions.

This is not the first time such a list was prepared and circulated by AP. The news organization published a similar list May 19, 2003—again, no attacks on Israel were included.

At the time this list was published, more than a thousand Israeli civilians had been killed by Islamic terrorists since the fall of 2000. Many thousands more had been injured. But none of this counts, according to AP.[2]

In 2002, following the 9/11 attacks, I was stunned to realize the *New York Times* no longer accepted as historical fact that a Jewish Temple once stood upon the Temple Mount in Jerusalem. Beginning at that point, news stories began referring to "the Temple Mount, which Israel claims to have been the site of the First and Second Temples."

In 2003, I noticed AP had followed suit.

We have a term in the news business for a standard paragraph of historical background information that you see in stories over and over again. We call it a "nut graph." Here's what the new nut graph at AP says about the Temple Mount: "Jews believe the mosques sit on the ruins of the first and second Jewish Temples, and revere as their holiest site a nearby wall believed to have surrounded the sanctuaries. Muslims say nothing existed on the hill before the mosques."

Let me get to the bottom line here for you: AP has lost its moral compass. The *New York Times*, a Jewish-owned newspaper, is leading the international, anti-Israeli pack journalism syndrome. And if you are reading virtually any newspaper in America today, you are tacitly supporting this kind of outrageous, vicious propaganda.

But why has this happened? How has this happened? Aren't the media attempting to be "fair and balanced"?

With the U.S. news media's growing infatuation with "fair and balanced" news presentations, it is losing sight of a principle far more important—truth. The Middle East is the perfect laboratory in which to view the failure of the "fair and balanced" experiment. Being "fair and balanced" in the Middle East prevents you from seeing or seeking the truth. In fact, I'm pretty sure it works this way everywhere. It's just easier to demonstrate the flaw in the Mideast.

Facts are facts. Truth is truth. If the news media stick to the facts and seek the truth, they won't have to worry about phony issues like "balance" when it comes to the Middle East.

How do you cover a murder with balance? Do we make sure we report the murderer's justifications for his crime? Do we investigate the victim to try to ascertain how he provoked the murderer? Nonsense. But that is how the United States and international news media approach coverage of the Middle East.

On the one hand, we have a historical fact with thousands of proof texts from archaeology. What is that massive platform upon which currently sit the al-Aqsa Mosque and Dome of the Rock in Jerusalem? We call it the Temple Mount because it is a historical fact—not an opinion—that the Jewish Temple once sat upon it.

Weighed against that are the red-hot rhetorical incitements over the years by people like Arafat, who, in their hatred for the Jews, insist no Jewish Temple ever rested there. They don't cite any studies, any history books, any archaeological digs, no scientific reports. They just say they know it was never there.

And that's enough for the *New York Times*, in its quest to be "fair and balanced," to begin addressing this issue simply as a matter of opinion.

Think about it this way. Let's pretend you're a reporter. You cover a traffic accident. You interview the two drivers involved. One tells you the truth, the other lies through his teeth. A "fair and balanced" report will give equal weight to the lie as the truth, right? Sometimes that may be the best we can do as journalists.

But this illustration shows why we must never settle for "fair and balanced." It falls far short of our mission to seek the truth.

Contributing to the distortion that results from the "fair and balanced" model of coverage in the Middle East is Israel's own semi-suicidal quest for peace at almost any price. Israel's concessions to Arab myth-making and the wholesale fabrication of reality has backfired. Israel's gravest mistake has been yielding to international pressure to compromise its own security for peace with people who have no desire to live with them in peace and harmony.

Today, as a direct result of that mistake, most people in the world believe that Israel represents the gravest danger to peace in the world—or so the polls tell us. How can anyone in their right mind believe the tiny sliver of a land called Israel, with fewer than seven million people, could actually represent the gravest threat to peace in the world?

We're living in a time when right is wrong and wrong is right, when truth is seen as a lie and lies are seen as truth. Clearly, to a great extent the world has gone mad. But at least part of this moral blindness is fed by the failure of the "fair and balanced" international press.

Here's the irony: Israel has done what no other nation in the world has done in the last three decades—sacrificed over and over again its own security interests and concerns in a breathtaking, selfless, and often ill-advised crusade for peace with duplicitous neighbors. For that, it is perceived not only as a pariah nation, but the biggest threat to peace in the world today—worse than Iran, worse than North Korea, worse than Syria.

The more efforts Israel makes for peace, the more it is seen as a warmonger. The further Israel goes in making concessions to its enemies, the more it is seen as the aggressor. The more evidence mounts that Israel is an embattled target in the Mideast, fewer can see the truth.

The term "moral relativism" often comes to mind in the discussion of certain domestic "social issues." But I've been seeing more and more evidence of it in the context of the Middle East conflict.

During the years I did a daily radio show and during some of my television interviews, I've had the opportunity to debate the Middle East issues with some of the best distortion artists and apologists for fascism Arabian-style.

When the moral relativists suggest that Israel is the real oppressor in the region, I usually try to ask a short series of questions (you can play along at home or use this technique with your moral relativist friends):

Do Arabs in Israel have the right to vote?

Do Arabs in Israel have full citizenship rights in every way?

Do Arabs in Israel have the right to speak out, dissent, publish newspapers?

Do Arabs in Israel have the right to worship as they please?

In case you don't know, the answer to all these questions is yes. Then I ask if Arabs in most Arabic countries have these same rights.

In case you don't know, the answer to that question is a big, fat negatory.

From there, all you need to do is ask if Jews in most Arab countries have any of these rights. The answer is clearly no.

Nevertheless, despite the answers to these questions and all they suggest in terms of an ultimate settlement of the Arab-Israeli conflict, there are still those who say we need another Arab country in the Middle East—a homeland for the "Palestinians," to ensure that these disfranchised people have the right to self-determination.

As an Arab-American, I am not without compassion for my brothers and sisters in the Arab world. What I want for them is freedom—the kind of freedom they know in no other country in the Middle East but the Jewish state.

Usually, what my opponent will say at that point is something like this: "You have an unbalanced view of the region and both sides have blood on their hands."

Why? Because that is where the moral relativists want the debate. There is no right. There is no truth. There is only compromise.

Is it technically true that both sides in the conflict have blood on their hands? Sure.

It is also technically true that both the United States and al-Qaida have blood on their hands.

The nature of conflict and war is that both sides get blood on their hands.

But it is an argument designed to suggest there is no good guy and no bad guy—no right and wrong.

I know there are people who believe this. But it is still shocking to me nonetheless. I can understand how someone truly uninformed about the Middle East would chalk up the debate to "both sides have a legitimate grievance" or "both sides have blood on their hands." But when people who have actually studied the history and viewed the present reality come to that conclusion, there are only three possibilities:

They are guilty of incredibly bad analysis of the facts.

They are evil and want to excuse evil and rationalize it.

They are moral relativists.

Even many Israelis can't face the truth. They are so well-conditioned in the art of moral relativism that they are just plain uncomfortable saying they are right—even when they are.

This is probably why I got fired from the *Jerusalem Post* a few years ago.

It all started when I wrote a column. But, of course, I write a column every single day. When I wrote this particular one for publication October 11, 2000, I didn't think it was anything special. But I was wrong. It was called "Myths of the Middle East." And its 750 words became some of the most well-read in my long writing career.

Several weeks earlier, an uprising began in and around Israel—an Arab uprising called an *intifada*. This rioting and mayhem and violence has never ended—not even six years later. I didn't think there was much point in trying to explain why the riots began or what caused it. I decided it was time to back up and deal with so much of the distortion that had been peddled by media and accepted by people around the world regarding this conflict.

I asked the rhetorical question: *What is this fighting all about?* Here is my rhetorical response:

If you believe what you read in most news sources, Palestinians want a homeland and Muslims want control over sites they consider holy. Simple, right?

Well, as an Arab-American journalist who has spent some time in the Middle East dodging more than my share of rocks and mortar shells, I've got to tell you that these are just phony excuses for the rioting, troublemaking, and land-grabbing.

Isn't it interesting that prior to the 1967 Arab-Israeli war, there was no serious movement for a Palestinian homeland?

Well, Farah, you might say, *that was before the Israelis seized the West Bank and Old Jerusalem.*

That's true. In the Six-Day War, Israel captured Judea, Samaria, and East Jerusalem. But they didn't capture these territories from Yasser Arafat. They captured them from Jordan's King Hussein. I can't help but wonder why all these Palestinians suddenly discovered their national identity after Israel won the war.

The truth is that Palestine is no more real than never-never land. The first time the name was used was in AD 70 when the Romans committed genocide against the Jews, smashed the Temple, and declared the land of Israel would be no more. From then on, the Romans promised, it would be known as Palestine. The name was derived from the Philistines, a Goliathian people conquered by the Jews centuries earlier. It was a way for the Romans to add insult to injury. They also tried to change the name of Jerusalem to *Aelia Capitolina*, but that had even less staying power.

Palestine has never existed—before or since—as an autonomous entity. It was ruled alternately by Rome, by Islamic and Christian crusaders, by the Ottoman Empire, and briefly by the British after World War I. The British agreed to restore at least part of the land to the Jewish people as their homeland.

There is no language known as Palestinian. There is no distinct Palestinian culture. There has never been a land known as Palestine governed by Palestinians. Palestinians are Arabs, indistinguishable from Jordanians (another recent invention), Syrians, Lebanese, Iraqis, etc. Keep in mind that the Arabs control 99.9 percent of the Middle East lands. Israel represents one-tenth of 1 percent of the land mass.

But that's too much for the Arabs. They want it all. And that is ultimately what the fighting in Israel is about today. Greed. Pride.

Envy. Covetousness. No matter how many land concessions the Israelis make, it will never be enough.

What about Islam's holy sites? *There are none in Jerusalem.*

Shocked? You should be. I don't expect you will ever hear this brutal truth from anyone else in the international media. It's just not politically correct.

I know what you're going to say: *Farah, the al-Aqsa Mosque and the Dome of the Rock in Jerusalem represent Islam's third most holy sites.*

Not true. In fact, the Koran says nothing about Jerusalem. It mentions Mecca hundreds of times. It mentions Medina countless times. It never mentions Jerusalem. With good reason. There is no historical evidence to suggest Mohammed ever visited Jerusalem.

So how did Jerusalem become the third holiest site of Islam? Muslims today cite a vague passage in the Koran, the seventeenth Sura, entitled "The Night Journey." It relates that in a dream or a vision Mohammed was carried by night "from the sacred temple to the temple that is most remote, whose precinct we have blessed, that we might show him our signs…" In the seventh century, some Muslims identified the two temples mentioned in this verse as being in Mecca and Jerusalem. And that's as close as Islam's connection with Jerusalem gets—myth, fantasy, wishful thinking. Meanwhile, Jews can trace their roots in Jerusalem back to the days of Abraham.

That was the essence of the column that caused reverberations around the world. Like I said, I didn't think it was anything special. I know it's not my best work on this subject or any other. Nevertheless, it hit a chord. Within days, the piece was making its way around the world, being translated into dozens of foreign languages. I was hearing from people I hadn't seen for decades who got a copy of this piece in their e-mail inbox and located me as a result. Suffice it to say this column was read by millions.

Shortly after it was first published, the *Jerusalem Post* asked permission to reprint it, which I gave them. About a week later I received an e-mail from the very excited publisher of the *Jerusalem Post.*

Here are his exact words, save for spelling corrections I made to save further embarrassment: "My name is Tom Rose. I am the publisher and CEO of the *Jerusalem Post.* We ran a piece of yours yesterday that has turned this country upside down. Our phones have been ringing all day. Hundreds of people. It is being discussed on Israeli talk-radio shows. How do we get you to write for us? There is a huge market for a syndicated column for you. Huge. The *Jerusalem Post* is owned by Hollinger International, publishers of the *Daily Telegraph* (London), *Chicago Sun-Times*, *National Post*, and on and on. How can we help you? You say what we can't. Just as only a Jew is free to criticize Israel without fear of being branded a racist, only an Arab can point out discrepancies and hypocrisies in the Arab world. You would be huge hit in our paper. Our U.S. weekly edition of the *Post* has 180,000 readers. It is very influential. You have the potential to be huge. To have incredible influence on American opinion and American policy. You must realize that. You and I need to talk. Tell me how and when. I am waiting to hear from you."

So I wrote to him. And we talked. Within a few days I had agreed to write a weekly column for the International Edition of the *Jerusalem Post* for a very modest fee. Two years later, my editor—a very amiable chap—told me I would be sending my column to a new editor. After that, I noticed my column stopped appearing with any regularity—even though no less than the publisher and chief executive officer of the Jerusalem Post had commissioned it.

I sent e-mails repeatedly to Rose, my new editor, and my old editor. Rose never responded. Straight answers were not forthcoming for days. Finally, I was informed that I had been fired— without notice, without explanation.

The Arab-American who had turned the country upside-down just as suddenly had worn out his welcome.

What do I think happened?

I think the *Jerusalem Post* wimped out.

I think the paper caved.

I think the publisher, who obviously couldn't even face communicating with me by e-mail anymore, yielded to pressure.

I think the editors lost their nerve.

I knew it wouldn't last at the *Jerusalem Post* because I'm not predictable. And the *Jerusalem Post* obviously wanted predictable.

Sooner or later I was bound to rub someone the wrong way. Sooner or later I was going to skewer some sacred cow. Sooner or later the very same people who hired me on the basis of one commentary were going to fire me on the basis of one commentary.

And that's too bad. Not for me—but for Israel. Because it needs to hear a voice of reason. It needs to be reminded that it has not outlived all the empires that sought to destroy it because it is so smart, or so well-armed. It needs to hear that it is still around because it is blessed—and because God has promised it a future. It needs to hear and read and see the truth.

Imagine if that local Ohio paper actually had dispatched a reporter out to interview Orville and Wilbur Wright. How do you suppose the journalist would have covered the story? Would he have sought the truth? Or would he have used the "fair and balanced" method of reporting? Would he have watched the airplane soar with his own eyes and relay that exciting news to others? Or would he present "both sides"?

I like to think I'm the kind of journalist who would recognize a flying machine when he sees one and not be afraid to report it because of scoffers. We need more journalists like that in the Middle East. We need more journalists like that in Israel. We need more journalists like that in the United States. We need more journalists like that around the world.

I think it would be amazing to see what would happen if truth became the new standard of the news media.

CHAPTER SIXTEEN

TAKING THE MEDIA BACK

"The theory of a free press is that the truth will emerge from free reporting and free discussion, not that it will be presented perfectly and instantly in one account."

—Walter Lippman, columnist and author

A T LEAST you have to admire the candor of ABC News reporter Bill Blakemore.

He says he doesn't "like the word *balance* much at all" when it comes to the global warming debate.

On August 30, 2006, he told the nation, or at least those who still get their "news" from the major networks, "After extensive searches, ABC News has found no [scientific] debate" on whether the planet is warming as a result of man's activity.

Then, two months later, as if we needed confirmation that he is no reporter but an advocate for the half-baked theory, he told a conference of the Society for Environmental Journalists there was no more need to seek balance in stories about the topic.

"It was very lazy of us for ten years when we were asked for balance from the [climate skeptic] spinners," he told a group of fellow activists posing as reporters. "We just gave up and said, 'Okay, okay—I will put the other side on, okay, are you happy now? And it saves us from the trouble of having to check out the fact that these other sides were the proverbial flat earth society."

He continues: "Does [extreme weather patterns] fit exactly within the predicted pattern that we projected almost thirty or forty years ago? This is the little logical problem that we journalists can still work on and solve."[1]

If indeed Blakemore was actually reporting on the topic of climate change ten years ago or twenty years ago or thirty years ago, he would know that the scientists and his media colleagues have changed their minds several times about what is happening.

In fact, in the 1970s, Blakemore's colleagues were telling us the real threat was global cooling. The hysteria then was about an impending ice age.

That was also true from 1885 through the late 1920s, when slightly warmer weather prompted the *New York Times* to report "the earth is steadily growing warmer."

Then in 1954, *Fortune* magazine was back promoting the cooling theory. The *New York Times* changed its mind in 1975, reporting "A Major Cooling Widely Considered to Be Inevitable."

Newsweek predicted an impending ice age. Some of the same activists today who are preaching doom from warmer weather were telling us then to expect global famines as a result of the cooler temperatures.

It wasn't until the early 1980s that the scientists, most of whom earn their keep from government contracts, and their shills in the media decided the real scare—and the real payoff—was in global warming. So they switched gears again.

On August 22, 1981, the *New York Times*, once again leading the pack, reported seven—count 'em, seven—government atmospheric scientists were predicting global warming of an "almost unprecedented magnitude."

So we're talking about four changes of direction on climate change in one century. We went from global cooling to warming, to cooling to warming again.

The only difference now is that some journalists and scientists are so rigid in promoting their theories that they refuse to accept any debate. They refuse to hear any dissenting opinions. They refuse to hear any evidence that contradicts their lucrative scam. They refuse to recognize that there is another side to the argument!

This is not as unusual as you might think. Back in 2000, the National Lesbian and Gay Journalists Association heard from speakers at its annual conference suggesting similarly that reporters shouldn't be required to get "the other side of the story" in news about homosexuality because, essentially, there is no other legitimate side.

There is this new form of rigid Stalinism sweeping into the big media. It is not just a grassroots phenomenon, for the organizations that justify this perverse thinking subsist on mega-contributions from the multinational media corporations that employ most of the "journalistas"—my term for activists posing as newspeople.

Once again, this is a worldview issue. People can only be expected to see the world through their own eyes, through the lenses they've been given, through the prism of their own belief system. It's a worldview issue both in the newsrooms and in the corporate offices.

I know. I know. You've heard all your life that businessmen are conservative—and that big corporations ultimately control the agenda of the press.

Let me disabuse you of this myth.

Big corporations in the United States are hardly promoting personal responsibility, national sovereignty, and free markets. On the contrary, we see the multinational corporations promoting just the opposite—open borders, global governance, socialism, and "alternative lifestyles."

Positive change in the media or anywhere else is not going to come from this sector. It's going to come in spite of it.

I worked for the Hearst Corporation for nearly nine years from 1979 through 1987. Hearst is one of the very largest privately held corporations in the world. It still has a reputation as a conservative enterprise. But as an insider, I can tell you it is anything but.

I was hired in the news department of the *Los Angeles Herald Examiner* by Jim Bellows in an effort to rebuild a dying paper from the ground up. That process involved differentiating the paper in every way from the bigger and dominant *Los Angeles Times*.

We ensured the paper looked different. We made sure we emphasized local news, while the *Times* emphasized national. We made sure the paper was lively and engaging to contrast with the *Times*'s dull and gray approach.

We did everything we could think of to distinguish ourselves from the competition—except speak with a different voice.

Early on I recognized the problem. In fact, I knew that our grand effort to save the *Los Angeles Herald Examiner* from extinction was doomed unless we recognized that we had to give the community a real alternative—a substantive alternative—and not just different window dressing.

I decided I would take the matter right to the top—the president of the Hearst newspaper division in New York. I presented my plan. I explained why staying the course we were on was a mistake.

Much to my surprise, my analysis got a good hearing in New York. Suddenly, this twentysomething news editor in LA was getting calls from the top Hearst execs in New York, not to mention William Randolph Hearst II, the son of the legendary "Citizen Hearst."

Their big idea in New York, however, was to make me the editorial page editor. That was how the newspaper would speak with a different voice. Unfortunately, I explained, that would not be enough. Because newspaper personalities are not shaped by their editorial page voices. They are shaped by their front pages. They are shaped by the stories they write and how they write them.

I turned down what was sure to be a very lucrative offer without even entertaining it. Even then, I was a man on a mission, not seeking job security and creature comforts. Even then I believed in the free press. I believed it was a vital part of our free society. I believed if America succumbed to an age of monopoly media—which we were rapidly approaching in the 1980s—in the long run, our free republic would be at risk.

Back then, Ben Bagdikian wrote a scary book about this subject, *The Media Monopoly*. He was both right and wrong in his dire predictions, which have continued to this very day as he ignores the burst of new press competition that began in the twenty-first century.

The preface to that first edition of the book, now virtually required reading in journalism schools around the country, provides a fitting metaphor for the rest of Bagdikian's highly ideological work. He tells of being inspired to reporting by the story of Sacco and Vanzetti.

In 1925, Nichola Sacco and Bartolomeo Vanzetti were Italian anarchists accused of a lethal payroll robbery in Massachusetts. Indifferent to the facts, the Soviet Union quickly set out to build a worldwide myth around the fate of the killers.

Literary figures like Upton Sinclair rushed in to plead the case in their writings. Nearly a hundred years later, there seems to be little doubt that Sacco and Vanzetti were guilty as charged. In 2005, a letter became public for the first time that suggests even Sinclair believed they were—even their defense attorneys did![2]

Nevertheless, the Sacco and Vanzetti myth continues today—and Bagdikian includes that first ode to the murderers in all subsequent editions of his book.

The problem with the U.S. media is not corporate control, it is worldview. Competition helps, as we've seen with the advent of the New Media. It gives voices like *WND*'s a chance to break through, to challenge the old guard, to level the playing field.

That's what was needed.

That's not to say the battle for the media is over. Hardly. Much of what we measure as progress isn't really progress at all.

Take the case of Rupert Murdoch, for example. With the *New York Post*'s formal endorsement of Sen. Hillary Clinton in 2006 and the media baron's decision to hold a fund-raiser for her, some were explaining it with this old phrase: "Politics makes strange bedfellows."

I guess it is strange and unexpected if you are among those who have deluded themselves into believing Murdoch is a right-wing ideologue and his Fox News Channel is really the distinctive alternative so many apparently believe it to be.

Murdoch has never lived up to his billing as a conservative. With Fox Entertainment, he is one of the biggest purveyors of pornography in the world. His News Corp. has been characterized by its reliance on sleaze for a generation. There are the nude page two girls in his British and Australian tabloids. There's the filth on his TV network that makes watching even sports programming, with its Viagra ads and constant promotions for prime-time licentiousness, dangerous for children and other innocent living things.

Do I really need to remind Americans that Murdoch sent money to John Kerry for his presidential bid and throughout his career in the U.S. Senate?

This is hardly the record of a conservative.

No, a great myth has been created around Murdoch—perhaps because his political preferences may seem more eclectic than other media moguls, who live and die with socialist politicians, whether they have a chance for victory or not.

Murdoch is not today, was not yesterday, and will not be tomorrow a freedom fighter. He is a man who has accommodated even the brutes of Beijing for access to that developing market.

A man who can make his peace with the totalitarian fascists in China will have no moral qualms hosting a fund-raiser for Hillary Rodham Clinton.

They are actually quite a pair.

Hillary is indeed an ideologue, but she has learned from her estranged husband the art of sounding mainstream, the art of positioning oneself as a political moderate, the art of…well…lying.

Clinton, as the front-runner for the Democratic presidential nomination in 2008 will become a chameleon. She will adapt to her surroundings—become whatever her audience wants her to be. She will tell people what they want to hear. If necessary, she will sound more conservative and more traditional in her thinking than her Republican opponents.

None of it, of course, means anything.

It's all about winning—winning at any cost.

Murdoch, too, is all about winning—in a different arena. While Hillary is an overachiever in politics, Rupert has an inexhaustible appetite for business success. He's a classic example of the guy who measures life by the standard: "Whoever dies with the most toys wins."

While Hillary is a true believer who masks her real agenda, Murdoch is a man who really doesn't care that much about politics at all—a man without real convictions. Ultimately they are two of the most ambitious people alive on the planet. And, if it suits the goal of meeting their own individual personal goals, they will help each other out.

You scratch my back, I'll scratch yours.

I am convinced the only reason Murdoch has ever employed "conservatives" and "conservative values" in his communication enterprises is because he recognizes it's good for business.

My own experience with Murdoch came in the early 1990s. His *New York Post* was still struggling as the number three paper in town. I decided I would take the fount of knowledge I had accumulated over the previous fifteen years and share it with this man in an effort to "save" this journalistic institution.

I put together my "Murdoch memo." It was a plan to turn the *New York Post* into a feisty paper that exposed government fraud, waste, abuse, and corruption at the local, state, and national level. I never expected to hear back from Murdoch. But I did.

One day, his secretary called me and asked if I would be willing to fly from my home in California to New York to meet with the top execs of the *Post* to present my plan.

"Sure," I said, having no idea of what to expect.

When I got to New York, I was ushered in to the office of Ken Chandler, then the Australian editor of the paper. He was polite but seemed perplexed about who I was and what I was doing there. But he also seemed to recognize that I had come at the request of Murdoch.

It turned out to be a thoroughly amusing day. I was offered several jobs, all of which I turned down, explaining the only job I would even consider at the *New York Post* was Chandler's. No, I was just here to help, I explained. I was just here to see if they liked the plan that I had developed—the plan that Murdoch had evidently blessed.

It turns out they did. They would soon launch an investigative reporting unit. After learning that I would not accept a job directing it, they asked who could staff it. I gave suggestions, and they actually followed them.

I never actually saw the *Post* put my plan into action, because it would have required the proper worldview in the newsroom and in the corporate boardroom—something I think is unlikely in any Murdoch-owned press institution.

But none of the endemic institutional problems of the news media will ever be solved by criticism. Nothing I can say about the *New York Post* or Fox News or CNN or the *New York Times* will make even the slightest bit of difference in the way those operations are run.

What will make a difference is competition. What *is* making a difference is competition.

I get frustrated when I hear media critics whining about the press being the root of our societal ills. The truth is that we are taking back the media.

I get frustrated, too, sometimes with the way certain stories are covered, the biases I see expressed, the ignorance I see displayed. But what we sometimes miss is that things are improving in the media. The additional competition of talk radio and the Internet and even cable TV has given each of us additional choices we didn't have a little over a decade ago.

The battle of the media is not over, but we are winning.

I used to tell people not to curse the darkness, but to light a candle. That's what we did with *WND* and some of the other media enterprises we've begun in the last decade.

So now it's time to stop complaining! Now that we have choices to make, it's time to make them. The candles have been lit. It really is past time to curse the darkness.

Fifteen years ago, I sat in the offices of my daily newspaper thinking about how "plugged in" I was to what was happening around the world with access to the Associated Press wire and supplemental news services and a daily reporting staff. Today, you, the average American with a computer and an Internet connection have far more information at your fingertips than I did—than the editor of the *New York Times* did, than even Rupert Murdoch did.

Hallelujah!

Now it's time to be wise media consumers. It's time to spend our money with moral companies that share our worldview. It's time to spread the word about these companies to our friends. It's time to celebrate the successful storming of the barricades of one of the most important cultural institutions in the world.

CHAPTER SEVENTEEN

LOOKING AHEAD TO THE NEXT DECADE

"Our republic and its press will rise and fall together."

—Joseph Pulitzer

TRUTH.

That's the destination.

Life is about a search for that destination.

It often involves twists and turns. Few of us have the luxury of finding the truth without some painful false starts.

My life was not exceptional in this sense.

I grew up in a loving working-class family headed by a second-generation American whose own parents immigrated to the United States from the Middle East to escape religious persecution and for the opportunities available to them only in this great country.

As a child of the 1960s, I was bombarded with lies. Let's just be honest about it. The decade of the 1960s was defined by deceit. We were told the United States was the fount of all evil in the world. We were told God was dead. We were told we could be anything we wanted to be if only we could discard the shackles placed on us by archaic religious values. We were told to "do your own thing." We were told, "If it feels good, do it."

These lies were the source of much horror.

My generation's adoption of those lies as moral code is still causing death and destruction to this day.

I believe the road to truth and salvation begins with repentance. I, along with most of my generation, have much to be repentant about.

Seduced by the lies of the media culture of the 1960s, like many of my generation, I rebelled against God and country. As a teenager, I was an activist for this cause—even a leader. I was jailed for my participation in civil disobedience demonstrations. I denounced my country. I supported the enemy.

In 1972, when Jane Fonda and her husband Tom Hayden were touring the country with their misnamed "Indochina Peace Campaign," I signed on as a bodyguard for the actress during a swing through the New York area.

Let me explain the horror of that one choice by a deluded teenager.

Fonda and Hayden had already been to Communist North Vietnam several times, where they encouraged—or, as we might say in another time, gave aid and comfort—to the enemy. She had posed for pictures on an anti-aircraft battery, looking through the sights, imagining herself shooting down a U.S. military plane.

With Fonda, despite her attempts to revise the historical record since, it was never about an honest American foreign policy disagreement. It was about working on behalf of the defeat of the United States by an evil enemy.

I have a simple litmus test for sorting out the honorable Vietnam antiwar protesters from the dishonorable ones.

After the U.S. troops pulled out, after the United States pulled the plug on all military aid to the South Vietnamese, and after the bloodbath that occurred as a result, what did the Vietnam War protester have to say?

The answer to that simple question defines for me who were the peaceniks and who were the agents working on behalf of the totalitarian communists in Hanoi, Moscow, and Beijing.

Some of the antiwar activists did speak out against the horrors, against the killing fields, against the refugee crisis that was created by the slaughter. Joan Baez comes to mind as one who spoke out. She even tried to enlist some of her former allies in the antiwar movement to join her—people like Jane Fonda.

Fonda didn't bite. Hayden didn't bite. John Kerry didn't bite.

This is how you separate the sheep from the goats of the antiwar movement. It's a simple, ingenious, nearly one hundred percent accurate way to sort the decent people from the treacherous.

There are a surprising number of antiwar activists who could never bring themselves to see the dark side of the totalitarian communists—even thirty-plus years later.

Positions like that make those responsible for them complicit in the horror.

Actions like that demonstrate a loyalty, a consistency to a dark ideology rather than to American ideals.

Actions like that suggest to me the people who hold them are evil.

Jane Fonda has been vilified and celebrated for a generation now for what she did. I use her only as an illustration. She was just one of millions of Americans who used their influence in the media to move our country further from truth, further from God, further from standards, further from morality.

I don't blame Jane Fonda for luring me into that immorality. I take full responsibility for it myself. But I also take full responsibility for repenting—turning away from that error.

Too many of my colleagues in the establishment press are still captives of that immoral worldview. But I believe God himself has given us the tools we need to combat it. Some of those tools, I'm convinced, are found in the New Media.

Ten years after founding *WND* and leading a small group of pioneers in this New Media, I think we've only just begun. I see evidence that we are winning the battle of ideas and information. Yes, there will always be a need to keep the media honest. But the media—particularly the New Media—are starting to become part of the solution rather than part of the problem.

I agree with Joseph Pulitzer, who said: "Our republic and its press will rise and fall together."

I think it helps explain some of the deep social, moral, spiritual, and intellectual voids our nation experienced in the past, when our press fell under the spell of people who perverted the historic mission of the free press, who allowed it to become captive to a worldview foreign to the American tradition.

But if the press and republic both fall and rise together, could the rise of the New Media herald a renaissance for our great country, for freedom around the world?

Call me an optimist, but I think so.

Who could have foreseen, for instance, even a decade ago the advent and influence of the blogging revolution? Today, you just can't get away with errors and distortion in the news media without correction. The Internet contains lots of errors—don't get me wrong. Just because something is published doesn't make it true. But with the plethora of information available on the Internet, any real truth-seeker can find out the real story.

Let's face it. It's getting harder and harder for the government-corporate-media complex to control the flow of information to the people. With the advent of the Internet and the synergy it has developed with talk radio, the hammerlock of control has indeed been broken.

I've seen it firsthand. The success of *WND* is a good example of what I'm talking about. A decade ago, what I first envisioned as an "Internet newspaper" was launched with little fanfare as an experiment in electronic publishing. Today it consistently is read by hundreds of thousands of different people every day—people representing every single country in the world. More than five million different people read it every month.

Why do they come? Because of our commitment to the traditional role of the press—the role the establishment media forgot. We believe the central role of a free press in a free society is to serve as a watchdog on government—to expose fraud, waste, corruption, and abuse wherever we find it.

The other twist that this new medium of the Internet provides is the ability to go where the news is—to utilize the resources of hundreds of English-language news services around the world. No longer are Americans reliant on one monopoly news agency—the Associated Press—for 90 percent of their information, as they have been for the last thirty years.

Is America on the cultural and political rebound as a result of the New Media's success? I admit, it might be hard to see the evidence for such a claim. Some will point to the 2006 midterm elections and what they have wrought on the country. If people are much better informed, some will ask, then how could Nancy Pelosi, a radical San Francisco Democrat, be elevated to one of the most powerful positions in government? How could marriage amendments simply defining the institution as between one man and one woman be defeated in at least one state and be opposed by 40 percent or more of the electorate in others? How could an abortion ban in South Dakota be defeated? How could human cloning and embryonic stem cell research be supported in Missouri?

These are good questions—and tough questions.

What I learned as a young radical on the other side of the barricades—much to my dismay—was that changing hearts and minds takes time.

Elections are useless as means of educating the public and changing the way Americans think—and feel—about issues. That work goes on daily, hourly, minute by minute. This is work done quietly and without fanfare by our cultural institutions—education, academia, Hollywood, press, churches, foundations, etc.

This is where the real battle for hearts and minds takes place. Politicians don't lead, they follow. They follow the direction of the cultural winds.

It's true that our culture is continuing to slide down a slippery slope of moral relativism. I believe this is largely a result of the destructive cultural trends of the last forty years, rather than a result of what is happening today.

Further, there is in our midst today—as I pointed out in my last book, *Taking America Back*—a growing remnant of Americans who truly get it. They operate within a Christian worldview. They shelter their children from the evil influences of our degrading culture. They seek out alternative information sources. They understand the principles of American freedom.

This remnant is small by the standards of electoral politics. It may be 5 percent or less. But 5 percent or less is a sturdy foundation upon which to rebuild a self-governing nation. Again, if we measure our success only through what happens at the ballot box, we're missing the big picture.

Good things are happening within our country. It's not time for gloom and doom. It's time to recognize the opportunities God has given us to expand freedom, to revive morality, to restore justice in our nation. Much of that good news is happening as a result of the New Media. It's a significant breakthrough—because only an informed, literate, and moral America can make the right choices in the future. That's what our founding fathers told us, and they were right.

So start the celebration! Join the party! We are living in perhaps the most exciting and challenging time in the history of the world.

We have stopped the presses. We have used new technologies to pursue truth in ways unimaginable a few years ago. We've got the government-corporate-media complex on the run. And, if I'm right—if Joseph Pulitzer was right, if our founding fathers were right—that heralds an imminent outbreak of God-given freedom in our country and throughout the world.

I pray I'm right.

NOTES

Chapter 2: Hillary's Nightmare Becomes a Reality

1. Joseph Farah, *WorldNetDaily.com* (*WorldNetDaily.com* hereafter cited as *WND*), January 5, 1998.
2. Rebecca Eisenberg, "First lady just doesn't get it," *San Francisco Chronicle*, February 22, 1998.

Chapter 3: How the Press Got This Way

1. World Values Study, Institute for Social Research at the University of Michigan, 1995–1997 survey.
2. John 8:32, King James Version.
3. "The most trusted man in America?" *WND*, July 10, 2000.
4. "Walter Cronkite—world federalist," *WND*, November 30, 1999.
5. "Walter Cronkite—flack for global elite," *WND*, February 1, 2000.
6. Ibid.

Chapter 4: A Brief History of the Free Press

1. Jerry W. Friedman, "Speaking of a Free Press," Newspaper Association of America Foundation, 1987.
2. "Confusion about role of the press?" *WND*, September 11, 2000.
3. Ibid.
4. John Hohenberg, *Free Press, Free People: The Best Cause*, (MacMillan Company, 1971), p. 8.
5. John 1:1, King James Version.
6. Hohenberg, *Free Press, Free People*, p. 9.
7. Hohenberg, *Free Press, Free People*, p. 17.
8. Marvin Olasky, *Telling the Truth: How to Revitalize Christian Journalism* (Crossway Books, 1996), p. 103.
9. Olasky, *Telling the Truth*, p. 107.
10. Hohenberg, *Free Press, Free People*, p. 40.
11. Olasky, *Telling the Truth*, p. 110.
12. Olasky, *Telling the Truth*, p. 114.
13. Hohenberg, *Free Press, Free People*, p. 48.
14. Marvin Olasky, *Prodigal Press* (Crossway Books, 1988), p. 18.
15. Olasky, *Prodigal Press*, p. 20.
16. Olasky, *Prodigal Press*, p. 21.
17. Olasky, *Prodigal Press*, p. 22.
18. Laurie Goodstein, "Disowning Conservative Politics, Evangelical Pastor Rattles Flock," *New York Times*, July 30, 2006.

19. Joseph Farah, *WND*, March 11, 2002.
20. Ibid.
21. Ibid.

Chapter 5: A Free Press for a Free People
1. Tribute to Ludwig von Mises by F. A. von Hayek at a party in honor of Mises, New York, March 7, 1956, Ludwig von Mises Institute, http://www.mises.org/misestributes/hayek.asp.
2. Joseph Farah, "I'm not a conservative, really," *WND*, February 2, 2000, http://www.wnd.com/news/article.asp?ARTICLE_ID=14906.
3. Pew Research Center for the People and the Press, http://people-press.org/reports/display.php3?ReportID=188, July 13, 2003, 1615 L Street, NW, Suite 700, Washington, D.C. 20036.
4. Associated Press (Associated Press hereafter cited as AP) Managing Editors, "New Attitudes, Tools and Techniques Change Journalism's Landscapes," the Pew Center for Civic Journalism and the National Conference of Editorial Writer, August 2001.

Chapter 7: Storming the Temple
1. Robert Stacy McCain, *Washington Times*, January 14, 2000. http://asp.washtimes.com/printarticle.asp?action=print&ArticleID=news2-01142000.
2. *Seattle Times*, August 8, 2003, http://archives.seattletimes.nwsource.com/cgi-bin/texis.cgi/web/vortex/display?slug=marco08&date=20030808.
3. "State-controlled media," *WND*, July 26, 2001, http://www.wnd.com/news/article.asp?ARTICLE_ID= 23792.
4. "Democrats favored in news coverage," *WND*, July 24, 2003. http://www.wnd.com/news/article.asp?ARTICLE_ID=33723.
5. "Wither CNN?" *WND*, April 21, 2003, http://www.wnd.com/news/article.asp?ARTICLE_ID=32155.
6. "Yahoo! buckles to China," *WND*, August 28, 2002.

Chapter 8: Google This!
1. "Google agrees to censor results in China," AP, January 24, 2006.
2. Ibid.
3. "Google map says Taiwan part of China," *WND*, October 4, 2005.
4. Ibid.
5. "Google's update of Taiwan map denounced," *China View*, October 19, 2005.
6. "Google money engine for Democrats only," *WND*, May 6, 2005.
7. Ibid.
8. "Google blocks ad for anti-Clinton book," *WND*, June 11, 2005.
9. "Google still runs anti-DeLay ads," *WND*, May 9, 2005.
10. "Google hosts 'boy love' site," *WND*, April 11, 2006.
11. "Google bars 'hate' sites' ads, but runs porn ads," *WND*, August 18, 2004.

12. "Christian Exodus banned from Google ads," *WND*, July 21, 2005.
13. "Google forgets Memorial Day?" *WND*, May 29, 2006.
14. "Google dumps news sites that criticize radical Islam," *WND*, May 23, 2006.
15. "No gun ads allowed at Google," *WND*, March 14, 2002.
16. "Google goes ballistic after getting Googled," *WND*, August 9, 2005.
17. "Google joins media elite," *WND*, May 4, 2005.
18. Ibid.
19. Ibid.

Chapter 9: The Drudge Effect
1. "*Drudge Report* sets tone for national coverage," ABC News Internet Ventures, October 1, 2006.
2. Ibid.
3. Ibid.
4. Leonard Downie, "*Wash Post* Editor Downie: Everyone in our Newsroom Wants to be a Blogger," *Editor & Publisher*, October 6, 2006.
5. John Harris & Mark Halperin, *The Way to Win* (Random House, 2006), p. 29.
6. Ibid.

Chapter 10: How *WND* Defeated Gore in 2000
1. Phil Valentine, "Why Gore lost Tennessee," *WND*, December 5, 2000.
2. Ibid.
3. Ibid.
4. Al Gore, "Gore: Country Straying from Principles," *Palm Beach Daily News*, March 14, 2006.
5. Al Gore, "Democracy Itself Is In Grave Danger," remarks as prepared for the American Constitution Society, June 24, 2004, Georgetown University Law Center, Washington, D.C.
6. Al Gore, "Gore Laments U.S. 'Abuses' Against Arabs," AP, February 12, 2006.
7. Ibid.
8. Al Gore, *Earth in the Balance* (Houghton Mifflin, 1992), p. 260.
9. Ibid., p. 128.

Chapter 11: The Other Scoops That Shook the World
1. Al Haig, C-SPAN, September 17, 1997, recorded and transcribed by author.
2. Joseph Farah, "Clinton rewrites the Constitution," *WND*, June 17, 1998.
3. The *New York Times*, July 5, 1998.

Chapter 12: Standards and Practices
1. "Will we see Gore TV," *Time*, June 18, 2003.
2. Ibid.
3. Helen Thomas, "Journalist Helen Thomas condemns Bush administration, MIT news office Web site, November 6, 2002.

4. Ibid.
5. Ibid.
6. Joseph Farah, "Why newspapers are dying," *WND*, January 20, 1999.
7. Ibid.
8. Ibid.
9. Joseph Farah, "The real civic journalism," *WND*, February 24, 1999.
10. Ibid.
11. Ibid.
12. Joseph Farah, "The press and the terrorists," *WND*, September 24, 2004.
13. Ibid.
14. Ibid.
15. Ibid.
16. Joseph Farah, "Vast left-wing conspiracy II," *WND*, May 6, 1998.
17. Joseph Farah, "Is prayer 'quirky'?," *WND*, July 29, 2006.

Chapter 13: From Jefferson to Washington
1. "*WashPost* editor's candid China interview," *WND*, March 13, 2005.
2. Ibid.

Chapter 14: Standing Up to the Press Police
1. Joseph Farah, "The Senate Press Rogues Gallery," *WND*, February 15, 2002.
2. Matthew Winkler, "What's a Bloomberg," *Columbia Journalism Review*, May–June 1995.
3. Joseph Farah, "Stalinists in the Press Gallery," *WND*, August 20, 2002.

Chapter 15: When Perception Becomes Reality
1. Joseph Farah, "What *Al-Jazeera* thinks of me," *WND*, July 28, 2004.
2. Joseph Farah, "Media's Israel double-standard," *WND*, November 23, 2003.

Chapter 16: Taking the Media Back
1. Joseph Farah, "Global warming: Media scam," *WND*, November 2, 2006.
2. Brenda Wineapple, "The Sunkist Utopian," The *Nation*, August 14, 2006.

INDEX

Jesus Christ, 4, 28, 50
Jewell, Richard, 136
Jewish Temple, 236
Job (Old Testament), 143
Jones, Clark, 145, 148
Jordan, Eason, 107
Jordan, Lara Lakes, 176–77
Journalism, and history, 44
Judicial Watch, 19, 22
Justice Foundation (U.S.), 227

K

Kaczynski, Ted, 179, 180
Keenan, Joe, 213, 216, 225–26
Kennedy, John F., 31
Kerry, John, 29, 83, 119, 130, 144, 257
Keyes, Alan, 62
KFBK radio station, 2
King, Larry, 37
Kissinger, Henry, 158
Klayman, Larry, 19, 22
Knight Ridder, 173–74
Koran, 241
Krane, David, 126
Krasnow, Bruce, 188
Kreep, Gary, 227
Kumler, Dan, 229–30
Kurtz, Howard, 184, 196

L

LaFon, Whit, 145
Lamestream media, 140
Lear, Norman, 31
Lebanon, 240
LeHane, Chris, 129
Lieberman, Joe, 119
Limbaugh, David, 9, 73
Limbaugh, Rush, 2, 3, 5, 8, 9, 23, 63,
    125, 162
Lippman, Walter, 201, 245
London Times, 110, 219
Los Angeles Herald Examiner, 6, 25,
    26, 60, 247, 248
Los Angeles Times, 20, 96, 219
Los Angles Times, 25
Lynne,Diana, 170–71

M

Madison, James, 17, 91
Mainstream media, 92, 140
Mather, Increase, 46
May Day demonstrations, 83
Mayzel, Mike, 120
McCain, Robert Stacy, 95
McCarthy, Eugene, 31
McClatchy Company, 1
McGovern, George, 83
McKinnon, Mark, 129
McLaughlin, Andrew, 116
McLuhan, Marshall, 102, 189
McVeigh, Timothy, 207
Media manipulation, 18
Media Matters for America, 67
Media revolution, 70
Microsoft/MSN, 115
Middle East, 83, 232, 237, 238
Miers, Harriet, 169
Mills, Elinor, 126
Milton, John, 46
Milton, Richard, 229
Mises, Ludwig von, 68–69
Moore, Michael, 106
Moral Majority, 105
MoveOn.org, 118
Moyers, Bill, 52, 54
MSN (Microsoft), 115
MSNBC, 55
Muhammed, John, 206
Murdoch, Rupert, 125, 132, 249-251
Murmers.com, 105
Muslims, 53, 193, 195, 206, 207, 235

N

Nader, Ralph, 43, 118
National Association for the
    Advancement of Colored People
    (NAACP), 169
National Association of Counties, 162
National Conference of Editorial
    Writers, 77
National Conference of State
    Legislatures, 162
National Governors Association, 162
National League of Cities, 162
National Lesbian and Gay Journalists
    Association (NLGJA), 173–74, 246

134, 182, 199, 219
USA Today, 173–74

V

Valentine, Phil, 145
Vanzetti, Bartolomeo, 249
Vietnam War, 82, 256
Vietnamese News Agency, 213

W

Wall Street Journal, 14, 19, 20, 96, 136
Wallace, Mike, 149
Walters, Barbara, 174
War Powers Act (1933), 164
Warnock, John, 197
Washington Post, 18, 31, 84, 94, 130, 139, 162, 214
Washington Star, 6
Washington Times, 14, 93, 95, 213
Watchdog role, of media, 71
Watchdog role, of *WND*, 205, 217
Watergate scandal, 84, 86, 188
Webster, Daniel, 229

Weekly Standard, 136
Western Journalism Center, 8, 14, 16, 22, 59, 201, 213, 221
Wolfe, Tom, 25
Woods, Keith, 186
Woodward, Bob, 84
World Federalists Association, 32
World Trade Center, 195
WorldNetDaily.com, 17, 42, 60–63
Wright, Orville, 229
Wright, Wilbur, 229

X

Xinhua News Agency, 213, 214
Xinhua Press, 134

Y

Yahoo!, 108, 109, 115

Z

Zenger, John Peter, 47–48, 134